SOME THINGS LAST...

DINO JONES

Some Things Last… Copyright © 2022 Dino Jones

All Rights Reserved. No part of this book may be reproduced, scanned or transmitted in any forms, digital, audio or printed, without the expressed written consent of the author.

ISBN 9798366146760

First edition, December 2022

For J. & R. This novel wouldn't exist without them both.

For Bobby. Take it easy my friend…like Sunday mornin'.

And for my grandmother, "Mema", Julia. Great supporter of my first novel. I wish she could read this one too.

D.J.

CONTENTS

PART I: QUESTIONS IN A WORLD OF BLUE

1	Movin' In On You	3
2	Albert's Disappearance	8
3	It's A Beautiful Day	17
4	Out To Lunch	26
5	Time For a Change	37
6	Supper With Sydney	46
7	On The Rooftop	54
8	Look To The Stars	66

FIRST INTERLUDE: HEAD OVER HEELS   79

PART II: YAWNING AT YOUR HEELS

9	Easy Like Sunday Mornin'	142
10	Creeping Shadows	160
11	Daddy-Daughter Day	175
12	Compression	200
13	This Letter To You	215
14	Fall Back Into Place	222

SECOND INTERLUDE: I'M FLOATING   243

PART III: ILLUSION OF HAPPINESS

15	Espers	307
16	Embracing The Truth	333

PART IV: ONE DAY AT A TIME

17	Now, I'm Back Again	349
18	Vivre Mon Rêve	374
19	Something To Live For	424
20	Wherever You Go	442

PART I

QUESTIONS IN A WORLD OF BLUE

CHAPTER 1
Movin' In On You

"Damn it, Al! What the hell are you doing, man!?" Sydney yelled to himself as he sped through the city streets of Lando. Rain heavily cascaded upon the Jeep he had borrowed from Olivia. It felt as if all hell was breaking loose around him. He fast approached a yellow traffic light that turned red. A minivan proceeded to drive forward slowly, and Sydney swerved to the right, narrowly avoiding it. "Watch where ya going! Ya fool!" he yelled. All the sake he'd thrown back at the restaurant had caught up with him. He was in no condition to be driving like this. He knew this, but he continued to press on.

Lightning forked across the angry sky above, followed by a deafening roar of thunder. *Jesus Christ! What a storm. I hope you're alright, Al. You've scared everyone half to death*, Sydney thought as he recalled being back in the restaurant just ten minutes before when he placed the phone call that set everything into motion.

"It's just you and me now, Syd," Sharon said as she moved close to him, staring seductively into his eyes.

"You know it, babe. Here…" Sydney reached for the teal-colored bottle of sake that sat on the table and poured him and Sharon another saucer full. "Kanpai!" he said, throwing back all of it in one gulp.

"You really can put this stuff away."

"What can I say? It's one of my favorites. I remember this one time when me and Al were in high school. I snuck a bit from my dad's private stash and got drunk off my ass. Of course, Al refused to have any, so I was the only one drunk. Ah, what a night that was."

"It sounds like you two were pretty close," Sharon said, smiling. "I wish I had someone like that growing up. I had my older sister, but we never really hung out like that."

"That's a shame, babe."

Sydney reached for the bottle of sake, aiming to throw back another shot, when he glanced over and saw Olivia returning from the restroom. "It's about damn time. I was beginning to think you'd fallen in."

"Oh, please! I wasn't gone *THAT* long! Hey, where's Albert?" Olivia said, turning around and looking at the buffet bar.

"He hasn't come back yet from getting his wallet…must have fallen under the seat or something…happens to me too from time to time," Sydney said, pouring Sharon another drink.

"Syd! Are you trying to get me drunk?"

Sydney smiled devilishly and replied, "Maybe."

Olivia looked out of the window, and a bewildered expression appeared. "What the hell…?" She muttered softly. "I'll be back, guys. Something's not right."

"OK, fine by me," Sydney said, laughing. Olivia exited the door and passed the window a few moments later.

"It's just the two of us again. What should we do, Syd? Oh, I have an idea…" Sharon said as she began to kiss Sydney's neck lightly. "Syd?"

"Yeah?"

"When are you going to leave your girlfriend for me?"

Sydney forced a laugh. "Soon, babe."

"Yeah? I wish you would. I want you all to myself. I can't stand the thought of her touching you."

"Please, Sharon."

"What's it like making love to her? I wanna know."

Some Things Last...

Sydney felt like he'd made a mistake giving Sharon so many drinks. When she'd get drunk lately, she would start with these questions. Sydney didn't want to answer them, let alone think about them. Whenever Sharon asked these questions, she would say, 'your girlfriend' this or 'your girlfriend' that. She'd never say her name. Victoria is her name, and Sydney didn't want to think about her right now.

Sharon began to kiss Sydney's neck harder. "Whoa, now. Go easy there," he said, stopping her.

"Let me out..."

"What?"

"I said, let me out!" Sharon said, visibly upset by Sydney stopping her.

"Alright," he said as he slowly rose from the brilliant red vinyl restaurant booth.

Sharon moved over and stood up. The two stood a moment beside the table when Sharon spoke. "I'm not a whore. I want more than this, you know, Syd."

Sydney slowly sat back down in the booth. "I know, babe. I'll take care of it."

Sharon laughed, "I've got to use the restroom. I love you, Sydney."

"I love you too," he said as she slowly walked away and turned the corner towards the restrooms.

He turned his head and looked outside the large circular ornate window beside the booth. *Christ alive. What have I gotten myself into*, he thought to himself as he saw a small red convertible speeding by on the street outside. *Wait a second...That car looked familiar. Nah, it couldn't have been mine.*

A moment later, Olivia ran past the window and burst into the restaurant. He turned around to see Olivia running toward him. "What the hell's going on, Olivia?"

"Syd!! Albert took your car! I don't know where he's going, but he had an old TV and...a gun with him!"

Questions In A World Of Blue

"Do what now!?" Sydney said, jumping up from the booth. "A gun and a TV?! Wait...a television set..."

"Do you have any idea where he could have gone?" Olivia said, her eyes wide with fear.

"Yeah, I think so. I gotta make a call. Can I borrow your Jeep?"

"If you're taking my Jeep, I'll come too!"

"No! I don't know what he's capable of right now, and I can't risk you getting hurt."

"Syd, You're acting as if he's a maniac! He wouldn't hurt us!"

"Look, he...was released from Duke's End not long ago. You know that place for the mentally unwell on the outskirts of town? I don't have time to explain this! Just trust me, Olivia! Stay here with Sharon, please. I'll be back as soon as I can."

Olivia looked down, reached into her purse, and produced the keys to her Jeep Wrangler. "OK, Syd...I trust you. I know the two of you are close. Just find out that he's alright."

"I will, Olivia. Don't you worry about that." The two hugged briefly, and Sydney ran outside towards the parking lot.

He found Olivia's lime green Jeep Wrangler parked next to where his red Miata was supposed to be. "Son of a bitch!" he yelled as he unlocked Olivia's Jeep and hopped in. He took out his cell phone from the pocket of his jeans and began to dial the only person he thought could help right now. The line rang...Once, twice, three times. "Come on! Pick up!" Sydney yelled.

"Hello?"

"Hey, Aunt Milly. Where are you?"

"Sydney? Is that you? What's going on? Is everything alright?" Albert's mother said with worry growing in her voice. From the sound of things, he guessed she was driving somewhere.

"Where are you?" he repeated.

"I'm on my way back from the grocery store right now. What's going on!?"

He paused a second, trying to find the right words. He didn't want to alarm her more than he needed to. "It's Albert...he took my car, and I think he's heading back home, but I'm not sure. He had an old TV with him."

"*WHAT?!* How long ago was this?! Where were you?"

"He left about ten minutes ago. We were eating at Akane Dragon."

"Weren't you, Victoria, and Olivia supposed to be with him?"

He paused a moment, then said, "Victoria?"

"YES! Victoria is there with you too. It was a double date, right?!"

"Yeah, that's right! Sorry. I'm gonna head for the house now."

"So am I! I'm almost there! Just a block away now. Sydney, please hurry!"

She hung up, and Sydney sat for a few seconds, gathering his thoughts. "Right! Let's go!" Sydney said, starting the Jeep and pulling out onto the road. He saw flashing blue and red lights and noticed several police cars in front of the pawn shop across the street. The place must have gotten robbed. *This is certainly one hell of a night*, he thought as he sped off down the road.

CHAPTER 2
Albert's Disappearance

Sydney slammed the Jeep to a stop in front of Albert's house and saw his aunt Milly's car parked alongside his Miata. The top was still down, and the heavens were raining down upon it inflicting permanent damage to the interior. "No, no, no!! Fuck sake!! Al, you're killing me, man!" He jumped out of the Jeep and ran towards his car. Sure enough, the interior was already halfway to becoming a swimming pool. He grabbed the top and hastily raised it. He sat on the tan leather seat and firmly secured the soft top. He slammed his hand down in anger upon the middle console. A loud bang came next from inside the house, and Sydney knew it wasn't thunder. He ran for the front door, soaked to the bone.

    He climbed the wooden deck steps leading to the front door and noticed it was ajar. He slowly opened the door and entered the cool interior of the house. Everything was quiet…too quiet for Sydney's liking. The raging storm was beginning to subside outside slowly. There was a dark hallway to his right. At the end of the hall was Albert's room. Sydney could see that Albert's door was open a crack. The light was on, casting an eerie light onto the beige carpet outside the door. He crept up the hall. Once he got closer, he noticed that the frame surrounding the door had been torn off, allowing it to swing outward or inward freely. "Hello? You there, Al? Aunt Milly?" He took a deep breath and slowly opened the door.

    Sydney stood for a moment in the doorway, looking over the scene in front of him. A large bookshelf lay on its side, barring half of the opening. Hundreds of books lay

Some Things Last...

scattered across the floor. Across from the shelf was Albert's reading desk, and an old television set sat upon it, much like the one Sydney had given Albert for a Christmas gift about five months prior. He stepped over the fallen bookshelf and into the room. Then, he saw his aunt Milly sitting beside Albert's bed, her eyes wide open and vacant. In front of her, on the floor, sat a silver revolver with a wooden grip. "Aunt Milly? What the hell happened?! Where's Albert?!" He noticed the TV screen was destroyed. Glass lay scattered about on the desk and all over the floor. Sydney ran over to the open bedroom window and stuck his head outside. "AL!? AL, ARE YOU OUT THERE!?" he yelled, looking left to right. He saw no one. The sky lit up, illuminating the side of the house for a moment. About fifteen seconds later, he heard thunder rolling in the distance.

Sydney turned around and knelled down to look at his aunt. "Aunt Milly? Are you alright? Speak to me! Say something! What happened!?" A moment later, Sydney heard a knock on the front door.

"Hello? Mrs. Oden, are you there? It's Mort from Duke's End..." Sydney stood there a moment, not knowing what to do. "We're coming in, ma'am."

A moment later, Albert's door revealed an intimidatingly large man wearing a white uniform. "Good evening, sir. I'm looking for Mrs. Oden."

Sydney looked into the man's beady eyes and said, "She's in here...but I don't know what happened." Mort stepped over the fallen bookcase, and Sydney expected him to slam his feet down upon the floor, but he didn't. Surprisingly, he moved pretty gracefully. Each step the lummox took was silent. This amazed Sydney, but he didn't have much time to observe Mort. Two more men appeared at the door behind Mort. These men were police officers.

Sydney spent the next hour and a half answering questions on everything that had occurred that evening. He

Questions In A World Of Blue

explained he had no idea what had happened at Albert's place before his arrival and that he had found his aunt unresponsive, sitting on the floor across from the blown-out TV. Sydney wondered why the police had been called in so quickly. He discovered it was because of Albert's theft from the pawn shop across the street from Akane Dragon. Albert ran off with the TV and the gun while the owner was in the back room. What he wanted with either of them was a mystery to everyone involved…except maybe his aunt Milly. She sure as hell wasn't talking, though. An ambulance was called for her, and she was transported to Lando Medical Center for further tests and observation. As for Albert, the police set out to look for him immediately.

After removing the busted television and revolver for evidence, they checked the house and premises for other clues as to where Albert could have gone. They discovered an empty bottle of his medication in the bushes opposite the bedroom window and determined that he was mentally unwell. They assured Sydney that Albert would turn up eventually one way or another…despite asking what they had meant by that, he already knew.

They assumed Albert had stolen the revolver because he intended to take his own life. Sydney didn't want to believe that he would do that…even if he had stolen the handgun, Sydney didn't think he'd actually use it. At least, that's what he wanted to believe. They grew up together, for God's sake. The thought of Albert ever contemplating that deeply saddened him. The last thing the police told him was that it would be a good idea for someone to stay at Albert's place in case he came home that night. Sydney agreed and said to them that he hoped that he would. He thanked the officers for everything and told them he'd let them know if Al showed up.

As soon as the police left, Sydney made a few phone calls. The first was to Olivia. Olivia answered immediately.

"Syd? What the hell is going on? Me and Sharon are still at Akane Dragon, worried sick."

"I...don't know all the details, but Albert's missing right now. I'm over at his place. The police are out looking for him right now, and they said I should stay here for the night in case he comes home."

"Missing!? Oh, my God...Why do you need to stay there tonight? What about his mother?"

"Well, I found her in his room...she's alright, but she's in shock or something...she's not saying anything."

"Syd...what the hell happened over there? What about that television...and the gun?"

Sydney thought about how to describe what had happened to the TV. "The police took them both away as evidence." He decided not to tell her about the TV. She was worried enough.

"Syd...do you think he's alright?" He could hear the tears in her voice.

"Yes, I do. He wouldn't do anything to harm himself. Whatever he's going through, he'll be OK. That's why I'm gonna wait here tonight. I have a feeling he'll come home eventually."

"Right. I believe that too," Olivia said, stifling several coughs. "Syd? Sharon wants to talk to you for a minute. Here she is."

"Are you alright, babe? I've been here with Olivia worried sick!"

Sydney took a seat on the sofa in the living room and took a deep breath. "Yes, I'm fine. I'm just over at Al's place for the night."

"Yeah, I overheard everything. We're going to get a taxi over there in a few minutes. You don't need to be alone. I'll stay with you tonight."

"Alright, what about Olivia?"

"She's gonna get her Jeep and go back to her place in case Al possibly decides to head over there. He never went there, but she mentioned where she lived to him."

"Ah, that's good thinking. You never know."

"Right, babe. Well, we'll be there soon. Have to go and call that cab now. I love you."

"I love you too…"

Sydney hung up, returned his phone to his pocket then sat a moment in silence. "Guess I better call Vicky and let her know what's going on," Sydney said to himself, breaking the silence. He stood up and walked over to the kitchen, and stood in front of the sink staring out the window at the night sky. The storm from earlier had passed, leaving the sky clear. Sydney stared out at the stars twinkling in the sky above and wondered if Al was out there looking at them himself. He took a bit of comfort in this thought.

Sydney took his phone out once again and dialed Victoria. The line repeatedly rang until he was greeted by the answering machine message. "You've reached Sydney and Victoria. Sorry, we're not available to take your call. Leave a message after the beep." It was a message that she had recorded the first night they spent in their apartment together. He looked at his watch, '10:37'. He then heard a beep and began to leave his message.

"Hey, Vicky, I guess you've fallen asleep. I'm spending the night at Al's place. Could you give me a call tomorrow morning when you wake up? Sleep well. I love you. Goodnight."

He ended the call and remembered one more call he needed to make. He dialed the number to his parent's house. This time the line rang only once when the high-pitched voice of his mother greeted him. "Hello?"

"Hey, Mom. It's Syd."

Some Things Last...

"Sydney? What are you doing calling at this hour? Your father and I were just about to head to bed. Is everything alright?"

Sydney took a deep breath and explained the evening's events one more time. When he finished, his mother began to cry. "Oh, my God...Albert. Where could he have gone...and Milly, you said she's at the hospital in town?"

"Yes, they took her in an ambulance to the hospital." The line went silent for a good five minutes. All Sydney could hear were far-off voices and loud bangs.

"Why didn't you call us earlier, Sydney?" his father finally answered.

"Dad...a lot has been going on. I'm sorry."

"Right...I'm sure it has. Your mother, God bless her, is in hysterics in the bathroom. We're going to the hospital first thing in the morning to see about your aunt. We expect you to visit her too. Try not to piss the day away, would ya?" His father hung up without even a goodbye. It didn't surprise Sydney. His old man had always been a bit gruff.

He slid his phone back into his pocket. After he put his phone away, he heard a car pull up outside. He looked out the front door's window and saw a taxi sitting in front of the house and Olivia and Sharon sliding out of the back seat. A knock came upon the front door moments later, and Sydney opened it to Sharon, who wrapped her arms tightly around him.

"I was *SO* worried about you, Syd!"

Sydney put his arms around her and replied, "I'm sorry. This entire night has been something else. Here, come on in." Sharon removed her arms from Sydney, walked inside, and sat on the couch. Sydney stood in the doorway, watching Olivia walk up the driveway and wave to him.

"Any word on Albert yet?" Olivia asked as she walked the steps onto the wooden porch and inside.

"Nothing yet...I'm sure we'll hear something in the morning."

"I hope so. Can you show me his room?" Olivia said, looking around the living room.

"Yeah, it's down the hall."

Sydney led both Olivia and Sharon into Albert's disheveled room. Each of them had to hop over the fallen bookshelf to enter.

"Good lord. How did THAT happen?!" Olivia said as she looked at the bookshelf.

"Beats me...I got here after everything had gone down."

"Wow...he loved to read, didn't he?" Sharon said in awe at the number of books scattered about the floor.

Olivia looked around Albert's room and opened his closet door. "So, this is his room, huh? It suits him."

"OK, ladies. I don't know if Al would want all of us poking around in here. He'll be back soon enough so let's head back to the living room..."

"OK, Syd...but do you think he'd mind if I grabbed one of his cardigans? It's a bit chilly out tonight."

"It's late May, Olivia. How is it chill-"

"No, you go ahead, Olivia. He wouldn't mind." Sharon said, flashing an angry look at Sydney.

"Alright, fine. Go ahead," Sydney mumbled as Olivia grabbed a black cardigan with gray stripes out of Albert's closet.

The three left Albert's room, and Sydney turned the light off and closed the door the best he could. They all sat silently on the living room couch until Olivia looked at the clock on the wall. "Oh, I better be getting back to my place in case Albert shows up. Syd, let me have my keys, please."

"Sure thing," he said as he reached into his back pocket and produced her keys.

"Thanks...if he shows up tonight, I want you to call me no matter the time. I'll race back over here."

"We'll call you the minute he shows up," Sharon replied and hugged her goodbye.

"Bye, Syd."

"You be careful," he replied as he lightly hugged her. Olivia closed the front door behind her and ran across the lawn to her Jeep while Sydney and Sharon watched. She started it up and sped up the road moments later.

"I don't know about you, but I'm tired as hell," Sydney said.

Sharon embraced him again. "I'm so glad to be alone with you finally...Syd, I meant to say that your clothes are pretty damp. Let's get you out of them..." she said as she began undressing him.

"OK, but we're just drying my clothes. I'm serious, Sharon. I'm way too tired to be fooling around tonight. Besides, I'm not even in the mood for that."

"Oh, alright..." she said, looking down, clearly hurt.

Sydney let out a sigh, "Look...Sharon, let's both get into bed and cuddle. I'll hold you close to me."

Sharon looked up and into his eyes. "That sounds nice, babe. Do you do that with her?"

Sydney looked away from her. "Let's not get into that tonight."

"You're right. I'm sorry. Let's not think about her. It's just you and me tonight."

"We're here for Al."

"Of course. I know that. I'm just happy we're together."

Sydney put an arm around Sharon. "Me too. I'm happy you're here. Now let's get these clothes off and into the dryer." Sharon smiled and nodded.

The two decided to sleep in Sydney's aunt's bed and slipped under its cool sheets shortly after Sharon undressed Sydney and threw his damp clothes into the dryer. The dryer was right across from his aunt's bedroom, and Sydney could hear his clothes turning and turning within the dryer as he lay naked next to Sharon. She was also naked and pressed into his side. She was really trying to get him going. He could feel her soft breasts pressing onto the side of his chest, but he could barely keep his eyes open.

"Sharon, please, babe. Another night. I can't stay awake."

"You're no fun…" she said as she turned away from him. "Goodnight," she said.

Within the darkness, Sydney rolled his eyes. "I'll make it up to you. I promise. Just come here and lie next to me."

"I am lying next to you."

"Don't be cute with me. You know what I mean. Get over here," he said as he pulled her close.

"Oh, Syd, I love it when you handle me like that."

He smiled. "I know you do. Don't let it get you going. As I said, I promise I'll make it up to you."

"OK, Syd. You better," Sharon said as she cuddled up close to him. She kissed his chest and told him, "Good night," once again. He never answered her. He passed out as soon as she cuddled up next to him.

CHAPTER 3
It's A Beautiful Day

Sydney slipped into a dream of a memory. He found himself sitting on the recliner back at his apartment. Victoria was across from him on the couch, laughing and smiling at him. Scattered all about the living room are dozens of cardboard boxes with labels such as CLOTHES, DISHES, and MOVIES. The labels are all in Victoria's lovely curvy handwriting.

"We can do anything we want, Syd! God, is this what it feels like to be an adult? If it is, it's pretty awesome. I think I might have cake for dinner tonight," Victoria said, bursting into laughter as he sat on the soft recliner, silent.

His eyes shift toward the window at the black abyss outside. It's as if nothing existed beyond the apartment. Within the window's reflection, he sees Albert staring back at him, sitting next to Victoria on the couch.

"Hey, I know what we can do tonight. Let's record our answering machine message!" Victoria said, diving into a box to locate the machine. She pulled it out, plugged it into the wall, and pressed a few buttons. "OK, it's ready. Aren't you going to say anything, Sydney?" He continued sitting in silence, staring at Albert's reflection in the window. "Fine. I'll record it without you," Victoria said, annoyed.

Albert sat with a look of profound sadness on his face. He looked at Victoria and then back at Sydney, shaking his head slowly in disapproval.

Sydney closed his eyes, and the darkness from the abyss enveloped him. When he opened them again, he found himself inside the apartment's bathroom, sitting on the edge of the tub. He sat there contemplating his situation. I can't be here too long. I gotta get back to Sharon. She's gonna wonder where I am. What the hell am I doing?

KNOCK KNOCK "You OK in there, Syd?" Victoria asked. Sydney could see the shadow of her feet from the bottom crack of the door. He didn't answer. He continued sitting in silence, then turned around and stared at the small window above the tub. An eerie light was shining into the room from outside.

He climbed onto the tub's sides and peeped out the window, trying to find the source of the light. Instead, he saw the exterior of Akane Dragon and Albert speeding by in the red Miata. As Albert sped by, his eyes locked upon Sydney's, and everything slowed down. Sydney noticed the television set in the passenger seat and the gun. He wanted to tell Albert to stop what he was doing and that everything would be alright. The words never came, though, and Albert disappeared into the darkness.

He turned away from the window to find himself back at the booth in Akane Dragon. Sharon was sitting next to him. Across from the two of them was Victoria.

"Hold me, Sydney," Sharon said, wrapping her arms tightly around him. Victoria watched with a blank look in her eyes. He couldn't bear to look at either of them, so he turned toward the sizeable ornate window next to the booth. He stared out the window for a moment then a blinding white light completely enveloped everything.

Sydney woke on the soft bed, the sheets slightly draped over him, hanging off the side. The sun shines down upon him from the two large bedroom windows. *Damn it, Sharon. Why'd you open the drapes?* he thought to himself as he climbed out of the queen size bed. He stretched for a moment and sat on the edge of the bed facing the window. The sun's warm rays shined upon his skin, slightly invigorating him, but he couldn't shake the feeling of the dream he just woke from...although nightmare might be more appropriate. *Jesus Christ...what a fuckin' dream,* he thought as he ran his hand through his hair. *It felt so vivid...as if I were really there again, but it was never like that. It was an enjoyable night...just Vicky and me. She actually did have cake for dinner...a chocolate cake I specifically went out and bought for her. I didn't even know Sharon back then. Honestly...it was a simpler time, even though it was only last year.*

The delectable scent of bacon wafting through the bedroom door brings Sydney back from his recollections. "Mmm, something smells good," he said as he stood up, walked over to the door, and stepped out into the small, darkened laundry nook outside the bedroom. Sydney lightly creeps to the doorway leading to the kitchen and peeps around the corner to see Sharon standing in front of the stove, wearing nothing but an apron and cooking bacon and eggs. She lightly sings to herself, wiggling her behind slightly back and forth. Sydney steps out from around the corner and stands, hypnotized by the two dimples above her behind. Sharon turns her head and grabs another egg from the carton sitting on the faux wood countertop beside the stove and is startled to see Sydney standing there.

"Well, hi there. Good morning, sleepyhead. Finally decide to join the land of the living?" Sharon says as she turns around, cracks the egg on the pan's side, and begins mixing it with several others inside.

"Yeah, the sun woke me up."

"Oh, I'm sorry, babe. Force of habit. I always open the drapes and let the sun in back home," Sharon said, giggling to herself and flipping over the strips of bacon.

"Right. I can see you're making yourself at home already here. Do you like to cook naked back at your place too?"

Sharon turns around slowly and looks into Sydney's eyes. "Well, if you stayed longer than the night, you'd know that...besides, I'm not naked..." Sharon moved her hands behind her back, slowly untied the knot behind her neck, and the black apron fell to the floor. Sydney continued watching her as she turned around and removed the bacon and eggs from the stove.

As she slid the eggs out of the pan and onto a plate, she stuck her behind out slightly and said, "Aren't you going to touch me, Syd?" He moved across the kitchen and put an arm around her soft, warm body. He held her close to his chest as he began to kiss her neck softly at first, then more aggressively. He could feel the excitement building inside of himself when Sharon spoke, "Yes...hold me, Sydney."

When she said that, Victoria's face flashed into his mind, and he recalled Sharon holding onto him tightly in his nightmare. "What's wrong, Sydney? Where did you go?"

He took a step back and hung his head. "Sorry, Sharon. Do you know how you don't remember things when you first wake up? I was thinking about Al...he never came back last night."

Sharon turned around and picked Sydney's head up. Her hazel-colored eyes glistened brightly in the morning rays of the sun coming in from the kitchen window. "Don't apologize. I understand you're worried about him. Wherever he is out there, I know he's fine."

"You think so?"

"I know so," she said as she wrapped her arms tightly around him. "I love you, Sydney."

"I love you too," he said as he held her tightly. He felt her soft breasts pressing into him as he buried his face in her short, velvety black hair.

The two decided to sit down and have breakfast together. The phone began ringing as they ate, and Sydney walked over and looked at the caller ID. The number belonged to Victoria. "Who is it, babe?"

"It's...Vicky." The light from Sharon's face immediately faded as she turned and looked out of the window next to the table. Sydney walked up the darkened hallway leading to Albert's room and answered the phone.

"Hello?"

"Syd? Hey, I tried calling your cellphone, but you didn't answer. What's up? Did you and Albert have a good time last night?"

Sydney took a deep breath and began to explain everything that had happened the night before. When he finished explaining, the line remained silent for a moment then Victoria finally spoke.

"Jesus...where do you think he went, Syd?"

"I don't know. There aren't many places he could have gone."

"He'll come back wherever he is. Don't worry."

"I'm trying not to."

"Why don't you come on back home for a while? We can have some lunch. I miss you."

"Yeah...I need to get some fresh clothes too."

"Well, don't let me stop you..."

Sydney stepped into the dark guest bedroom up the hall from Albert's room and leaned against the cool side of the wall. "I'm sorry, Vicky. I miss you too. I'll be by soon. I gotta lock up over here."

"Alright. Be careful. Watch out for the crazy people on the road."

"Haha. Don't you know? I'm one of them too."

Victoria laughed and replied, "Syd, I love you."

"I love you too. See ya soon." He hung up the handset, took a deep breath, and walked back up the hallway.

He returned to the dining room table to find it cleaned off, and the plates were sitting in the kitchen sink. Sharon was missing. "Sharon? Where did you go? Don't tell me you've disappeared too!" He began to hear the sound of footsteps and rustling coming from his aunt's bedroom. He walked to the bedroom and opened the door to find Sharon getting dressed. She was finishing buttoning her blouse and sliding her feet into her shoes. "Sharon? What the hell?"

"Don't talk to me," she said as she stood up and grabbed her purse. "We were having a nice breakfast together until *SHE* called. Then you had to go and not only answer the phone but actually say her name!" Sharon stopped and sat down on the edge of the bed. "I heard you...you said you loved her, and you were laughing."

Sydney began to see tears fall onto her black jeans. "Sharon, I was just talking to her. She said she loved me. What could I say?"

"YOU DON'T SAY IT BACK! THAT'S WHAT!" she yelled, tears in her eyes. "Do you really love her, Syd? Does all of this mean nothing to you?"

"Of course not, Sharon."

"Of course not to what? This meaning nothing to you...or you loving her?"

"Sharon, please."

"Don't 'Sharon, please.' me! I want to hear you say it. Do you love her, Syd?"

Sydney sat for a moment and replied, "No."

"Really? What took you so long? Did you have to think about it?"

"No...I'm just worried about Al, OK."

"Don't you use Al as an excuse for this! You know how I feel! Yet you still did this!"

"I'm sorry. I'll make it up to you."

"Make it up to me? Where have I heard that before? You're like a broken record, Sydney!"

He looked into her eyes and said, "Have I told you lately how beautiful your eyes are?"

"Syd..." she said as she looked away.

"They are. They were the first thing I noticed about you that night at the Sexothèque. You walked out on that stage, and those eyes just...drew me in."

"I thought you said it was my dimples..." she smiled.

"Well, those were a close second...I noticed those when you turned around." She began to laugh, and Sydney moved in close and sat beside her on the bed. "Look, babe. I said I'd take care of things between her, and I meant it. I need some time to sort some stuff out and get things settled...plus this whole thing with Al has got me all fucked up. I'm sorry for everything. I tell you what...you and me...Let's meet back up here later tonight. I'll cook you up some of my shrimp kabobs, and we can throw back some sake."

"What about her? Won't she be wondering about you?"

"You let me worry about her." Sharon began to smile, and Sydney hugged her tightly. "There's that smile. OK, how about I drop you off by your place, and we'll meet later."

"Are you gonna go out like that?"

Sydney looked down and realized he was still naked. "Right! No, I don't think I'd get far like this." The two laughed as Sydney retrieved his clothes from the dryer.

Sydney opened the front door, and Sharon walked out upon the front porch. He walked out next and closed the door behind him. He locked it with the spare key he had found hanging on the key rack in the kitchen. "The sun feels so good on my skin. Feel me...touch my arm. Feel how warm I am?" Sydney looked at Sharon for a moment. She stood within a shaft of sunlight beaming through the tree limbs above. He ran his fingers over her warm skin, and goosebumps began to form. "Oh, Syd! Your hands are like ice!"

"Sorry, babe. I just splashed some cold water on my face before we walked out."

"It's OK...I liked it. It gave me a thrill."

"Let's save the thrills for later," Sydney said as he walked down the steps and walked over to his Miata. He opened the driver's side door and surveyed the damage from the previous evening's flood. Before he even sat down, he could already tell the interior was still soaked. "Damn...fuck me."

"I thought you said to save the thrills for later?" Sydney turned around to see Sharon standing with a grin on her face.

"I did…Damn it. Al really did a number by leaving the top down. It's still sopping wet in here."

"Sopping wet, you say? Oh, Syd…"

"Alright, alright. Enough of that. I'm gonna have to let this air dry in the sun for the day…" Sydney said as he put the top down on the Miata, letting the warm rays of sunshine into the interior. "I hope this dries it out…It should be alright to leave here. Let me call us a cab."

"A cab? I wanted to ride with the top down, though…It's a beautiful day, Syd. The sun is shining, and I feel like no one can stop us."

"Stop us from what? What do you mean?" Sydney said as he removed the dripping wet floor mats, laying them upon the concrete driveway.

"Anything we want to do, babe."

He took a seat on the tan leather seat and leaned back, looking up into the brilliant blue sky above. Several robins flew by overhead, gleefully chirping. "Yeah, it is a beautiful day, isn't it? I suppose it'll be OK to drive it. The wind should help dry it out too."

Sharon hopped into the passenger seat, leaned over, and kissed Sydney. "Let's drive, babe. I want to feel the wind in my hair. It makes me feel so alive."

Sydney sped through the streets of Lando as Sharon's hair glistened in the noonday sun. Sharon was quite an intriguing girl. He began to wonder what this feeling was she had felt. The sun felt terrific shining down upon him, but other emotions alluded him. The only tangible feeling he had was his worry for Albert. *Wherever you are, Al. Hurry home*, he thought as he sped past the Lando Community Library. Sharon lived in an apartment building with a pool not too far from the library and not that far from his apartment. She lived too close to his liking. He tended to

Some Things Last...

stay away from her place because he was paranoid that Victoria might drive by and see him parked there. There weren't many bright red Miatas in town. Sharon had invited him for a swim several times, but he had yet to dip a single toe in the turquoise water.

Sydney pulled into the parking lot of Sharon's apartment building and stopped the car. She looked into the sky for a few moments and sighed, "It's time to part ways for now, huh, babe?"

Sydney leaned over and grabbed her hand, and squeezed it. "Don't worry. I'll be seeing you tonight. Bring your appetite because we're gonna be eating a lot."

Sharon smiled. "What if I get a little belly? Will you still love me?"

"Of course, I will. What a thing to say."

"Good. Because I might have one after tonight." She smiled as she squeezed his hand back, leaned over, and kissed him.

"I love you, Syd."

"I love you too, babe. Bye for now." Sharon exited the car and walked up the pathway next to the pool to her apartment. Sydney watched as she reached the entrance door on the ground floor. Before going inside, she gave a little wave with her index finger then she was gone. She lived on the seventh floor. He imagined her walking towards the elevator, her steps echoing in the old lobby.

Sydney turned around in the parking lot and then headed back onto the road toward his apartment. On the drive over, he tossed about in his mind what Sharon had asked repeatedly, more often here lately. *When are you going to leave her for me?* It was a question he liked avoiding at all costs. *After tonight's romantic dinner, I hope Sharon will lay off with the questions.* He continued to cruise through the streets, growing ever closer to his apartment and Victoria.

CHAPTER 4
Out To Lunch

Sydney pulled into his usual parking spot next to Victoria's Chevy Cavalier. She had received it from her parents as a graduation gift from high school. *Christ, has it been five years already!?* Sydney thought to himself, realizing it was almost that time of the year again. Another year had passed since he'd left Lando High behind him. He looked at her car and thought it looked much better after Victoria had re-painted it bright yellow. She put back money here and there from her substitute teaching gigs and finally managed to save enough about six months back. The car gleamed in the afternoon sunlight. She loved her car, washing it regularly and even giving it a name, Alex. He had asked her where she had gotten the name Alex from, and her response was, "Nowhere in particular. It just popped into my mind." Sydney let out an audible sigh and looked towards the second floor, where his apartment was. He could see the drapes were open, letting in the sunlight. "I've wasted enough time. Time to head on up..." Sydney muttered to himself. He turned around and reached for the handle to pull the top back over the Miata. He secured the soft top, stepped out onto the hot asphalt of the parking lot, and locked the driver's door behind him.

He climbed the stairs, footsteps echoing in the stairwell leading upwards. He reached the second floor, made it to his door, and then pulled his keys out of his back pocket. He slowly opened the door and found Victoria watching TV on the recliner. "Vicky, I'm home," he said with a maniacal grin.

"You sound just like Jack Nicholson when you do that. It's uncanny," Victoria said, laughing.

"I told you I was one of the crazy people, didn't I?" Sydney said, falling onto the couch across from Victoria.

"Yes…speaking of crazy. I still can't believe what you told me over the phone earlier. Have you heard anything new about Albert?"

Sydney turned away from her, facing the couch. "No. I haven't…Vicky?"

"Yeah, Syd?"

Sydney sat up. "How about I take you out for lunch today? I don't wanna overthink about Al right now."

"I'm sorry. You know you can talk to me about it. I'm here for you, Syd. I'm just as worried about him as you are."

He leaned over and grabbed her hand. "I know…Hey, how about we hit up QL's for lunch? I could go for some of their pizza."

"Mmm, that sounds fuckin' good. I'm craving some chicken, though."

"You can have whatever your heart desires." The two of them stood up, and Sydney gave Victoria a big hug before she headed off to their bedroom to get ready.

While Sydney waited, he grabbed a quick shower and slipped into a fresh set of clothes. After that, he sat on the recliner and began watching TV. He found a show about far-off destinations across the globe. The screen started to pan over a beautiful view of an exotic island in The Caribbean called The Isle of Elise. The narrator described the place as a romantic hot spot for honeymooners. "That place looks beautiful." Sydney turned around to see Victoria dolled up and ready to hit the town. She wore a black spaghetti strap dress with red and blue flowers and a pair of black heels. A silver necklace Sydney had bought her for her previous birthday hung from her neck. A white daisy sat in her wavy brown hair, which hung past her shoulders. He sat a moment admiring her.

"My, my…damn, you look great, Vicky."

"Thanks, Syd. Do you like the flower? I got it out of the planter on the balcony," Victoria said, lightly blushing.

"I love it. It ties the whole look together."

Victoria let out a small laugh, "Well, let's head out. I'm starving," she said as she walked over to the TV and pushed the power button. The screen went black, and Sydney stood up.

"You got that right," he said as he walked towards the door. As he shut the door and followed Victoria down the stairs, he couldn't shake the island from the TV out of his mind. *The Isle of Elise…I swear I've heard of that place somewhere before.*

"We taking the Miata?" Victoria asked as they approached the cars.

"Yeah, babe," Sydney said, still in thought. He walked over and opened Victoria's door.

"Uh, Syd…it kinda smells a little funky in here. Why does it smell all mildewy?"

Sydney leaned down and took a deep breath. It certainly did have a bit of a smell. "Fuck…I was hoping that wasn't going to happen."

"Why does it smell like that? Does your top have a leak?"

Sydney leaned against the car. "No…you know that big storm that rolled through yesterday evening? Well, it was around that time that Albert borrowed my car."

"What? Why did you lend him your car?"

Sydney didn't want to go into all of the specifics about them being on a double date at Akane Dragon. "We went out to get some Chinese, and he said he forgot his wallet in the car. I lent him the keys, and he took the car without me realizing until he was long gone."

Some Things Last...

"How the hell did you not realize it? ...Were you drinking again, Syd?"

He turned away from her, filled with shame. "...Yeah. I had a bit too much sake."

"I see..." was all that Victoria could say.

"Al took off in the Miata, leaving the top down when he got back to his house."

"It's gonna smell like this for weeks, I think," Victoria said, stepping away from the car.

"We can put the top down, Vicky. You won't be able to notice it with the top down."

Victoria stood for a moment staring at Sydney. "Syd, look at me."

His eyes surveyed her up and down. "Yeah? You look amazing."

Victoria let out a small sigh, "Thank you, and I wanna keep it that way. I'm not riding with the top down. I just fixed my hair. I can't have the wind mess it up, and I know how you drive. You fly like a bat outta hell."

"Alright...we won't take the Miata then," he said, closing the passenger door and locking it. "Guess that leaves Alex then," Sydney said, eyeballing Victoria's ride.

The two arrived at QL's after a leisurely drive through Lando. Victoria specifically took the scenic route, soaking up the lovely late spring views of Lake Lethe. Sydney nodded off along the way. "We're here," Victoria said flatly.

Sydney awoke with his neck in pain. "Ah, fuck...my neck," he muttered as Victoria closed her door and walked towards the entrance. *Ah, damn it. I didn't mean to fall asleep on her*, he thought as he shook the sleep off of himself and ran to catch up with her. He managed to grab the door for her and let her in. It was a start, a small way to make it up to her. She quickly walked inside without thanking him. He walked behind her to the counter where a woman wearing an apron stood ringing up an older woman's meal.

"One sec, my loves. I'll be right with yas. You can go ahead and take a seat in the dining room."

"OK, thank you," Victoria said as she walked through a door to her right into a warm dining room decorated with many articles of local history. A large mural was painted on the back wall that featured Lake Lethe and Lando along its banks. A thin veil of fog hung over the lake, and the morning sun peaked over the distant mountaintops. Sydney had always loved this painting and wished he could see this view through his eyes. He could never find out where the artist's vantage point was located. Once, he had asked the owner about it and was told that the artist had sadly passed away. It seemed the secret of the mural was one that would never be answered.

"You know I hate it when you leave me alone while I drive."

Sydney was brought back by Victoria's statement. "Right...I'm sorry, Vicky. I just had a hard time sleeping last night." He lied. He had slept like a baby next to Sharon. That old familiar feeling of guilt crept up within him again. He turned away from Victoria and looked at that lovely mural again, trying to distract himself from all the lies.

"I'm sorry. I should have realized that. Let's enjoy our time together, Syd. It's been ages since we've been out. What, with my school work and our jobs cutting into our time. It's hard to see you like I used to."

Sydney smiled and took her hand. It was warm and reminded him of simpler times. "I'm happy that we're here together, Vicky. Once you finish your teaching degree, we'll be able to do this more often."

She squeezed his hand. "One more year left to go, and I'll be finished. I'll be glad when I can stop driving back and forth between Lando and King City several times a week."

"Yeah...me too."

"What do you think you'll be doing this time next year, Syd?"

Sydney thought about that a moment. "I don't know. I suppose I'll still be working with your dad and brother. I like building people's porches and decks. Waylon mentioned teaching me how to build houses in a few months. I'll stick with helping the family business grow, I guess."

Victoria's brother was a master carpenter who owned his own business, Tesson's Carpentry. After graduating high school, Sydney was hired on, not knowing what else to do with his life. Victoria's older brother, Waylon, gladly gave him a job and took him under his wing, teaching him the tricks of the trade. Victoria's father, Wayne, also worked there in his spare time, helping with odds and ends. Sydney immensely enjoyed the job and imagined he'd be a master carpenter someday if he could stomach taking the classes for it. School and Sydney never really mixed well.

"Sorry, my loves, been a busy one today. What can I get yas?" Sydney ordered a Pepsi and a pepperoni pizza, and Victoria ordered a Diet Pepsi and a chicken dinner. She loved her white meat. Sydney was a dark meat man. He especially loved the legs, but today pizza was calling his name. The waitress hurried away towards the kitchen, leaving the two alone again.

"Kinda odd she said it was busy. It's a ghost town in here right now," Victoria said, looking at the empty tables.

Sydney looked at the clock beside the door the waitress had just exited. It was 1:30. "I guess we missed the lunch crowd. I'm glad, honestly. I hate all the chatter and small talk you hear with so many people crammed in here. It's pretty peaceful now."

"Yeah, it is. It's nice. It's just you…and me," Victoria said, softly grabbing one of Sydney's hands and holding it. He looked into her eyes, and she smiled brightly at him.

The two sat there momentarily, looking at each other, when Sydney's cell phone rang in his pocket. He took his free hand and removed it. "Just a sec, Vicky. This might be about Al," he said, flipping the phone open and answering it. "Ahoy-hoy?"

"Syd...I miss you."

Sydney separated his hand from Victoria's and tried to remain composed. "What's that? I can't hear you very well. Just a second." He rested the phone on his lap and looked at Victoria. "Give me a few minutes. I need to take this call."

"You can't take it here? Is it the police?"

He stood up and began to walk towards the door. "I'm not sure. I'm getting bad reception...I can't hear them."

"OK, I'll be here," she said, her brown eyes bright and curious. Sydney didn't want to take any chances on Victoria overhearing anything, so he walked outside to the parking lot.

Before he placed the phone to his ear, he could already hear Sharon repeatedly asking if he could hear her. "Hello, Sharon? Yes, I can hear you. What are you doing calling me right now?"

"Did you not hear? I said I missed you...I want to see you. It's so lonely here in this apartment. I'm all alone here wearing nothing but my robe...and now I've slipped out of that too. I've been sitting here imagining your hands upon me. Feel me, Syd. I *need* you."

Sydney put his fist on his forehead. He couldn't let her do this right now. "Sharon, I will see you tonight. Can you be patient?" The line was silent for what felt like ages. Sydney stood there with the sun beating down upon him. Sweat began to bead upon his forehead.

"Do you think I'm a whore, Syd? A dirty whore you can fuck and cast aside whenever you damn well please?"

Sydney rolled his eyes. "No, Sharon, I don't."

"Then why don't you come to me? I call you putting myself out there. Do you think I'm lying when I tell you these things? I'm standing here naked…both physically and emotionally."

"I believe you. It's just…"

"Just what? You're with *HER*, aren't you? Are you out with her right now?"

Sydney began to pace back and forth. As the minutes ticked by, the excuse of a wrong number flew out the window. He would have to concoct yet another lie. Lies, lies, lies. His life was fast becoming nothing but one big lie.

"Well?! Are you out with *HER* or not?! I want you to say it. Say you're with her."

"Sharon…please."

"Fuck you, Sydney," Sharon said, slamming the phone down and ending the call. Sydney thought about calling her back but knew there wasn't any time for that. The food was probably already at the table, and he had left Victoria alone for at least fifteen minutes. He let out a loud sigh as he ran back inside.

When he returned to the table, sure enough, the food was there. "I waited a good five minutes for you, Syd, but the chicken was getting cold, so I started without you," Victoria said, wiping her mouth with a napkin.

"That's OK, Vicky. Thanks for waiting as long as you could." He retook his seat and laid his eyes on the delectable pizza before him. "Damn, this looks good," he said, grabbing a slice.

"So, who was it that called?"

Sydney had hoped that by some stroke of luck, Victoria wouldn't ask him that question sparing him from having to lie to her once again. No such luck. None at all. While pacing back and forth in the parking lot, he had prepared a lie that he hoped would work. "It was the police. They told me to go back to Al's place and watch out for him again tonight."

"I was wondering why it was taking so long. Did they mention anything else?"

"No, they didn't have any new information."

"Oh, that's too bad. Well, maybe I'll go over with you tonight."

Sydney's stomach dropped at her saying this. "What?"

"Maybe I'll come over with you to Al's place. I should be there with you. You don't need to be alone."

"But what if he decides to come over to our apartment? Someone needs to be there just in case."

"We'll leave a note on the door. We'll tell him we're at his house. I highly doubt he'd go all the way over there anyway." This wasn't good. He had promised Sharon they were going to have the night together. Even though she had hung up on him, he felt she'd calm down before the evening came. "It's decided. We're spending the night at Al's together. I've missed sleeping with you," Victoria said with a mischievous grin on the side of her face. "Whether or not Al shows up…we can still have a nice evening together."

"Yeah, I can't wait," Sydney said as he looked at his pizza again. A few minutes prior, he had been starving, but now he had a great knot in his stomach. His appetite had vanished. He forced down two large slices of pizza while contemplating the night's events.

Sydney decided to take the rest of his pizza home for later. Victoria was concerned that he couldn't eat the entire pizza. "You usually eat everything, Syd. You even eat the crusts! Are you feeling alright?"

"I'm alright, Vicky…just worried about Al," he replied. This wasn't a total lie. Some people would argue against that, but Sydney took a tiny bit of solace that he wasn't entirely lying to Vicky this time. He boxed up the remains of his pizza, and the two sorted out the bill.

After, Sydney held the door open for Victoria once more. "Such a gentleman."

"That's me," he replied, forcing a smile. He felt like shit. He hoped Victoria wouldn't notice. The two were halfway through the parking lot when Sydney's phone rang again. *Oh, sweet Jesus. Not again. Not now*, he thought to himself.

"You better get it, Syd. It might be important," Victoria said as she continued walking towards the car. Sydney reached into the pocket of his jeans and grabbed his phone. The phone slipped through his fingers and flew towards Victoria. It landed at her feet. "Whoa, Syd! Hold on, let me answer it for you."

"WAIT! I mean, I can get it. It's alright," he said, but Victoria had already flipped the phone open and pressed it to her ear.

"Hello?"

This is it. So, this is how it ends. Funny, I always pictured it differently. Victoria stood facing away from him. Sydney stood there looking down at his feet. He prepared himself for the storm that was to come.

Interestingly enough, he didn't feel any fear. What he felt instead was a great feeling of resignation. Everything that came his way after this was something that he deserved. All the lies he had told and his secret double life were bound to catch up with him eventually.

"Syd?"

Oh, God. Here it comes. "Yeah?" he said, still looking down at the gray asphalt beneath his feet.

"Is there something you want to tell me?" He stood there in silence, unable to find the words. His mind was racing. He wished he could be anywhere but here. He felt like running away but couldn't move. He was frozen in place. "Syd? Did you hear me?"

"Yeah," was all he could manage to say.

"So, my question is…when were you going to remember Albert's mom?"

Sydney looked up, his eyes wide in shock. "What?"

"Albert's mom, Syd! She's at the hospital! That was your dad just now. He called, wondering where you were. He said you were supposed to visit her today!" Sydney almost fell but regained his balance. "Syd? Are you alright?"

He looked into Victoria's beautiful brown eyes. He was reminded of the first time he looked into her eyes and how he felt. It astonished him how he felt at this moment. He put his arms around Victoria and squeezed her tightly. "I'm sorry, Vicky! I've...had a lot on my mind today, but it's not too late."

"Syd...why are you crying?"

He quickly wiped his eyes with the back of his hand. "I'm just a bit overwhelmed, is all. I love you, Vicky." He held her tightly as he rested his head upon her shoulder.

Victoria stood there in silence. She was stunned by Sydney's sudden change in behavior. "It's alright, Syd. I understand you've been under a lot of stress since Al...We'll just head to the hospital and check in on his mother. You're right. It's not too late. Visiting hours don't end until nine."

Sydney held back the tears he felt welling up inside of him. Now wasn't the time for them. He got a hold of himself and regained his composure. "Let's head on over then, Vicky!"

"Syd?"

He turned toward her. "Yes?"

"Here's your phone."

"Oh, thanks. I almost forgot. Here let me turn it off. I don't need it ringing in the hospital." He turned the phone off and felt he'd be none the happier if it stayed that way forever.

CHAPTER 5
Time For a Change

The drive over wasn't a long one. Sydney had hoped the red lights would catch them through town, but it was so typical the one time he wanted red, they would all be green. He wanted a bit of time to reflect...to think about things. On the drive over, he put his hand on Victoria's leg as she drove. Her skin was warm and smooth. He began to caress her leg. It made him happy to hear her jokingly say, "Fresh!" It had become his habit to place his hand upon one of her legs while driving, no matter who was behind the wheel. Before he knew it, they had arrived at Lando General Hospital. Victoria pulled into an open space in the visitor's parking lot, and the two walked down the sidewalk toward the hospital's entrance. As soon as they stepped onto the reflective linoleum floor, their footsteps began to echo through the vast reception area.

"Your dad said she was already in a room on the second floor. Room 217."

"Alright. There's an elevator. Let's head on up."

When they exited the elevator, they followed the signs down a hallway until they found room 217. The room's door was closed, but he could hear voices on the other side. He knocked three times on the door and waited.

"Come on in," his father said. He could tell his old man was already in a bit of a mood.

He entered the room and saw his parents surrounding his Aunt Milly. She looked the same as she had the previous night. *God, has it only been just one night?* Sydney thought. She had the same vacant, far-off look in her eyes.

"Look who decided to grace us with his presence. It's about damn time."

"Sorry, dad."

"Sorry? Yeah, I bet you are."

"Now, Harry, please. The important thing is Sydney is here now. Hello, Vicky. I'm glad you came."

"Hello, Lolita. Harry."

"Ah, it's always great to see you, Vicky. I wish this knucklehead would bring you around more often. Instead, we get to see you like this," Harry said as he hugged Victoria.

"How is she?" Victoria asked.

"The doctor said she's in shock. Whatever happened yesterday evening really traumatized her," Lolita said as she leaned over and took Milly's hand.

"The doctor said if you keep her company and talk to her, she should come out of it," Harry said. "We've been here all day with her. Talking to her. No change as of yet…"

"How long do you think she'll be like this?" Sydney asked as he continued to stare at her eyes and slightly open mouth.

Harry gave Sydney a loud slap across the back of his head. Victoria jumped a bit at the sound. "None of this would have happened if you'd kept an eye on your cousin. Albert wasn't well! What the hell were you thinkin' lettin' him take your damn car! You know he doesn't even have his license!"

"I didn't let him take the car. He said he needed the keys because he left his wallet in there."

"Harry, please…" Lolita began.

"No, Lo, the boy needs to hear this. You coddle him too much. If he'd kept an eye on Albert, his mother wouldn't be lying in that godforsaken bed right now!"

Sydney took a step back. He felt like yelling back at his old man but held it in. "You don't think I know I fucked up,

Dad? *I'm* the one that has to live with that. I don't have to put up with this shit."

Sydney turned around and walked out of the room. He walked back down the corridor towards the elevators. Across from the elevators were two large tinted windows overlooking the parking lot. Sydney stood there staring at his reflection. He tried to put what his father had said out of his mind and focus on the good. He still had Victoria. She felt like the one good thing he had left in his life.

It's not too late. There's still a chance to turn things around! Yes, we're gonna spend the night at Al's. Just the two of us. When we get outta here, we can go to the grocery store. I'll make Vicky my shrimp kabobs instead of Sharon. She hasn't had those in ages, Sydney thought as he continued to stare out of the large window. As he stood there going over his plans for the evening, he saw Victoria come around the corner behind him. He looked at her through the reflection.

"Syd...your dad didn't mean what he said. He's just upset. He told me to tell you he apologized."

"Did my mom ask you to tell me that?" Victoria looked away.

"It's OK. I'm not worried about him," Sydney said as he stared out onto the brightly lit parking lot outside.

"What are you thinking about?" Victoria asked as she walked over to him, looking out at the parking lot.

He wanted to grab and kiss her at that moment, but he knew that would be too much. He didn't want to act out of the ordinary. "Just thinking about supper."

Victoria turned towards him and said, "Supper?"

"Yeah. What do you think about having shrimp kabobs tonight?"

Victoria lit up, "Ohhh, you haven't made those in a while! They're so good."

"I know...I tell you what...How about I make them tonight for you? We'll get a nice cheesecake for dessert too."

"Syd, you're spoiling me. It isn't even my birthday yet! What's the occasion?"

"I just wanna make up for not seeing you much lately."

"Oh, Syd...I love you."

"I love you too, Vicky."

"Hey, I can see Alex from here," Victoria said. "He was easy to find."

"Oh, yeah? Why's that?" Sydney asked.

"He's the only yellow car out there."

The two laughed, and Victoria said, "OK, let's go. It's fuckin' freezing in here."

Sydney looked at the goosebumps on her arms. "You poor thing. Alright, let's get outta here. We can go over to the grocery store and pick up our stuff for tonight."

"I'm already thinking about those kabobs."

"Me too, Vicky. Me too."

The two pulled into the parking lot at Food Paradise. It had been a while since the two of them had gone shopping together. Because of Victoria's busy schedule the past five months, the two had more often than not decided to go to a restaurant to eat to save time cooking. Sydney truthfully had missed this time they used to spend together. As he walked beside her to the store entrance, he grabbed her left hand and held it tightly within his. Victoria looked over at him and smiled. She squeezed his hand, and the two entered the cool air-conditioned interior of the supermarket.

Sydney looked to his left and grabbed onto a shopping cart. As he pushed the cart over to Victoria, he could hear the constant beeps of items being rung up over the supermarket's checkout lanes. Sydney followed behind Victoria as she began to walk toward the fresh produce section. As they walked by the lettuce and cabbage, he heard thunder from a small speaker in the corner of the display. A few seconds later, water came spraying out of the overhead sprinklers covering the produce in a fine mist. Sydney always enjoyed this aspect of Food Paradise. He couldn't help but feel a bit melancholic about it today. The thunder had made him think briefly of the previous night's storm...and Albert. He pushed the thought from his mind as he continued pushing the cart along, as Victoria gleefully added all sorts of goodies into it.

"Hey, Vicky. Why don't I grab that cheesecake while you finish up here?"

"OK, baby. I'll be here. You know what kind I like," she said with a wink as she began to walk over to the zucchini.

Sydney walked to the bakery and eyeballed the cakes behind the display counter. "Good afternoon, sir. What can I help you with?" A black gentleman wearing a white uniform and red apron said from behind the counter.

"Hi, I was hoping to get this cheesecake here." Sydney pointed to a small cheesecake in the middle of the display.

"Ah, I see. Just the right size for two people." Sydney looked over to see Victoria pushing the cart down the spice aisle. She smiled and waved to him. "That your girlfriend there?" the man asked, looking at Sydney above his glasses.

"Yeah, that's her," Sydney said, smiling lightly.

"She's a cutie. If you don't mind my saying so, sir."

"Not at all. I'm sure she'd enjoy hearing that."

"I tell you what, sir..." The man leaned over, grabbed a sticker from the counter, and attached it to the top of the cake. "I label the close-to-expiry goods with these stickers. You can get half off with this."

Sydney looked down at the sticker and smiled. "Is that so? Well, that's good of you."

"Think nothing of it. It warms my heart to see young love. I've been married going on thirty years now."

"We've been together almost ten years."

"Ten years? That's great. When are you gonna make an honest woman of her?" Sydney stood there for a moment in silence. "Oh, I'm sorry, sir. You'll have to excuse me. That's none of my business."

Sydney smiled and looked at the man. "It's alright. You know...you're right about that. That's something to think about."

"Excuse me, sir. Again, I didn't mean to say that."

"Sydney. My name's Sydney Lee. My friends call me Syd," Sydney said with a smile and produced his hand.

The man took his hand and shook it firmly. "Nice to meet you, Syd. I'm Henry Stone."

"Nice to meet you, Henry."

"Well, don't let me hold you up. You better catch up with your lady."

"Yeah, you're right. I don't wanna leave her alone for too long," Sydney said as he walked towards the spice aisle.

"Hey, Syd!" Sydney turned around to see Henry holding out his cheesecake. "Don't forget your cake."

"Thanks, Henry."

Henry gave Sydney a quick wink and a smile. "Take it easy, Syd."

"Like Sunday mornin'," Sydney said with a laugh as he went to find Victoria.

Sydney walked to the spice aisle, but Victoria was no longer there. He looked down each aisle but couldn't find her. A feeling began to overcome him. He was reminded of a time when he was barely five years old, and he was out with his parents grocery shopping at Yonders Blossom, a small mom-and-pop shop in uptown Lando. He wandered off from his parents and felt he would never find them again. He panicked and felt like he would be alone for the rest of his life. It had turned out that they were an aisle over, and he had only been separated from them for five minutes. It had felt so much longer than that, though. It's incredible how space and time can seem much more significant when you're a child. Sydney pondered over these thoughts as he continued his search for Victoria.

As he continued his search, he got sidetracked in the magazine section. A tabloid rag's bold headline caught his eye, and he felt compelled to stop and pick the magazine up and read it.

ABDUCTED MAN RETURNED AFTER INTERGALACTIC VOYAGE

Sydney flipped through the magazine to the cover story and began reading an incredible tale of a man who claimed to have been abducted by aliens. The man described waking up in a spaceship, climbing out of some sort of metallic sleep pod, and stumbling over to an impossibly large window looking out into open space. He witnessed a planet coming up on the horizon, and as it grew closer, he identified it as Saturn. He described how gorgeous the rings were and how photos could never do them justice. As he stood in awe in front of the window, he became incredibly sleepy and passed out. When he awoke, he found himself lying on the grass outside his home, looking up into the night sky as a bright light ascended into the heavens, disappearing moments later. When he stumbled to his feet and went inside, his family crowded around him and embraced him tightly. He was told that he had been missing for an entire week.

What a load of shit. These people will print anything for poor hapless sons of bitches to read out there. Sydney laughed as he returned the magazine to the rack. He stepped away from the magazine rack and accidentally walked into a kid reading a comic book.

"Whoa, I'm sorry. I didn't see ya there, big man." Sydney crouched down and picked up the comic the kid was reading. "Hmm, Gross Point? Looks pretty scary," Sydney said, looking at the comic's cover. It depicted two menacing young kids on a street corner sitting down at a table peddling "soft drinks" to passersby. The bright red "soft drink" was held within an enormous glass dispenser for fifty cents a glass. Four leather-clad vampires lined up, eager to get a taste.

The kid took the comic back and replied, "Not really. It's actually pretty funny. You should read it sometime, sir."

Sydney smiled, "Maybe I will, kid."

"The name's Danny, sir."

"I'm sorry...Danny." Sydney looked down to the end of the aisle and saw Victoria walk by with the cart. "Oh, sorry, Danny. Gotta run. Enjoy the comic!"

"Sir?!" Sydney quickly turned around, and Danny had his cheesecake in his hand. "Don't forget this!"

"Oh, thank you. That's the second time I almost forgot this." Sydney turned and ran, hoping he would catch up with her this time.

He turned down the canned goods aisle and spotted her putting a few cans of honey carrots in the cart. He felt a great sense of relief wash over him. "Yo, Vicky, I've been looking for you. I got the cheesecake!"

Victoria turned around and smiled. "Looking for me? I saw you down the magazine aisle reading a few minutes ago. Did you think you'd find me in the magazine?"

Sydney hung his head for a moment. "No, I got sidetracked reading about some dude who said aliens abducted him."

"I see. Those tabloids always have caught your eye. Oh, why's there an expiry sticker on the cake? I wanted you to get a freshly baked one."

"The guy in the bakery, Henry, put it there to save us some cash. It's still fresh."

"Henry? You're on a first-name basis with the bakers here?" Victoria said, letting out a laugh.

"Oh, I just met him today. He seems like a cool dude. So, did you get everything?"

"Let's see..." Victoria eyeballed the cart and looked back up at Sydney. "Yep, that's everything we need."

"Alright. Let's go pay and get outta here." Sydney followed Victoria as she pushed the cart toward the checkout. Standing in line, he began looking at her and thinking about what Henry had said. *When are you gonna make an honest woman of her?* Henry's words echoed within his mind. *That certainly is something to think about. We've been together for ten years in October. Maybe...it's time for a change. What about Sharon, though? What the hell am I gonna do about her?*

"Syd? You wanna grab the bags?" Victoria said as she was paying for the groceries.

"What? Oh, sure thing," he said as he came out of his thoughts. He grabbed onto four sizeable brown paper bags and walked towards the exit. He pushed the door open and held it for Victoria. The two entered back into the humid late afternoon air. The sun hid behind the building and cast a long shadow onto the parking lot. He loaded the groceries into the trunk, and they climbed back into Alex.

"You ready for supper, Vicky?"

"Yessss. Can you hear my stomach?"

Sydney put his head down towards her stomach, and sure enough, he could hear it rumbling. "Hehe. Yeah, I hear it. Patience, my pet," he said as he rubbed her stomach.

"Syd! Quit it," Victoria laughed as the two began the drive to Albert's house.

CHAPTER 6
Supper With Sydney

"It's been a while since I've been over here," Victoria said as she entered the front door.

"Yeah, it has," Sydney replied as he walked inside and carried the groceries to the kitchen.

"It's so quiet. It's kind of eerie."

"It kinda is. Do you think Al's mom will come out of it?"

Victoria took a seat on the couch. "I hope so. Did you see her eyes? They just looked…lifeless. Like she wasn't even there." Sydney remembered his aunt lying in her hospital bed and how his father had blamed him for everything. "I shouldn't have brought her up. We should focus on supper," Victoria said, forcing a smile.

"Yeah, that sounds good to me."

Sydney began prepping the food with Victoria's assistance. "It's great to have you back in the kitchen as my sous chef, Vicky," he said, smiling.

"It's great to be back, but the chef forgot to wash two dishes in the sink."

Sydney looked over and saw the two dishes from that morning's breakfast. He had utterly forgotten them after Sharon had put them in there. "Yeah, Al and Aunt Milly left those... I'll wash them up real quick, babe." The lie flowed seamlessly out of him. It was a bit scary to him how easy it had become to create these lies. As he stood there washing the dishes, Victoria hummed quietly as she prepped the food. He thought about the morning again. Sharon stood in almost the exact spot humming as well. He finished washing the dishes and tried pushing the thoughts out of his mind.

The two worked closely together, and before long, everything was cooking, and the entire house became filled with a delectable aroma. Sydney carefully removed the kabobs from the oven and left them to cool a bit on the stove.

"Mmm, they smell divine," Victoria said as she leaned over the stove, breathing deeply of the heavenly aroma.

Sydney looked over at Victoria. Her dress was clinging to her body in all the right places. "Yeah, now that I think about it, though, I'm kind of in the mood for some rump roast."

"Rump roast? Why's that?"

"Because the best meat's in the rump!" Sydney said as he pinched Victoria's behind.

"Syd, stop it!" She said as she began to giggle hysterically. "Later...you have to wait."

Sydney looked into Victoria's eyes and saw the fire begin to ignite deep within them. "Sure, Vicky. I can wait. Until then, let's eat." He leaned over and pulled her close to him, and kissed her.

"Why don't you go grab a seat at the table, and I'll fix your plate, baby," Sydney said, smiling.

"Alright, that works for me." Victoria left the kitchen, and Sydney began plating the kabobs.

A few minutes later, he exited the kitchen holding two plates loaded with fragrant kabobs. Victoria had raised the blinds over the window and was staring out onto the back deck. "Dinner is served, Vicky."

She continued to sit staring out the window. In the reflection, Sydney noticed a thoughtful expression on her face. "Hey, Syd. You ever wonder about those far-off stars in the sky? Like, if there's another world out there and on it, people are staring back right now at their sky, and they can see a tiny pinpoint of light in the sky, not knowing that's us?"

Sydney couldn't help but think about the tabloid article he had read earlier that day. "I suppose I've looked up off and on and wondered plenty of things. Me and Al used to lie down and look up into the night sky in my backyard growing up."

"How romantic."

Sydney turned away, stifling a laugh. "Yeah, yeah. We did that a lot back in the old days. I wonder if he's out there looking up at the sky tonight?"

Victoria turned away from the window and leaned over, and embraced Sydney. "Let's eat, baby. The kabobs are gonna get cold."

"Yeah, let's do it," Sydney said as he took the seat opposite Victoria.

As the two were starting on their second kabobs, a knock came from the front door. "Who the hell is this?" Sydney said, lowing a kabob from his mouth.

"I don't know…want me to go check?" Victoria said as she was about to stand.

"No, you eat. I'll check it out. Maybe it's the cops?"

"Ah, maybe. OK, you go check."

Sydney walked over to the front door, looked out of the diamond-shaped window, and saw no one standing outside. The front porch was cloaked in darkness. He switched the light on, and although the porch was illuminated in a bright light, he still saw no one. He slowly opened the door, and a figure hidden off to the side wrapped its arms around him.

"Hello, Syd. Surprise!"

Sydney's eyes grew wide with surprise. "Sh-Sharon?!" he whispered. He turned around and closed the door behind him.

"Haha. Yeah, it's me! I haven't heard from you since our…talk this afternoon. I tried calling you earlier but couldn't get through to you. I felt bad, and I knew you were going to be here tonight. I could smell those kabobs when you opened the door. So, you made them after all? You knew I'd be by, didn't you? You know me so well. You know I can't stay away."

His mind was reeling. *Oh, shit! This is not good. She can't be here right now. No, no, no!*

Sharon moved close to Sydney and whispered in his ear. "Is everything alright, babe? You look like you've seen a ghost. I know I surprised you but was it that bad?"

"No, I'm alright. It's just..." A moment later, Sydney heard the front door slowly open. He immediately pushed Sharon away from him. Sharon stumbled a few steps backward. Sydney turned to see Victoria standing in the doorway, eating a shrimp kabob.

"Is everything alright, Syd? Who is this?"

Sydney stood speechless for a moment. "This? She said her car broke down a few blocks over, and she asked to use the phone to call for a tow truck." Sharon looked at Sydney and Victoria.

"Is that right? I'm sorry. Would you like to come in and use the phone?"

Sharon stood there and forced a smile, shaking her head in agreement. "Thank you. I was...worried that I wouldn't get anyone to help me," Sharon said, stepping past Sydney and into the house.

"Well, we'll help you out. In fact, that happened to me one time a few years back. On my way home from the university, I got a flat tire in King City."

"You go to KCU?"

"Yeah, I'm studying to become an English teacher."

"That's cool. How much do you have left?"

"Only one year, thankfully." Sydney couldn't believe his eyes. Sharon and Victoria were having a conversation together in the living room. It felt like he had entered the Twilight Zone when he opened the front door.

A few minutes later, Sharon finished her call. She had gotten on the phone and given directions to where her car was supposed to be. Sydney had no idea who she called, but he knew damn well that she wasn't on the line requesting a tow truck. Her acting was phenomenal. It rivaled even his own.

"I sure do appreciate your help. I must be getting back to my car, though. I have to meet them there."

"Oh, before you go, would you like a kabob? Syd and I made enough to spare."

"You made them yourselves? Together?"

"Oh, yeah. We love to cook together. I'll go wrap one up for you." Sharon looked at Sydney, and he could see the profound sadness in her eyes. He wanted to apologize for all of this. He never wanted her to be a part of any of it.

Victoria came back from the kitchen with a kabob wrapped in tin foil. "Here you go…um, I never caught your name."

"Sharon. Sharon Moon."

"Sharon, you be careful out there. Glad we could help."

"You've been very nice. I have to be leaving now. Enjoy your evening." Sharon exited the cool air inside Albert's home and entered the humid night outside. Just like that, she was gone. Sydney sat on the couch, wondering if what had happened genuinely occurred or if he had imagined the whole thing.

"I hope she gets back home, OK."

"Huh?" Sydney said, looking up at Victoria, who was standing looking out of the diamond-shaped window of the door.

"Sharon. Well, she's gone now." Victoria switched the light off outside and returned to the dining room table. "And on that note…how about we finish our supper?"

"Right," that was all Sydney could think of to say. He sat back down and picked up the kabob he was going to eat earlier but found that he had lost his appetite.

"I'm gonna jump in the shower," Sydney said as he stood up from the table.

"Shower? What about dessert? Don't you want some cheesecake?"

"I'll have some when I get out."

Sydney decided to use his aunt Milly's bathroom to shower. Albert's bathroom was always a bit too closed in for his liking. It also didn't come equipped with a window which added to the sense of claustrophobia. He entered the bathroom and began to undress. He let his clothes fall to the floor in a pile and stepped into a large tub with a small rectangular window above it. He reached up and rotated the handle letting in a fresh breeze of air from outside. He turned the handles on the faucet, adjusted the temperature to his liking, and stepped into the warm stream of water. He closed his eyes and listened to the sound of the water rush down the drain at his feet. *Sharon...I'm sorry.* He thought about the look of immense pain in her eyes. *Vicky had no idea who she had met tonight. Christ, I'm a terrible person. When did I get to be like this? Lying all the time...It didn't use to be this way.*

He stood there, letting the water cascade over his body, wholly lost within his thoughts of self-loathing for what felt like ages until he was brought back by Victoria's voice.

"Is there room enough for two?" Sydney looked over to see Victoria peeking at him from around the shower curtain.

"Yeah, Vicky. There's always room for you."

"Good. One sec." She disappeared behind the curtain and reappeared a few moments later and hopped into the shower. Sydney moved out of the warm stream of water and let Victoria step into it. She began to wet her long wavy hair. She had kept her hair in pretty much the same style for all these years. He loved it, though. It certainly suited her perfectly.

"Do you wanna scrub my back, Syd?" Victoria turned around, and Sydney admired the curvature of her spine as the water ran down it. He grabbed a bar of soap, ran it between her shoulder blades, and built a nice lather. He ran his hands over her back, feeling her warm skin slide over his fingertips. "That feels so nice," she said as he continued to wash her back. "Syd, do you want me?" she said, turning around and looking up into his eyes.

"Yes, more than anything," he said as he pulled her close to him. Her body pressed into his, and the excitement between them rose to a fever pitch.

"Let's go to the bedroom, Syd," Victoria said as she hopped out of the shower and hastily dried off. He followed closely behind her, and the two jumped onto his aunt's bed and began to make love. It had been a while since the two had made love together. Sydney found himself trying to avoid thinking about Sharon. He had made love to Sharon more these past few months than Victoria, and those thoughts kept creeping into his mind. He cast them aside and focused on the here and now. He wanted to make Victoria happy. She deserved every second of pleasure that he could give to her.

After the two of them finished, they embraced one another. They lie in the cool, comfortable darkness of the bedroom. "That was amazing," Victoria said, breaking the silence.

"You were amazing."

Victoria placed her head upon Sydney's chest. Her hair was still damp from the shower and felt nice against his warm skin. "I can hear your heartbeat."

"Oh, yeah? You know what it sounds like? Vic-ky! Vic-ky! Vic-ky!"

Victoria giggled, "How did you get to be so cute?"

"Years of practice." Victoria became quiet again.

"Everything alright?" Sydney asked.

"Yeah, just listening to your heartbeat. It's soothing." She turned her head and kissed his chest. "I love you, Syd."

"I love you too, Vicky." His eyes grew heavy as he lay there with Victoria's head upon his chest. He found himself within a random world of dreams. The day's events unrolled before him in broken flashes.

CHAPTER 7
On The Rooftop

Sydney was woken several hours later by a loud sound emanating from the living room. His sleep-fogged brain struggled for a few moments to identify it. As the fog subsided, he recognized it as the phone ringing. It kept ringing over and over. He lay there hoping it would stop. He had a bad feeling about what lay on the end of the line. Nobody calls in the middle of the night unless it's bad news. That's always been the case. He was content where he was. Victoria slept soundly next to him. A light snore would come from her every few moments as she exhaled. She would never believe she snored. Sydney had told her once, but she took great offense to it. Maybe it had been the way he had worded it. She didn't snore like a bear. He thought she sounded downright adorable. Victoria was out like a light. Usually, any slight noise would wake her, but tonight, she slept blissfully, unaware of the never-ending ring of the telephone.

He began to count the rings of the phone. It rang ten, fifteen, and twenty times before finally becoming silent. *Thank Christ for that*, he thought to himself when the phone began to ring again a moment later. It was starting to drive him mad. He hopped out of bed as quietly as possible, opened the bedroom door, and slowly closed it behind him. He bolted to the phone beside the couch on an end table and answered it without even looking at the caller ID.

"Hello?" he spoke into the receiver, audibly annoyed. There was nothing but silence until Sydney began to listen closer and could hear the sound of sobbing on the opposite end of the line. "Who is this? Hello?"

"It's me, Syd. You sound angry. I'm sorry. I didn't mean to wake you."

"Sharon? What's going on? Is everything alright? I'm not mad…you don't need to apologize."

"Were you in bed with…her? Did you make love to her tonight, Sydney?" Sydney took the phone away from his ear and looked behind him at the door to his aunt's bedroom. He hoped to God that Victoria would continue to sleep blissfully. "Why did you go? Why did you turn away from me?" Sharon sobbed into the phone.

Sydney closed his eyes and took a seat on the couch. "Sharon, I'm sorry. You weren't supposed to see any of that."

She let out a laugh. "So, you were going to do all that and lie to me about it? Is that it?"

"I didn't say that."

"You didn't have to. I know you. You're a liar…and you're very good at it. You scare me sometimes at how stone-faced you can look at me and lie."

"Sharon, I don't lie to you."

More laughter. "How can you say that? Do you not respect me at all? I guess I really *am* just a whore to you. A plaything for your amusement."

"That's not true. I care about you, Sharon." There was a long moment of silence then. Sydney sat listening intently. He thought he could hear the sound of doors closing and other far-off sounds on the opposite end.

"Sydney…I want you. Come to me. Leave her there tonight. Please, come. I'll be waiting…for you."

Sharon hung the phone up, and Sydney sat there for a minute, listening to the sounds of the house settling. He looked at his watch. It read 3:17. A car passed by on the street outside, casting its headlights through the diamond-shaped window of the door for a brief moment. He stood up and thought about what she had said. Sharon didn't sound well. He couldn't leave her alone like that, not in good conscience. *I'll go over and calm her down. I'm gonna end this tonight. I can't keep living this double life. I'm not that great of a guy. I know damn well a beautiful girl like her can find a guy who can be with her every day, all day, and give her all the love and affection she desires.* He nodded in affirmation and crept back to the bedroom to collect his clothes in a pile on the bathroom floor.

He slowly opened the door, and it let out a sound that made Sydney think of a crypt door. *This damn door picked a hell of a time to cast me as the crypt keeper. Good evening boils and ghouls...* he thought to himself as his eyes were fixed upon Victoria cloaked in shadow. He listened intently to her breathing. She was still letting out those quiet little snores as before. *Hot damn. She really is out...Thank God for that.* He walked across the room into the bathroom, collected his clothes into his arms, and slipped back into the hallway, closing the door behind him.

He threw his clothes on as quickly and quietly as possible, walked to the front door, and entered the humid night air. Then, he realized he would have to take Victoria's car. He had forgotten that he'd left his Miata at their apartment. He let out a string of curses, went back inside, and flipped the switch for the overhead light in the living room.

Sydney noticed Victoria's purse on the marble coffee table in front of the couch. He walked over and slid his hand into it, hoping to feel the metallic coolness of keys, and breathed a sigh of relief when his fingertips stroked the cool ridges of one of them. He retrieved the keys, slipped them into his back pocket, and high-tailed it outside.

He ran over to Alex and unlocked the door, and slid onto the cool surface of the cloth driver's seat. He said a prayer as he started the car and pulled out onto the street that Victoria wouldn't awake until the morning. As he hit the road, he threw the car in drive and sped off down the dark city streets of Lando towards Sharon's apartment on the other side of town. He prayed as he drove like a bat out of hell that no cops would be around and Sharon would be alright when he got there. Even though he had had barely any sleep, he was operating on pure adrenaline at this time. He drove like a man possessed.

Sydney pulled into the parking lot of Sharon's apartment building in record time. He flew into a parking space, slammed the brakes, turned the car off, and looked up at the building in front of him for a moment. He'd only ever entered it a handful of times, but he remembered perfectly where Sharon lived, Apartment 717. He got out, locked the door, and ran for the main entrance. He grasped the golden handle of the ancient door and entered the cool lobby of the building. His footsteps echoed off the walls as he hurried along to the elevator.

Once he reached it, he found the doorway adorned with a large sign.

OUT OF ORDER - Take the stairs

"Damn it to hell!" he softly said to himself.

He took to the stairs and scaled them two at a time for the first two floors but then quickly began to tire as he continued upward. Once he reached the seventh floor, he was about ready to give out but pressed onward. He got his second wind when he went around the corner and saw her apartment in view. He knocked on the door and waited a moment catching his breath, when he noticed a white slip of paper stuck between the door and the frame. He grabbed it and yanked it out. On the front of the paper was his name in Sharon's handwriting. He opened the letter, unsure of what was inside.

MEET ME ON THE ROOFTOP... - SHARON

Below her signature was a kiss mark in bright red lipstick. He looked at the letter a moment, intrigued by what she was doing up there. As he traversed the three remaining floors to the roof, he thought back to the last time they'd been up there together.

It was a few months prior, in April. He remembered it was right before his cousin Albert had been released to come home from Duke's End. Sydney frequented the Sexothèque almost every night, while Victoria had decided to stay in King City for a week with friends at their apartment, studying for important exams. He had gone out with Sharon every one of those nights, and they ended up back at her place a few times. They'd ended up back at his place one time too. He'd overdone it and couldn't make it out the door, so Sharon decided to escort him home. She loaded him into his Miata and found out where he lived from his driver's license. When he awoke the following day, he was in his bed and looked over to see Sharon lying naked, close beside him. Ever since that night, he explained to her that it was too risky to spend time at his place. He promised to spend time at her place...which he did. He just didn't spend the night there.

He had come close, though, on that final night before Victoria was to come home from King City. Sharon had been off work that night, and Sydney met her at her apartment. She hopped into his Miata and told him to drive around the lake. She wanted to watch the evening fog roll in and see the twinkling lights of the lakefront homes on the opposite shore. She explained that when she was a little girl, she dreamed of living in one of those palatial estates overlooking the city below. He promised her he'd build her dream home in those hills one day. She was so happy to hear him say that. Later that night, when they returned from their scenic drive, Sharon randomly laughed all the way to her apartment. On the elevator ride up, Sydney finally asked her, "What are you laughing about, babe?" She replied, "Nothing. I'm just happy."

They entered her apartment, and he tore the clothes off of her in a frenzy. Sydney sunk his teeth into her neck and kissed every square inch of her body. Just when Sydney was about to make love to her, Sharon told him to stop, and she threw on her blue robe and told him to follow her. She led him down the hallway to the staircase, traversing the three flights of stairs leading to a door labeled ROOF ACCESS.

She swung the door open, threw her arms out, and spun around laughing. "This is my secret place. I come up here to look at the stars." She walked towards the edge and sat down on the raised concrete platform. Sydney watched in amazement as her robe slowly came open, and Sharon gazed into Sydney's eyes with a sultry look. "Make love to me beneath the stars, Sydney. I want to look up into the night sky and feel like I'm falling into it."

He rushed over to her, took her in his arms, and made love to her on the rooftop. She clung to him as she sat on the edge as they made love. After a while, she stopped clinging to him and leaned ever closer to the edge. Sydney was lost in the moment, and with one thrust, Sharon fell backward. Sydney quickly grabbed her robe with both hands and pulled her towards him. He fell back, pulling her on top of him. They lie there for a moment in shock. If he had reacted a second slower, she'd have fallen all the way down...he didn't want to think about it. He put his arms around her and held her tightly. The two of them lay on the roof, not uttering a word, but he could feel her tears pooling upon his shirt. As he lay there, he closed his eyes and cried silently too.

Sydney reached the top of the stairs and came upon the familiar door again. He slowly opened it and stepped out onto the pitch-black rooftop. As he looked around, a gust of wind blew through his hair. "Over here, babe!" a voice called out in the darkness. A bolt of lightning illuminated the sky, and in the distance, on the opposite end of the roof, he saw a figure standing on the edge. It was Sharon dressed in her blue robe just as she had been that night a month prior.

Christ's sake! he thought as he ran across the roof, making it halfway when Sharon yelled out to him, "Don't come any closer! Stay...away!"

He did just as she asked. "Sharon, what are you doing? Come off of the ledge, babe. It's dangerous. We can talk about this." Another flash of lightning lit the sky, and the wind intensified. On the street below, Sydney could hear the branches of the trees moving steadily in the gusts. He took another step closer, and Sharon took a step back closer to the edge. "Jesus Christ, Sharon!"

"I told you not to come any closer! I'll step right off this ledge, Syd! I swear to God above I will!"

Sydney stood helplessly, not knowing what to do. "Tell me what you want, Sharon! What will make you come down from there!?"

"You know what I want. I want *YOU*! I've *ALWAYS* wanted you! Why don't we just vanish? Disappear into the night just the two of us. Albert did it! Why don't we join him!?"

"You say that like I know where he is. I don't know where he went! Where do you think we could go? We can't just up and leave."

Sharon hung her head. "Yes, it's a lovely thought, isn't it? Oh, I've been such a gullible fool. I was willing to believe every single promise you made me when I knew deep down...that you'd never be able to give me anything. You'll never leave HER...*VICKY* for me! The way she looks at you...she looks at you the same way I do. I have to wonder, though...does she realize how good she has it? She's smart, beautiful, and kind. She has a bright future doing whatever she wants for her career and has the love of her life beside her for it all...I wonder if you'll build her that house you promised me. That house that we'll never live in. The love we'll never have to fill it with. The sound of little feet..." she trailed off and began to sob.

Sydney ran over before she could realize it and grabbed her off of the ledge and got on top of her. She looked up at him with hatred in her eyes. She kicked and screamed as loud as she could, but a deafening thunder roared overhead, and the sky unleashed torrential rain upon them. She began to yell over the storm into Sydney's face. "WHY CAN'T I EVER BE GOOD ENOUGH FOR YOU!? WHY DON'T YOU JUST LET ME DIE!? I CAN'T LIVE LIKE THIS, SYDNEY!! LET ME KILL MYSELF! YOU WON'T HAVE TO CHOOSE BETWEEN US THEN!"

Sydney grabbed her and began to shake her, and yelled, "STOP TALKING LIKE THIS! YOU'RE A BEAUTIFUL GIRL WITH YOUR ENTIRE LIFE IN FRONT OF YOU! YOU'RE JUST AS SMART AND BEAUTIFUL AS ANY WOMAN OUT THERE! YOU DON'T NEED ME TO GIVE YOU THE WORLD! YOU CAN TAKE IT RIGHT NOW!!"

Sharon lies speechless, looking up at Sydney. The hatred in her eyes began to disappear, replaced by indifference. A few minutes passed, and she finally spoke to him. "Alright…let's go inside. We'll talk more in the apartment."

Sydney warily moved off of her but held onto her right arm. "Alright. Let's get down from this roof," Sydney said as he led her by the arm to the stairwell.

They reached the apartment, and Sharon reached into her soaking-wet robe, brought out the keys, and opened the door. She cast the soaking wet robe at her feet and fell naked into the couch face down. She lies there motionless.

"You want some coffee?" No reply. "I'm gonna make some coffee." Sydney went and fixed up a pot of coffee and returned to find Sharon lying on her back with a vacant look in her eyes. It scared him. It was the same look his aunt had possessed at the hospital. "Sharon? Baby? Talk to me."

"Don't call me baby. I'm not your baby."

"Now you're talking to me, baby. That I like." It wasn't the time for some macho swagger. He knew that, but he hoped it might lighten the mood.

"Sydney?"

"…Yes, Sharon?"

"Did you ever love me?"

He fell onto the loveseat beside the couch. "Of course. I still do."

"Were you ever going to leave Victoria for me?" He sat there momentarily, trying to find a way to answer. "Your silence speaks volumes to me." How was he supposed to respond? He had spent ten years with Victoria! They had grown up and experienced so much together! "If you're not going to talk, you'll have to leave. I don't need a one-sided conversation, although I know this isn't going anywhere. I know you've been with her for all these years. You've grown comfortable with her and don't want to take a risk with…me. I imagine you think things will be more difficult with me. Your cushy job with her family's business would be gone. All of that easy money you've grown accustomed to would disappear. You don't have to say it. You probably came over here to tell me all of this anyway. Well, I don't need you to tell me. It doesn't matter if you love me. I want more, but you're never going to give me more. Just go…have a good life. I'll figure things out…I always have."

Sydney leaned over and tried to touch her. "No, don't touch me! I'll die if you touch me." He pulled his hand away and stood up. Through the apartment windows, he could see the first golden rays of sunlight peeking into the room. "Wow, would you look at that. It's morning. You finally stayed the night. You should be getting back. She'll wonder where you are if you stay much longer." He looked at his watch. 5:47, it read. "Syd, just go. Thank you for coming here and trying, but let's be honest, we were doomed from the start."

Once upon a time, Sydney would have had about a million things to say to Sharon. Right now, when it counted, he had absolutely nothing. She was right…about everything. He didn't want to accept it, so he kept stringing her along. This was the cold honest truth, though. "You're right, Sharon.

You're right about...everything. I'm a coward. I couldn't even tell you what I already knew."

"Sydney, please go. The longer you stay, the more difficult this is for both of us." He turned away from her and walked towards the door. He placed his hand upon the cold knob, turned it, and stepped out into the hallway. Sydney began to turn around when the door slammed shut behind him. He could hear her sobbing on the opposite side of the door, and a part of him desperately wanted to go back and hold her and tell her it would all be alright, promise her the world and everything in it. They would be nothing but empty promises, though. He knew that, and he was finally facing that fact head-on.

As he drove back home, he felt exhausted. All he wanted to do was sleep to forget. He didn't want to hear Sharon sobbing anymore. As he drove back to Albert's, it felt like he couldn't get her sobbing out of his mind. He passed the Lando Community Library, glanced at it, and thought of Albert. Something within himself snapped, and he began to sob, but he managed to regain control of himself and push down these chaotic feelings. He didn't want to think about Albert right now, along with Sharon. It was far too much for him to handle.

He returned to Albert's, parked Alex, and headed for the front door. He was so tired he barely felt like dragging himself up the steps. He entered the house with his eyes closed and breathed a deep breath. "Sydney?" He fell backward into the door banging the back of his head on it. Victoria sat in the rocking chair, wearing a blue robe next to the couch. The first thought through his sleep-addled mind was, *What the fuck is with all of these blue robes?* "Where did you go? You've been gone for hours."

Sydney took a seat on the couch. "Hey, Vicky."

"Syd, answer me. Where the hell have you been?" He closed his eyes and drifted off. "Sydney!"

He jolted upwards. "Oh, hey, Vicky."

"Stop fuckin' around! Where were you!? I woke up to the sound of the car starting and realized you had taken it. That was close to three thirty! It's after six now! Now TELL ME!"

"I was out looking for Albert! I had a bad dream about him and couldn't sleep until I drove all over Lando looking for him!"

"Really? Syd...do you promise me that's what happened?"

"Yes, Vicky. I promise."

"Do you swear to me?"

"Yes," he said, closing his eyes. She got up from the rocker and ran down the hallway toward Albert's room. She returned a few minutes later with a Bible. "Put your hand on this. Do you swear that you were only looking for Albert?"

Lord, forgive me for this, he thought as he placed his hand upon the cover and answered. "Yes, I swear."

"You didn't go anywhere else?"

"Where would I go to at that hour?"

"I don't know...how about the Sexothèque?"

He maintained his composure. He was going to see where this was going. "The what?"

"It's a strip club downtown. Alexis and John told me about it. I tried calling you a lot when I was out of town last month, and you barely answered me at night. They said they bet you were down at the Sexothèque at that hour. They were kidding, of course. I mean, no man of mine would go to a strip club, especially one called something as ridiculous as that."

What the fuck? How would they even know about that place? he thought, maintaining a perfect poker face, but on the inside, relief washed over him in an awesome wave.

"Sydney, I'm sorry...I just have this feeling that something is wrong between us. Please, tell me that's not the case. When I woke up and knew you had left me alone here without a word, it was as if you were sneaking off somewhere to do something you didn't want me to know about. I love you, Sydney." She stood up, sat beside him on the couch, and took his hand. She held it firmly and looked him in the eye. "Tell me everything is OK. Are we not the same as we used to be?"

Sydney felt the comforting warmth emanating from her hand. "Vicky, everything is fine. I love you too."

"Really? Then why do I feel this way? You're the other half of my heart. How could I go on without the other half of my heart?"

"Vicky," he spoke softly and firmly, "I love you now just as much as the day I met you almost ten years ago. Nothing is wrong between us."

She embraced him tightly. "Alright, I believe you. I love you, Sydney. Hold me. Never let me go."

"I love you too, Vicky." He held her tightly there on the couch for a long while.

As he held her, he felt like a real piece of shit. He didn't deserve to be in the warm embrace of Victoria's loving arms. He deserved to be out there all alone with the rest of the lonely people of the world. He wanted so badly to let the dammed-up emotions within him burst out, but he didn't want to burden Vicky with his guilt about Albert. He didn't deserve to be comforted by her anyway. He would have to find a way to work out all those feelings in time. More than anything, at that moment, all he wanted was to fall asleep.

CHAPTER 8
Look To The Stars

Over the following month, Sydney took one day at a time. He made Victoria's happiness his priority as he dealt with everything with Albert and Sharon on his own. He didn't like bringing up Albert, but he was never far from his mind. After a week of looking out for him at his house with Victoria, they were advised by the police to go home. If they came across any information, they would immediately let Sydney know.

Summer came in full swing again, and with it, Sydney took Victoria out to local parks they hadn't visited since they first began dating. It was an excellent way to help rekindle his feelings and reinforce that he still loved her with all of his heart. During one of these dates, his cell phone "accidentally" fell out of his pocket and into the lake. He got another one the following day and only gave Victoria and his family his new number.

Mid-July fast approached them, and they realized it had almost been a year since they had first moved in together. Victoria had written it down, flipped back through her papers, and found it was July 17th. They decided to invite all of their family over for dinner. Victoria didn't mention Albert, but it was an unspoken detail between them. She had repeatedly asked Sydney if he wanted to talk further about what had happened, but Sydney was too afraid to delve into it in case he should let anything slip about that night he didn't want her to know. He just wanted to leave it alone.

The two reached out to their respective families, and Sydney quickly discovered that his side of the table would be rather bare. His mother and father were preoccupied with moving Albert's mother into their home to watch after her themselves. It was such a sad thing. His aunt Milly had remained, for the most part, unresponsive. Besides being able to be moved short distances on her own feet while being led and eating when you fed her, she could not do anything else for herself. Sydney was glad that his parents, his mom mostly, would be watching after her now. Maybe if she were around family, she'd come around in time? He prayed that that would be the case. He told Victoria it would just be her family and asked if she could invite Alexis and John along. He didn't mind. In truth, he loved John. The dude was always worth a laugh. Alexis was, too, but she played the straight "man" most of the time.

The 17th came quickly, as Sydney knew it would. He was going to have that rump roast for real this time. The two stocked up on all the supplies, and when the day arrived, he acted as head chef and Victoria his sous chef again. Things couldn't have gone smoother with the preparation of everything. Everything was pretty much finished by the time people started arriving. Victoria's parents, Wayne and Greta, showed up first. He answered the door and greeted them both. "Hope you guys brought your appetites. We're having rump roast tonight."

"Oh, that sounds delicious, my son," Wayne said, smacking his lips comically. He always brought laughter with him. Sydney loved Wayne. In all honesty, he loved him more than his own father. Wayne wasn't perfect and would sometimes get irritable, but Sydney understood that he worried a lot about Victoria's older brother and the carpentry business.

"Hello, my love. I've missed ya. Oh, that smells heavenly. We can't wait to dig in."

"Great to see ya, Mudder," Sydney said. Victoria's mother was named Grace, but she called her mother

"Mudder," and it stuck with Sydney. He had grown to be another son to her. In the past, he found himself getting her to sew holes in clothes that his mother couldn't do. She was an easygoing person whose main goal was to win the jackpot on the local TV bingo. So far, she had won several smaller pots, but the jackpot remained elusive.

A few minutes later, Victoria's older brother Waylon arrived with his wife, Claire. "Hey, Waylon, Claire. Glad to see ya. We're having rump roast."

"Oh, you cook the rump roast?" Claire asked him.

"Well, me and Vicky together. She was my sous chef."

"I'm looking forward to it, Syd. I just finished building a deck on the north part of the lake. Thing was massive. So, I hope I can have seconds."

"Of course, you can, man. We've got a lot of sides too. Vegetables, fruit, salad, cheesecake."

Waylon smiled brightly, "Ah, Victoria asked you to buy a cheesecake, eh?"

Sydney smiled back, "You know how she loves those things."

"Right on. Well, you know what they say. Happy wife, happy life. You're learning that early." Waylon gave him a pat on the back and proceeded to the table of ever-growing chatter. Waylon was a hard-working man. From the ground up, he built his business, Tesson's Carpentry, and became the best carpenter in Lando. If you wanted an expansion on your house, or an entire house for that matter, Waylon would build it to your specifications. Sydney looked up to him and could never thank him enough for taking him on after graduating high school. Waylon molded, or rather carved, him into what he is today.

His wife Claire also worked for the company. She was Waylon's secretary and answered all the calls throughout the day. Once upon a time, Victoria helped her with the office work, but within the past year, she'd given it up to pursue her teaching career.

Another knock came upon the door, and Sydney opened it to Victoria's grandparents. "Hello, Syd, my son. How you been gettin' on?"

"Hey, Pop. I've been doing OK. Hope you're hungry," Sydney said as he shook Pop's hand. The man was 81 years old, but damn did he have an iron grip handshake, like Burt Reynolds and shit. Sydney feared what a handshake would have been like in his prime. He imagined Pop could take a lump of coal and squeeze it and produce a diamond.

"I brought my appetite alright. Now, is it ready?"

"Almost, Pop. Go have a seat."

"Alright, hope it's not much longer."

"We'll get there, Pop. We'll get there," he said with a grin.

Behind Pop came Nan. She was a small-framed woman who was a bit soft-spoken. Every time she spoke to Sydney, she'd always be very friendly and never failed to send him a birthday card signed 'Nan & Pop' every year. "Hi, Nan. Glad you could come," he said as he hugged her.

"Is this everyone, Victoria?" Wayne asked.

"No, Dad. We've got two more people showing up," Victoria called out from the kitchen.

Right on cue, a knock came upon the door, and Sydney opened it to see the bespectacled John with Alexis by his side. "Yo, John. Good to see ya, man."

"Oh, looks like everyone is here already," Alexis said, looking at everyone sitting at the table.

"We're fashionably late, Alexis. Hey, Syd."

"Hope you guys are hungry. We're having rump roast."

"You know what they say. The best meat's in the rump."

"Yes! That's exactly what they say! A man after my own heart. Get in here, you two."

Alexis and John took a seat across from Nan and Pop. Victoria came over and began chatting with them. She then

Questions In A World Of Blue

said to Sydney, "Can you keep an eye on the food for a few minutes?"

"Yes, dear," she narrowed her eyes at him, and he smiled mischievously. She didn't like it when he said that.

He stood in the kitchen listening to all the chatter when Victoria came in and asked him a favor. "Hey, can you run down to the mailbox and check it? I forgot to check it today, and John and Alexis said they sent us a postcard from their vacation they just got back from last week."

"Sure thing, baby. Hey, come here…"

She walked over to him and looked into his eyes, "Yes?"

He leaned in and kissed her and gave her butt a light smack. "I'll be back, Vicky. The food should be about ready. You can probably start serving it now."

Sydney walked downstairs to the mailboxes located around the corner from their apartment block. It was a lovely summer evening with a light breeze in the air. As he walked, he could hear the sound of children playing in the distance mixed with the hum of lawnmowers and the central air units around the apartment complex.

When he got to the box, he slid the key into the hole and opened it. Sure enough, they had some mail. Within the box was a small pile of letters. One of them was the postcard from John and Alexis. They had just gotten back from a week in The Bahamas. The postcard showed a lovely beach with beautiful clear blue water and the sun sitting high in the sky. Dozens of people sat beneath umbrellas enjoying the scenery with their tropical drinks. He decided to read the postcard with Victoria when he got back upstairs.

He flipped through the other pieces of mail and found the rest to be junk mail except for one curious letter. It was in a plain white envelope addressed to him with no return address. This was intriguing to him. The postmark read July 15th, 1998. He placed the other pieces of mail back into the box and opened the letter. There was one piece of lined notebook paper that smelled familiar to him. He unfolded it and began to read.

Dear Sydney,

I hope this letter finds its way into your hands and only your hands. I don't want to disturb your life with Victoria. I hope she never sets eyes upon this letter, but I have to risk that she might. For you see, I had to write this letter to you. After you left that night, I cried my eyes out for hours until I fell asleep. I slept for fifteen hours, woke up, showered, and listened to the silence of my apartment. This was a sound that I had to become well accustomed to. I went to work at the Sexothèque that night and couldn't perform. I went out on that stage and truly felt naked for the first time in my life. I called out your name like a fool, hoping you'd be out there to protect me. To give me strength, but of course, you weren't there. I froze up, and the men yelled some horrible things at me. Luckily Olivia, Joe, D.B., and the rest of the girls shut them up. Olivia took me back home, and I told her about how things ended between us. She said she would look after me while I took some time off for myself. Joe, bless his heart, understood and told me to come back when I felt better. Everyone has been so lovely to me, but I don't feel worthy of their time. I honestly don't feel worthy of anyone anymore. Olivia has visited each day for a while this past month before going to work, but she's been out of town to see her family in King City this past week. She's called, but I don't want to answer the phone. Each day I've sat here listening to the silence, and I've come to the conclusion that without you in my life, I have nothing. The silence truly is deafening. I miss the sound of your voice, our laughter, and those drives in your Miata with the top down. Those times we spent together I'll always hold precious. You, me, Olivia, and Albert. We made quite the team. Another thing has been on my mind especially. That night you and I were on top of the roof that first time. You know how I almost fell off the edge when we were making love, and you caught me? I wish you hadn't. I wish I could have fallen…fallen right into the sky that night and become one with the stars above. Next time you look up into the night sky, Syd, look for the star twinkling the brightest. That's me up there shining down upon you forevermore, my love. I'll always be with you. Just look to the stars.

Yours forever,
Sharon

The letter slipped out of his fingers, and he watched it fall to the ground in slow motion. *Dear God, no. This can't be real. Tell me she didn't actually do it!* He spotted a newspaper box up the street and ran for it. He shoved fifty cents into the coin slots, grabbed onto a paper, and began to flip through it.

An article on the third page made him lose his footing and fall onto the cool grass beside the sidewalk.

WOMAN FALLS FROM ROOF OF LOCAL APARTMENT BUILDING

He scanned the article and saw Sharon's name and her family's arrangements for her funeral. The viewing was happening tomorrow, and she was to be buried in Pine Grove Cemetery the following Monday. Another thing the article said was there was no suicide letter left behind.

The letter! He ran back to the mailboxes, picked up the letter from the ground, and looked at it again. This was Sharon's final mark on this world, and it was left to him. It was his cross to bear. He stood there and cried as quietly as he could for a few minutes. "God damn it! God damn it! …God damn it!" he yelled out. He couldn't hold it in anymore. Sharon was gone. Her fire was forever extinguished. He slid the letter back into the envelope and slipped it into his back pocket. He grabbed the mail and left the newspaper sitting on the ground beside the trashcan. He was sure someone would happen upon it and take it.

As he walked back to the apartment, he noticed stars beginning to ignite overhead. He stopped and looked up at them and saw one twinkling brilliantly. "Well, hi there, babe," he said as he continued looking upwards. He couldn't be sure, but he swore the star twinkled even brighter after he said that. It wasn't much comfort, but as he walked back to the apartment, he patted his back pocket and thought, *I'll hold onto your letter, Sharon...I'm so sorry. God, please, forgive me...*

He entered the apartment's cool air and frenzied voices. "It's about time you got back. Did you get the mail?"

"Yeah, right here, Vicky. The postcard was in there."

"Really? Ohh, let me see. Did you read it yet?"

"No, I was waiting for you so we could read it together."

"Ah, that's sweet," Alexis said as Victoria sat beside her. Sydney stood next to Victoria as she read the postcard, but he didn't hear a word. He smiled, nodded, thanked them for sending it, and excused himself to wash his hands.

Before he hit the bathroom, he made a detour into their extra room. It contained boxes of things they'd never unpacked. One box contained a plethora of old photos from Sydney's childhood, with Albert in many of them. *This will be a great place to stash it*, he thought as he slid Sharon's letter into one of the photo album pages. Young Al looked back at him with a smile spread across his face. *I miss you, buddy. I hope you're not up there with Sharon.* He closed the album and returned it to its box.

He washed his hands and splashed some water on his face. *Time to put on my party face. Don't let them see you cry out there. Don't let them see you cry.* He opened the door and rejoined the festivities, acting the role of host perfectly. No one would have ever suspected the heavy burden he carried within himself. Not even Sydney himself knew of the burden. Not yet, but he'd find out in due time.

FIRST INTERLUDE

HEAD OVER HEELS

Sydney lay snugly underneath two layers of bedsheets. He was content as he lay in the darkness of his bedroom. He didn't want to roll over and look at his alarm clock. *So comfortable...Hopefully, I won't have to get up for a while.* KNOCK KNOCK *Oh, no...I jinxed it*, he thought as he clinched his eyes shut and pulled his blanket over his head.

"Sydney, are you up yet?" He continued to lie there, pretending not to hear. A moment later, more knocks came upon his door. "Sydney? Time to wake up!"

He let out a sigh and finally rolled over, and the alarm clock's red numbers mockingly shone into his sleep-filled eyes, momentarily blinding him. "Yeah, mom. I'm about to get up."

"Alright, dear. There's bacon, eggs, and some pancakes in the kitchen for you. Come on. You don't wanna be late for school."

Sydney begrudgingly cast the sheets off his body and threw his legs over the side of his bed. His bare feet touched upon the icy surface of the hardwood floor below, and the shock cleared his cloudy brain. "Woo! How are these floors so cold? It's only early October!" he said as he stepped across the ice rink that was his bedroom floor and switched the overhead light on. He walked to his window, peeped out of a slant in the blinds, and saw the sun barely peeking over the horizon. "Man, I could have slept another thirty minutes or so. Why you gotta do me like that, Mom? Eh, well, may as well hop in the shower."

After Sydney finished his shower, he quickly threw on a black turtleneck and jeans with his favorite high-top sneakers. By this point, Sydney's stomach had begun to growl, and he was looking forward to breakfast. He exited his room, walked up the hallway to the kitchen, and found his father sitting at the table reading the newspaper.

"Mornin' Dad," he said as he grabbed a plate and began to serve himself.

"Mornin', Syd. Took ya long enough to get out here. Your mother and I didn't get you that alarm clock for decoration. It's there to wake you up, so your mother doesn't have to. She does enough around here, you know." Sydney took a seat across from his father. He looked down at his food, feeling guilty that he had forgotten to set his alarm again. "Well? Do you hear me, Syd?"

Sydney looked back up at his father, "Yes, Dad. I'm sorry. I'll remember to set it next time."

"You do that...I have to get to work. I'll see you and your mother tonight." Sydney watched as his dad quickly walked past him and down the hall to the front door. A few moments later, his father closed it behind him.

Sydney sighed and began to eat his breakfast which was already a little cold. *Maybe if you'd woken up on time, it'd be warm*, his father's voice rang in his head. He imagined his old man giving him a smack on the back of the head, and he pushed his plate away from him. His appetite disappeared.

Sydney had a complicated relationship with his father. His father was a serious man who worked Monday through Friday each week at Micky's Glass, installing new windows and mirrors into homes and businesses across Lando. Each night he'd come home and fall onto his recliner and crack open a "cold one," as he called it, watch the news until supper was ready, and then join Sydney and his mom at the table. Most nights, Sydney's mother, Lolita, would lead the conversations. During the week, his old man would be pretty quiet, mainly listening to Sydney and his mother discuss their day.

A few weeks prior, the weekend came, and his father came home from work on top of the world. He walked

Some Things Last...

through the door with a dozen roses and handed them to Sydney. Sydney had said, "Gee, dad, for me? You shouldn't have."

His father rolled his eyes and replied, "Damn it, Syd, those aren't for you. They're for your mother. I just had to grab the groceries I picked up."

His father walked back inside with a large bag. "What's inside, dad?"

His father grinned, "Rump roast, son." That night his father revealed that he had been promoted to assistant manager. They ate and celebrated. His father had pulled him aside after supper and explained that he would need to be more responsible soon. He told him he'd be putting in more hours at work and wanted Sydney to help lessen the load on his mother. Sydney promised that he would. His father extended his hand, and Sydney shook it firmly and looked his father in the eye just as he had been taught when he was younger. Later, his father put some records on, and his parents danced together. Sydney looked on, smiling from the doorway of their den. He never wanted that night to end…but it did.

The weeks continued, and his father grew ever busier with his new responsibilities. Most nights, he'd come home past sunset and not even say anything. Sydney would try joking with his old man, but he'd tell him to leave him alone and finish his homework, even if he didn't have any. If he did have some, he'd rather not look at it. Usually, math work followed him home, which was the last thing he wanted to see.

Since Sydney entered the 7th grade about a month earlier, his grades had plummeted steadily. His parents didn't know about it, which Sydney was relieved about, and he hoped they wouldn't find out. He had begun to dread going to school each morning and hoped his mother would forget

about him and he could stay home. His plan so far had only resulted in his father becoming increasingly irate at him. Sydney looked over at the time on the stove. It was 6:50. He closed his eyes and laid his head on the cool wood of the tabletop.
"Syd? Are you feeling OK?" his mother asked.

He didn't answer. He heard the jingle jangle of her car keys and knew that it was time to go. Thoughts of pretending to be sick flashed through his mind, but he didn't feel like trying to pull a fast one on his mother. She was, after all, a pharmacist, and it took quite a lot to convince her that he was ill. "Yes, mom. Just a little tired, is all."

"If you didn't stay up so late watching TV, you'd be more rested."

"Yes, mom."

"Please, try to remember to set your alarm tonight. Your father doesn't need to tell you again."

"Yes, mom…"

"Alright, let's go. It's time to drop you off for school."

"Yes, mom."

"And don't 'Yes, mom.' me like that."

As he went to grab his backpack, his words echoed over and over in his mind. *Yes, mom. Yes, mom. Yes, mom…*

"Alright, Syd, have a good day," his mother said as he hopped out of the backseat and onto the concrete sidewalk which led to the entrance of Hubbard Middle School. He quickly walked along the pathway, not looking back. He didn't want to come off as a "Mama's Boy" to anyone who might be watching. He traversed the five steps leading to the open set of double doors and entered onto the smooth reflective wax surface of the long linoleum hallway leading to the central atrium of the school and Sydney's current destination: the gymnasium.

His footsteps echoed along the walls as he continued onward. A young woman exited into the hallway from a doorway to Sydney's left and greeted him, "Good morning, Sydney. How are you today?"

"Fine, Mrs. Stuermer." She was Sydney's math teacher. How lovely it was for her to be the first person he saw today. "Do you have a few minutes, Sydney? I'd like to talk with you."

Sydney wanted to say that he was pretty busy. He wanted to make up some bogus excuse not to go, and that's what he did. "No, ma'am. I actually have to…use the restroom quite badly. Breakfast isn't sitting well."

Mrs. Stuermer's eyes grew wider, and she said, "Oh, I'm so sorry to have held you up. Go ahead." Sydney lowered his head to her and briskly continued down the corridor. When he was a few feet away, she said, "We'll talk after class today!" It seems he'd only prolonged the inevitable.

He turned the corner, continued past the front office, and walked towards the restroom. In case Mrs. Stuermer was to follow him for whatever reason, he wanted to make sure she saw him go inside the bathroom, as he said. He needed some time alone anyway. He pushed the heavy wooden door open and entered the chilly restroom. The interior was decked out in a checkerboard of green tiles along the floor and walls. It seemed perpetually dim inside, with the faint smell of piss always lingering in the air. He walked over to one of the large mirrors hanging above a white porcelain sink. The sink's inner crevices were off-white. It seemed the janitors always failed to scrub those spots. He looked into the mirror and stood there a moment. He closed his eyes, leaned back, took a deep breath, and exhaled.

A moment later, the door was pushed aside, and a heavyset young boy strode in, smiling at Sydney. He had a messy head of short black hair and wore a white t-shirt with suspenders and jeans. "Yo, Syd, I seen ya chattin' up Mrs. Stuermer. Damn, she's lookin' good in those black pants.

They really show off her ass, man. I'm already sportin' a mean chub."

Sydney continued to stand in front of the mirror, unmoved. "I hadn't noticed, Roland."

Roland moved next to Sydney to the sink and mirror alongside him. "You hadn't noticed my chub or her ass?"

Sydney broke into a smile. "Neither, you damn fool."

"Haha, alright, my man. So…what were you two lovebirds talkin' about?"

"I was telling her about how you clipped her photo out of the school faculty listing and pasted it beside your bed to keep you company on those long nights. She told me to tell you to call her up sometime. She'd be more than happy to keep you company herself."

Roland took a step back. "R-Really?!" His right hand was moving slightly in his pocket.

"Jesus *Christ*, man! Get your damn hand outta there! Of course not! She's a married woman, for God's sake! You think she'd wanna mess around with *you*?!"

Roland hung his head. "No…I guess not." The excitement in Roland's voice faded.

Sydney placed his hand on Roland's shoulder. "Look, man. I'm sorry. I see how she looks at you in class when you're not looking."

"What?"

"Yeah, man. She looks at you with this fire behind those dark eyes."

"But…I'm always looking at her, and she never looks at me…"

"She watches you leave, bro. She hates to see ya go but loves to watch ya leave."

Roland immediately perked up. "Hot damn. I knew I felt her eyes on me!"

"Yes, yes. You're a regular Don Juan de la Nooch."

Roland smiled brightly, "Thanks, Syd. So...what were you two really talking about?"

Sydney turned away from Roland. "She wants me to stay after class today and talk for a few minutes."

"You lucky bastard...why can't I stay after class?!"

"I'd trade places with you if I could."

"The world ain't fair, my friend. Not at all." Roland's words ring hollow in his ears. He knew he'd gotten himself into this situation by his own hand. "Hey, Syd, I was wonderin' why don't you ever talk about any girls? You aren't...you know..."

Sydney turned toward Roland and stared at him with serious eyes. "No, I don't know, Roland. What are you asking here?"

"You know...you're not a peter puffer, are ya? That's what my dad calls it."

Sydney turned away from Roland and looked into the mirror. "Roland, your dad sounds like a fuckin' clown."

"You have no idea how right you are about that one...Look, man. I'm sorry. If you were...you know. I would think nothin' of it. As long as you didn't try to put any moves on me."

"Oh, my God...shut the hell up, Roland. I like girls...it's just I haven't found any around here I'm interested in. I'm waiting for my thunderbolt."

"Thunderbird? My uncle has a thunderbird, but what does that have to do with chicks?"

"Damn it, Roland. Thunder*bolt,* not *bird!*"

"Alright...I'm still not following."

Sydney signed, "My old man sat me down, and we watched The Godfather a while back. In the movie, the main guy sets eyes on this beautiful woman, and they instantly fall in love. I want that, Roland! *My* thunderbolt!"

"Jeez, Syd, I never pegged you for that romantic crap."

"Yeah, well, there you go, Roland. Keep it to yourself."

"Well, Syd, I gotta get over to the lunch room real quick and have some breakfast. You wanna join me?"

Sydney shook his head, "No, man. You go ahead. I'll see you in homeroom in a bit."

"Alright, I'll see ya…Mr. Thunderbolt," Roland said with a cheeky grin.

"Fuck off," Sydney said, laughing slightly and kicking the air.

Sydney had met Roland Torfilio after Christmas break had ended in 2nd grade. Sydney got to class that first day back and noticed this chubby kid sitting in the corner by himself with short black hair. He thought the kid could use a friend, so he went over and began to chat with him. The two hit it off pretty quickly, both being class clowns of sorts. Roland was just a bit shy at first.

He hadn't changed much during these five years since then. One thing that certainly hadn't changed was his penchant for older women…going back to the very beginning with Ms. Gamble. She was a young woman with shoulder-length blonde hair, but her nose drew Roland to her.

Sydney couldn't understand it, but Roland certainly was sad when the day came that she got married and changed her name to Mrs. Hawk. On the playground, he wept behind a tree. Sydney had offered him a pack of candy to lessen the blow. Roland inhaled them all yet still cried. Roland remained depressed for a good week which was a long time in those days.

Now that Sydney was alone in the dimly lit bathroom, he took a moment to enjoy the silence. The morning sun was just slightly peeking into the restroom's rectangular window. He didn't have a watch, but he figured it must be at least a quarter after seven. Judging by the mounting sounds outside the heavy wooden door, he'd consider it might be even later. Sydney smiled slightly, thinking about Roland's insatiable appetite for Mrs. Stuermer. *That woman doesn't have any interest in you, you pudgy fuck...but God love ya for dreaming. Boy, I'd trade places with ya in a second. You can talk to her all damn day.*

Sydney paced back and forth a bit, not wanting to head for the gym. It was rather nice in here, despite the slight undertone of piss. He stood in the bathroom and listened as the chatter within the gym grew to a roar. *Well, I guess it's about that time...may as well start to head for my locker.*

He pulled on the cold metal handle of the bathroom door and exited into the brightly lit main hall of the school. His eyes had to adjust to the change in lighting, and he was momentarily blind. He unknowingly walked right into someone and went head over heels onto the cold, smooth surface of the floor. "Whoa, I'm sorry about that. I didn't mean to..." Sydney stared across from him and lost all words. His mind went blank at the sight of a young girl with long, wavy, dark brown hair and matching eyes.

He quickly rose to his feet and offered a hand to her. She smiled slightly and gladly took it. Her hand was soft and warm within his. He felt rooted to the spot and stood there, unable to form any words. She looked at him with wide eyes, but they weren't full of anger from Sydney's foolish collision with her. They were warm, if not surprised. Lovely eyelashes accentuated her eyes that Sydney felt he could admire for hours. It felt as if time slowed to a crawl in this moment of composure.

Time has a bad habit of trudging forward, whether you liked it or not, and the mystery girl brushed herself off and walked away towards the office. She quickly turned her head around briefly and smiled the sweetest smile Sydney had ever seen. His heart fluttered, and he felt every part of himself ignite. *Why did I choose to wear a damn turtleneck today of all days! It's so hot in here!* Without thinking, he spoke out loud, "Hot damn. Who *was* THAT?!"

He had become so lost in thought that he didn't realize the bell had rung. He was quickly surrounded by a river of students from the gym heading down the hallway toward the seventh grade classrooms. He tried to move on from his brief encounter, but that smile...those eyes...every detail was imprinted upon his mind's eye, and every time he closed his eyes, he'd see her in slow motion turning and smiling at him.

Sydney took his seat in the middle of Mr. Scally's classroom. He still couldn't shake the thought of the mystery girl. He cursed himself that he never spoke to her, let alone got her name.

"Sydney Lee? Sydney Lee? Sydney?" He was still lost in his thoughts. "Excuse me, Mr. Lee? Do you mind answering roll call?"

Sydney looked up at Mr. Scally. He was a tall man with shoulder-length black hair and a thin build with light stubble on his chin. He eyeballed Sydney over a pair of horn-rimmed glasses. "Sorry, sir. Present."

"Thank you, Syd. Now...Albert Oden?"

"Present." Sydney looked over to his right and looked at his cousin Albert. He wore a black baseball cap pulled low, almost hiding his face. Sydney could tell that Albert looked a bit concerned from what little of his face he could see.

Albert began to whisper, "Hey, Syd, is everything alright? I tried talking to you outside at our lockers, and you completely ignored me. Now you're not answering roll. What's going on?"

Sydney peered behind him and saw Roland mirror Albert's look of concern. "We'll talk later, Al. Now's not the time." Sydney returned his gaze to his desk, still obsessing about the mystery girl.

"OK, class, before we get any further, I want to introduce you to a new student. She comes from King City and moved here at the end of last week. Sydney raised his gaze toward the front of the classroom, and as he did, his eyes widened in disbelief. "Allow me to introduce Victoria Tesson. Is there anything you wanna say to the class, Victoria?"

Victoria...so THAT'S her name!! Sydney sat with his eyes wide open, waiting, hoping, praying to hear her speak.

"Hi, everybody," Victoria said with a silly wave. Some people giggled at her, including Sydney. "So, yeah, I'm Victoria, and, um, my friends call me Vicky. Um, I'm not sure what else to say...Nice to meet you?" she said, grinning.

Oh, lord. Take me now, Sydney thought as he sat there enraptured by her.

"Haha. OK, Victoria, how about you take the empty seat right over there in front of Sydney." Victoria looked over at her desk and behind it at Sydney. Their eyes met again, and she stopped a moment and then walked towards the desk. She kept her head down but looked up briefly at him and smiled that same smile from before, then took her seat.

As homeroom proceeded, Sydney had his eyes on the back of Victoria's head, admiring the color and contrasts of each strand of hair. He'd never felt this way before in all of his life. He wanted to get a hold of himself, reel his heart back in, and hold onto it tightly, but it was feral and couldn't be contained.

Homeroom ended, the bell rang, and Victoria quickly rose to her feet and exited the room without looking behind her this time. She entered the river of students flowing by outside Mr. Scally's room and was gone...at least for now. He knew her name now, and her voice rang like sweet music in his ears. Sydney wanted to follow her but was held back by Albert and Roland's concerned voices.

"Yo, Syd, what the hell is wrong with you, man? It's like you're drunk or somethin'. I've seen my old man act like this on Saturday nights," Roland said as Albert rolled his eyes at him.

"Yeah...I must agree with Roland you are acting very strange, Syd."

Sydney continued watching the door as Roland said, "Yo, we gotta get goin', Syd. I can't be late for class again. I already got my last warning this month about that... besides my lady is waiting for me."

"Yeah, Roland, right behind you," Sydney muttered, half listening. Albert waited for Roland to leave and turned and spoke to Sydney, "This is about that girl, isn't it? Victoria?"

Sydney turned and looked at Albert. "How'd you know, man?"

Albert grinned, "It's pretty obvious. You were staring at her pretty hard. Roland's pretty dense not to see that one. Besides...there was something about that look that reminded me of...something. I can't explain it. Just made me think of better times."

Sydney smiled at Albert, "You're a weird guy, Al, but damn if you're not right."

The two had to part ways, but they agreed to speak at lunch in detail about what had occurred earlier that morning. Sydney headed for his most dreaded class of the day...math with Mrs. Stuermer. *I'm looking forward to this like a kick in the balls,* he thought as he opened the door and entered right as the tardy bell rang.

"So, nice of you to join us, Sydney. I was beginning to wonder if you'd skipped out on us," Mrs. Stuermer said, grinning.

Sydney forced a laugh, "Nah, I'm here. Wouldn't miss this for the world, Mrs. S." She smiled and walked to the chalkboard as Sydney took his seat behind Roland beside the large windows which looked out on the baseball field in the back of the school.

"OK, class, let's begin."

Sydney sat in the confines of his old wooden desk. As Mrs. Stuermer droned on about pre-algebraic equations and how to solve them on the board, his attention kept drifting away. He looked down at the wooden desktop and noticed several initials and doodles carved deep into its wooden surface. He began to trace around the letters of a few names but quickly grew bored. His attention went next to the field outside the window. In the early morning P.E. class, a group of kids were trekking out onto the field in their uniforms, getting ready to play softball. He felt a little bad for the people who had that class first thing in the morning, but right now, he longed to be one of them out there and far away from this torture.

"Sydney? Can you come up here and solve this equation, please?"

Sydney's head bolted towards Mrs. Stuermer. "Huh? Me?"

The class let out a light giggle, and Mrs. Stuermer quieted them. "Yes, Syd. Come on up here."

Fuck me, runnin'. I don't even know what we're doin', Sydney thought as he walked towards the board. Mrs. Stuermer handed him the chalk, and he finally looked up at the problem. The equation on the board stretching out before him read, '$2x + 9x - 3x + 8 = 16$'

"I want you to find x, Syd," Mrs. Stuermer said.

Sydney stood for a moment, looking over every part of the equation. He felt his back begin to grow hot, and a layer of sweat began to pour out of him. His turtleneck began to stick to his skin as he heard someone clear their throat. A grin broke out across his face as he thought maybe this was a trick question and he was overthinking it. He took the chalk and circled each 'x' in the equation, and stepped away, turning around, facing everyone, and noticed they all were smiling. Roland was the first to laugh, and then everyone else joined in. "I found it, Mrs. S.," Sydney said, smiling.

"OK, class, that's enough. Yes, Syd, you certainly found it alright...very funny. Now, how about you really find x, huh?"

Sydney's smile faded, and he turned around and began to look at the equation again. It felt like it had grown while he had his back turned. All eyes were on Sydney, and he felt each one boring into him, waiting for him to make a move. He couldn't take it anymore. He placed the chalk below the board and hung his head, "I...I'm sorry. I don't know." He returned to his seat feeling amazingly dumb.

The class ended, and everyone began to pile out of the room. Sydney looked up and noticed that Roland was leaving without even saying anything. He caught Roland looking back with a big smile on his face. *Good for you, bro...at least someone's smiling when they get outta here.*

"Sydney, come over to my desk, please."

Fucking hell. Here we go... Sydney thought as he dragged his feet across the carpeted classroom and sat in front of Mrs. Stuermer's desk.

"OK, Sydney, I'm sure you already know why I asked you to stay after class this morning." Sydney nodded in agreement but sat silent, waiting to see what exactly she had to say. "Your grades have been steadily declining since the beginning of the semester. Your current grade for this course is a 53." Sydney's eyes widened a bit. He was surprised it wasn't lower. "The good news is that it's not too late to turn things around. We have a unit test coming up next Friday and another two weeks after that. You'll be passing once again if you study hard and pull in at least a C to a B on each one. If you don't manage to attain those marks on the next exam...I'll have to contact your parents next weekend."

Sydney hung his head a moment and thought of his father answering the phone on Friday afternoon after a long week and receiving the news his son was a failure. He

Some Things Last...

promised his father he'd help out around the house and make things easier. So far, his promise was crumbling apart.

"Do you understand, Syd?"

Sydney looked up into Mrs. Stuermer's dark brown eyes and replied, "Yes, ma'am. I'll study and get those marks. Please don't contact my folks. They don't need to know about this."

She smiled, and for one brief moment, he could see why Roland was so smitten with her. "I won't contact them, Syd. This will stay between you and me. Just promise me that you'll study and if you want, we can meet up after school, and I can tutor you for about an hour."

Sydney gracefully declined her offer but promised he'd study hard. As they were about to wrap up their business, the tardy bell for the next class of the day rang, and Mrs. Stuermer came out from around her desk and placed her hand on Sydney's shoulder. "Syd, I'll be here anytime if you change your mind about the tutoring. I love you, and I want you to do your best." Sydney took a step back and thought, *Whoa, this is gettin' a bit weird.*

He quickly told her goodbye and made for the door. "Wait, Syd." He stopped and slowly turned around. "You'll need this tardy pass."

He plucked it from her hand and said, "See ya tomorrow, Mrs. S!" as he bolted from her room, thinking as he hurried along to his English class, *Roland's not gonna believe this one.*

As the day continued, Sydney's P.E. class arrived, and within this class, he met back up with Roland and Albert in the gymnasium. He entered the boy's locker room and found Roland slipping into his blue shorts and red t-shirt, adorned with the school's Native American mascot and name. "Yo, Syd, did you see Mrs. Stuermer put her hand on my shoulder this morning and smile when I solved that equation? Man, I had to take my seat fast because I was already gettin' a mean hard-on!"

"Nah, I guess I missed that, bro. Good for you."

"Good for me? Come on, man. Don't worry about not knowing how to solve that shit. I just got lucky. Besides, you're not the downer of the group...Al is."

"What did you say about me, Roland?" Albert said, coming around the corner from the shower room.

"I said you're a downer, Al! Glad to see you in here with the rest of us and not hiding away in the shower room getting dressed so no one can see your tighty whities."

Albert's face turned pink, "I-I don't wear tighty whities!"

Sydney smiled and began to unlock the combination lock of his gym locker. "It's no big deal, Al. We've all worn them at some point," Sydney said, undressing and revealing a blinding white pair of briefs. "And some of us still do. Lay off Al, Roland. You know damn well you wear 'em too...along with those cute little alien pea pod pajamas you wore last time you came over."

Roland quickly ran over and placed his hand over Sydney's mouth. "Shhh," he said as he looked around, hoping no one had heard. Albert watched, stifling a laugh. Sydney pushed Roland off of himself and quickly finished dressing into his uniform.

"Alright, gentlemen, let's head on out," Sydney said, leading the way to the bleachers.

The trio sat on the bleachers and waited for Coach Perkins to start class. Coach Perkins was a man in his 40s with a hairline way past receding. He had all of it on the sides and none of it up top. He mostly kept his dome covered with a bright red Hubbard Middle School baseball cap. Another distinguished attribute was his thick mustache. Sydney liked to call him Burt - As in Burt Reynolds. He got a few laughs, mainly from his crew, but he took what he could get.

Some Things Last...

Coach Perkins came out from his office a few minutes later, just as the bell rang, and took his place in front of the class. He looked at everyone through his wire-frame glasses and began to speak. "Alright, boys! We planned to go out and play some softball today, but there's rain forecast, and it's already begun to drizzle out there. SO!" he said, slapping his hands together, "We're gonna be playing dodgeball today with the ladies." Sydney looked to his right at the second set of bleachers where the girls sat, listening to Coach Laurel convey just what Coach Perkins had said.

"OK, we're gonna divide you guys into teams now so we can get started," Coach Perkins said as he came together with Coach Laurel. He began reading names off the list and directing each person to move either to the left or right side of the gym. Sydney was moved to the right side along with Roland, but Albert was placed on the opposing team.

"Oh, yeah, I'm going straight for Al as soon as I get a ball in my hands," Roland said, beaming.

"You're a real bastard. You know that, man?"

"Sure am!" Roland happily replied.

Sydney closed his eyes and moved to the corner, waiting for all this nonsense to end. He had no interest in dodgeball until Coach Laurel yelled, "Victoria Tesson!" His eyes flew open, and he saw Victoria walk down onto the gym floor. "Left side!" Coach Laurel said as Sydney's heart fluttered. The butterflies were back in full force.

"Hey, lookie lookie, it's the new girl! She's pretty cute in those little shorts…look at them legs. Hoo Ah!"

Sydney smacked him across the back of the head. "You stay away from her. She not for you…and don't look at her like that either."

Roland began to rub the back of his head, "Ceeripes, man! Alright, she's all yours. I wasn't serious. You know where my heart lies." Sydney felt a little bad for smacking

Roland, but he knew how depraved he was. Victoria wasn't going to be talked about that way. Not at all.

Everyone was divided up evenly, and Coach Perkins stood in the middle of the gym laying out the dull red balls, placing seven evenly spaced out. Sydney stood in the corner, eyeballing Victoria. She had moved to the same corner Albert had, directly across from Sydney and Roland. Albert paid her no attention, though. He had pulled his cap down over his eyes and resigned from the game. Sydney sympathized with him. The balls were placed and ready. Everyone was eagerly waiting for the game to begin when Coach Perkins blew his whistle and yelled, "Let's get it on!"

Balls began to fly left and right, and Sydney continued standing in his corner, hoping Victoria, and to a lesser extent Albert, would be alright. A ball came rolling next to Roland, and he picked it up and set eyes on Albert in the corner, but Victoria was standing several feet in front of him. Sydney could see the menace in his eyes. He was about to yell out to him, but it was too late. He threw the ball, and it flew directly toward the back corner and Victoria. Sydney looked on in horror as the ball continued its path. As Victoria was about to be beamed, she jumped out of the way. The ball hit Albert, causing his hat to fly off his head. "Hoo, yeah! Did you see that, Syd?!" Roland yelled, turning around to face Sydney. He completely left himself open, and a ball was lobbed and hit him in the back of the head, sending him flying forward.

Everyone had almost been knocked out at this point. Only a handful of people were left on either side, and Sydney continued standing in his corner until a ball came rolling up. As he bent down to grab it, two more people fell on his team and two others on the opposing side. Sydney looked around and couldn't believe it, but he was the last man standing…and on the opposing team stood Victoria with a ball in her hand. They both stared at each other. There

Some Things Last...

was only one way this was going to end. One of them would have to hit the other. Everyone was cheering them on. Victoria threw her ball, and Sydney barely moved out of the way in time. He looked up at her with surprise, and she stood, smiling with a cheeky grin. He looked over at Roland on the sidelines and could see him mouth the words, *Throw the fucking ball*. Sydney began to smile too. He did just that.

This back-and-forth went on for a good while. Each time one of them threw a ball, the other would dodge it. Neither of them tried to catch a ball. The crowd was going absolutely mad on the sidelines. Sydney knew this couldn't go on forever. There had to be a way to end it. He wanted Victoria to win, but he felt like giving everyone a bit of a show first. He felt he'd done that in spades. Now, he wanted an out, and he believed he'd found it. It was to appear like a complete mistake, a bit of a technicality, if you will. He saw a ball right in front of him. It was just slightly over the dividing line. He'd be declared out if he placed just one foot on the other side. He decided it was now or never and took off for the ball.

He ran forward and could hear Roland's voice mixed in with the crowd. He saw Albert sitting in the bleachers. His hat was still off, and his eyes were wide, watching every moment. Sydney made for the ball, and Coach Perkins's whistle cut through the air. "You're out, Syd! You went over the line!" The gym erupted in a frenzy of cheers from the opposing side and sneers from his team. Either way, Sydney was glad it was all over. He looked up and saw that Victoria had disappeared.

Son of a bitch! Where'd she go? he thought as he rejoined Roland. "That was crazy, bro! You could have had her, but Burt over there cheated ya."

Sydney smiled, "It's all good, Roland. Did you see where Victoria went?"

Roland pointed toward the girls' locker room. "She ran back in there, I think. Damn, man. That was fuckin' intense!"

"Yeah…" Sydney mustered and made his way back toward the locker room. He could see Albert was gone from the bleachers. *Must be inside changing already, h*e thought as Roland kept talking his ear off about the game.

The locker room erupted in a frenzy of noise as Sydney changed back into his regular clothes. Many guys told him it was "one hell of a game." No one knew he'd purposely thrown the game. He was happy about that. He was also happy that it was lunchtime. After that intense game, his stomach was growling fiercely. Sydney looked around for Albert, but he must have slipped out in the commotion. Albert was never one to be a part of chaotic situations. Sydney figured he must have gone ahead to the lunch room.

Sydney and Roland walked down the hallway from the gym to the lunchroom. Sydney threw open the wooden door with its cold reflective handle and stepped into the noisy lunchroom. He looked over to the table they usually sat at during lunch. Albert was sitting there with his teal-colored lunch box in front of him. Sydney smiled and was glad to see him. Albert looked up and gave him a quick thumbs up. Sydney returned the gesture. "What are you two queerbaits doin'?" Roland said, snickering.

"Get the hell outta here," Sydney said, laughing.

"OK, sorry to interrupt your special moment," Roland said, taking his place in line.

The two made their way through the lunch line and grabbed some spaghetti with some bread and some chocolate milk. "Nice! Spaghetti day's the best," Roland said as he began slipping some noodles into his mouth. Sydney just stood watching, shaking his head in astonishment.

The two finally took their seats as Albert was halfway finished with his lunch; a ham and cheese sandwich, potato chips, and a fruit punch juice box. Albert gave Roland a dirty look as he sat down. "What's with the dirty look, Al?"

"You know exactly what it's about. What's the matter with you? You have any idea how hard you threw that ball?"

Roland let out a little chuckle, "Yeah, I beamed ya real good. No use being a pussy about it. You'll live."

Albert's eyes lit up, and he was about to argue with Roland when someone stopped next to their table and spoke, "Excuse me?" Sydney looked up from his lunch, and his eyes grew wide. Victoria stood next to their circular lunch table, smiling. "Would you mind if I sat here?"

Sydney looked at the empty seat beside him and blurted out, "Yes."

Victoria stopped smiling and answered, "Oh, I understand. I didn't mean to bother you guys."

She turned and began to walk away when Sydney said, "Wait!" She turned around, surprised. "I meant to say yes. You can sit hear. We don't mind at all. Right, fellas?" Sydney looked over at Roland and Albert, who both looked surprised. "*Right*, fellas?" Sydney repeated.

Both Roland and Albert replied in unison, "No!"

"See? We don't mind. Have a seat," Sydney said, standing up, grabbing the empty chair, and pulling it out for Victoria.

"Thank you…Sydney, right?"

"Yep, that's me. My friends call me Syd…And you're…Victoria."

Victoria scooted closer to the table and shook her head up and down. "That's right! Well, Syd, please call me Vicky. It's what *MY* friends call me."

Sydney smiled brightly, "Right. I remember you mentioning that earlier."

"What are your friends' names? It seems they've gotten quiet since I came over. Don't mind me, guys."

Sydney looked over at Roland and Albert, both sitting with the same wide-eyed look of surprise. Sydney had almost forgotten they were there. His attention had fallen solely upon Victoria. "These guys? They clearly have no manners. If they did, they'd have introduced themselves." Sydney cast a displeased look at Roland and Albert.

Roland cleared his throat and spoke, "I'm Roland Torfilio."

Vicky smiled, "Torfilio? Is that Italian?"

"Yeah, I'm part Italian."

"That's cool. My family originated in France. One day I'd like to go there."

"I've thought of going back to the old country myself. Maybe one of these days, when I get the hell out of Lando, I will."

"Well, good luck with that trip back," Victoria said as she opened her carton of chocolate milk. "And what about you? What's your name?" Victoria asked, looking over at Albert.

Albert had his cap pulled down, but some of his eyes were still peeking out below the bill. Sydney could sense that Albert didn't want to talk. He had a thing with meeting new people. He struggled to open up to them. The guy was practically a genius when it came to his schoolwork, but when it came to social situations, he failed almost every time. "This is my cousin Albert! Don't mind him. He's a bit shy, but when you get to know him, he's a good guy."

"I understand that. It didn't use to be easy for me to approach people. I was pretty shy when I was little. To a certain extent, it still isn't easy," Victoria said, taking a sip of her milk.

"I never would have guessed that. You came over to us pretty easy," Roland said.

"Well, I came over to you guys mainly because of Syd. I was looking for a place to sit, and I still don't know anyone yet, but I remembered Syd from our epic dodgeball game," Victoria said, laughing.

"YEAH! You guys sure did have one hell of a game!" Roland said. "I still think we were robbed, though. Syd could have gotten you out. I know it."

"Oh, you think so? What do you think, Syd?"

Sydney thought for a moment. "I think the game went down the way it was supposed to, Roland. It's best to let it go. Vicky here won fair and square."

Roland tossed a piece of bread at Sydney, "Yeah, yeah. You *WOULD* say that while she's actually here."

"Shut *up*, man!" Sydney said as Victoria began to giggle at the both of them.

"Ah, well, whatever. There's something else I need to know about, Syd. What happened with you and Mrs. Stuermer after class today?" Roland asked.

Sydney wanted to avoid this conversation while Victoria was around…at least the whole thing about Mrs. Stuermer saying she loved him. He knew Roland wasn't going to let it go, so he decided to tell him why he got held after class. "Nothing interesting really happened. We just talked about my grades, OK? Let's drop it."

"Your grades? What do ya mean, man? Is this about that joke you made about finding x? That was brilliant stuff, bro!"

Sydney sighed, "No, it wasn't about that. Let's forget it, man. I don't wanna go into it right now."

"Is it because of Vicky being here? Come on, man. Don't mind her. If something juicy happened between you two, I wanna *hear* this!"

Sydney sighed again, "I told you it was about my grades. Now, let it go."

"I don't understand."

"What's there to understand, Roland? I'm failing math. Is that what you wanna hear? There ya go. Damn."

"Way to go, Roland," Albert finally spoke up.

Albert and Roland bickered back and forth a bit before lunch finally wrapped up. The two of them took their trays over to the trash and left as Sydney stood up. "Syd?" Victoria said softly.

"I'm sorry about Roland, Vicky. He's a good guy at heart. Just a bit…misguided."

"Oh, he seems nice. Albert too. They both really care about you. I can tell. It's nice to have friends like that."

Sydney smiled, "Yeah, they're all you could want in a crew."

"Could I join the crew?" Victoria asked.

"Well, we weren't looking for new members…" he said with a grin, "but I suppose I can pull some strings. You can hang out with us anytime. We've got your back."

Victoria laughed and said, "That's good. When I left my old school, I was unsure if I'd ever meet anyone like my friends there. Now, I know I have. Oh, and that offer of watching each other's backs goes both ways."

Sydney's brow raised, "Oh, yeah? How do you mean?"

"I mean, I can help you with your math issues. I'm really awesome at math, and if you'd like, I can meet you at the library or something and go over things with you."

Sydney looked at Victoria briefly and replied, "That would be really cool. Only if it's no trouble for you and your own work."

"It's no trouble at all. I'll talk to my parents about it, and we can meet there this afternoon if you'd like."

"That sounds great."

"It's a date then…study date, I mean!" Victoria said, forcing a laugh and blushing lightly. "I'll see you later, Syd," she said, then quickly took her tray to the trash.

"Yeah, see ya later," Sydney said as he watched her walk away.

Sydney spent the remainder of the day eagerly waiting to meet up with Victoria at the library. The second half of the day mercifully went by quicker than the first, and soon the final bell rang, ending the day. Sydney met up with Albert at their lockers, hurried over to the sidewalk where he was dropped off that morning, and waited for Albert's mom to arrive to pick them up. Sydney would typically be dropped off at school by his mother and then get a ride home from his aunt.

"Yo, Al, would your mom mind dropping me off at the LCL today?

Albert turned around with a surprised look on his face. "No, because that's where I was going myself."

"What? Why are you going down to the library?"

"To read! What about you?"

Sydney turned, blushed a bit, and said quietly, "Um, I'm meeting Vicky there."

"What? I couldn't hear you."

"I said I'm meeting Vicky there!"

"Oh, right! Why's that?"

"She's helping me…study."

Albert smiled, "That's good, Syd. I could have helped you out, you know."

"No offense, Al, but when a beautiful lady offers to help you. There's no competition there. You'll understand one of these days."

Albert furrowed his brow and turned away, "Right, I understand that. She seems nice."

"Yeah, she is," Sydney said, smiling. The two spoke no more on the subject.

Albert's mom arrived a few minutes later and eagerly greeted the two of them. "Hop on in, Alby and Syd!"

Albert rolled his eyes as Sydney chuckled a bit. "Hey, Aunt Milly, would you mind dropping me off at the LCL? I've got some studying to do."

Sydney's aunt smiled brightly, "Not at all, Syd. I was gonna drop Alby off there anyway. He loves to go down there and read the latest books they get in."

"Ma, what have I told you about calling me Alby? I'm not a little kid anymore." Sydney's aunt turned the radio up and began driving, ignoring Albert's words. The local radio station played some synth-pop hits, and Sydney enjoyed it. He sat beside Albert, bobbing his head as Albert sat with his arms crossed, looking quite displeased.

They pulled into the side parking lot of the brown brick library five minutes later. They hopped out, and Sydney's Aunt Milly told them to be careful walking home. Albert took off for the main entrance without saying goodbye to his mother. She looked visibly hurt by his coldness.

"Don't mind him, Aunt Milly. He's just eager to get to those books!"

His aunt Milly smiled, "Thanks, Syd. I know he doesn't mean it. He'll be fine later…I'm making his favorite for supper tonight. Steaks."

"Whoa, now. I'm jealous. I think we're having chicken alfredo or something. That'll perk Al up for sure."

"Keep it a surprise, Syd."

"You got it, Aunt Milly."

Sydney walked around the corner as a gust of wind blew through the trees planted along the sidewalk in front of the library. He looked up into the limbs noticing the brilliant-colored leaves clinging to the branches. He always enjoyed this time of year and the burst of color it brought with it. He didn't have time to admire the leaves, though. Victoria could very well be inside waiting for him, and he certainly didn't want to keep a lady waiting. He reached the front entrance of the library. A large sign out front read 'Lando Community Library'. Everybody around town usually just called it "The LCL". It was a grand tan brick building located in uptown Lando. Sydney couldn't remember the last time he'd set foot there. *Must have been back when me and Al took that field trip here way back in second grade.*

He stopped reminiscing, flung the door aside, and entered the warm lobby of the LCL. He scanned over the place and saw no signs of Albert or Victoria. The place certainly hadn't changed much. It still had the distinctive smell of old books permeating the air.

He continued to look around and saw no sign of Victoria. His heart began to sink. *Where is she?* he thought as he felt that she hadn't been able to make it. Then, he heard a voice, "Psst, Syd." Sydney looked around and saw no one. He thought he was losing his mind when the voice spoke again, "Up here!" He looked up and saw Victoria looking down from the floor above. Her long wavy brown hair hung over the banister. She smiled brightly, motioning for Sydney to come upstairs.

He wasted no time and quickly scaled the stairs, finding Victoria waiting at the top. "Hey, Syd. That was pretty funny. I called out to you, and you were like," she said, mimicking how he looked around aimlessly, and then she laughed.

Sydney laughed and agreed that it was pretty funny. "So, where are we doing this? I see a few small desks up here, but this is the children's library. We'd have better use of the desks downstairs."

"We're not sitting at those little desks. Come this way! Wee!" Victoria said, skipping over to a series of rooms off to themselves with the blinds closed. "I asked the librarian downstairs, Delores, I think her name is, and she said that the best place to study without any distractions was up here!" She opened one of the rooms, and he saw that she'd already set out some pencils and paper, and her backpack was sitting by the door.

"This looks like a nice spot. We have a nice view of the back of the library too. Look at all of the colors of the leaves."

"Yes, Syd, they're lovely," she said as she walked over and lowered the blinds. "We're not here to admire the leaves, though. We're here to save your grade. Now, let's have a seat and begin."

Sydney proceeded to share the details of his current situation with Victoria. She sat and listened intently. When he wrapped it up, she cleared her throat and reassured him that they would work together and get him back on track. They would meet up after school and study each day leading up to Sydney's exam that following Friday. Sydney could immediately tell that she meant business. He had to admit, though, that he felt terrible that he was even in this situation in the first place. Another part of him guiltily relished the notion of being able to see her each day after school.

They spent the following days meeting up just as they discussed. Sydney was quickly picking up on how to solve for x and no longer circling it. They both had a good time with one another and found themselves laughing together more and more. He was saddened when Friday came because he knew he wouldn't see her until Monday.

As their last study session of the week ended, Sydney sprung a question onto Victoria. "Hey, Vicky, I was wondering…"

She finished packing her supplies and turned to him, "Yeah, Syd?"

"Could I have your number? You know, in case I have trouble with my homework over the weekend." Sydney had finished his homework up earlier that day without any issues. He was so happy to be able to understand things finally.

"Oh, yeah, sure. I'll give it to you. …Is that the only reason you want it?" she said, smiling as she jotted it down onto a piece of paper within one of Sydney's notebooks.

He laughed, "Maybe I'd like to call you and talk about other stuff too."

"Other stuff?"

"Yeah."

She blushed lightly. "OK, I'd like that." She looked at her watch and said, "I gotta be going, Syd. Mudder's probably out there waiting for me."

Syd looked at her curiously, "Mudder? What do you mean?"

Victoria laughed and quickly replied, "Sorry, my mother. I call her "mudder". I gotta go, Syd. Have a good weekend."

Sydney watched as she quickly ran down the stairs and out the front entrance. Her footsteps echoed on the linoleum floor of the large lobby below then Sydney was left with silence. He missed her already.

He went downstairs and caught Albert on the way up, holding a thick tome. "Whoa, that's quite the book you got there, Al," Sydney said as Albert quickly walked by, looking visibly flustered.

"Yeah, it's an encyclopedia. I'm going to flip through it a bit before I go…"

"Right…you have fun with that. Are you still on to come over to my place tonight? Roland's supposed to come over too."

"Yeah, I'll be there. See you later, Syd," Albert said from the top of the stairs. *Alrighty, time to get back to the house,* Sydney thought as he set off for his home.

Roland and Albert arrived at Sydney's place around seven o'clock. The guys usually came over on the weekends and hung out each Friday night. Roland always loved coming over and having some of Sydney's mother's home cooking. His favorite was her fried chicken, and that's just what they had for supper.

"Mmm, Mrs. Lee, I swear you could put the colonel out of business with your chicken," Roland said as he licked the savory juices from his fingertips.

"Thank you, Roland. What about you, Albert? Did you get enough to eat?"

"Yes, Aunt Lolita. I certainly did," Albert said as he patted his stomach and groaned lightly.

Sydney's father laughed, "My thoughts exactly, Albert. Now, I'm gonna go put my feet up for a while and maybe watch a movie. What do you boys have planned tonight?"

"We're gonna watch a movie too, Dad," Sydney said, finishing his supper.

"Alright. Just don't turn it up too loud in there. It's hard for me to keep up with two movies at once…like last Friday night."

"Sure, Dad," Sydney said as he helped his mother clear the table.

After he helped clean some of the dishes, he met up with Roland and Albert in his bedroom. Roland was spread out on his bed, and Albert was sitting on his desk chair reading what looked like a horror novel. Sydney walked over to his television set and put his hand on top of its faux wood paneling. "Alright, gentlemen, I have a movie here tonight that I'm sure we'll all enjoy. It stars one of our favorite actors…AL FUCKIN' PACINO! And trust me, you're gonna hear a lot of the 'F word' tonight. From 1983, directed by Brian De Palma: Scarface." Roland and Albert both gave Sydney's introduction a short applause. "We'll start the film in just a bit. There's just one thing I wanted to do first before it gets too late."

Roland and Albert looked at each other. "What do you have to do that's more important than Scarface, bro?" Roland asked, legitimately concerned.

"I have a phone call to make."

"This must be some phone call. I never thought I'd see the day that a phone call would take precedence over Al Pacino," Albert said.

"Yeah...Sit tight, boys. I won't be long."

Sydney left Roland and Albert and walked into the kitchen, where he thankfully found it deserted. He could hear his parents in the den already watching their own movie, his father laughing loudly. He was glad that his old man was in a good mood tonight. It also put him in a good mood and gave him the confidence to call Victoria. He slipped his hand into his pocket and took out a folded-up piece of paper from his notebook. He unfolded it and read the number Victoria had written down.

He took the phone off the receiver on the wall and inputted each number slowly. With each digit, his confidence became muddled by the butterflies in his stomach. He reached the final digit, and the line began to ring. Once, twice, it rang in his ear. He came close to hanging up halfway through the third ring when a man's voice spoke on the opposite end, "Yello?" Sydney stood silent when the man repeated, "Yello?"

Finally, Sydney answered, "Can I speak to Victoria, please?"

"Victoria? Who's calling?"

"I'm Sydney, a classmate of hers."

"Ah, OK. Hold on just a sec now." The man put the phone down, and a moment later, Sydney could hear him yell out, "Victoria! Phone call!"

A minute later, he heard another phone pick up and Victoria's voice, "Hello?"

"Vicky?"

"Syd?"

"Hey, there! How's it going?" Syd said, smiling. He heard the phone on the other line hung up.

"I'm good. I just finished having supper before you called. What's up? Having some homework issues?"

Sydney began pacing a bit. "No, I finished up my homework without any problems. I just wanted to call and…chat a bit."

"Chat, huh? I suppose we can…chat a bit," she said, giggling. He took a seat at the kitchen table and was about to speak again when he heard the sound of another line being picked up and hung up almost immediately after. "Did you hear that? It sounded like someone picked up on another line," Victoria said.

"Yeah, I heard it…was that your dad who picked up earlier?"

"Yeah, that was him. He wouldn't pick up again, though…and my mom's down to the bingo hall with Nan."

"I see," Sydney said as the line picked up again. This time he heard some laughter in the background and then the sound of the receiver being abruptly hung up.

"There it was again! What's going on, Syd?"

"I might have an idea. Let's give it another minute." The two listened quietly for a few moments, and the receiver was picked up again. This time the laughter was louder, and the person was making random noises. Sydney knew where it was coming from now. "Will you excuse me for a minute, Vicky? I'll take care of it."

Sydney laid the phone down on the table, quickly walked to his bedroom, threw the door open, and saw Roland on the bed with the handheld receiver to his ear, laughing. Albert was sitting in the same spot, continuing to read his horror novel.

Sydney ran over to Roland and started whaling on him. "OW! Damn it, Syd! It was just a joke, man! I got bored waiting for you! I didn't hear nothin' juicy between you and Vicky, I promise!"

Sydney noticed the phone was still on. "Shut the hell up, Roland! Damn it!" He quickly hung the phone up and slid it into his pocket. "What the hell is wrong with you? I'm trying to have a private conversation, and you're in here acting like a jackass, as usual! No wonder you can't get any girls to talk to you!"

"Whatever! Mrs. Stuermer talked to me today, AND she put her hand on my shoulder the other day! She totally wants me, man!"

Sydney laughed and put his hand on his forehead. "Oh, my GOD! Well, let me tell ya somethin'! After class the other day, *your* lady touched *my* hand AND told me she loved me! Don't fucking ask me why she said it, but there ya go!"

Roland sat in stunned silence for a moment. Albert even looked up from his book, shocked by what he'd just heard. "Liar! That's a lie! She...wouldn't tell you that. She loves ME!"

"Look, man, I don't want her. I'm only interested in one girl, and that's Vicky...SHIT! I forgot she was waiting for me on the phone! He quickly ran out of the room and back to the kitchen. "Vicky?"

"I'm here, Syd. Sounds like you got Roland. Is everything alright now?"

Sydney let out a sigh of relief, "Yeah, everything's all gooood. I put an extra o in the good 'cause it's so good."

Victoria laughed, "That's pretty lame, Syd...But cute."

Sydney's cheeks flushed, and he forced a laugh, "I'm glad ya liked that."

With Roland sorted out, Sydney and Victoria began to chat properly. They talked about some of their favorite shows on TV. They both were fans of Miami Vice, and Sydney shared that one day he wanted to own a sports car with a convertible top and some pop-up headlights and cruise around Lando and feel the wind in his hair like Crockett. She said she'd like to have him drive her around.

He imagined that, and the thought put a big smile on his face.

Another thing he learned about was some of her favorite movies. She was really big into horror. Friday the 13th was her favorite. Sydney explained how he liked "gangster flicks," as he called them. His absolute favorite was The Godfather. He didn't go into the whole thunderbolt bit for obvious reasons, but it was undoubtedly on his mind. He went on to explain that he had Roland and Albert over to watch Scarface, and he looked over at the clock and noticed that an hour had already passed.

"Whoa, have we really been on the phone for an hour already?"

"I guess so! Time goes by fast when you're having fun...were you gonna leave Albert and Roland alone for too much longer? You said you guys were gonna watch Scarface, right?" Sydney closed his eyes. He honestly didn't mind keeping those guys waiting, especially Roland. "Syd?"

"Yeah, I'm here. It's true...They are waiting on me."

"Syd, I wasn't aware of all that. I don't want to hold you up. You go and watch your movie. We can talk again soon."

Sydney felt disappointed. "That's true. It's been fun, Vicky. I enjoyed our chat."

"So did I, Syd. Well, bye for now."

"Bye for now." He heard her hang up and placed the phone back on the wall.

He returned to his room and found Roland passed out on his bed, snoring. Albert was nowhere to be seen. *Lord...he's good for the night. It'd take a stick of dynamite to get him up. Guess I'll be sleeping on the floor...I deserve that, I suppose.* He felt awful about the things he said to Roland. He didn't mean to tell him about Mrs. Stuermer in that way. He had intended to tell him and Albert later that night before they went to bed in a shocked, what the hell, kind of manner, but he blurted it out in a hurtful way.

He closed his door and walked to the den, where he found his parents sitting on the couch under a blanket, watching Blue City. "What's up, Sydney?" his father asked.

"Have you seen, Al?" Sydney asked.

"I think he might have stepped out into the backyard a little while ago, dear," his mother said, turning her attention back towards Judd Nelson riding down the highway on his motorcycle. Sydney turned around and walked to the back door.

He entered the brisk autumn evening and immediately saw Albert sitting on a lawn chair, looking up into the cloudless night sky full of stars. The moon was a crescent high above and filled the backyard with dim light. "What are you doin' out here, Al?" Sydney said, grabbing an adjoining chair, placing it immediately next to Albert's, and falling onto it.

"Just looking at the stars, Syd. I finished my book, and Roland fell asleep. He passed out a bit after you left the room."

"Oh, yeah? Did he say anything about what I said?"

"No, he just kind of grunted a bit and turned toward the wall."

Sydney let out a chuckle, "That sounds like him."

"Yeah, he'll be fine. He knows you were just mad at him for messing with the phone. I told him not to do it."

Sydney leaned over and gave Albert a light slap on the shoulder, "Of course you did, bro. I know you wouldn't do stupid shit like that…How was your book? You seemed pretty into it. Hope you don't have any nightmares tonight."

Albert's gaze remained fixated on the stars, "Eh, don't worry about that. The stuff from my novels doesn't frighten me. I'm more frightened of being alone."

Sydney looked over at Albert, "Alone? You're not alone, buddy. I'll always be here for ya."

Albert's face remained emotionless. "I don't mean that. I mean..." he trailed off. Albert closed his eyes, removed his black baseball cap, and placed it on his lap. He then looked over to Sydney. "You ever feel that there's more out there than people know about? Like...somewhere far, far away but close at the same time?"

"You mean like aliens, man?"

Albert frowned, "No...well, I don't know...It just sometimes feels like there's something I've forgotten...or rather *someone*...I'm sorry. Let's just forget it."

The two sat silently for a while, staring upwards when a shooting star zoomed across the sky. "Wow, you see that, Al? Did you make a wish?"

"Yeah...I did. Did you?"

"Yeah, man. I hope it comes true."

Later that night, as Sydney lay on the floor next to Albert, he smiled in the darkness as he thought of the wish he'd made. He wished that he'd continue to grow closer to Victoria. It was a simple wish he felt wasn't asking too much from the heavens. He drifted off, thinking of how Victoria had called him cute. *Oh, Vicky*, he thought as sleep enveloped him.

As the days progressed, Sydney continued to meet up with Victoria at the library. They would meet and study, then talk on the phone each night. The two were quickly growing closer to each other, and Sydney thought of the wish he'd made that night with Albert under the stars. He wondered if Albert's wish had come true as his had. He hoped so.

Sydney's first exam approached, and he usually would be filled with dread the night before as he lay in bed, and he'd wake up feeling terrible from tossing and turning all night. This time though, he woke up completely rested. He had even begun setting his alarm clock properly, which made his old man pleased. He was happy to live up to his promise to his father and planned to continue by knocking this exam out of the park.

Mrs. Stuermer placed the exam on Sydney's desk and quietly wished him luck. Roland looked over at him with angry eyes. *Fuck sakes. Now, I have to smooth things over again with this jealous bitch*, Sydney thought as he put Roland out of his mind for later. He looked over the equations and was delighted to see they weren't anything special. With all the help he'd received from Victoria, he quickly solved each equation. After checking over his answers a few times, he stood up, walked to Mrs. Stuermer's desk, and turned in his exam. He returned to his seat and spent the rest of the class taking a much-deserved nap.

The bell woke him a short time later, and he had a quick stretch and then proceeded to leave. As he passed Mrs. Stuermer's desk, she said, "I saw that you finished your exam pretty quickly. I hope you did well, Syd."

Roland pushed Sydney aside, placed his test on top of her desk, and said, "Here's mine, Mrs. S."

"Thank you, Roland. Have a lovely day," she said, smiling at him.

"You have such a lovely smile, Mrs. S. You have a lovely day, too," Roland said, smiling and giving Sydney a smug look.

Lord...this guy is somethin' else, Sydney thought as he headed off.

At the end of the day, as Sydney and Albert were walking down the main hallway, Mrs. Stuermer called out to Sydney. "I'll catch up, Al...*don't* tell Roland about this." Albert laughed and agreed.

"Hi, Syd. I wanted to let you know what you made on your exam. I saw you walking, and I didn't want to leave you hanging until Monday. You made a...94! You did really well! You must have studied a lot."

Sydney smiled and thought of meeting up with Victoria. "I sure did...but I didn't do it alone. I had a lot of help from a special someone."

Mrs. Stuermer smiled brightly, "Oh, I see! They certainly seem very special indeed to help you study like this! I'm very proud of you, Sydney. You'll only have to make around a C on the next one to pass again. You're very close right now. You keep completing your homework correctly and passing the quizzes, and you'll be just fine. You can do it. I'll see you on Monday, Syd. Have a good weekend."

Sydney rushed off to meet with Albert and tell him the great news. He couldn't wait to tell Victoria later that night. She would be the proudest of everyone.

That night after supper, he hopped onto the phone and called up Victoria. He had cleared the entire night to chat with her. No Roland or Albert this time. He was relieved not to have to deal with Roland this time around. When Victoria got on the line, Sydney shared the good news. She was incredibly proud of him. The entire night felt like a dream to him. Time seemed to flow so slowly as they talked, but before Sydney knew it, he looked up, and it was midnight. His parents had long since gone to bed, and the house was still and quiet. The two had to part ways for the time being, but Sydney knew they'd be talking again before he knew it.

As October continued, Sydney's school had become decorated in all things spooky. Paper ghosts and witches hung outside teachers' doors and spider webs, both natural and fake, hung in the hallways. Pumpkins lined the entrances as he stepped into the school each morning out of the steadily chilling air outside. Sydney and Victoria continued to meet and study. The situation had become less dire, and Victoria even left the blinds open, allowing Sydney to watch as the once golden leaves withered to a dark brown and began gradually falling from the large tree outside the window.

Test number two arrived, but Sydney and Victoria knew that he would do just fine on it, and he did more than that. He scored a 91 on the exam and brought his grade well into the passing range. Now that he had accomplished his goal, he wanted to do something special.

That Friday afternoon, after he found that he'd passed the exam, Sydney happily walked through the hallway to meet back up with Albert when a poster caught his eye. It was an advertisement for a local amusement park called Miracle Pier. It was partially built over a bit of Lake Lethe, the large lake that Lando was built around. The font on the poster had the letters all bloody.

MIRACLE PIER HALLOWEEN CELEBRATION '88!! WEAR A COSTUME GET IN FREE!!!

Sydney's eyes lit up. *That'd be the perfect thing for us to do! Maybe I can even get Albert and Roland to tag along!* Sydney grabbed the poster off the wall, tucked it into his backpack, and ran outside.

That night after Sydney proudly revealed he had passed his second exam, he sincerely thanked Victoria and asked if she had any plans for Halloween. She said the only thing that she had planned was to hand out candy. She'd decided to give up trick or treating that year. She felt she was almost a teenager and was too old for it. He then explained to her what he'd found out about Miracle Pier. Before he was even finished, she was on board.

"I'd love to go! I saw the posters around school, but I was unsure if you'd be down to do it since I heard you talking to Albert about trick or treating..."

"Well, we usually go around the neighborhood and eat candy into the night, but this sounds so much better than that." Victoria agreed. "You wouldn't, by chance, know of any girls you could invite? ...For Albert, I mean!"

"Just one? What about Roland?"

Sydney cleared his throat, "Um, don't worry about Roland. He's already got his eyes on someone."

"Oh, alright then. I know this one girl I could invite. She's pretty nice. I think she and Albert would get on well."

"Awesome! That sounds great. So, what kind of costume are you gonna wear?"

"I have one I was going to wear around the house to hand out candy. I'll wear that one!"

"Yeah? What is it?"

"You'll have to wait and see, mister."

Sydney laughed, "Alright, fine. Should be good."

"What about you, Syd?"

"I've got something in mind…I think you'll enjoy it."

"Ooo, nice! I'm sure I will. I can't wait to see it."

As Sydney lay in bed later that night, he couldn't believe how October had flown by. It had been an eventful few weeks. Halloween was only two days away. He wished it fell upon the weekend instead of a Monday, but it couldn't be helped. He knew that he'd have to call Albert and Roland the next afternoon and explain that the usual plans had changed. He wondered how Miracle Pier would be. He'd never actually been there. It was mostly a tourist spot, and couples visited there from what he remembered. He'd always been captivated by the enormous Ferris wheel that rose high above the pier. *Soon, I'll be on it…with Victoria next to me*, he thought and felt both excited and nervous.

The following day Sydney gathered his costume together. He had an idea for a while of what he wanted to dress up as, but it just so happened that Victoria would love it too. He gathered up some old clothes and purposely got them dirty and tattered. He got some big black boots and borrowed his dad's old hockey mask to complete the look. He donned the outfit, stood in front of the mirror in his room, and was quite pleased with the results. He knew for sure that Victoria was going to love his Jason Voorhees costume.

Halloween morning arrived, and Sydney tried to keep his excitement in check and not think so much about going out with Victoria, but he couldn't keep a hold on his heart. His mind continuously wandered throughout the day, and he was eager to see what her costume would be. He found his gaze shifting to clocks on the walls of his classrooms throughout the day. It appeared at times as if time was inching backward. He played it cool, though, around Roland, Albert, and especially Victoria. He didn't want her to know how excited he was to go out with her…albeit with Albert and her friend.

The afternoon arrived after an excruciatingly long day at school. His mother picked him up. She had decided to take off early from her job at Lethe Pharmacy after Sydney had explained his plans for the evening.

It had been Sunday night, and Sydney's mom had asked him during supper what his plans were going to be for Halloween. As they sat eating some of his mother's vegetable stew, his mother sprung the question upon him. "Are you gonna be going out with Albert and Roland again this year?" she asked.

Sydney took another spoonful of vegetable stew to his mouth and replied, "Um, well, I'm not going trick or treating this year, Mom. I'm gonna be going out to Miracle Pier with Albert and some other friends."

"Miracle Pier? Where do ya think you're gonna get the money to get in, son?" his father spoke up.

"It's free, Dad…as long as you wear a costume."

"Ah, well, have fun then, Syd. Don't be out too late."

His mother's eyes went wide, "Harry?! What do you mean?"

"What? He's almost a teenager, Lo. We gotta let him spread his wings sometime." His mother threw her foot out and kicked his father's leg.

"Ow! What did *I* do?"

"You could at least ask him who he's gonna be with, Harry!"

"...Yes, dear. You're right. OK, son, who are you meeting up with? Besides Al..."

Sydney was hoping he wasn't going to have to go into this. *Damn...* he thought as he put his spoon down into his stew.

"I'm meeting up with another friend of mine...a girl named Victoria, and a friend of hers."

A smile began to spread across his mother's face. "A girl, huh? Who is *Victoria*?"

Sydney began to blush lightly. "She moved here from King City about a month ago. We've been talking for a few weeks now."

"So, that's who you've been talking to until midnight..." his father said, lightly laughing. "Makes sense. I didn't think you were on the phone like that with Al or Roland. No offense but those two aren't great conversationalists," his father said, smiling. Sydney shook his head in agreement.

"Well, where does she live, Sydney?" his mother asked.

"She told me a little while back that she lives on Lookout Hill."

"Ah, I know where that is," his father said. "How about your mother and me go along and pick her up tomorrow evening? We can drop you guys off at the pier."

"That's a great idea, Harry!" his mother said. "It'll give us a chance to meet your girlfriend and her parents. Plus, that's too far for you to walk anyway."

Sydney looked down into his stew, and his reflection stared back at him from the silver handle of the spoon. *Girlfriend? Is Vicky really...my girlfriend?* He tossed about the term in his mind for the rest of the night until he was in bed and drifted off to sleep.

He stood before his mirror again, reflecting on his mother*'s words.* He smiled as he flipped the hockey mask down over his face. He stood as tall as possible, trying to look as menacing as he could. He wanted to really frighten Victoria with his outfit. As he stood there, he almost frightened himself. *Yeah, this is good,* Sydney thought as a knock came upon his door.

"Syd? You ready, son? Your mom is ready to go...She's been ready ever since you got home. Come on out."

Sydney flipped his mask up and winked at his mirror. *It's showtime.*

He opened the door, flipped his mask back down, and took heavy steps up the hallway to the den, where he found his parents sitting on the couch. "Ohhh, no! It's Jason! Everybody clear out!" his father said, laughing to himself.

"You're gonna wear those grubby clothes over to meet Victoria's parents?"

Sydney flipped his mask up. "It's a costume, Mom. They'll know these aren't my regular clothes."

"Yes, true...but still. Do they have to be so dingy?"

"It's part of the look, Mom!"

"Fine, fine. I'll have to put a towel under you in the car. Let's go, Harry."

"Alright, come along, Jason," his father said, smiling and patting him on the shoulder.

The ride to Victoria's didn't take too long, but his mom wasn't wrong about it being too far to walk. On foot, it would have taken thirty minutes or longer in his soot-heavy outfit. In truth, Sydney was excited, and a bit relieved that his parents were along for the ride. He was pretty nervous about meeting Victoria's folks. He thought his parents might make it a little easier as long as his mom didn't embarrass him. *Just don't break out the baby pictures...*he prayed silently.

His father drove their family station wagon along a private road directly next to a part of Lake Lethe. There were a few homes scattered about on the banks of the lake, and Sydney could see that the road dead-ended ahead. It was right before the dead end that his father turned right. He drove up a short hill that led to two small homes which looked out upon this part of the lake. *Lookout Hill…A perfect name for it*, he thought as his father parked the wagon, and they all hopped out. "This is a lovely spot they have up here. Right on the edge of the woods, too," his father said, admiring the view.

"Which is it, Syd? I don't see any numbers on the front," his mother asked.

Sydney turned and looked over at the house on the right. "This one. I remember Vicky mentioning the living room windows and the Halloween decorations." He stepped onto the pathway that led to the dark brown porch and noticed the jack o' lantern staring out at him from the top of the porch. It was a bit of a gory pumpkin. Victoria had mentioned it to him earlier when he explained he would come over with his parents. She had said to look at the pumpkin before he came in. He did just that and noticed a knife sticking out of the side of it with some red paint. Its face was bruised, and it was missing teeth. Blood had been splattered over the gaping holes in its mouth. Sydney was quite impressed by the pumpkin.

"Ew, this pumpkin is too much," his mother said, eyeballing the pumpkin as she turned away from it.

"Oh, Lo, it's not that bad. Wow, look at that knife. Killer. Who made this, Syd?" his father asked.

"Vicky did. I think her dad helped a bit with the knife."

"She sounds like a cool girl." Sydney smiled brightly under his mask. He was thankful for the mask. It made him feel more at ease.

Sydney approached the door and rang the doorbell. Inside, he could hear the typical DING DONG, and the butterflies fluttered again. Through the darkened glass of the door, Sydney could see some movement. Someone was coming, but he was unsure who it was. A moment later, the door slowly opened, and out stepped, "Victoria?" Sydney said as he looked at her in full costume.

She wore a pointy black hat, a buttoned-up black top with a long skirt, and black boots. Her skin was painted a light green. "Yep, it's me! And you're Jason Voorhees! Wow, awesome costume, Syd! I love it!" Victoria then looked up, seeing Sydney's parents behind him, smiling at her. "I'm sorry! Hi, Mr. and Mrs. Lee! I'm Victoria," she said with a smile. Her teeth stood out against her green skin. Sydney's parents were thrilled to meet her, and she quickly led them all inside. "Would you guys mind slipping your shoes off out here?" Victoria asked. They all slipped out of their shoes. Sydney took a minute to undo his tight boots. "Come on, Syd. My parents have already met yours!" she said, lightly ribbing him.

"I'm coming, Vicky! Just one more tug…there we go," he tossed his boot aside and entered the kitchen.

"Took you long enough, Sydney. Come on into the living room," his mother said from across the room. The kitchen led directly into the living room, and Sydney saw his parents sitting on the couch and two other people sitting across from them.

In the recliner sat a man with dark brown hair and eyes that mirrored Victoria's. He knew that this must be her father. The man rose from his recliner and lightly smiled at Sydney. "You must be the young fella that keeps calling asking to speak to Victoria," he said, extending his hand.

Sydney took it and grasped it firmly. He looked into the man's warm eyes and introduced himself, "Yes, sir. That's me. Sydney Lee, nice to meet you, sir."

"Sir? Haha. Wayne will do just fine, Sydney."

"Right, Wayne," Sydney said, looking over at the woman smiling beside Wayne.

"Oh, it's so nice to finally meet you, Sydney. Victoria talks about you all the time!"

"Mom!" Victoria said from behind Sydney, her eyes wide with embarrassment. Everyone would have seen her blushing brightly if not for her green skin.

"Oh, it's alright, Victoria. I'm sure he knew that already. I'm Grace, my love," Grace said, wrapping her arms around Sydney and hugging him tightly.

"Nice to meet you, Grace," Sydney said.

"Waylon! Come out here a minute and meet Sydney!" Grace yelled out.

"Victoria's brother is in his room right now. He's going out too, but I wanted him to meet you before he left."

"OK, sounds good," Sydney said as he heard a door open from the hallway past the kitchen. A thin guy with a small mustache came walking into the kitchen. He politely waved to everyone and said, "Hello." He approached Sydney and extended his hand, "Nice to meet you, Sydney. I'm Waylon." Sydney shook his hand and introduced himself.

Sydney's mother said, "Waylon looks a bit older than Victoria."

"Yeah, it took us six years to get over him," Wayne laughed. Waylon excused himself and returned to his room.

The parents took some time to chatter back and forth while Victoria decided to give Sydney a tour of her home. She led him through the kitchen, briefly pointing out such fascinating amenities as the stove and fridge and her family's kitchen table. She then led him down the hallway past Waylon's room. They walked past a door across from Waylon's room and up the hallway a bit. Sydney wondered why she skipped over it, but he went along with the tour. She pointed out her parent's bedroom and the bathroom,

Some Things Last...

and lastly, the laundry room. She showed him into the laundry room, which had a door that led out onto the back porch. They stepped outside for a few minutes.

"So, what do you think of my family?" she asked with a smile.

"They seem great. Really friendly."

"Yeah, they liked you."

"It seems you like me too...according to your mom."

Victoria started laughing and lightly hit him on the shoulder. "Oh, look! It's my grandparents...Nan and Pop!" she said, pointing to an old couple walking over to the side entrance of the house next door. "Come on. You can meet them too real quick!" she said, grabbing him by the shoulder.

"Hey, Nan and Pop!" The two turned and looked over at Victoria, who slightly startled them.

"Who's that? Victoria?! Oh, I didn't recognize ya for a minute there! Who's this you got with ya?" her grandfather asked.

"This is a friend of mine...Sydney."

Sydney stepped over to her grandfather and extended his hand. Her grandfather took his hand and tightly squeezed it, almost too tightly. When he released his hand, Sydney could still feel his grip around his hand for a good hour. "That's a nice handshake, my son. You take care of Victoria," he said, smiling. Sydney smiled and agreed that he would, and her grandfather made his way up the steps and into the house.

Followed close behind was Victoria's grandmother. "Nan, this is Sydney!"

Sydney smiled, and the older woman returned the smile. "Oh, nice meeting you, Sydney." She then followed her husband into the house. "Your grandfather has quite the iron grip handshake," Sydney said, rubbing his hand.

Victoria laughed and said, "You gonna be alright, Syd?"

He stopped rubbing his hand and smiled, "Of course…it wasn't *that* bad!"

They returned to Victoria's home. "Now, I know what you're thinking. I skipped over a room! Well, I saved the best for last!" Victoria said, leading him to the room she had skipped across from Waylon's and opening the door. "Here's *MY* room! She said, showing off her posters of various bands and horror movies. Sydney was certainly impressed. "Check this out…" she said as she turned the lights off. "Look up, Syd!" He looked up at the ceiling and saw it adorned with dozens of glow-in-the-dark stars, and around the light was her name spelled out in bold letters.

VICKY

A knock came upon the door, and Victoria quickly turned the light back on. She opened the door to find her mother standing in the hallway. "Victoria, what are you two doing in there with the light off?" she said, one eyebrow raised.

"Nothing, Mudder. I was showing Syd my room and the stars on the ceiling…I only had the door closed for like a minute!"

Her mother shook her head and smiled. "Alright, come on out so we can get a photo of you two in your costumes. It's getting dark out."

The two returned to the living room and stood in front of the large window. Sydney admired the view a moment while Victoria fixed her hair a bit. The view really was quite scenic in this part of town. He could see light waves crashing against the shoreline in the distance. Ripples stretched out on the water's darkening surface.

"OK, Sydney, look forward," Grace said, looking through the camera's viewfinder. "Say cheese!" The two smiled, and a bright flash momentarily blinded Sydney. He returned his gaze out the window and saw that the final rays of the sun

Some Things Last...

were disappearing. Night had finally arrived, and it was time to head out to pick up Albert.

Sydney and Victoria sat in the backseat chatting as the station wagon moved along through Lando. He could already see kids wandering the streets in many different costumes. Some guy in a Michael Myers outfit menacingly stood on a street corner. As they passed him, Sydney could swear those soulless black eyes were laid upon him. Sydney quickly laughed a bit at himself. He realized it was just some guy in a costume, much like himself.

They pulled into Albert's driveway and got out. "We're not gonna be here long. Let's get Al and head over to pick up your friend, Victoria," his father said. Sydney walked behind his parents as his mom knocked on the door. A moment later, his Aunt Milly opened it.

"Hey, Lola! Come on in, guys!" his aunt said happily as she held the door open for his parents. "You must be Victoria! Albert mentioned you! He also said you were going to be bringing along a friend for him. Where is she?"

"Yes, we'll be going to get her after this," Victoria said, smiling.

"Ah, I see. What's her name?"

"Abigail," Victoria replied.

"Abigail. That's a nice name. Come on in, you two! Alby's in his room, reading."

"Thanks, Aunt Milly. We'll go get him."

Sydney led the way down the darkened hallway. Albert's room was at the end of it. A warm glow shone from the cracks of the door. KNOCK KNOCK. Sydney knocked lightly. He looked over at Victoria, who smiled at him. A moment later, the door opened, and Albert stood wearing a bright red jacket, a white t-shirt, blue jeans, and a pair of brown boots.

"Dude, you're supposed to be in costume, remember!"

Albert rolled his eyes, "I am, Syd. Don't you remember that movie we watched a while back? The one I rented for movie night?"

Sydney thought a moment, "Nah, I'm drawing a blank, bro."

Albert sighed, "Rebel Without A Cause! I'm Jim Stark!"

Sydney scratched his head, "Still drawing a blank."

"I'm James Dean! Lord almighty!"

"Oh, yeah...Nice costume."

"It's a great costume, Albert," Victoria said, giving Sydney a light shove.

Albert smiled and nodded, "Thanks."

"Yeah, yeah. Hey, you're not gonna wear your black hat tonight? You wear that thing everywhere. Come to think of it...you weren't wearing it at school today either."

"Oh, no. I threw that out this morning. I don't need it anymore."

Sydney took a step back, "You alright, Al?"

"Yeah, Syd. I'm great. Why do you ask?"

"Um, just wondered. So, you ready to meet up with Abigail tonight, bro?"

"She's really nice, Albert. I think you'll like her."

Albert lightly smiled, "Right, I'm sure she is...will you two excuse me a moment. I need to use the bathroom before we leave." Albert quickly left his room and entered the bathroom down the hallway.

"Is it me, or does something seem...different with Al?" Sydney said.

"He does seem a bit different. I'm sure he's alright, though. Probably just nervous about meeting Abigail."

"Yeah, I guess so..."

"Sydney, is Alby ready?" his Aunt Milly called from up the hallway.

"He's in the bathroom," Sydney said, pointing at the bathroom door.

Some Things Last...

"Alby, come on out. I want a photo of you guys!" Albert exited the bathroom a moment later and walked up the hallway.

"Hey, boss man! Good to see ya! You decide not to wear a costume this year?" Sydney could hear his father talking to Albert.

"OK, Vicky. Let's get this photo over with so we can get going."

"Yeah, Abigail's gonna be wondering where we are."

The two entered Albert's living room, and his Aunt Milly took out a Polaroid camera. "OK, you guys. Give me a good pose! The three of them posed in front of the couch.

"Wait a second, Ma." Albert zipped his jacket up a quarter of the way and popped his collar. "OK, now."

She snapped the photo, and it popped out of the camera a moment later. She began to shake it back and forth, and the image slowly revealed itself. "Memories!" she said and placed the photo on the end table.

"OK, guys, let's head on out. Bye, Milly. We'll be back over on Thanksgiving!" Sydney's father said, exiting the house.

"Alright, Harry! Alby, have fun with Abigail. Remember what I said about the Ferris wheel."

Albert closed his eyes and nodded, "Sure, Ma. See you later."

After leaving Albert's place, everyone went and picked up Abigail. She was a quiet, soft-spoken girl. Sydney could understand why Victoria would invite her for Albert. When she introduced herself to Albert, she smiled and complimented his jacket. "Nice jacket. Who are you supposed to be?" Albert thanked her and then looked away. "What do you think of my costume?" Abigail was dressed as a cat.

"Nice," is all he said. Sydney might have said something to him about that, but he was too busy talking and laughing with Victoria.

The four sat close together in the backseat as they finally made their way to Miracle Pier. "I've never been out to Miracle Pier," Abigail said. "Have you, Albert?"

Albert shrugged and simply said, "Nope."

"Yeah, neither have I, Abigail," Victoria said.

"I've wanted to go for a while but never had the opportunity," Sydney said.

"That's not true, Syd. Me and your mom have been a good bit of times. It's been a while, but you've been there too. When you were a baby, we have this family photo we had taken in front of the Ferris wheel ages ago…your mom will have to find it for ya."

"Well, Dad, that doesn't really count since I don't remember it!"

"Fair enough, son. Well, you can say you've been there now…since we're here."

Sydney looked through the window and saw groups of people steadily entering the main gate. Above the entrance was a large sign which read:

MIRACLE PIER

Its edges were adorned with large, flickering white lights. *Wow!* he thought as his father parked the car in front of the entrance.

"OK! Everybody out! I already got a car behind me!" The four of them piled out of the car.

Sydney held his hand out to Victoria, helping her exit the station wagon. "Thanks, Syd," she said, winking at him.

Albert hopped out of the car and walked around to where Sydney was. Abigail joined a second later. "Thanks, Albert," Abigail said. Albert looked off at the main entrance, totally ignoring her.

Some Things Last...

"Alright, Sydney. I'll be back here at ten. You make sure to meet me out here then."

"I will, Dad. Al's got a watch."

"I do, too, sir," Victoria said, raising her left sleeve.

"That's good. Alright, I'll see you four later. Oh, Syd, come here a minute..." Sydney ran over to the driver's side door. "Get her a bite to eat, Syd. She'll appreciate that." Sydney's father discreetly slipped him a ten-dollar bill.

"Thanks, Dad."

His father nodded and smiled. "Bye, guys!" Sydney's mother said as his father pulled away from the entrance and drove home.

"Let's head on in, guys," Sydney said as Victoria walked next to him. When they reached the gate, Sydney saw a guy wearing a uniform that read *Miracle Pier Staff* on the front. He was looking over everyone and seeing if they were in costume by the looks of it. They got in line and made their way along.

"OK, you're good. You're good. Alright. Go ahead," the guy kept saying quickly to everyone in line. "Wait a minute. Who are you supposed to be, red?" Sydney turned around and saw the guy eyeballing Albert. Albert looked like he didn't really care. "Yo, come on, pal. I asked ya a question."

Sydney stepped over, "Can't you see he's the guy from that movie..."

The guy looked Albert over. "Oh, yeah...Rebel Without A Reason"

"Cause," Albert said.

"Reason, cause? Whatever. Go on in."

"Thanks, Syd," Albert said.

"Anytime, man."

Finally, they all stood in the main concourse of the pier. The place was divided into three sections. To their right lay various carnival games nestled closely together, along with a variety of small food stands. There was everything from ring toss to darts and hot dogs to funnel cakes. To their left was the haunted castle. The siding of it was a light gray color with dark gray shingled awnings over the windows. The entrance led to the far left into a spooky tree with a warped face upon it. The tree had long, pointy limbs, but it didn't scare Sydney. It was almost comical to him. Lastly, directly ahead lay the Ferris wheel that loomed high above them. Its many illuminated cars slowly turned around. The lights along its frame flashed rhythmically.

"How about we check out the haunted castle first, Syd?" Victoria asked.

"I thought you'd want to check it out first," he smiled. "Let's go, guys. Vicky wants to check out the haunted castle." They joined the long line stretched out in front of the spooky exterior.

"It's a shame Roland decided not to tag along," Sydney said.

"Maybe he felt like a fifth wheel?"

"Nah, he told me in the hallway after school that he didn't want to go to Miracle Pier. He'd rather enjoy the peace and quiet at home…whatever that means. He's a weird guy."

Victoria laughed, "Syd, what does that say about the guy who's his friend?"

"It says…that I'm a charity case." Victoria's mouth opened, and she poked him. "Come on now! You know Roland, and I go way back. I'm sure he's fine. Maybe he's growing up like all of us…"

"Oh, we're next, Syd! Come on, guys!" Victoria didn't hear the last part of what he had said. Just as well. He didn't want to get all serious. Tonight was about fun.

The four of them piled into the darkened entrance of the warped tree, and one of the guys working instructed them to walk slowly through the dark and that things would be popping out randomly. They then entered the darkness of the haunted castle. A few feet in, a flash of light illuminated the cramped hallway, followed by thunder. Victoria jumped and grabbed onto Sydney's arm. *Nice*, he thought as they continued forward through the darkness. They turned a corner and were greeted by two hefty ghosts wailing through a hole in the wall. Sydney felt embarrassed that he jumped a bit at this one. "Damn! That one got me!" he said over the wailing.

They pressed onward into a dimly lit corridor. Sydney looked up and saw that the ceiling had spikes on it. As they slowly walked ahead, a panel on the floor slightly went down, and the ceiling suddenly dropped a few feet and then quickly stopped. Victoria latched onto Sydney, and they both fell to the floor. They looked into each other's eyes for a moment but quickly looked away, laughing. He looked over at Albert and Abigail. She was latched onto his arm, but he looked unimpressed.

After that final scare, they exited the haunted castle and came out to the opposite end of the entrance. "That was awesome!" Victoria yelled.

"Yeah, that was pretty bitchin'."

They all made their way back to the main concourse, and Sydney found himself gravitating toward the smell of sweet funnel cakes. "Hey, Vicky, you wanna grab a funnel cake?"

"Hell yeah, Syd! They smell awesome."

"Come on, Al and Abby," Sydney said, following the scent of the delectable funnel cakes to a small stand in the center of the carnival games. "OK, we'll have two funnel cakes," Sydney said to the lady running the stand. She quickly made them, and he handed her the ten-dollar bill his father had generously given him.

"These smell like heaven," Victoria said as she bit into hers. The powdered sugar stuck to her lips. Sydney imagined kissing her soft lips and tasting the sugary sweet powder. The thought made him blush, and he quickly turned away to see Abigail trying to talk to Albert.

"Can I order a funnel cake, Albert?"

Sydney could barely hear Albert over the frenzy of the games around them, but he thought he heard him say something like, "Got no money for that."

"Hey, Abigail, I'll buy you one. I'm good for it," Sydney said.

"Aw, thanks, Sydney. You're sweet. Unlike some people..." Abigail said, casting a dirty look in Albert's direction.

The group decided to walk through the games as they ate their funnel cakes. Sydney looked over at Victoria and saw that the sugar around her mouth was gone. He was slightly disappointed at this. "What? What is it, Syd?"

"Nothing, Vicky. Did you enjoy your funnel cake?"

"Yesss, I did. It was awesome."

"That's good."

As they walked through the games, an annoying voice cut through the crowd. "Hey! Yeah, you, dingbat! Get ova here!" Sydney stopped and looked over at a rough-looking clown sitting in a dunk tank. His hair was sticking up, and he wore a massive pair of oversized pants and suspenders. There was a sign over his booth.

DUNK THE RUDE CLOWN!! WIN A PRIZE!!

Sydney watched as a big muscle-bound guy paid for a handful of balls and tossed them at the target. He came close but missed every one of them. "*YOU LOSER!!* Look at ya. Guess your muscles can't get ya everything, huh? Get outta here. They call *ME* the clown. Look at you. Here's my impression of you. I got little legs and a huge upper body! You look like a freak! I bet you take supplements. Yeah, I bet you got a micro penis too. *HEEEEY YOOO!!!* High and dry!!" The muscle-bound guy promptly flipped the clown off, and the clown laughed, calling out to the man, "*WOAH! WHAT A BIG MAN WE ARE!!* Too bad you're mister tiny downstairs! *HEEEEY YOOO!!!* Alright, who's next?! What

Some Things Last...

about you?! I see ya watching there with your girl. She's a cutie. What's she supposed to be a witch? I can tell what she is, but what the hell are you?"

"Syd…I think he's talkin' to you," Victoria said with a shocked look.

"Nah, I'm sure there are other witches around here…let's go."

"Yo, where ya think you're going to! Don't you *dare* ignore me! *I KNOW YOU HEAR ME!! I'M TALKING TO THE GUY NEXT TO JIM STARK! REBEL WITHOUT A CAUSE, BROTHER!! LOVE THAT MOVIE! YOU GET A PASS, BUT YOUR FRIEND IS A B-E-M BUM!!*"

"See! I knew someone would know who I am!" Albert said, laughing. It was the most he'd said all night.

Sydney turned and looked at the clown. Their eyes locked. "There you are, you little peter puffer. Get your little ass over here…NOW! Tell me who you're supposed to be!"

Sydney approached the booth. "I'm Jason Voorhees, numb nuts!"

"*OHHH*, numb nuts! I like that! I'll have to remember it for later! So, you're Jason, huh? Where's your machete and your hockey mask?!"

"I couldn't bring a machete into the park, jackass!" he said, lowering his hockey mask.

"OH, there's Jason! I can see the intensity in your eyes. Yeah, use that! Come on, big man! *DUNK ME!*"

Sydney gave the attendant one dollar for four balls. Victoria stood beside him and spoke to him. "Dunk that damn clown, Syd."

He smiled, "You got it, Vicky." He threw one ball and completely missed the target.

"*WOAH!* Are you blind? What are you aiming at?!" He tossed the second ball and hit the outside of the target. "*OH, SO CLOSE! COME ON, BUDDY BOY! DUNK ME! I'M BEGGIN' YA!*" Sydney raised his mask and tossed the next ball, which also fell short of the target. "You got one ball left, but I'm just gonna cut to the end already. *HIGH AND DRY!! HAHAHA!!* Hey, why not let Jim over there have a go? At least he's got glasses. Maybe just maybe, he'll do better than you? But let's be honest. If he hit inside the marker at all, he'd do better than you!!! *HEEEEY YOOO!!!*"

"Al, wanna have a go?" Sydney asked.

"Sure, Syd. Why not." Sydney passed the final ball to Albert, who promptly threw it dead center and dunked the clown. The three of them stood for a moment with their mouths ajar. Albert went over to the attendant, who handed him a teddy bear. He stared down at the bear's small reflective eyes and gave it to Sydney. "Here, Syd," Albert said and walked away from the dunk tank. The clown climbed back onto the platform and remained quiet as he watched Albert walk alone down the path.

Sydney caught up with Albert, who was already walking towards the Ferris wheel. "Wait up, Al!" Sydney called out to him. "Where the hell did you learn to do that?!"

"My dreams, I guess," Albert said, looking down at the bear in Sydney's hands. "Take good care of Tony."

"Tony? Who the hell are you talking about, man?"

"The bear. I'm sorry. I mean…he looks like *our* Tony. Me and…Elly's." Albert turned away from Sydney. Sydney watched as he slowly walked towards the Ferris wheel. Victoria and Abigail caught up a moment later.

"Is everything alright with Al?" Victoria asked.

"I don't know. He seems alright…I suppose."

Abigail began to laugh, "He's far from alright. He's been nothing but selfish and disinterested all night. I thought he was shy at first, but there's more to it. He told me earlier that he was already with someone, or at least he felt he was. I don't know what that means but I'm going home. I can't do this anymore. I'm going to call my parents to pick me up. Goodnight, Vicky…Syd." Just like that, Abigail was gone.

Some Things Last...

You really hit a homer today, Al, Sydney thought as they watched Abigail walk towards the front entrance where the payphones were located.

"Guess that's that for Al and Abby. Too bad. I thought they'd hit it off," Victoria said glumly.

"Yeah, me too. Well, chin up. Al's an eccentric guy. He's always a little...odd. It just takes a while for him to open up."

"You really love him, don't you?"

Sydney turned away and watched Al standing beside the line to the Ferris wheel. "Yeah, he's my brother."

Sydney and Victoria caught up with Albert. "Hey, Al, wanna ride the Ferris wheel? It's almost time to go. We should be able to go around on it a bit before we gotta take off," Sydney asked.

Albert stared up at the Ferris wheel and the lights flashing above. "I guess so, Syd. Here, I'll hold onto the bear. What did you guys decide to name him?"

"How about Al?" Victoria answered.

Albert laughed, "If that's what you want. Al, it is. Come along, Al. We're going for a ride," Albert said with a smile. Sydney could see him smiling, but as Tony Montana had said in Scarface, 'The eyes, chico. They never lie.' Albert's eyes were full of sadness. Sydney wished he knew what was on his mind.

Albert climbed into an empty car with Al and fixed the bear in a seatbelt. He gave Sydney a quick thumbs up, and Sydney returned it. Sydney then followed Victoria to the second car behind Albert and took the seat next to her.

Finally, I'm here, he thought as the wheel slowly turned and let other people on. They began to rise higher into the air, and Victoria grabbed Sydney's hand, squeezing it tightly. The entirety of Miracle Pier started to come into view. "Hey, someone else is trying to dunk that damn clown!" Sydney said as the clown fell into the water again. "Got 'im!" he said, as they both laughed.

As they rose to the peak of the Ferris wheel, Sydney could see out across the entirety of Lake Lethe. He saw the lighthouse's beam briefly shine out over the lake. He noticed the moon was a quarter full in the starry sky above, and its light shone down upon the water's dark surface. The hills in the distance surrounding the lake were peppered with the glowing lights of the large cliff-side homes overlooking the lake.

"Wow, the view is beautiful up here," Victoria said.

He looked over at Vicky. Her eyes reflected the lights around them. "Yeah, I agree..." he didn't look away from her this time. He inched closer and closed his eyes. His lips touched her's for a moment, and that was all, but Sydney felt he could live in that moment forever. As they began to descend, he continued to look into Victoria's eyes and held her hand tightly. Sydney's heart felt very happy.

In the distance, Sydney failed to notice gathering thunderclouds. He was too busy watching Victoria. Their laughter masked the low growl of thunder in the distance. Albert noticed it all, though. He knew a storm was coming, and it would be there soon.

PART II

YAWNING AT YOUR HEELS

CHAPTER 9
Easy Like Sunday Mornin'

In the darkness of the night, a massive crack of thunder cut through the air. Sydney awoke from his deep sleep, his eyes wide open, as he bolted upright in bed. He looked to his right and saw three bright flashes in quick succession from the sides of the curtains. Another loud clap of thunder followed immediately after, and he involuntarily recoiled from it.

"What's going on, Syd?"

"Just a storm, baby. I'm sorry. The thunder woke me up. I didn't mean to startle you," Sydney said, reaching over in the darkness and rubbing Victoria's bare shoulder.

"It's OK, sweet thing. I know storms like these make you uneasy..." Victoria said, trailing off. She was already drifting back to sleep.

It was true Sydney didn't like storms like these. They reminded him of the past, and he didn't like to think about that. He liked to focus on the present. Sydney slid back down under the covers and emptied his mind. He listened to the sound of falling rain outside the window when another crack of thunder, although paling in comparison to the ones prior, cut through the air.

A knock came on the bedroom door a few seconds later. Sydney could hear light sobbing coming from behind the door. He hopped out of bed, slipped some flannel pajama pants on, and walked across the room. He slowly opened the door and saw a pitiful sight.

"Daddy? The lights went out, and the thunder's scary. Could I sleep with you and Mommy?"

Sydney crouched down and smiled, "Of course, you can, honey." Another crack of thunder cut through the air causing Sydney to jump slightly and the child to leap into his arms. "Oh, Vivian. It's alright. Daddy won't let the thunder get you," he said as he kissed the top of her head. He walked over to the bed, placed her next to Victoria, and then slid back into bed himself next to Vivian.

She quickly sighed and said, "Good night, Daddy. I love you." Sydney smiled and listened as her breathing became deeper. She was fast asleep. He lay there in the dark listening to the rhythmic sound of falling rain upon the roof for at least a half hour. After a while, the rain began to slacken, and the storm faded into the night. He tried slipping back to sleep but try as he might, he couldn't get there.

He decided to get up and head out into the living room. He gingerly slipped out of bed, careful not to wake Vivian and Victoria. Stealthily, he slipped out of the bedroom and left the door ajar so as not to cause any noise. He entered the kitchen, opened the fridge, and drank several mouthfuls of water from the jug. Victoria wouldn't have been happy about him drinking out of the container, but he was parched and didn't feel like fumbling for a glass in the dark. He felt he could drink the entire gallon of water but stopped after about four mouthfuls. He returned the jug to the fridge, went through the darkness to the living room, and fell onto the recliner.

He leaned back, put the footrest up, and looked at the darkened ceiling. *Damn, was I thirsty. This happens every time I order a dinner all legs. Ah, it's so worth it, though.* His mind began to wander as he thought about going out earlier that night.

They had met up with Victoria's family at a local restaurant called QL's for supper. It had become a weekly tradition for them all to meet up there and spend time together, going back to Sydney and Victoria's middle school days. They usually met up around seven every Saturday night; that night was no exception. Sydney always enjoyed it, though. He always ordered a big plate of chicken legs and fries and was content to sit and listen to Wayne and Waylon discuss the family business. When Vivian came along, his attention shifted to helping Victoria get her to eat.

That night he recalled sitting at the table as the usual business chatter came from Wayne and Waylon. They were discussing a job lined up to build a house for someone in town in the coming week. Tonight, Sydney wasn't in the mood to think about work, so he tuned out the rest of their conversation and looked at Vivian. She sat between him and Victoria. She was busy drawing in a notebook Victoria had given her to keep her preoccupied until supper arrived.

Vivian looked up from her doodle and smiled, "Look, Daddy! I drew you eating a chicken leg!" Vivian said gleefully.

Sydney looked over at the drawing, and he could kind of make out a figure holding something resembling a chicken leg. It was all drawn in red crayon. Sydney smiled, "Aw, it's beautiful, Vivvy. I love it." Vivian ripped the paper from the notebook and handed it to Sydney with her tiny hand.

"We'll have to put it on the fridge when we get home," Victoria said, smiling. Sydney nodded in agreement as he folded the doodle and placed it into his wallet for safekeeping.

The food came out a few minutes later, and everyone began to eat. Vivian thankfully ate her meal without any coaxing from her parents this time. She sunk her tiny teeth into a juicy chicken leg and some fries. When they were ordering, she told the waitress, "I want a dinner all legs like Daddy!" Everyone had laughed, and Victoria talked her down to just two legs knowing full well that Vivian would never be able to eat six chicken legs.

The evening began to wind down, and the time came when everyone proceeded to the counter to pay. When they lined up, something caught Victoria's mother's eye. She pointed and said, "Look at that, Victoria. Doesn't that bring some memories back?"

She was pointing to a poster on the wall beside the counter. It had a photo of a familiar Ferris Wheel on it and, in bloody letters, read:

MIRACLE PIER HALLOWEEN CELEBRATION '05!!
WEAR A COSTUME GET IN FREE!!!

"Do you remember you and Syd's first date, Victoria?"
Victoria looked at Sydney and smiled, "Yes, Mudder, of course, I remember it."
Sydney's eyes went wide for a moment in realization. "It's hard to believe it's been almost seventeen years ago. Oh, hell. Time does go by," he said.

As Sydney sat in his recliner, he thought a bit more about that realization. *Seventeen years...so much has happened since that night. God, we were all so young. Oh, Al...I miss you, brother.* As he sat reflecting on the past, the power came back on. The microwave and stove both let out quick beeps, and he could hear the fridge's hum begin again. *Ah, thank Christ. Let there be light*, he thought as he quickly set aside his reflection. He needed something to take his mind off things. He decided to get another sip of water and then see what was on television. Sleep, he'd accepted, wasn't in the cards for him tonight.

Sydney took the water jug over to the kitchen window and began to sip on it. He laid it down on the faux wood counter and looked out the window. He could see the sky starting to brighten a bit, and he knew that sunrise wasn't too far off. As he stood there, he saw in the reflection of the window a small figure come from around the corner.

"Daddy? Why did you leave?" Vivian said, followed by an enormous yawn.

"Hi, Vivvy. I just wanted some water. All that chicken from earlier made me thirsty."

Vivian looked at the water jug next to the sink. "Mommy doesn't like you drinking out of the jug."

Sydney smiled, "Yes, I know. Let's keep that between the two of us, sweetie."

"OK, Daddy. Can I have some?"

"Sure thing." Sydney went to grab a glass for her from the cupboard.

"No, Daddy! I wanna drink from the jug too!"

"Alright, Vivvy. Just a little bit, though. We don't need you wetting the bed."

After Vivian's drink of water, Sydney carried her back to her bedroom. He took her through the living room and down the hallway. Pausing next to the bathroom, he asked, "Do you need to go, Vivvy?" she shook her head no. He continued into her bedroom, placed her on her bed, and tucked her in. "Good night, Vivvy," he said and kissed her forehead. Vivian smiled, and her light brown eyes closed.

He returned to the living room, fell back onto his recliner, and noticed that the sky was growing brighter. He sat there for a few minutes and decided to turn the television on. As he grabbed the remote, he heard a floorboard creaking up the hallway, and then he saw Vivian's little face peep around the corner at him.

"Daddy?"

"Yes, Vivvy?"

"I can't sleep. Can I lay with you on the recliner?" Sydney moved over a bit, and Vivian ran over and jumped up with him. She rested her head on his chest, and he began rocking slightly. A few minutes later, she was fast asleep.

He sat and listened to the sound of her breathing. He looked down at her wavy light brown hair. *Same as her mother's*, he thought. As he looked down at her, he felt immense contentment. It was enough to bring a few tears to his eyes with the sheer love he felt for her. He leaned back, continued listening to Vivian's steady breathing, and found himself slipping steadily back to sleep.

He awoke several hours later to the smell of breakfast being cooked. His eyes gradually opened and adjusted to the bright morning light cascading through the window opposite him. The morning sun cast a bright diamond shape upon the couch through the front door window. He looked down and saw Vivian still nestled beside him on the recliner. He didn't want to move her, but he needed to use the restroom. All of that water had caught up with him. He tried to slowly move her off of him and slip out of the chair, and for a minute, he thought he'd succeed, but she began to stir, and her little eyes slowly opened and quickly shut, blinded by the bright morning light. "Where are you going? You're leaving me again, Daddy?" Vivian said, pouting.

Sydney picked her up in his arms, hugging her tightly. "No, sweetheart. Daddy has to use the bathroom. I was going to come right back."

He continued holding her tightly when he heard the sound of the oven timer going off. "Vivvy, I think your mother has some breakfast for us. Are you hungry?"

Vivian looked into his eyes and smiled, "Yes, but I'm thirsty!"

Sydney laughed, "Thirsty, huh? Well, Mommy can help you out with that. I'm gonna use the restroom real quick." He lowered Vivian to the floor, and she toddled off toward the kitchen.

In the meantime, he walked up the hallway and into Vivian's bathroom. They thought of it as her bathroom, but she was a tad young still for it to truly be hers. When she became a teenager, she would need her own space, and this was to be hers. Vivian as a teenager…it was a distant time that he didn't want to contemplate. He was content with her being the age she was now. She thought the world of him, but would she still feel that way when she got older? Once upon a time, he thought that way about his parents. As he grew older, though, his opinion of them diminished, especially the one of his father. He never wanted Vivian to think of him like that.

After he had used the restroom, he looked in the mirror. The bags under his eyes were a bit more pronounced this morning. People used to say he looked younger for his age, but the way he looked this morning, it seemed that time was catching up with him. *I suppose time catches up with everyone eventually. One way or another*, he thought as he looked down at his slightly protruding stomach. *Yep...one way or another. One too many chicken legs...but I can't help myself.* He rubbed his belly and sucked it in a bit, then breathed out, returning it to its regular size.

He thought about starting a workout routine when a knock came on the door. "Syd? You alright in there?" He opened the door to see Victoria standing in her lime-green robe. Her hair was all over the place, and she had no makeup on. Sydney thought she looked amazing. It took every bit of his self-control not to rip her robe off and ravage her. "Good morning, sweet thing," she said, smiling.

"Mornin', sexy," he said, leaning in and kissing her soft lips. "Something smells good...besides yourself, I mean."

Victoria laughed, blushing lightly, "I made some bacon, eggs, and mini pancakes. Vivvy is already sitting to the table eating. She was awfully thirsty. I think that chicken from last night is to blame."

"I know how she feels," Sydney said, chuckling.

After breakfast, Sydney washed the dishes and put them away. He looked out the kitchen window and saw that it was a gorgeous day out. He looked over at the clock on the stove. '11:23', its bright green numbers read. An idea popped into his mind. He walked to the living room to see Victoria and Vivian sitting on the recliner, watching Vivian's favorite cartoon.

"Hey, I had a great idea just now." The two of them curiously looked up at him. "Since it's such a nice day out, how about we go feed the baby goats?"

Vivian's eyes lit up at this, and she quickly leaped from the recliner. "Yay, Daddy! I can't wait! I hope Perkins the Horse is out today too!" Vivian speeded up the hallway, into her room, and then back again. She was a bundle of energy. Victoria and Sydney watched in amazement as she ran up and down the hallway squealing in delight.

"I better get her dressed if we're going," Victoria said, smiling.

"I'll go get ready, too," Sydney said as he returned to their bedroom and walked over to the closet. He opened the door and looked over his wardrobe. Most of the closet was taken up by Victoria's clothes, but he certainly didn't mind. He found a blue t-shirt and threw on a pair of jeans and a light jacket. As he was tying his shoes, a knock came on the door. "Come on in!" Sydney said, tightening his laces.

The door opened, and Vivian walked in, followed by Victoria. Vivian was wearing a peach-colored long-sleeved t-shirt with a ginger cat on it, looking into a mirror. Above the cat, there was a thought bubble that read, 'I'm purrrfect!'. She wore a black beanie on her head and a pair of light brown corduroy pants. With each step she took, Sydney could hear the corduroy rubbing together.

"OK! You and Daddy go to the living room and let Mommy get ready."

"Try not to take too long, Mommy. You're already pretty."

Sydney laughed and looked at Victoria, "You heard the little lady. You're already pretty," he said with a wink.

Not long after, Victoria joined them in the living room. She wore a track jacket, jeans, and a green plaid shirt with matching green sneakers. Sydney couldn't help looking her up and down. Victoria noticed his glance. "What do you think?" she asked.

"You're always so pretty, Mommy."

"I agree with Vivvy."

Victoria smiled, "Aw, you two are so sweet."

Sydney smiled and headed for the kitchen. "I'm gonna grab some jelly beans and carrots for our buddies." He loaded the snacks into a bag and walked to the front door.

The three of them left the house and headed for Victoria's car. "Alex" had certainly been around for a good while. Despite this, the vehicle was well-maintained. Sydney walked to the passenger door and waited for Victoria to open it. She unlocked the door, and Sydney placed Vivian in her car seat. Once she was secure, he took his seat in the passenger seat. He enjoyed sitting back and letting Victoria drive. It offered him the chance to enjoy the scenery a bit more, and where they were going, it would be a bit of a scenic drive. As they pulled out of the driveway, he glanced at his bright red Miata. *Man, today would be a great day for a drive…Oh, well.* He dismissed the thought and looked ahead.

The baby goats and horses lived on a nameless farm that stretched over dozens of acres on the scenic cliffs on the edge of Lando. The land owner usually allowed their livestock to graze during beautiful days like this one. Sydney and Victoria had never met the owner, but the baby goats were always happy and healthy. Their only real complaint was that Perkins the Horse's mane was always in tangles. Perkins was always in great spirits, though. Sydney had been the one to name him. Perkins had a thick mustache over his mouth, which reminded him of a certain P.E. coach from the past.

Victoria drove onto the stretch of road, which led to where their goat buddies usually "hung out." The road was unpaved and very bumpy. They had to drive very slowly,

Some Things Last...

and Vivian was already impatient. "Faster, Mommy! By the time we get there, they'll be gone!"

"Alright, Vivvy, settle down back there. We'll be there in a minute. It's just around the next corner," Sydney said as he looked at the sprawling open landscape. There wasn't much to look at out here. Other than the bumpy dirt road, there were a lot of areas of tall grass, fields of wildflowers, and open expanses of fields.

As they turned the next corner, they approached an open field where the goats usually grazed. Sure enough, they saw the baby goats running and playing. Victoria stopped the car and got out. Sydney stepped out and quickly unbuckled Vivian as she eagerly hopped out of the vehicle. Sydney reached into the floorboard and grabbed the goodie bag. He turned around, and he saw that the goats had already begun to gather around. They knew they were in for a treat. One of the larger goats noticed the bag and began to approach him. He didn't want the goats to get too excited and bump into the car, so he yelled, "Over here!" He shook the bag as he walked further into the field. He felt like the Pied Piper of the goats for a moment.

"Hand me some candy, Daddy! I wanna feed the goatlings!" Sydney laughed and gave a handful of jelly beans to Vivian and Victoria. They each began to feed them to the little goats quickly. A big brown and white goat began to shove the smaller ones aside and hog the candy. "NO! You wait your turn!" Vivian said, lightly pushing the big goat.

"Easy, Vivian, don't push him. He might headbutt you," Victoria said, eyeballing the big goat.

"That's OK. If he does, I'll headbutt him back!" Vivian said.

Sydney shook the bag, trying to lure the big goat over to him, and luckily he took the bait. Sydney focused on feeding him as the smaller ones gathered around Vivian. Sydney turned to the bully goat and softly said, "If you headbutt

Vivian, you won't have her to worry about ya greedy bastard." With his slanty eyes, the goat looked at Sydney for a moment, and Sydney swore he had understood him.

"OK, Syd, we're out of goodies! Let's go see if Perkins is up the road!"

"Alright, sounds good!" They all piled back into the car and slowly drove further up the dirt road. Sydney noticed the goatlings watching them drive away.

"Aw, bye-bye, goatlings!" Vivian said as she looked out of the window.

"Don't worry. We'll be back to see them again. Maybe next weekend if the weather is good," Victoria said as she drove around another winding corner. The open field the goats grazed in was followed by tall grass on both sides of the road for a bit, then finally, the right side opened up to an expanse where Perkins was usually left alone to enjoy himself.

They arrived at the expanse, but Perkins was nowhere in sight. Sydney raised his window down. "Honk the horn, Vicky. Maybe he's out further in the field today." Victoria honked the horn, and then they waited. As they were sitting, Sydney began to hear a sound. When Perkins galloped from behind the tall grass, he knew it was the sound of his hoofs.

"Perkins!! He *IS* here!" Vivian said in awe.

Perkins galloped over to the car and almost stuck his head inside to grab the bag of carrots. "Whoa, now, buddy! Hold on a minute!" Sydney said as he quickly slipped out of the car.

As Sydney slipped out and stepped away from the car, a gust of wind struck him. He was thankful he had decided to bring a jacket with him out here. He had made the mistake of not bringing one the last time they had come out here a few weeks prior and regretted it. It was always breezy up here on the cliffs overlooking Lando, and the wind could be especially chilly this time of year. *Woo! Winter is certainly on the way. I can feel it*, he thought as he zipped his jacket up. Despite the chilly breeze in the air, the sun was beaming down directly overhead.

Sydney looked over at Victoria and Vivian, stepping from around the car and out into the field where Perkins had returned after Sydney had stepped out. "Let's go feed him!" Vivian yelled as she took off towards Perkins.

"Hold on there, Vivian! You don't want to frighten him!" Victoria said, chasing after her. Sydney grinned and clutched the bag of carrots tightly.

He quickly caught up with the two, and Victoria had Vivian in her arms. Vivian was stroking Perkins' mane softly with her hand. Sydney handed Vivian a carrot. Perkins turned his head, moved his lips towards the tip of the carrot, and then bit down on its top half. It produced a loud crunch that made Vivian lightly squeal. "Watch his teeth, sweetheart," Sydney said as Perkins finished chewing the top half of the carrot. He returned for the bottom half, Vivian held out the rest by the base, and Perkins quickly ate it.

Each of them fed Perkins some carrots as Vivian remained in awe of him. She never took her eyes off of him the entire time. After a while, Perkins ate the whole bag of carrots and slowly turned and galloped back to the deeper part of the field, where he began to drink from a large barrel of water. "Such a majestic beast," Victoria said, shielding her eyes from the sun.

Sydney looked at his watch, '2:33,' it read. "We should be getting back," he said as Vivian frowned.

"Aw, but we just got here."

Sydney laughed, "We've been out here almost an hour, Vivvy!"

"REALLY? I don't know about that," Vivian said as she stared at Perkins in the distance. He had finished his drink and was nibbling on some hay.

"How about we head by Food Paradise on the way home and pick up something good for supper tonight?" Victoria said, looking down at Vivian.

"Can we get a cheesecake?" Vivian asked.

Sydney leaned down and picked up Vivian. "Like Mother like daughter," he said, giggling. They headed back to the car and loaded up. As they all drove away, they looked over as Perkins galloped closer. Sydney raised his window down and waved.

"BYE, PERKINS!" Vivian yelled from the back seat, waving her tiny hand. Perkins watched them leave as the goats did. Sydney saw him in the side mirror. Perkins stood alone as another gust of wind blew through his mane. A moment later, they turned another curb, and he was gone.

After another scenic drive back into town, they arrived at Food Paradise. It had become their go-to place for their groceries with its aisle of plenty. They all piled out of the car and headed into the cool interior of the store. Sydney was again thankful that he had worn a jacket because even in the summer, Food Paradise could be a bit brisk inside. He placed Vivian into the child seat in the shopping cart, and he followed Victoria as she walked along through the store. They had decided to make some meat and potato stew. Victoria began loading the cart with the ingredients and a couple of other things the house needed.

Soon, the cart was halfway full, and Sydney grew bored of following along. "Why don't I go get that cheesecake, Vicky? It'll save us a bit of time."

"I wanna go with Daddy too!"

Victoria placed a few more items in the cart and looked at Sydney. "You just wanna go see your buddy Henry don't you?"

Sydney looked down at Vivian. "Yay! We get to see Henries!"

"Yes, we're gonna see Henries today!" Sydney laughed.

Some Things Last...

"Alright, you two. I'll meet you over there. I gotta get some milk and cereal."

Sydney lifted Vivian from the cart and placed her upon his shoulders. She laughed and held on tight as Sydney walked to the bakery on the other side of the store. He arrived at the counter, and a familiar face greeted the two. "Well, if it isn't Ms. Vivian Lee and her father, Syd! It's nice seeing you two looking so well!"

"Nice to see ya again, Henry. How have you been?" Sydney said, smiling and extending his hand. Henry took it and shook it firmly.

"Takin' it one day at a time, brotha," Henry said with a big smile.

"That's all you can do," Sydney said.

"So, what can I help y'all with today?"

"We want a cheesecake, Henries! That one!" Vivian pointed to a large cheesecake inside the cake display counter.

"Hold on now, Vivvy. We don't need one *THAT* big. This one here will be more than enough," Sydney said, pointing to a much smaller cake.

Henry laughed and replied, "I know that's right! Maybe when it's your birthday, you can get the big one, Vivian."

"I guess so…my birthday's a long time from now, though," Vivian said glumly.

"Vivvy, your birthday is a little over a month from now. It will be here soon."

"How old will you be this year, Vivian?" Vivian thought a moment and extended one of her hands. "My lord. You're gonna be five this year! Time has gone by! I still remember when your parents first brought you in here. You were so tiny. You're growing up."

"Don't remind me, Henry. I don't wanna think about it," Sydney said.

"Hi, Henry," Victoria said, pushing the cart beside the glass cake display. "I hope these two haven't bugged you too much."

"We didn't bug Henries at all, Mommy! He was telling me about how I used to be a tiny little baby. Now, look at me! I'm a little lady!"

Henry began to laugh, "She is precious. Let me get your cake for you." Henry opened the display and handed Victoria the small cake Sydney had pointed out. "I made this cake this morning. I hope the three of you enjoy it later. "

"Thanks, Henry, we certainly will," Victoria said, placing the cake in the cart.

"Alright, don't let me hold you up. I'll see y'all again soon. Take it easy, Syd."

"Like Sunday mornin'," Sydney said, smiling just as brightly as Henry.

He'd always liked Henry. From the moment they met, Henry had always been so cheerful and full of life. Seeing him each time they came in to shop was always a pleasure. Sydney thought about inviting him to Vivian's 5th birthday party the next time they came in. He thought Henry would love an invite. He hoped that he would remember to do that when they came back.

Victoria pulled into the driveway and parked next to Sydney's Miata. They all exited the car and carried the groceries inside. Vivian even helped bring some of the lighter items. After Victoria and Sydney organized all of the groceries, Sydney decided to fix supper. Since Victoria made them all breakfast, he felt he should make supper in return. "Vicky, I want you to relax on the recliner and let me handle everything with supper, OK?"

"That's easier said than done with a bundle of energy bouncing around," Victoria said.

"Put on her favorite show. That usually helps calm her down a bit."

"Oh, nooo. If I gotta watch that space unicorn one more time, I swear," Victoria said, rolling her eyes.

"Yeah, I know…but at least she sits there and doesn't run around the house."

Victoria let out a large sigh. "Guess it's time for Celeste The Space Unicorn…again." Sydney wrapped his arms around Victoria and kissed her. "Syd…maybe later, after we put Vivvy down for the night, you and I can have some alone time."

"Sounds good to me, sexy," Syd said as he freed her from his arms. As she walked away, he gave her a quick slap on her behind.

Later that night, after they all had their supper, Vivian began to lose steam from a day worth of running around. She sat on the carpeted floor of the living room, drawing Celeste the Space Unicorn. Sydney and Victoria were watching the ending of Leon: The Professional on TV.

Sydney looked down at Vivian and saw that she had fallen asleep holding onto her pink crayon. He motioned to Victoria to look over at Vivian. They smiled and tried to contain their laughter when Vivian dropped her crayon. Her eyes slowly opened, and she picked up her crayon and continued drawing for a few moments when she fell asleep again.

"You should tuck her in, Syd," Victoria said.

"Yeah, I will. Precious little angel," Sydney said as he got up from the couch. "OK, little one, time for beddy-bye."

Vivian opened her eyes and yawned, "OK, Daddy, I guess I am kinda tired."

"You've had a busy day, Vivvy, " Sydney said as he picked up Vivian and carried her down the hallway.

"Put Celeste…on the fridge…OK, Daddy?" Vivian said, falling asleep in Sydney's arms. He entered her bedroom and turned on her nightlight. The small bulb filled the room with a dim glow. He leaned down, placed Vivian on her bed, and tucked her underneath the soft sheets. She remained still, her breathing steady and deep. Sydney could tell she was fast asleep. He leaned down, kissed her head, and quietly exited the room, closing the door behind him.

He returned to the living room to find the television off and Victoria MIA. "Yoo hoo…" Sydney turned around and saw Victoria standing beside the dining room table. She was wearing her lime green robe. She moved her index finger, beckoning him to follow her as she slowly turned and disappeared around the corner. He followed her into their bedroom, where she was already waiting naked on the bed. Her robe lay on the floor beside the bed.

"Oh, baby…" Sydney said, locking the door behind him. He took a moment to enjoy the view. She was magnificent.

She looked at him seductively, "Turn the light off, Syd…and come and give it to me."

"You don't gotta ask me twice," he said, quickly flicking the light off and tossing his clothes aside. He jumped onto the bed and got on top of her. He began to kiss her neck and lightly blew into her ears. This always drove her crazy.

She let out a loud moan and whispered into Sydney's ear, "Fuck me."

The two made love and lay breathlessly next to each other. "Oh, Syd, I fucking love you."

He leaned over and kissed her shoulder, "I fucking love you too."

"It's been a while since we've been able to be alone," Victoria said.

"Yeah, you never know what's gonna happen with Vivian. At least we don't have to go out for a drive and show her that fountain with the neon lights."

Victoria laughed softly, "Yeah, her little eyes would light up as she watched the water shoot into the air. She loved the colors, I believe. Maybe that's why she likes that Space Unicorn show so much."

Some Things Last...

"You know you might be on to something there. I think Vivvy will sleep through the night. She certainly was out of it when I tucked her in. She wanted me to…Oh, damn. I forgot to put her drawing on the fridge." He moved to get up, and Victoria grabbed him and pulled him back down.

"Leave it…we'll sort it out in the morning. I just want to lie here with you for a while. You're a great dad. You know that?" He moved closer to her, and she put her head on his chest and listened to his heartbeat.

"You're a wonderful mom…" Sydney hesitated a moment, then decided to say what else was on his mind. "Vicky, I was afraid, honestly, when you found out. I remember I was watching a movie at the time, and you had been late for about a week or so…"

"Yeah…I took the test, and it came back positive. I had never been so afraid in my life. Having a kid was something I didn't know if I really wanted…but I'd never trade it for the world now. Vivvy is so amazing."

"She is. You and her are what I live for…" Victoria kissed Sydney's chest.

"I love you, Syd."

"I love you too, Vicky."

"OK, Sweet Thing, we should try to get some sleep. We've both got work in the morning. I hope we get to do this again soon." The two re-positioned themselves. Sydney put his arm around her from behind and put one of his legs between hers. As they lay there, he breathed in the smell of her hair and thought just how great the day had been. He continued to hold her close as his eyes grew heavy, and he drifted off to sleep.

CHAPTER 10
Creeping Shadows

The sun rose slowly over the horizon and gradually began to shine its brilliant light over the town of Lando. Within her bed, Vivian stirred as the first signs of light brightened the sky. Her eyes slowly opened, and she thought, *Good morning, Mr. Sun.* She kicked the sheets off of her body and hopped out of bed. She opened her door, walked to her bathroom, and used the toilet. The seat was cool to the touch as she sat upon it, clearing the sleepy fog further from her mind. She finished up, flushed the toilet, and walked out into the darkened hallway. The house was chilly and silent. A feeling of unease began to fill her. She didn't like being alone in the darkened house, so she decided to go and wake up her parents.

Sydney and Victoria lie in bed, blissfully asleep. The alarm had been set for 6:30, which was a half hour away. As they lay in bed, a knock came on their bedroom door. It was soft at first and then grew in intensity. Victoria's eyes slowly opened, and it took a moment for her to realize where the knocking was coming from. She sat up and looked over at the alarm clock. The glow of the red numbers left a brief imprint within her eyes as she closed them and threw on her robe.

Victoria turned the light on and opened the door to find Vivian standing there, her eyes wide open. "What's wrong, Vivvy?"

"I woke up and had to use the bathroom. Then it was dark and quiet. I was scared."

Victoria knelt and picked Vivian up, and held her against her chest. Vivian hid her face beneath Victoria's long wavy hair. "There, there, Vivvy. There's nothing that's gonna get you out here," Victoria said as she rhythmically patted Vivian's back. "Come along. Let's have some breakfast. You can help me crack some eggs." Vivian continued hiding her face away, but as they turned to leave the room, she peeked out at her father, who was still blissfully asleep.

Before long, the front yard was lit up with the sun's early morning glow. Mother and daughter prepared breakfast together. Vivian cast off her fears as she cracked several eggs into a clear bowl. Victoria placed the eggs in a pan on the stove, and Vivian noticed that her father had yet to wake. "Daddy sure is being lazy," Vivian said, crossing her arms and pouting her lower lip.

"Why don't you go and wake him up, Vivvy?"

Vivian smiled and quickly ran out of the kitchen and to her parent's bedroom. She pushed the door aside and jumped upon the bed and onto Sydney's chest. "Wake up, Daddy! Get out of bed!"

Sydney's eyes flew open, and he looked down at Vivian. "Five more minutes, Vivvy," he said, smiling, closing his eyes.

Victoria looked into the room and laughed. Sydney opened his eyes again and looked at her. "Get out of bed, Daddy!" Victoria said, mimicking Vivian's voice.

"Alright, alright, ladies. Daddy's getting up. Just let me get dressed, and I'll be out."

"You better hurry, Daddy. Me and Mommy made breakfast. We might just eat it all. I'm starving!"

Sydney smiled, "Did you now? I have to try Vivian's home cooking! I can't wait." Vivian smiled brightly and hopped off the bed. Sydney threw his legs over the side of the bed and sat a moment. As he sat there clearing the sleep from his mind, the alarm clock began to go off. He quickly reached and silenced it. It was 6:30 AM, and Sydney had to get to work by eight.

Sydney left the house an hour later. The crisp late October air hung lightly as dew cloaked every inch of his Miata. Even though a coolness filled the air, he threw the convertible top back and hopped into the driver's seat. He could feel the cold of the tan leather seats beneath him, even through his jeans. He sat a moment, letting the engine warm up, and watched Victoria load Vivian into her car seat in the back of her vehicle. She was on her way to her job at Hubbard Middle School.

She had accomplished her dream of becoming an English teacher. He knew that she loved her job. Teaching had been something that had interested her even before the two of them had met. Sydney knew from the early days of their relationship that she'd eventually accomplish her goal. Two years of work at Lando Community College and then two years at King City University certainly paid off. She was so happy the day that she walked across the stage and accepted her degree.

As for Sydney, he was still working at Tesson's Carpentry, her brother's business. Even though Sydney never envisioned his life's work as a carpenter, he immensely enjoyed what he did. He loved working for Waylon and Wayne and felt fulfilled with his work. It also didn't hurt that the job paid very well. Sydney started learning the basics and then moved on to more advanced projects, such as building porches and decks. After some time, he helped build houses. As his skills grew, so did the company. Lately, Sydney had become a supervisor and was in charge of building a substantial home on the outskirts of Lando. A few weeks prior, Waylon had told him that Sydney was close to becoming a master carpenter. Sydney was proud to hear that he would be in the same class as Waylon shortly.

Some Things Last...

Sydney took a deep breath of the fresh morning air and looked at Vivian, waving to him. "Bye-bye, Daddy!" she yelled out from the back seat. Victoria was going to be dropping off Vivian at preschool on her way to work. She was already super bright. She could read basic words and had a comprehension of a child at least a year or older than herself. Sydney knew that she got that from her mother. As he watched Vivian continue to wave, the car began to back up, and he looked at Victoria. She smiled and waved goodbye to him. Sydney sat a moment longer as he watched the yellow Cavalier slowly disappear from sight. A cloud rolled across the sun casting a shadow over the yard. A cold wind blew through the Miata, chilling Sydney. He reached over and turned the heat on. "Time to go," he said as he pulled out onto the street and began the trek to his job site.

It was a typical day for Sydney. The beginning of the workweek brought its fair share of complaints from everyone, including Sydney, about the weekend going by too quickly. As he worked on setting up the "bones" of the house, he listened to the typical "macho bullshit," as he liked to call it, go back and forth between his co-workers. The younger guys would usually discuss the sexual escapades they had over the weekend in great detail. Sydney tended to stay out of those conversations, but sometimes they'd ask him to regale them with stories of what it was like to be a family man. Truthfully, he enjoyed telling them what it was like to come home to a beautiful wife and daughter. As soon as he entered the door, he felt loved. Some of the guys would tell him they were envious of him and that he was so lucky.

Of course, there were others who had no interest in the family side of things and were only curious about his sex life. He always made up some excuse to get away from these conversations when they turned toward the sexual side of his marriage. He had no intention of sharing his sex life with

Victoria. He was more than happy with it. Every time they made love to one another, Sydney thought it was better than the time before. He figured that came with time. After a while of being with someone, you know what to do to please them.

As he hammered some nails into place, he thought of some other hammering he'd much rather be doing. *Oh, Vicky...* he thought to himself as he put the hammer down firmly on his thumb. Pain shot through his hand in a burst of speed as he dropped the hammer and began throwing out some rather colorful language. Luckily, no one was around to see the fool he'd made of himself. He slowly removed the work glove from his hand to survey the damage he'd done. His thumb looked fine, but it hurt fiercely. He decided to take a break while his thumb continued to throb.

As the day rolled onward, lunchtime approached. Sydney returned to his car, put the seat back, and sat for a few minutes. He had some leftover stew from the night before in a bag resting on the passenger seat. He glanced over at the bag but decided to wait a bit before he began to eat. He gazed up into the sky at the gathering clouds overhead and could tell that rain was on the way. *I hope it holds off until I get outta here. It sure has been raining a lot here lately. We've gotta get this place closed up before the winter comes.*

Sydney closed his eyes and took a deep breath. His left thumb continued to throb, but the pain had almost subsided. He was close to dozing off when his cell phone began to ring. His eyes opened, and he checked his pockets but couldn't find it. He then remembered that he'd left it in his glove compartment. He reached over and opened the latch, and grabbed his phone. Without looking to see who it was, he answered and placed it to his ear.

"Ahoy-hoy?"

"It's about time you answered your phone! What do you even have one for?"

Sydney leaned back in his seat and sighed, "Always nice to hear from you, Dad," he answered sarcastically.

"Don't you give me any of that, Syd. I've been calling you off and on the past few hours."

"I'm at work, Dad. I left my phone in the car. Is everything alright?" There was silence for a moment on the other end of the line. "Dad?"

"I'm still here, Syd...Could you come by here this evening? Your mother and I need to talk to you about something."

"OK...why not just tell me now?"

"Because...it would be best to discuss this in person, Syd. Just come over when you get off."

"Alright, Dad, I'll come over around 5:30."

"We'll see you this evening, Syd."

His father hung up without saying goodbye, as he usually did. Sydney fixed his seat and sat upright, thinking about the phone call. *What could they want to talk about? I just don't know...* He looked at his watch, '1:27 PM'. *Three and a half hours...until I'm outta here. What the hell is going on?* Sydney sat pondering his father's cryptic call as he ate his leftovers. The stew churned about in his unsettled stomach, and he felt ill. He wanted to leave then and there and see what his father wanted, but he knew he was obligated to oversee the men's work. Waylon had entrusted him with supervising this site as he was across town sorting out another one. Like it or not, he knew he couldn't leave just yet.

Sydney quickly clocked out and ran to his car. He had spent the past few hours worrying about what his parents wanted to discuss with him. As he thought about what his father had told him, he noticed that they only wanted to speak to him. He quickly drove through town, making great time, and before long, he pulled up to his old home. It had been a few months since his previous visit, but he wasn't looking forward to hopping out of the car and running up to the front door.

He sat for a few minutes, looking at the front of the place. He watched the window of the living room for movement. He saw that the lamp beside the front window was on, but he saw no trace of shadows moving about inside. *I may as well get out and go in. See what this is all about. I'm sure it's nothing THAT serious.* His thought offered him a small amount of reassurance, enough to get out and knock on the front door anyway. He knocked three times and waited. A few moments later, his mother answered the door.

"Hi, sweetheart. Glad you came over. Me and your father have been waiting for you. Come in. He's in the kitchen."

"What's this all about, Mom? I can't stay too long. Vicky will worry. Plus, I don't wanna leave her to look after Vivian by herself."

His mother ushered him along through the living room. The local news was on the TV and the meteorologist forecast more rain in the coming days.

"This won't take too long…it's something we got in the mail today."

Sydney followed behind her, thinking, *Something in the mail? What the hell is it?*

He entered the kitchen to see his father sitting down at the table. "Have a seat, son," his father said solemnly. Sydney didn't object. He sat across from his father. His mother stood in front of the sink, looking out the window at the dim evening sky. Sydney could see her reflection in the window; it looked like she was about to cry.

"Alright, what's going on here, Dad? Enough of this cryptic crap."

His father sighed, reached into his jacket pocket, and placed an envelope on the table. "This letter came in the mail today, Syd. It's a letter about…your cousin."

Some Things Last...

Sydney stared at the letter, but he didn't grab it. A feeling of dread enveloped him. "About...Al?!" Sydney said.

His father shook his head and continued, "Yes...he's been gone for over seven years. They've pronounced him legally dead, Syd."

Sydney sat stunned for a moment, then spoke, "What?! He's not fucking dead!"

"Keep your voice down. Your aunt is in her room watching television," his father whispered.

"Does she know about this?"

"What do you think, Syd? The woman has been mute ever since the day he vanished. She can barely take care of herself...Her knowing about this wouldn't help her condition in any way. Hell, it could make it worse. So, keep your damn voice down."

Sydney grabbed the envelope and removed the piece of paper inside of it. He quickly read over the document, and it declared what everyone had feared all of these years. They'd given up looking for Albert.

"What do you think about this, Dad?"

His father looked away from him. "Honestly? ...I'm relieved. We can finally embrace what we've known for a long time now. Al...isn't coming back. God rest his soul. I knew that the day he disappeared."

"How...how can you say that? Do you feel the same, Mom?" Sydney looked at his mom. She was still turned away from him.

"Oh, Syd, I'm sorry. I know how much you loved Albert. We all did."

"What's with the past tense? Do you really believe Al's not coming home? Don't lump me in with you two. I've never given up hope! Why do you think I decided to live in his old place?! It wasn't because Aunt Milly couldn't live by herself anymore. It was because I knew that *ONE* day...he'd return. One day he'd knock on the front door and say, 'I'm home,'!"

"I told you to keep your voice down, damn it. Do you want your aunt to hear you?"

Sydney leaned back in his chair, defeated. "I need to use the bathroom," he said and quickly left the kitchen.

Sydney walked down the hallway outside of the kitchen to the bathroom. Along the way, he passed his old bedroom. The door was slightly ajar. He peeked in through the crack and saw his aunt turned away, watching the flickering screen of her TV. His aunt had been moved into his old room after she came home from the hospital. He decided to pay her a quick visit.

He knocked on the door and said, "Aunt Milly? It's Syd. I'm coming in." He entered the warm room and sat across from her on the bed. His aunt sat motionless in her chair. Her eyes held the same haunted stare they had the evening he found her on Albert's bedroom floor. "Hi, Aunt Milly. It's been a little while," he said solemnly. "I'm sorry if you heard my old man yelling at me again out there…some things never change, huh?" he said, forcing a smile.

His aunt continued to sit staring at the television screen. She was watching a program about the rural out-port towns of Newfoundland. Sydney continued, "I'm sorry I didn't bring Vicky and Vivvy with me…they miss you. You should see Vivian. She's getting so big. She's already super smart…takes after her mom in that department. Can you believe it'll be seventeen years next week that we've been together? I still remember that Halloween when we came over and picked up Al. He was wearing that bright red jack-" he cut himself off and realized that maybe he shouldn't be bringing up Albert to her.

He looked at his aunt and noticed that her eyes didn't appear as haunted, and he could swear she was slightly smiling. He decided to continue to talk to her about Albert.

"I remember he loved that jacket, and he'd always wear that black ball cap back then too…and boy did he love to read! I never knew anyone who loved to read more than Al…Except maybe Vivvy."

As Sydney was reminiscing, the program ended, and another began about a tropical locale. Sydney looked over at the screen and said, "I wouldn't mind going there." Tears started to form in the corners of his aunt's eyes, and Sydney became alarmed. "What's wrong, Aunt Milly?!" he grabbed her hand and squeezed it. "It's gonna be OK. I'm sorry…I shouldn't have brought Al up like this…" Tears began to stream down her face. The smile that had formed upon her face had faded, and that haunted look returned. Her sadness was profound. He wished there was something he could do.

"What's going on?!" his mother said as she entered the bedroom. "What happened, Syd? Why is she crying like this?"

His father entered behind her. "Come here, Syd!" he said, grabbing Sydney by the shirt collar and dragging him out of the room. He took him to the living room and released him from his grip. "What the hell did you say to her? Did you tell her about the letter?"

Sydney struggled to find the words, "No! I was just visiting with her. I got to talking about Al, but-"

"For God's sake, Sydney! Why did you bring Albert up to her?! You know that's a very hurtful topic for her! She doesn't need to be reminded of what happened! No wonder she was crying!"

"No! You don't understand! She was smiling! She enjoyed me talking about the old days with her!"

"Then why the hell did she start crying?! You told her, didn't you? It's time for you to go. I bet your mother and I will be up calming her all night."

Sydney became angry and yelled. "She was fuckin' smilin'!"

He quickly exited the house and returned to his car. This visit was a disaster, from his parents' quick acceptance of the terrible news to his father thinking the worst of him. It filled him with immense disgust, but at the same time, he was overwhelmed with shame. He knew he played an integral role in how his Aunt Milly ended up in such a state. If only he hadn't been drinking that night…if only he hadn't been out that night, period. None of this would have ever happened.

Those thoughts plagued him repeatedly throughout the subsequent years since Albert's disappearance. The thoughts haunted him as he sat in the driver's seat, but he looked at his watch and saw that he didn't have any more time to spare for these apparitions. He quickly started the Miata and sped off toward his home…Albert's home.

He drove like a bat out of hell, running at least two traffic lights. He pulled into the driveway and killed the engine. He noticed the evening stars were twinkling brilliantly. One, in particular, caught his eye. It was the brightest star in the sky. He averted his gaze and slammed his fist upon the steering wheel. "DAMN IT!" he yelled.

From the kitchen window, he could see two familiar faces looking out at him. His heart began to swell. *Vicky and Vivian*, he thought as he struggled to compose himself. *I can't let them see me like this.* He breathed deeply and got a hold of himself. After a few deep breaths, he hopped out of the car and waved to the both of them. They both smiled widely at him. He quickly put the top up on his Miata and ran inside to join them.

Sydney entered the warm glow of the living room and was immediately greeted by Vivian, who wrapped her tiny arms around his legs.

"Daddy! I was worried about you! You're always home before the stars come out."

He placed his hand upon her head and began to rub her soft hair lightly. "Don't worry, sweetie. Daddy just paid your Pepaw Harry and Nanny Lo a visit. Oh, and your great Aunt Milly too!"

She looked up at him with sadness in her eyes, "What? Why didn't you come get me?"

"I'm sorry, Vivvy. I went right after work. We'll see them again pretty soon."

"Pretty soon? How long is that?"

"Probably next week sometime."

Tears began to flow down Vivian's face, "Next week?! What'll I do til then?"

Victoria came out of the kitchen and intervened. "You can start by getting ready for supper, young lady. Now go wash your hands and dry those eyes!" Vivian released her grip around Sydney's legs and obeyed her mother's words.

Sydney fell upon the couch and looked up at Victoria. She stood there smiling. "What is it, Vicky, darling, light of my life?"

"You need to get ready for supper too, Mr. Lee."

"Oh? I'm the kinda man who likes to know what he's havin' for supper, Vicky."

"It's not a matter that concerns you. At least, not at this point," she said, holding back a laugh.

"Anything you say, Vicky! Anything you say!" They both began to laugh, and Sydney arose from the couch. He embraced her tightly. "I love you, Vicky. You know that?" he said, kissing her softly.

Victoria smiled and replied, "I know. Now go wash up."

Sydney returned to the living room after he finished washing the dishes. Victoria ran a bath for Vivian, and he was left to himself for a brief while. Sitting in his recliner in the darkened living room, he looked over at the fireplace. He had been waiting for a suitable night to use it again. There was a slight chill in the air, so he decided that tonight was the night he'd light it up. He ignited the log within it and stoked the flame until it was nice and steady. He closed the grate and sat on the couch just as Victoria returned.

"Ooo, a romantic fire. Syd, you know our anniversary isn't until next week, right? You couldn't hold off on lighting the fire until then?"

Sydney chuckled, "I'm always lighting the fire, baby. Speaking of babies...where's Vivian?"

"I put her to bed. She was falling asleep in her bath."

"Aw, that's precious. Well, I guess it's just the two of us. Come join me."

Victoria took a seat on the recliner and sat looking at the fire. It crackled and popped as she watched it. She could feel the warmth of it beginning to fill the room. "This was a great addition you built, Syd."

"I think so too. I imagined it would really make for a nice spot to read."

Victoria looked over at him, "I see." They sat silently, watching the fire for a moment, when Victoria said, "Syd? What happened at your parent's earlier?"

He closed his eyes and continued to listen to the embers popping.

"Syd?"

"Yes, dear?"

"Don't 'Yes, dear,' me. What happened? You've been acting 'off' all night."

He sighed, "I didn't want to go into it with Vivian around...but my dad called me this afternoon. He said to come by later. I did. Turns out...they got a letter...it was about Al." He stopped and watched the flames dance upon the ceiling.

"About Albert? What did it say? Did the police find out something?"

Some Things Last...

He took a deep breath, "Yeah, they did. Apparently, since he's been missing this long, he's not worth looking for anymore. So, they've pronounced him legally dead."

"What?...that's not true," she said. Sydney could hear the tears in her voice. She crawled over on top of him on the couch and held him. "Sydney, I'm so sorry. I know...that you built this fireplace with him in mind. I know you've looked after this entire place...for him."

"Yeah, it's my cross to bear."

She grabbed his face and looked at him. "Don't you ever think that way. What happened that night wasn't your fault. Don't blame yourself, Syd." He tried to look away, but she forced him to look into her eyes. "Look at me. You're a good man, Sydney.

He felt sick to his stomach. *If you only knew how wrong you were.*

The two of them lay on the couch together for a while as the fire slowly began to die. "Syd, let's head to bed. It's getting late. We've both got work in the morning."

"Yeah, let me put this fire out, Vicky. I'll be right behind you." Victoria entered their bedroom as Sydney threw water onto the smoldering log. He listened to the loud hiss as the water extinguished the embers, followed by silence.

Outside, a gust of wind blew against the house. He walked over to the diamond-shaped window and looked at the street, illuminated by a row of street lights. He stood watching, hoping that Albert might decide to stroll by out of the night.

"Syd? You coming to bed?"

He turned around to find Victoria in her nightgown. "Yeah. I'm coming," he answered.

"What are you looking at out there?"

"...Nothing," he answered and followed her to their bedroom.

Yawning At Your Heels

    Sydney slid underneath the cool sheets and felt the warmth of Victoria's body next to him. He got behind her back and put his arm and leg over her. He always joked that she was a Vicky brand heater. She always kept him warm on chilly nights.

    "Good night, Syd. I love you."

    He squeezed her tightly and said, "I love you too, Vicky." As he held her close, he began to slip into a deep sleep and found himself drifting through that darkness to a familiar diner from his past.

CHAPTER 11
Daddy-Daughter Day

Sydney took a seat at an empty booth. It's freezing cold, and a puff of steam comes from his mouth as he exhales. He looks around and sees that he's the only customer at this desolate diner. Turning his gaze, he stares out the large window next to him onto the parking lot. His Miata is parked across from him, and Albert sits in the driver's seat. The headlights pop up, and Albert reverses. He stops and looks over at Sydney, giving him a thumbs up. Sydney stands up and tries to motion for him to stop as Albert speeds off down the pitch-black road disappearing into the black abyss surrounding the diner.

He falls back onto the cold, hard bench and slams his fist down on it. "Why? Why did you die?"

"Excuse me, sir. Are you two ready to order?" Sydney looked up and noticed someone had taken the seat across from him. The person across from him sat silently, hidden behind a sizable menu emblazoned with the name **Danny's Diner**. *"I'll come back in a few," the waitress said and walked away.*

Sydney turns to look at her. She had short dark hair. He's unable to catch her face, but he has a strange nostalgic feeling.

"Who's died?" Sydney looks back to the person across from him. The menu sits folded upon the table.

"A-Al?!"

"Who else would I be? Have you been drinking that sake again, Syd?"

"N-no...I gave up that shit after that night."

"Oh, you mean the night I left? I see. Took you long enough. Maybe if you'd done that sooner...among other things...I'd still be here. Not gone into the abyss."

Sydney looked away from him. The waitress stood across the diner, wiping a table down. She was facing away from him, but within the reflection on the window, he thought he could slightly make out a bit of her face. What was strange, though, was the fear he felt growing within him as he continued staring at her.

"I see you're still ignoring what I'm saying to you," Albert spoke.

Sydney turned towards him, full of anger. "You think you're so god damn high and mighty, Al? What the fuck do you know?! It hasn't been easy for me going on like this year after year wondering what the fuck happened that night!"

"What do you think happened? Do you believe I've died as well, Syd?"

Sydney sat in silence, unable to look at Albert. He looked beneath the table into the darkness. He felt himself being drawn to it. Almost...falling into it.

"Excuse me, sir. Are you ready to place your order now?"

Sydney looked up and noticed that Albert was gone. Was he ever there to begin with? "I'm sorry I...I..." Sydney looked up at the waitress and froze in terror.

"Is everything alright, babe? You look like you've seen a ghost."

The waitress wasn't any waitress at all. She was Sharon. She stood before him, wearing nothing but a white apron. Sydney had wondered why the diner was so cold. This place was full of the ghosts of his past, and he wanted out. He tried to get up, but Sharon blocked his exit. She smiled at him with a ghostly grin. She had a suggestive look in her hazel eyes, surrounded by dark blue eyeshadow.

"Oh, Syd, it's been such a long time since I've seen you. I've been waiting for you to come back to me...I've always known that she couldn't satisfy you. You'll never forget me, will you? Just look up...you know that star. I'm always watching you. Now, feel me, Syd! Hold me."

Some Things Last...

Sydney moved further away from her in the booth. He found his back to the window. Sharon began to climb into the booth slowly. Hurt began to fill her eyes. "Where are you going? Are you leaving me again? Don't go...Stay with me." She moved closer and began to climb onto Sydney's lap. He pushed her off him, and she fell backward onto the reflective surface of the diner's linoleum floor.

A moment later, she rose, and blood began to pour from her forehead and down into her eyes. The blood mixed with her tears, and she began to scream, "WHY CAN'T I EVER BE GOOD ENOUGH FOR YOU?!"

Sydney continued to press his back against the glass of the window. He closed his eyes, and he fell backward. He opened his eyes for a moment and saw darkness accompanied by a single shining star.

"I'm always watching you," Sharon whispered, then he hit bottom.

"Syd? Where are you?" Sydney opened his eyes and moaned. "What are you doing down there?" Victoria said, offering him her hand. He took it, and she helped pull him up. "You must have fallen out of bed. That hasn't happened in a while. Is everything alright?"

Sydney sat on the soft carpet beneath him and tried to gather his thoughts. "No...I had this nightmare. The worst one I've ever had..."

Victoria helped Sydney back onto the bed and put her arm around him. "What happened, Syd?"

"Al was in my dream. He was in my car, and I watched as he drove off in it into this darkness. Pitch black...he disappeared into it." He couldn't explain the rest.

"Syd, that was just a dream."

"Yeah...I know," he replied. He knew that but thought of sitting with Albert and what he'd said. Albert's words rang true, and he couldn't shake the terrifying ghostly apparition that Sharon had become. Seeing her like that sent a shiver down his spine. *I'm always watching you*, her words echoed in his mind.

"I need a shower, baby. What time is it?" He looked over at the alarm clock. '7:35,' it read. "Whoa, I didn't know it was *that* late!"

Victoria sat up, walked to the closet, and removed a black blazer from a hanger. "Yep, I was trying to get Vivvy up, but she said she wasn't feeling well. She was being really fussy this morning. I gave her some medicine, and she's lying in bed again. Could you call my mom to come over and get her in a bit?"

"Sure, I'll call Mudder. Why not just let me watch after her today? They can make it one day without me at work. I'll give Waylon a call and tell him Vivvy's sick."

"Alright. If you're sure things will be alright. I have to go, or I'll be late. Make sure Vivian takes some more medicine later. I'll try to call this afternoon."

"OK, don't worry, Vicky. I've got it under control." Sydney stood up and hugged her tightly. "I love you, Vicky. Have a good day," he said, kissing her.

"I love you too, Syd," she replied, giving him a quick smack on his butt. "Try not to sit around watching TV all day," she said, smiling.

"I won't. I'll get some things done around here."

Victoria headed for the front door and left. Sydney peeped out of the blinds as she hopped into her car and quickly took off down the road. Sydney stood beside the window for a moment, naked, and thought of Sharon's ghostly words again. *I'm always watching you.* He quickly headed for the shower and tried putting the nightmare out of his mind.

After a quick shower, it began to fade from his mind mercifully. He opened the small rectangular window above the tub and stepped out of the steam-filled bathroom. He slipped into a black t-shirt, green plaid boxer shorts, and pajama pants. *Guess I better see how Vivian is doing*, he thought as he exited the bedroom.

As he entered the nook outside the bedroom, he began to hear a sound coming from the living room. He stopped and listened closely and immediately recognized the source of the sound. He quickly walked out into the living room, and what he saw confirmed his suspicions.

Vivian was lying on the recliner, stretched out, and watching her favorite DVD of Celeste, The Space Unicorn. "Someone looks like they're not sick at all," Sydney said, folding his arms.

Vivian sat up and smiled, "I'm all better, Daddy!"

Sydney laughed, "Oh, I bet you are. Vivvy, be honest. You weren't sick at all, were you?"

A mischievous grin began to form on Vivian's face. "No…but, Daddy, I had a good reason to fake it!"

"Oh, is that so? Well, go ahead and tell me."

"Daddy, who's Albert?"

Sydney's eyes flew open, and he looked at Vivian. "What did you say, sweetheart?"

"Who's Albert? I heard you and Mommy talking last night…you said you didn't want to tell me about Albert. Who is that?"

Sydney took a seat on the couch and took a deep breath. "Ah, so you heard us talking. You've always been the sneaky one."

Vivian's lip pouted, "I wasn't sneaking around, Daddy! I wanted you to read me a story, but then I heard you and Mommy talking."

"OK, Vivvy, I'm sorry. You're just curious. You want me to tell you about Al, huh?" Vivian smiled and shook her head quickly up and down. Sydney sat a moment. "Al's your uncle."

"He's like Uncle Waylon?"

"Yep, that's right."

"I have two uncles?!"

"Yep."

"Wait...if that's true. Where is he? Where is Uncle Al?"

"He's...gone away."

"Where's he gone to, Daddy?"

Sydney thought a moment. He couldn't tell his four-year-old daughter the truth, so he concocted a story to shield her instead. "He's out traveling the world, sweetheart. He's an adventurer."

Vivian's eyes grew wide, and Sydney swore they sparkled for a moment. "An adventurer? Like Celeste?"

"Yes, honey. He travels around having adventures like Celeste...except his are here on Earth and not out there in space."

Vivian leaped from the recliner to the couch and back again. Sydney's explanation greatly excited her. He began to regale her with tales of Albert's exploits across the globe. Vivian's DVD of Celeste the Space Unicorn continued to play, but Vivian became so enraptured by Sydney's stories about Albert that she paid no attention to it. Sydney never thought he'd see the day. He enjoyed talking about Albert, albeit a fictionalized version of him.

"Why haven't I ever met Uncle Al? When was he here last?"

"He hasn't been back home since before you were born...you know, Vivvy, this used to be his home," he said, opening his arms and looking around the room.

"Really?"

"Oh, yes. And guess what? His room is now your room."

Vivian let out a scream and began to jump back and forth again. "Does that mean I'll grow up to be an adventurer too?!"

Sydney smiled brightly, "Maybe, baby."

Some Things Last...

"Daddy, do you have any letters or postcards from Uncle Al?"

"No, Vivvy. He's not much of a writer. He's not like Celeste." During Celeste the Space Unicorn, each episode has an end segment where Celeste's family reads quick postcards from her detailing her latest adventure.

"What about any photos? You have photos up of everyone but him!"

"That's true…come with me. I'll show you some." Sydney rose from the couch and walked down the hallway to their storage room. The storage room used to be a spare bedroom where Sydney stayed when he spent the night with Albert. It was located up the hall from Albert's room.

"Where are the photos, Daddy?" Vivian asked excitedly.

"I have them put away in here, Vivvy."

Sydney pushed the door open and hit the light switch. Rows of boxes were on the guest bed. This room hadn't been used as a guest bedroom since Sydney's high school days. The box that Sydney was after wasn't located on the bed. It was tucked away underneath it in the darkest corner. He leaned down and looked under the bed and saw the box. The rest of the boxes were cardboard and labeled with their contents, but this one was flat and plastic and lay unmarked. Sydney reached for it and grabbed onto it.

"Hurry! Hurry!"

"Alright, Vivvy. Hold on a second," Sydney said, pulling it out into the light. The box hadn't been moved once since Sydney slid it there a little over seven years prior. That was shortly after he and Victoria had moved in.

"Open the box, Daddy!"

Sydney removed the top of the container, reached inside, and pulled out a navy blue, leather-bound photo album. "Follow me, Vivvy." She eagerly obeyed as they went back out to the couch.

They sat down, and Sydney opened the album revealing photos he'd not looked upon in a long time. "That's your uncle, Vivvy," Sydney said, pointing to a picture of Albert taken when he was in high school.

"Wow…That's him?"

"Yep, there he is," Sydney said, looking over the photos.

"Who's that?" Vivian asked, pointing to another photo.

"Oh, that's our old buddy Roland. He hung out with Daddy and Uncle Al back in middle school."

"Is that Mommy with Uncle Al?" Vivian asked, pointing at a photo of Victoria and Albert taken during her and Sydney's housewarming for their old apartment.

"Yes, that's Mommy. She's known him a long time. We all went to school together."

They continued to flip through the pages of the photo album. Sydney noticed the growing sadness on Albert's face as time went on. When they reached the album's end, Sydney couldn't restrain himself from tearing up.

"Daddy, what's wrong? Why are you crying?"

Sydney took his shirttail and dried his eyes. "I miss your Uncle Al is all. It's been a long time since I've seen him."

"Don't cry, Daddy. He's out there having fun! He'll come home again!" Vivian chirped.

Sydney forced a smile and put his arms around Vivian, hugging her tightly. "That's right, sweetie. He'll be back! Thank you for that." Sydney looked at the clock on the wall. It was half past nine. "Hey, how about we get out of here for a while, Vivvy? Let's have a daddy-daughter day! Where do you wanna go?"

Vivian smiled and replied, "Let's go to the mall!"

Sydney stood up and bellowed, "If that's where Vivvy wants to go, then *THAT'S* where we shall go!"

After putting away the photo album and returning the box from whence it came, Sydney got Vivian dressed in her favorite shirt, a black long-sleeve, with Celeste standing on the rings of a planet similar to Saturn. In the background was a spaceship blasting off. The flames of the spacecraft were holographic. Vivian wore that shirt almost everywhere despite her closet being full of other clothes. Sydney didn't feel like fighting with her on it. He slipped the shirt over her head and let Vivian slip her arms through the sleeves. After he dressed her, he quickly got dressed. He tossed on a dark gray dress shirt and black pants.

Since Victoria was gone in her car, that left Sydney with his Miata. Sydney hoped they wouldn't run into any police along the way, or he'd have one hell of a ticket to pay off for driving with Vivian in his car. "Alright, hop in, Vivvy!" Sydney said, opening the passenger door for her.

"We're going in your Yata, Daddy?" she said, her eyes wide.

"Yep, that's right. You're gonna be a big girl today and ride in the passenger seat. So, while you're in the passenger seat, you sit still and let Daddy drive, OK?"

"OK, Daddy!" Vivian said, hopping in the car and buckling her seat belt.

"Good job, Vivvy. Keep it up, and you'll get a treat at the mall. Why did you pick the mall, anyway?"

"Because I wanna see the fountain!"

"Fair enough. Alright, to the mall we go!"

Sydney, who usually sped through the streets of Lando, took his time. He leisurely drove along, trying not to draw any unwanted attention to himself, and left the top up for the first time ever. They pulled into the parking lot of the Lethe Plaza Mall ten minutes later, and Sydney parked across from the main entrance. True to her word, Vivian sat still and quietly. It wasn't until he let her out of the car that she became rambunctious.

"Come on, Daddy! Let's hurry inside! I wanna see the fountain!"

"Alright, young lady, we'll get there. Now, grab my hand, and let's go." Vivian put her small hand in his, and he held it tightly.

The automatic doors slid open, and they entered the brightly lit interior of the mall. The air was warm inside the mall, and Sydney felt even warmer as the sun beat down on him through the windows high above. Vivian clenched Sydney's hand tightly as they continued to walk onward. They reached the railing that looked out upon Lethe Plaza's vast glass center atrium as they continued forward. Sydney stopped and looked out on the food court below.

"Man, it's pretty slow in here today," Sydney said as he noticed only a dozen or so people at the various eateries and tables scattered around the large fountain in the center of the food court.

"Lift me up, Daddy!" Vivian cried.

Sydney laughed, "Alright, sweetheart. Up you go!" he said as he picked her up and placed her upon his shoulders.

"Wow, I can see everything from here! Look at the fountain, Daddy!" she said, pointing.

Dozens of streams of water were being shot at least twenty feet into the air into the center of the fountain. Surrounding the streams were circular lights that illuminated the fountain. Within the very center, where the streams culminated, a color-changing light shifted through all the colors of the rainbow. Standing there watching the fountain, Sydney could understand why Vivian wanted to come just to see this. It was pretty spectacular.

"Let's go down. I wanna see it up close!" Vivian said.

"OK, but first, let's get you a cookie and an Icee for your treat. Then we'll sit at one of those tables and watch the fountain."

"An Icee? OK, Daddy!" she said, smiling.

After the two visited the cookie stand upstairs, they ventured to the elevators, which overlooked the fountain. "I

Some Things Last...

wanna push the buttons!" Vivian happily cried as she sipped on her banana-flavored Icee. She reached up and slowly pressed the down button, and a moment later, the reflective metallic doors slowly opened. A couple departing the elevator looked down and smiled at Vivian, who smiled back in return. She stepped into the elevator, followed by Sydney, and the metal doors slowly shut.

She looked up at the buttons and furrowed her brow. "Do you know which one to press, sweetheart?" Sydney asked.

She continued to look and then smiled, "This one!" she said, pressing the '1' button.

"Great job, Vivvy. You're very smart," Sydney said, placing his hand on her shoulder. She looked up at him and beamed as the elevator slowly began to move downward.

"Daddy, look, we can see the fountain getting closer already!" Vivian said, looking out of the large glass window of the elevator.

The elevator slowed to a stop, and the doors opened again, and Vivian ran out onto the reflective gray tiled floor. "Hey, wait, Vivvy!" Sydney yelled as he ran after her. She was pretty quick, but Sydney caught up to her as she reached the fountain's base. The streams of water shot high above them. It was even better up close. Vivian stepped close to the edge and held her hand out, trying to grab one of the streams. "Vivian, don't get too close now. Let's go grab a seat and enjoy our cookies."

The two sat at a table under a large umbrella directly next to the fountain. Sitting there eating his chocolate chip cookie and sipping on his cherry Icee, he listened to the fountain. He had forgotten how peaceful it was. Usually, when they visited the mall, it was packed full of people who drowned out the serene sounds of the fountain's water. Today was a slow day, though, and he was pleased by this fact. He leaned back, closed his eyes, and almost drifted off to sleep.

"Daddy? I finished my Icee," Vivian said. Sydney's eyes slowly opened, and he stretched a moment. "Are you sleepy?"

"A little bit. Daddy didn't sleep too well last night."

"Were you dreaming of Uncle Al?"

Sydney looked over at the fountain's center and watched as the color changed from a warm pink to a cool blue. "Yeah, I see him sometimes in my dreams."

Vivian reached over and grabbed Sydney's hand. "It's OK, Daddy. He'll visit you again."

A smile broke across Sydney's glum face. "Let's go for a walk, Vivvy. This fountain is putting me to sleep." Vivian hopped up, and he took her hand.

They wandered for a bit through the mall, not looking for anything in particular. Sydney was just happy to have his daddy-daughter day. Days like this didn't come around very often for him as he was usually busy with work during the week, and they spent time together as a family on the weekends.

Sydney began to notice a curious sound coming from around the corner ahead. As they drew closer, the sound became louder and more identifiable. It was the squawking of birds. They turned the corner, and he began to look around, wondering where the sound was coming from. He noticed a store tucked away in the far corner of the mall. They slowly approached the storefront. The place's name was lit up in bright yellow neon lights above the entrance.

Olivia's Pet Shop Birdy Birds

"It's a pet shop, Daddy!! Can we go in, please? I wanna see the animals!" Vivian said, squeezing his hand tightly and looking up at him wide-eyed.

"Alright, Vivvy! We'll check them out! We're not buying any, though!"

Some Things Last...

"Yay!! Let's go in!!" Vivian said, dragging Sydney into the store. He imagined they must be quite a sight. A grown man being dragged along by a child.

They entered the noisy pet shop, and the squawking of the birds was magnified within the enclosed space. "Look at all the birds, Daddy!" True to its name, the shop had a fair portion of exotic birds. They were situated within the back portion of the shop.

Sydney noticed the shop was full of other animals too. Along the right wall were tons of tropical fish. They swam through the water, their bright colors shimmering in the lights over their tanks. On the opposite side of the shop, a few puppies and kittens were up for adoption.

"Welcome. Can I help you?" Sydney turned and noticed a young short Asian woman behind the counter. She wore a gray and blue t-shirt emblazoned with the shop's logo.

"Me and my daughter are just looking today."

She smiled brightly, "I understand. Would you like me to show your daughter our birds? She seems pretty keen on them."

Sydney looked over and noticed Vivian had walked over to the bird cages. Her eyes were alight with curiosity. "Sure, that would be great."

The woman walked over to the bird cages and reached up to a basket on a shelf above them. She reached in and pulled out a pop-sickle stick adorned with many bits of birdseed. She stuck it through the side of one of the cages, and the tiny birds within began to come over and peck at it.

Vivian began to giggle. "Can I feed them?" she asked, looking up at Sydney.

"Go ahead. Just watch your fingers." Vivian eagerly took a stick from the woman. She gingerly put the stick into the cage. They cautiously approached and began to peck away at the seeds. Vivian watched, entranced by the birds until they finished.

"Do you want to feed my birds, sir?"

"Do you have any talking birds?" Sydney asked.

"No, sir, we don't have talking birds here currently. Personally, I don't even like talking birds."

"I see," Sydney said, a bit disappointed.

"Here, why don't you feed Barney? He's our oldest cockatiel. He's like the mascot for the store. He always enjoys being fed."

Sydney looked at the bird. His cheeks were bright orange, and the feathers on his head were sticking straight up. "I guess so," he said as he grabbed a stick from the woman. He slowly put the stick in the cage, and Barney eagerly approached. He began pecking away at the seeds at the top first and quickly began moving downward.

"He loves it, Daddy!" Vivian gleefully cried.

Sydney turned to look at Vivian, whose eyes were wide, and then he felt a sharp pain from one of his fingers. Barney pinched his beak down hard on the tip of Sydney's thumb. He yanked it out of the cage quickly. "Ow! I think you guys should have named him Bitey instead of Barney!" He noticed a small trickle of blood begin to come from the tip of his thumb.

"Oh, I'm so sorry, sir! Barney has never bitten anyone!"

"First time for everything," Sydney said as he noticed the blood beginning to run down his thumb.

"Come this way, sir. The manager has a first aid kit in her office." Sydney and Vivian were led to the back office. "One moment, please, while I inform Miss Olivia!" Sydney and Vivian waited outside the office. "Excuse me, Ma'am, one of the customers has been bitten by Barney."

"What?! Barney bit someone? Have them come in. I have the first aid kit right here!" The woman returned and motioned for Sydney to enter the office.

Some Things Last...

When he entered, he saw the manager standing by her desk next to some bandages and rubbing alcohol. A moment later, he exclaimed, "O-Olivia!?"

"Syd!?" she said, her eyes wide with surprise.

A few minutes later, Sydney sat across from Olivia at her desk with his thumb bandaged. "Good as new. I'm sorry about Barney. I'm just as shocked as Li."

"Li? Oh, her. Yeah, she seemed pretty surprised. She's pretty enthusiastic about the birds out there."

"She is. I was fortunate to find her. But anyway...I can't believe it's you, Syd. How long has it been?"

"Seven years...You did good, Olivia. I mean...you own your own business. Amazing....The name could use some work but other than that..."

Olivia rolled her eyes, "Thanks, Syd. We haven't been open for very long. Since the summer, actually."

"I see. I don't usually get the opportunity to visit the mall much these days."

Olivia began to laugh, "I'd imagine not. I'm sure your little girl keeps you busy...still, I can't believe you have a daughter now!"

"What's so hard to believe about that?"

"Well...you were a wild one. We used to party pretty hard down there at the Sexothèque."

"Damn, that's a name I haven't heard in years," Sydney said solemnly.

"Yeah, I'd imagine not. Syd, can I ask you something?"

Sydney looked into Olivia's eyes. "Yeah, go ahead."

"Whatever happened with...Albert?"

Sydney turned away from her and sighed, "Al, huh? You still think about him after all this time? I'd have thought you'd moved on by now. That ring on your finger tells me you have."

Olivia ran one of her fingers over her gold wedding band. It gleamed in the fluorescent light overhead.

"Yeah...in some ways, I suppose I have...but there will always be that place that Albert left behind. He reminded me of myself, you know? I thought he was broken like I was at that time. At least I thought so...I thought he lost someone very close to him like I did."

Sydney stood up, walked over to her, and placed his hand on her shoulder. "I remember you briefly mentioned that once...your fiancé and his car wreck coming home on the highway from King City... That was shortly after I met you, if I recall...right after New Years..."

"I'm surprised you remember...you were pretty out of it in those days."

Sydney chuckled, "Yeah, I'm surprised I do too...but I remember plenty from those days."

"You have a ring on your finger too...and your little girl out there looking at the birds...but...I'm sure you still think about her too."

Sydney walked over to the wall across from Olivia's desk and leaned against it. "Like I said...I remember plenty from those days. Some things I wish I could forget..."

"Do you mean that? She cared so much about you. Do you really wish you could forget about Sharon?" Sydney felt an unbearable sadness begin to rise within himself. "Syd...can I show you something?"

Sydney turned and noticed Olivia holding out a photograph. He reached over and grabbed it. The picture was of Sydney and Sharon sitting beside one another at a booth in a diner. Sat across from them were Albert and Olivia. Everyone was hamming it up except for Albert, looking out the window with his brow furrowed, his face full of sadness. Sydney had his arm wrapped around Sharon, and he was kissing her cheek.

"When the hell was this taken?" he asked, his hands shaking as he looked into Sharon's eyes.

"I see you don't remember everything. This was taken the week before Albert...left. We used to go to that diner every week, remember? I've not been back there since that photo was taken. I drive by it on the way home, though. Sometimes I think of stopping in, but I just can't do it. All I can do is glance over and see that booth of ours."

"So...Danny's is still there, huh? I tend to stay away from that part of town."

"Bad memories, Syd?" He handed the photo back to her, ignoring her question.

"Every time I look at it, it makes me feel blue. I long for those days, Syd. God help me, but I do. Things just felt brighter back then, I guess...more hopeful. Don't get me wrong...I love my husband more than anything. Maybe it's not so much me loving Albert, but that particular time. I don't know...I guess I never will...but that's OK."

"Why are you telling me all of this? Why not talk to your husband?"

"Syd, after everything that happened with Sharon, I cut ties with the club. I never went back. I suppose Joe understood. He mailed me my final paycheck with a note that said, *Good luck, Olivia. Follow your dreams.* So, I went back to school and did just that. When I transferred to King City University, I met my husband shortly after. I never told him about my time as an exotic dancer. No one knows about that...not even my family."

"I suppose it's easier if they don't know."

"Yeah, it is. I knew you'd understand. I'm sure you've been through the same things I have." Sydney stood in silence, not answering her.

Olivia began to rub her palms together anxiously. "Syd, I noticed you never mentioned what happened with Albert. Do you think he killed himself?"

"Christ, no! Why the hell would he!?" Sydney said, losing his composure.

"He had a revolver with him that night. He had this crazed look in his eye. He said he was gonna be with Elly, one way or another. She must have been very important to him."

"Yeah...she was. Maybe he's with her right now, huh? Having all kinds of fun. Either way, don't you go thinking he's gone."

"Oh, Syd..." Olivia hugged him tightly, "There was one other thing he said that night. I forgot to tell you. He said for me to tell you that he was sorry and that he always thought of you as a brother."

Sydney took a seat once again. "Is that right?" Sydney said, fighting back the tears.

He sat a minute in silence, composing himself, then said, "You were right, Olivia. About...Sharon. Sometimes she pops into my mind. Although I differ from you. I don't long for those days back then. I'm happier now than I ever was then. I should never have put Sharon through that hell. Now...because of me...she might very well be there for real."

"Syd, I blamed myself for her taking her life too. I was out of town the week she did it. That will stay with me forever. I thought that if I had only stayed here in Lando and not taken off to visit my folks in King City, she wouldn't have gone up to that roof...Honestly, I think she would have done it either way. It wasn't just you, Syd, that haunted her. She went through a lot growing up with her family. Things that a kid shouldn't have gone through."

"Yeah, she told me about plenty of things...but still."

"Have you visited her?"

"Visited?"

"Her grave. Have you paid your respects? She's buried up in Pine Grove underneath a tree towards the middle of the cemetery. Next to her is a large Japanese maple. I went there a lot after everything happened. Even now, I visit each summer. You should go...maybe it will help with your feelings."

"Maybe...maybe. Either way, I should be getting back to Vivian. It's about time we head out."

"OK, I'll see you two out. Just a minute. It's a little chilly out there on the sales floor." Olivia walked over to a door in the corner of the room and pulled out a black cardigan with gray stripes that she slipped on. The cardigan was baggy and looked well-worn.

"I'm not sure when we'll be back...but it was good seeing you again."

"You too, Syd." The two embraced for a moment. "Remember what I said, Syd. Go and visit her." Sydney exited the back office, followed closely by Olivia.

"Daddy! Miss Li let me feed the fish and more birdy birds!"

"OK, Vivvy, sounds like you had quite a time out here."

"Is your thumb all better now?"

"Yes, sweetheart," Sydney said as he patted her head.

"You're a real cutie, Vivvy. I'm sure you keep your dad busy," Olivia laughed. Vivian smiled brightly at this.

"Alright, Vivvy. It's about time we head back."

"Ohhh, alright, Daddy. We'll come back though soon, right?"

"Maybe."

"Then I can get a little birdy bird?"

"We'll see..."

"You can come back anytime and feed the birds, Vivvy!" Olivia said.

Sydney picked Vivian up and put her on his shoulders. She waved goodbye to Olivia and Li as Sydney turned and walked out of the pet shop. The squawks of the birds increasingly grew quieter and quieter as they walked along through the mall's neon-lit walkway. Olivia's words echoed through Sydney's mind as they passed through the food court and waited for the elevator to arrive.

Go and visit her? Christ...maybe today's the day I will. I've been putting this off for so long now...sometimes no matter how much you wanna get away from something, there's no escaping it. No matter how much you run and put it out of your mind, it still manages to find you and drag you right back to the place you wanted to escape. Sharon...I'm coming.

Sydney exited the warm interior of the mall and entered into the cool autumn air that lurked outside. "Hey, Vivvy, since we still have a few hours before Mommy gets home, why don't we go by the park for a bit?"

"The park? Yay! Let's go!"

"Alright, young lady, remember what I said earlier. You sit still and behave in the car."

"OK, Daddy."

After buckling Vivian's seatbelt, Sydney hopped into the driver's seat and headed for Pine Grove Park. Located directly next to the park was Pine Grove Cemetery. The park was erected at the same time as the cemetery back during the late 40s. The original idea was that while funerals were taking place, children would have a place to play. Children generally would be antsy and unable to comprehend the complexities of life and death, so off to the playground, they would go. Local stories say that the spirits of children buried in the cemetery come over and play in the park late at night.

Sydney didn't know what to believe about that, but the park was one he had never wanted to visit. Lando had a hand full of parks scattered about the town, and whenever he took Vivian to play, they usually visited the park a few minutes from their home. Pine Grove was on the other side of town. The side of town Sydney didn't frequent. Driving along to the park, Sydney passed by his old apartment building.

"Mommy and Daddy used to live there before you were born, Vivvy," Sydney said, pointing at the apartment complex as they drove by it.

Vivian looked at it with wide eyes, "You lived in that big building?" she asked.

"Yes, sweetheart. On the second floor." A few blocks over, Sydney turned his head to the left to see another familiar apartment complex. Carved into the concrete frame surrounding the main entrance was the name of the building.

Shallow Stream Apartments

He looked over and wondered exactly where she had fallen but turned away, unable to look at the building any longer.

A few minutes later, Sydney pulled into the small parking lot beside the park, and Vivian tried to contain her excitement as best she could. He was pleased to see the parking lot empty. Considering school hadn't let out yet, he figured most of the children must still be in class. He exhaled a sigh of relief. He desired silence for what he needed to do.

"Come along, Vivvy," he said, taking her hand into his and leading her up the pathway to the entrance. Next to the main entrance was a large wooden sign.

PINE GROVE PARK

Upon entering, Sydney surveyed what lay inside the park and saw that a concrete walking track surrounded the outskirts of it. In the distance lay a pond with a wooden bridge built across the center. On the banks of the pond were several ducks.

"Let's go see the ducks, Daddy!"

"No, Vivvy. You've had your fill of birds for the day." Vivian poked her lower lip out. "Now, don't pout. Maybe we'll see them before we go."

Sydney's gaze shifted to the left, and he noticed the cemetery's side entrance across from the pond. In the distance, on a hill, he saw a brilliant red tree that he thought might be the tree Olivia had mentioned. *Is she there under that tree?* Sydney wondered.

"Let's go to the playground, Vivvy."

Vivian ran ahead of him and reached the swings. "Push me, Daddy!" she said, smiling. Sydney got behind and began pushing her, but he continued staring off at that brilliant red tree in the distance.

He continued pushing her a few minutes longer until he couldn't stand it any longer. "Vivvy, go play on the slide for a bit. Daddy has to run over to see a friend next door."

She turned around and looked at him, "Next door?" She looked over at the cemetery. "OK, Daddy…I'll be on the slide."

"That's my girl. I won't be gone long." He leaned down, kissed her head, and quickly walked towards the cemetery's side entrance.

Along the side of the cemetery leading to the entrance were thick hedges covering the old iron fence surrounding the cemetery. Sydney reached the entrance, surrounded by a rusty metal archway with the name of the cemetery spelled out.

PINE GROVE CEMETERY

He climbed a short series of stairs leading to a paved pathway toward the middle of the cemetery. Once he reached the main path, he turned around and saw Vivian at the top of the slide. She turned and noticed him, and he waved to her. She threw her arm in the air and quickly returned his wave, then slid down the winding plastic slide. Sydney smiled to himself and turned around. He saw the bright red tree in the distance. It beckoned to him.

He exited the pathway and cut through the various plots of many individuals laid to rest there. Scanning some of the headstones along the way, he noticed that some people had long since been gone. Some had only been gone a brief period, and the grass had yet to grow over the recently placed dirt.

After passing a dozen or so headstones, he reached the tree. It was larger up close. Its brilliant red leaves blew softly in the autumnal breeze upon the hill. One came gently falling and landed upon the tip of Sydney's shoe. He bent down to pick it up and noticed something metal beneath the various leaves that had fallen. He slowly brushed away the fallen leaves…and then he saw it. It was her's, Sharon's headstone. He hadn't realized it, but he was standing directly above her. He quickly moved off of her grave and backed into the tree trunk, shaking a few more leaves off the limbs in the process. He bent down and ran his hand over the damp leaves, removing them entirely from her headstone. He stood a moment, unbelieving of what he saw.

SHARON ISABELLA MOON
JULY 27, 1976 - JULY 15, 1998
FOREVER IN OUR HEARTS

"Sharon…so, this is where you've been all this time," he said, breaking the stillness of the air. He sat down next to her headstone, not moving his eyes from it. "No, that's not right. You're not *really* here…I hope you are up there sleeping with the stars. Every time I look up, I can't help but see you. Can you see me?" He reached out and felt the cold metal of the plaque. He ran the tips of his fingers over each letter. As he did so, he felt tears stream down his cheeks.

He began to sob lightly when he felt a hand fall upon his shoulder. He fell forward and looked behind him. It was Vivian. "Why are you crying, Daddy?" She was standing under the tree holding a bright yellow wildflower. As she was standing there, a shaft of sunlight fell upon her through the tree limbs above.

"Where did you get that, Vivvy?" he asked, drying his eyes and regaining his composure.

"I found it growing beside a statue of Jesus. I wanted to give it to your friend." She knelt and placed the yellow wildflower upon Sharon's headstone.

Sydney smiled at this. "She would have loved that. Yellow was her favorite color."

Vivian sat down next to Sydney and began to read the headstone. "Who was she, Daddy?"

Sydney turned away and looked into the branches of the tree. "She was a friend of me and your Uncle Al's."

"What happened to her?"

"You don't need to worry about that, Vivvy. Just know that she's OK."

"Alright, Daddy. I'm glad she'd like the flower I found."

"She certainly would. In fact, I bet she's smiling right now."

"How do you know?" Vivian smiled.

"Just a feeling."

"How about we head on home, Vivvy? Your mom will be home in another while. We don't need her to know about our adventures today. Let's keep all of this a secret between the two of us, OK?"

Vivian furrowed her brow and looked at Sydney. "Why a secret, Daddy?"

"Your mom will get angry with me for taking you out in my car. You're far too young to be sitting in the front seat."

"But you don't have a backseat! It doesn't count!"

Sydney laughed, "I wish it worked that way, honey, but it doesn't. So, let's keep all of this fun to ourselves."

"...Alright, I won't tell her," Vivian replied softly.

"Let's get back home, sweetie!" Sydney said, lifting Vivian onto his shoulders.

He didn't look back at Sharon's grave. He kept forward. He had finally paid his respects and felt a slight relief by doing so. *Now, maybe I won't have more of those terrible nightmares,* he thought as he buckled Vivian up again. Before he backed away from the park, his eyes shifted back to the distant looming red tree. *Goodbye, Sharon,* he thought as he headed off down the quiet road.

CHAPTER 12
Compression

As the week moved forward, Sydney went about his life as usual. Over the years he'd grown quite well at preoccupying his mind so as not to think about the past. He would throw himself head on into his work during the day and at night focus on his family. It was quite easy for him to forget about the overwhelmingly emotional day he'd shared with Vivian. He acted as if nothing were out of the ordinary. Beneath the surface though he was still very much haunted by his past and each day it grew more apparent that something was wrong.

Sydney awoke in a cold sweat. He bolted upright in bed and noticed the early rays of sunlight peeking along the sides of the drapes.

"Syd? Are you alright?"

He turned and saw Victoria, who was on her side turned toward him in the bed. Her eyes were open halfway, still full of sleep. She was so beautiful. "Yeah…just a bad dream."

Victoria reached over and placed her warm hand upon Sydney's back. She began to rub his still moist skin softly. "Another nightmare? Syd, what's on your mind? Talk to me…is it Albert?"

Sydney kicked the sheets off of his legs and placed his feet upon the cool floor. "A lot's been on my mind lately. Ever since that letter came in the mail." Victoria moved over to Sydney and got behind him. She held him tightly. He could feel the warmth of her body enveloping him. He felt her soft breasts pressing beneath his shoulder blades. He wished he could stay there forever in that moment. All of his worries felt so far away.

"Syd, don't let that letter get to you. He's alright."

Sydney took a deep breath and exhaled, "I'm sorry that I've been having these dreams these past few nights...each night I swear they get more vivid..."

"What do you dream about?"

"I can't really remember...I'd rather not think about it. Anyway, we gotta get up. TGIF..."

"Maybe we can go away for the weekend? Just the two of us? We can get your parents to watch Vivvy for the weekend. We could go to the Lando Inn just like our honey moon. We can go to Miracle Pier too...ride the Ferris wheel...share another kiss there..." she said as she began kissing his back.

"You know what? That sounds like a great idea."

"You know what else sounds like a great idea?" Victoria moved her mouth to Sydney's left ear and seductively whispered, "You...fucking me."

Sydney turned around and saw Victoria stretched out upon the bed. Her naked body was illuminated in the lemon colored honey glow of the dawn. She looked at him, biting her lower lip. He loved it when she did this. He pounced on top of her, kissing every inch of her supple body. He admired every detail of her body and strove to give her everything he had. Everything outside of the two of them became nonexistent. His worries about Albert and Sharon disappeared.

When their passion reached its climax, the two debated staying in bed all day but the responsibilities of adulthood beckoned; breakfast had to be made, Vivian had to be dressed and dropped off at preschool and they had work. They begrudgingly rose from their bed and began to prepare for the day ahead. As he was getting dressed, Victoria came into their bedroom and kissed him deeply.

"Bye, sexy, " she said, with a smile.

"See you tonight, Vicky…"

He hopped into his Miata and threw the top back. He slid the key into the ignition and started her up. While waiting for the motor to warm, he leaned back and stared into the light blue sky above. *Life is good. Damn, I wish every day could start like this one. Just gotta make it through to the evening and then we can hit up the hotel. Mmm, I can't wait.* As he sat there smiling, images of Victoria's body flashed in his mind. The curve of her spine, her nipples, her lips and her hair. As he thought about making love to her, images from his nightmare began seeping back into his mind.

He found himself standing above Sharon's open grave looking down into it. The grave stretched into an infinite darkness below. As he stood there looking into it someone pushed him and he fell into that darkness and immediately woke up. Each night since his visit to Sharon's grave, he'd have some variation of being within the cemetery. He'd fall into her grave but he'd never see her. *God damn it. Why am I thinking about this shit right now? Vicky! I need to be thinking about her! I made my peace with Sharon damn it! Stop haunting me!* He slammed his fist down on the steering wheel. He closed his eyes a moment and pulled out into the street. *It can't be helped. I gotta get my mind off of this crap before tonight. It's a total mood killer…*

The day went by relatively quickly. He did what he always did, threw himself into his work without thinking much about anything else. Pretty soon it was lunch time and soon after it was time to go home.

As he pulled up to his house a familiar car was parked in front of it. *What the…what are mom and dad doing over here?* he thought as he pulled into the driveway. *Hmm…Oh, yeah. Vicky must have called them to pick up Vivian. Ooo, I can't wait to get to the hotel room…* Sydney exited his car, pulling the top up and gleefully headed inside with a smile.

Some Things Last...

Before he opened the door he looked through the diamond window to see his parents sat upon the couch. Victoria was sat on the recliner beside them. As he turned the handle of the door all of them looked over and smiled at him, besides his father. Sydney wasn't surprised by this. He entered the warm interior of his house and greeted everyone.

"Heyyy, I wasn't expecting to see you guys today. What brings you over? Did you come to pick up Vivvy?"

His father frowned and said, "Why would we pick up Vivian?"

Sydney crossed his arms and replied, "Because Vicky and I were planning to go out tonight..."

"Oh, honey, we could take Vivvy tonight for them. Isn't it you two's anniversary in a few days?" Lolita said with a smile.

"Ohhh, that's true isn't it. I guess we could. It has been a little while since we've had her over for a sleep over," Harry said, finally smiling.

A moment later Vivian came rushing down the hallway wearing a bumble bee costume. "Look what Nanny Lo and Pepaw Harry brought for me, Daddy! It's my Halloween costume!" Vivian happily said as she circled Sydney and wrapped her arms around his legs. "You know what you are, Daddy?"

"A flower?"

"Nooo, silly. You're my knees, Daddy! You're my knees!"

Everyone began to laugh and Sydney placed his hand upon her head. "The bees knees, eh? OK, you better go change out of your costume. It's still a few days until Halloween. You're going to spend the night with your grandparents."

"Really? Let me get packed!" Vivian smiled and quickly buzzed off down the hallway to her room.

Their smiles quickly faded after Vivian left. "What's with the glum looks?" Sydney said falling onto the couch beside his mother.

"Well, son, we didn't come over to get Vivian as you well know."

"Yeah, so why are you guys here exactly?" Sydney leaned back and closed his eyes.

His father paused and continued, "Well, son, your mom and I have been talking and we want to get your cousin something to remember him by…a headstone over in Pine Grove."

His eyes flew open and he was completely taken aback by this. His mother shook him, "Are you alright, Syd?"

"Am I alright?" he said, sitting up straight on the couch, "No, I'm not alright! Not in the slightest! You two seriously have given up on Al!? What's the matter with you guys?"

"Now Syd…" his mother said, placing her hand upon his arm.

"Don't touch me!" he said, shaking her hand from his arm and standing up.

"Syd, don't make a scene, son. Vivvy doesn't need to overhear it."

Sydney exhaled and shook his head. "No, she doesn't," he managed to say.

"We didn't just come over to tell you this. We were hoping that you could give us a photo to use for the plaque," his father continued.

"Yes, dear, ever since everything happened with your aunt, you and Victoria moved in here and you packed away all of the photos of him. We just want to look through them and find a good one for his memorial."

"You wanna look through Al's photos to slap on a *memorial*, huh?"

They shook their heads in agreement. "Where are they, Syd? Victoria here doesn't know," his father asked.

Some Things Last...

"Even if she knew she wouldn't agree to this. Right, Vicky?" Sydney looked over to Victoria who up to now had been silent.

"Well, I don't know..."

Sydney's eyes grew wide. "You don't know? What's there to know? This isn't right. Al isn't dead. You've said this countless times to me."

"Yes, and I agree with that. It's just that...it's been almost seven and a half years Syd. Would it hurt to have a plaque made?"

Sydney clenched his hands into fists tightly. "YES, IT WOULD! I DON'T AGREE WITH THIS AND YOU won't BE GETTING ANY SUPPORT FROM ME!" He turned around and grabbed the door handle.

"Where are you going, Syd?!" Victoria called after him as he walked outside.

"FOR A DRIVE!" he yelled.

"Sydney! You get back in here!" His father ran out after him. Sydney entered his Miata and slammed the door and locked it. "Open this door! Get back inside and apologize." He started the engine. "Listen, Syd. Is it so wrong to want to remember Albert with a headstone. Maybe he's still out there? Maybe not? If he is he certainly isn't studying us! I think it's time to start thinking about the possibility that he might not be coming back!" He put the car in reverse and backed out into the road. "Don't run away from this, Sydney! It's not gonna go away! Get out and we can talk about it, damn it!" He put the car in gear and peeled out down the street. He didn't look back and wanted to put some distance between him and everything behind him.

He drove aimlessly throughout Lando for hours, lost in his thoughts. He mainly thought of Albert and the time leading up to his disappearance. *Christ, if I hadn't have been caught up in my bullshit I could have helped him. I could have helped him damn it! If I hadn't have been drunk that night..as well as all those other nights I would have noticed something was wrong!*

Without realizing, he looked over and noticed he was in front of the Lando Community Library. He smiled to himself and pulled around to the side parking lot. *Fuck, I haven't been here in a long time. I should really take Vivvy to the children's library. She'd make you proud, Al! She's such a smart kid. She'll be leaps and bounds ahead of me before too long. I know it.* He sat a moment hoping by some twist of fate that Albert would come walking around the corner as he had done on those Friday afternoons before their escapades at the Sexothèque, or more correctly *his* escapades. *Why am I waiting for you like this? You're not here, Al…yet, for some reason I'm sitting here hoping that you are. It's been like this for a long time now.*

He looked at his watch and saw that it was approaching eleven. "Holy shit…I need to get back home. When the fuck did all this time pass. Feels like the world is passin' me by…" He started the engine once more and slowly drove home.

He pulled into the driveway and was relieved to see that his parent's car was gone. *Thank God for that…but I hope Vicky's alright. I forgot my damn phone. I think she'll forgive me after everything that happened earlier…I hope so.* He exited the car and slowly walked towards the front door. There was a stillness in the air. The only sound was the steady chirp of crickets in the distance. As he approached the door he looked through the window and saw no one in the living room. He thought it odd that Victoria wasn't sitting there waiting for him. He entered the house and quietly shut the door behind him.

He felt for the light switch and found it casting light upon the living room. "So, you decided to come home did you?"

Sydney quickly turned around to see Victoria sitting on the recliner, a frown upon her face. It wasn't the look of someone happy to see him. "Hey, Vicky...I'm sorry for taking off like that...it's just everything my parents were saying was bullshit and-"

"Sit down," Victoria said, cutting him off.

He obeyed and slipped onto the couch. "Did you put Vivvy to bed?"

"She's with your parents tonight."

"Yeah? So, do you still want to go to the hotel tonight or wait until tomorrow?"

"Syd...I have a question for you," Victoria said, flatly.

"OK, Vicky...What's up?"

"Who is Sharon?"

Sydney tensed up. He wasn't sure he heard her properly. He hoped he had misheard. "What?" he asked, cautiously.

Victoria raised her right hand and pointed to an off white envelope sitting upon the coffee table in front of the couch. "Look at that letter..." she said.

Sydney slowly reached for it and opened it. Within the envelope was a single lined piece of notebook paper. He unfolded it and the memory of when he'd last held the piece of paper came flying back to him. He couldn't bring himself to read it but the ending line caught his eye.

Yours forever,
Sharon

It was her final mark upon this world.

"That letter was addressed to our old apartment. It's from over seven years ago and was inside an old photo album." Sydney sat in silence, staring at that final line. His mind began to drift to another place, thinking back to that evening when he'd slipped this letter into that photo album. *Christ...I forgot I kept this...how could I forget...*

"Syd! Look at me!" He was brought back to the present and quickly looked up at Victoria. Her eyes were wide with anger and hurt. "What the hell is this? You were fucking *cheating* on me!?" she said standing up from the recliner and grabbing the letter from Sydney's hands.

"Don't!"

Victoria stopped and looked at Sydney with even more hurt in her eyes. "Don't what? Don't rip up your precious letter from your whore?"

"She wasn't a whore!" Sydney said, defensively.

"I can't believe you're actually defending this girl right now."

She was about to rip apart the letter when Sydney yelled, "STOP! It's a suicide letter!"

Victoria stopped and looked at the letter. "What? What do you mean?"

"Vicky…she…Sharon wrote that before she…"

"S-suicide?! Oh, my God, Sydney…What the hell happened?" Sydney hung his head in shame and proceeded to explain everything to her.

After he unburdened himself with every sordid detail they both sat in silence.

"I…can't believe this. How could you lie to me like this? For all this time?" Victoria finally said, breaking the silence.

"Vicky…I…" Sydney stammered.

"Do you realize what your actions have done? Because of your selfish, juvenile escapades you directly contributed to Albert's disappearance and your aunt being in a catatonic state! …And let's not forget how you strung that girl along for those months…*toying* with her! I don't even know what to think of you right now. These past seven years I've worried about you *so much*. Those nightmares…were you ever dreaming of Albert or were they all about Sharon?"

"…Half and half…"

"I see…More lies from you…that's great. How can I ever believe what you say again?" He didn't have the words. "Sydney, I want you to pack a bag. I can't have you here."

"What?! This is *our* house...*Albert's* house! He wouldn't want you to kick me out like this!"

Victoria angrily replied, "Don't you dare bring him into this! Albert doesn't give one fuck about what happens here! You know why? BECAUSE HE'S NOT COMING BACK, SYDNEY! HE'S *GONE!*" Victoria stopped and tears began to stream down her face. "I see you standing there looking out that damn window every night before we go to bed. You think I don't know what you're looking for? You're looking for him to come walking up the street back home! Syd... it's been *seven years.* When are you going to accept that he's *not* gonna be looking back at you from the window?"

She wiped her tears and continued, her feelings spilling out of her. "You know...I've wanted to go to France for a long time. When I finally became a teacher I thought maybe one day I could go there and teach English. Each year I hoped that we could go there as a family and have this big adventure together...I wanted you to leave this place behind. Being here year after year hasn't been good for you...but each year comes and goes and we're still here in this house shackled by the ghosts of your past."

Sydney was absolutely taken aback, "Vicky, do you really feel this way?"

Victoria paced back and forth, "I don't know how I feel right now. All I know is I can't do this anymore."

Sydney heard the sound of a car pull up outside and people talking. "Who's out there?" he said as she looked out of the diamond shaped window.

"It's Dad and Mom...I called them right before you came in. I needed to see my Dad. Needed him to talk to. To help me feel better."

Sydney wasn't pleased to hear this. "What? You didn't need to involve them in this! We could have talked this out!"

"Right! Because you're doing *such* a great job of that." Sydney stood in silence, with his head held low, as the front door swung open and Wayne and Greta entered the house.

"What's going on, Victoria? You sounded pretty upset on the phone." Wayne said as Greta closed the door behind them.

"Sydney cheated on me…"

"What?!" Wayne said, completely flabbergasted.

"Oh, Sydney, no…" Greta said, her voice filled with immense disappointment. Sydney stood there unable to believe what was transpiring. It felt as if the world was being fast forwarded and he was standing there on pause.

"Syd, go and pack. Victoria doesn't want you here and after hearing this I can't say I disagree… Syd…you've broken all our hearts," Wayne said, placing his hand upon Sydney's shoulder. Sydney shook his head and averted his eyes from Wayne's.

He walked to their bedroom and opened their closet door and plucked out two bags. The first was a large black travel bag with wheels and handle. The second was a lime green duffle bag. He opened the large black travel bag and began slipping shirts into it when Victoria entered the room. She walked over to him and leaned down, grabbing his left hand. "Let me get this before you go," she said, grabbing his wedding ring and slipping it off of his finger. He was amazed that she took it from him but much like everything else that was happening he felt he was on the outside looking in. She pocketed his ring and left the room again, leaving Sydney to finish packing.

He finished packing the duffle bag when Victoria returned. He zipped the bag closed and stood up.

"Are you finished?"

"Yeah…" he replied.

Some Things Last...

"Alright..." she said, approaching him, "Why did you do this, Syd? Didn't I give you everything you ever wanted?" She wrapped her arms around him tightly.

"Yeah, I'm sorry, Vicky."

She squeezed him and said, "That's not good enough," then let him go. She exited the room again and he followed behind her.

As he returned to the living room, he felt the eyes of her parents boring into him. He walked to the front door and grabbed the cold doorknob, tightly in his hand and slowly opened it. He stepped outside, and Victoria cried out, "He's not even going to say goodbye!" She immediately burst into tears and ran back toward their bedroom.

Sydney turned around and tried going back inside when Wayne stopped him. "It's too late for that." Indeed it was. He could see that Wayne had no intention of moving and he didn't have the gumption of pushing him aside.

He turned and was about to walk down the steps when Wayne spoke again, "Here, Syd...I didn't want to just throw this away...considering what it is. It can't stay here so do with it what you will. Syd...were things serious between you and this girl or were you just playing around with her?" Wayne asked as he handed him Sharon's letter.

Sydney stared into his eyes a moment, they looked weighed down and full of immense sadness and disappointment. He didn't answer his question. Sydney placed the letter inside of his duffle bag and trekked onward with his two bags in tow towards his Miata. He loaded the bags up and entered the car. Wayne continued watching him from the porch as he started the car up and took off into the night.

Sydney didn't know precisely where to go. He'd been kicked out onto the streets, justifiably so. *Guess I'll give Mom and Dad a call...* He reached over and plucked his cellphone out of his duffle bag and gave his parents a ring.

After several rings he heard the grumpy voice of his father on the opposite end. "Hello?"

"Hey, Dad...sorry to call so late."

"Well, well, look who it is. The least popular man in Lando...maybe 'man' is a bit of a stretch."

"What are you talking about?"

"Me and your mother heard about your little dalliance with this Sharon girl. We were there when that letter was found! How could you do it? You broke Victoria's heart."

"Dad...I *know* that!!"

"Don't yell at me, Sydney. What are you calling for at this hour? What's happened?"

"Vicky...kicked me out and I was on my way over to the house. I thought maybe you and mom wouldn't mind if I stayed a few days until I've sorted this out with Vicky."

"Ah, I thought this might happen...Well, you thought wrong, Syd. You dropped the ball on this one and I'll be damned if I'm gonna clean this mess up. Come by tomorrow and maybe we'll talk. You gotta learn from your mistakes, son." His father hung up and Sydney was left alone once again.

"Guess I'll be staying at a hotel tonight after all..." Sydney sighed.

He turned around and headed across town to the very hotel he and Victoria were going to stay at had the past not caught up with him. It didn't take very long for him to reach the hotel. He pulled off the darkened streets into the warm glow of the antique street lamps surrounding the parking lot of The Lando Inn. He pulled into a space across from the entrance and killed the engine. He grabbed his bags and then walked towards the front entrance. The sound of the wheels from his large bag echoed throughout the still air of the parking lot.

He approached the front entrance and grasped the large metallic handles upon the glass doors but they remained

Some Things Last...

firmly in place. *Shit, they must lock the entrance after hours.* He looked to the left and saw a security camera that looked out over the front entrance and beneath it was a black button and intercom. A sign was posted next to the speaker.

DOORS LOCKED AFTER 10 PM - PRESS BUTTON FOR ASSISTANCE

He pressed the button and a few moments later a woman's voice came over the intercom, "Yes, sir? What do you need?"

"I was hoping to rent a room. Sorry to be coming by so late."

"No problem, my love. I'll buzz you in." A moment later the door unlocked and Sydney opened it.

Sydney stepped inside and approached the front desk. An older woman with graying brown hair stood behind the counter, smiling at him. He placed his bags next to him upon the luscious red carpet in front of the check-in counter and breathed a sigh of relief.

"Good morning, my love. You said you wanted a room for the night? When will you be checking out?"

"I'm not sure at the moment. Let's just reserve it for the weekend."

"OK, check out will be Monday morning at 11. Is that OK?"

"That'll work."

"What kind of room would ya like?"

"Um, I guess a single…whatever is cheapest."

"A single and double are about the same price if you want a double."

"Make it a double then…may as well."

The woman fixed the reservation and took Sydney's payment then directed him to his room. "It's straight ahead down this hallway here." She handed him his key-card. It was for room 237.

"Thank you," he said as he picked his bags up again and quietly walked down the hallway.

He found his room towards the end of the second floor and slid his key-card into the lock. The light on the lock lit up bright green and he slowly opened the door. The air was cool inside compared to the warm air out in the corridor.

He placed his bags inside the closet next to the door and found the light switch. He switched it on and a lamp in the corner illuminated the room in an off white glow. He looked at his watch and saw it was approaching three in the morning. He kicked his shoes off and eyeballed the closest bed. In that moment he believed he felt more tired than he had in his entire life. "My God…my God…my God…" he said as he fell onto the soft sheets of the bed and drifted off into a familiar dreamscape.

CHAPTER 13
This Letter To You

He was there again in Sharon's apartment. Upon her couch lay her blue robe but she was nowhere in sight. He walked across the room and grabbed the robe, squeezing it tightly within his hands, and began to rub it across his left cheek. Tears began to fall from his eyes upon it and he stopped himself. He wondered why it made him so incredibly sad. "Where are you, Sharon?!" *he called out but received no reply. As he walked down the hallway towards her bedroom he began to hear sobbing come from behind the door. He stood there listening, wanting to help but unable to bring himself to enter the room. It's too late for that, he thought to himself.* What? What the hell do you mean? It's too late? She's in there! She needs me.

He gathered his courage and pressed his body firmly into the worn wooden door frame and fell onto hard concrete. He rolled over and stared upwards into the night sky. There were millions if not billions of stars overhead. It felt as if he were staring into the depths of space.

"*Hello, Syd.*" *He snapped out of his awe and looked ahead. He was on the roof of Sharon's apartment complex.* "*Do you like what you see?*" *He stared at her unable to respond. She was standing away from him, naked, at the edge of the building, arms spread across as if she were about to fly.*

She slowly turned around and smiled at him. "*I meant the stars you perv...not me. Although I can see you like that too,*" *she said with a giggle.* "*Oh, Syd...so, she finally found out about us?*"

"*How do you know about that?*"

"I know you remember. You always had such a great memory...I suppose that's a curse these days for you all things considered."

He hung his head a moment. "Yeah, I remember. Come away from the edge, Sharon."

"A bit late for that don't you think? You always make a move too late. That's why I'm lying in that coffin in Pine Grove right now. It was your fault."

"I thought you were up there with the stars, Sharon." As he said this each of the brilliant stars above began to disappear into the void. "What...what the hell's happening!?" One by one they all faded away until one remained, the most brilliant of them all. It too slowly faded until there was nothing but darkness.

"This is what I really see, Syd. Darkness and nothing more," she said as she took a step backward. Sydney bolted across the rooftop as Sharon fell backward off the roof. He reached the edge and saw her body down below contorted in a pool of blood.

"NOO!! Why, Sharon!? Why..." He stood up and climbed onto the edge and looked down once again.

"Because of you!" Sharon said, behind him, pushing him off the edge and free-falling toward the sidewalk below.

Sydney screamed as he rolled over off the bed and onto the carpeted floor. "Wh-where am I?" For a moment he failed to remember where he was but it all came rushing back to him. "Vicky...I remember. That wasn't the pleasurable night's sleep I wanted here at the Lando Inn. Lord, what time is it?" He looked at his watch and saw that it was after noon.

Why...why was I there again? Up on that damn rooftop with Sharon. I refuse to believe that she's in the dark and nothing more...right? He lifted himself off the floor and entered the bathroom, waking himself up a bit. Looking into the mirror, a broken man looked back. "Looking a bit scruffy there," he said rubbing the backs of his fingers across his cheeks. The right side of his face was moist with cold drool. He looked away and looked back at the bed he'd passed out on. A large wet stain, where his head had been, surprised him. "Damn...I really passed the fuck out didn't I?"

He walked across the room and fell onto a comfy dark brown chair in the corner under the light. *OK, I've wasted enough time here. Can't go thinking about that dream right now. I gotta get on the phone and call Vicky. Maybe we can still talk this out. God, I hope so...*

He looked around for his bags a moment and remembered he dropped them by the door inside the closet. He delved into his green duffle bag and pulled out his cellphone. He flipped it open, eagerly hoping he had tons of missed calls, but there were none. *Oh, boy...that ain't a good sign*, he glumly thought.

He sighed and called the house phone. It rang five times when the answering machine picked up. "You've reached Sydney and Victoria. Sorry, we're not available to take your call. Leave a message after the beep." It had been a while since he'd called the house. Hearing Victoria's voice in that message tugged at his heart strings. He couldn't help but tear up a bit.

He cleared his throat after the beep and said, "Vicky...are you there? If you are please pick up. I want to talk about everything that happened. I really messed up but I don't want to lose you. I love you." He closed his phone and returned to his chair. He placed the phone upon the small table in front of him and waited patiently for it to ring.

Thirty minutes passed and his phone sat silent. He didn't want to pester her by calling over and over so he decided to jump into the shower and clean himself up a bit. He noticed that the battery was running low so he plugged the phone into the charger and left it on the table.

As he was lathering up his hair his phone began to ring and he quickly hopped out and wrapped a towel around himself, leaving a trail of water behind him.

Yawning At Your Heels

"Hello?" he quickly answered.

"Sydney?"

"Mom? Hey, what's wrong? I can barely hear you. You'll have to speak up. I'm wearing a towel," he said trying to lighten the mood. He could clearly tell that something was the matter.

"Sydney, we got a call this morning from Victoria. She told us that it was your fault…everything that happened with Al and your aunt Milly. That can't be true." He sat on the edge of the bed in silence. "That's not true, right, Sydney? Please tell me it isn't."

"Mom, now isn't the best time to talk about all of that. I'm waiting on a call from Vicky…"

"Sydney…can you just tell me if what she said is true?"

"I'll call you this evening, Mom…please. Just give me some time."

"Alright…this evening. Are you OK? I heard about everything…"

"Yeah…I'm fine. I'm at the Lando Inn right now. I gotta go, Mom. I love you."

"OK, bye, Sydney. Love you too."

He quickly closed his phone and tossed it onto the bed. *Damn. They didn't need to know about that!* He returned to the shower and finished up, hoping his phone would ring again, that Victoria would call, but it remained silent.

He finished up his shower, got dressed and decided to step outside for a little walk around the building. He dropped his phone into his back pocket and grabbed his room key. He closed the door behind him and continued down the carpeted hallway towards the front entrance.

He reached the front and noticed a young couple checking in. The girl made Sydney stop for a moment. From behind she looked just like Victoria. It was her hair and the way that she carried herself. She turned around and their eyes met for a moment. She smiled at Sydney and he returned the gesture as he pushed the front doors aside and stepped out into the cool autumnal air outside.

Across the street Sydney noticed the trees were all a plethora of bright colors. This time of year always reminded him of some of the happiest times in his life. He hated to think that autumn days from now on might take on a tinge of sadness much like summer had for him. He shook off the notion and breathed in deep of the crisp air. It filled his lungs and rejuvenated his mind. He planned to call Victoria once again when he went back inside and he needed a clear mind in case she answered.

He proceeded back inside to his room and entered the long hallway. In the distance he noticed the couple from before slip into a room. As he made it upon their room he noticed they just so happened to be staying next to him. For a brief moment he was happy for this. He felt a piece of Victoria was close to him. He chuckled a bit at this foolish thought and entered his own room.

He fell onto the seat once again and called Victoria. No reply at all. The answering machine didn't even cut in. *Does that mean she's at home? She got the message…but didn't call me back…* He decided to call her cellphone this time and he immediately received the message that played when her phone was turned off. "The customer you have dialed has turned their cellphone off or is out of the service area." It seemed Victoria was in no mood to talk.

He went back inside and sat down. He stared at the glass screen of the television set and saw his reflection staring back at him. A lone man in a hotel room. He was supposed to be sharing this weekend with Victoria. They should be ringing in seventeen years together, instead they were separated.

He walked over to the window and opened the drapes letting the late afternoon sun cascade into the dreary room. In the golden rays of the sun, he noticed a small computer desk beside the entertainment center. Upon it were two pens emblazoned with the hotel's insignia and beneath them some hotel stationary. *I've got to express these thoughts of mine or I'm going to go mad.* He took a seat at the small wooden desk and grabbed one of the pens and pieces of stationary, and began to empty his mind.

Vicky,

I'm in a small hotel room across the bay. I've been trying to reach you for most of the day. I look out of the window here and see the trees alight with fiery colors. They remind me of the day we got married. Seeing you in your dress that day, you looked so incredibly happy. That night we drove here…and made love like it was our first time together. I had hoped we would be here like we were back then but now I'm not even sure if you'll speak to me again. That was probably the second happiest day of my life directly behind the day Vivian was born. I remember looking into her eyes for the very first time and I swear I could see the universe in them. You and her are my universe. Without you, I have nothing. I know I've done some terrible things. Things you'll never forgive me for. If I could turn back the years I would make so many different choices…but I can't. I have to own up to what I've done. I can't run away from it all like I tried to do for these past seven years. Well, this letter has gone on for long enough. The sun is beginning to set outside. I'm not sure if you'll read this. I hope to talk to you later and discuss all of this with you. Until then…goodbye, I love you.

Sydney

Sydney took the letter and eyeballed it a moment. He hadn't written a letter in a very long time but he felt satisfied with it. He looked around for an envelope and opened the drawer beneath the top of the desk and found a neat stack within it. He wrote on the outside of the envelope:

Victoria Tesson Lee
402 Duke Avenue
Lando, Alabama 35250

He noticed the postage was paid on them. *Not like it matters…I'm not gonna be mailing this letter. This was more of a way of making me feel better…I do feel a bit lighter but still…not by much.*

He decided to call Vicky one last time before driving over to the house. Unsurprisingly, she didn't answer. He looked at his watch and saw it was coming up on six. *I've waited long enough. Time to go over there.* He reached into his black bag and pulled out a gray blazer and slipped it on then grabbed his keys and wallet and headed out the door.

As he made it to his Miata the final inklings of sunlight were fading from the sky and Sydney could see thick clouds rolling in. Some of them were alive with flashes of light. "That's just great…that's all I need tonight," he sighed and started the car. A minute later he began making his way across town.

CHAPTER 14
Fall Back Into Place

He mulled over everything he wanted to tell Victoria. Normally, he'd speed through the city streets of Lando with the top down but tonight he wanted to take his time. He needed to be ready to address many things that he'd been avoiding for quite a long time.

As he grew closer, he noticed that the wind was beginning to pick up. He had hoped that the weather would improve, that maybe the clouds in the distance would move away from the city. He turned down his street and his Miata rocked within the strong gusts outside. *That's not a good sign.* As he rolled up on the house, lightning pitchforked across the sky followed by rolling thunder in the distance a few seconds later. He pulled into the driveway and another brilliant flash of lightning forked across the sky. He couldn't help but be reminded of a certain night from the past. *There was a storm brewing just like this that night…*

He came out of his memories and noticed that Victoria's car was gone and the house was devoid of life. "Where could she be? Her parents? I…can't face them right now…I need to talk to her alone. Maybe she'll be home soon," he said to himself. He thought briefly of going inside and waiting for her but he didn't want to make her angry. "No…it's best not to surprise her. I'll go out for a little ride in the meantime. She's got to be home soon!"

He backed out into the street and looked over at his home. Flashes of the night Albert disappeared came to him. He shrugged them off and decided to head downtown for a little drive down memory lane.

He was driving through the streets of downtown Lando five minutes later. He cruised slowly through the dimly lit streets, partly because he couldn't believe that he'd returned after so long and also partly because the streets were in serious disrepair. He was dodging potholes left and right but couldn't avoid a few smaller ones. Once upon a time this part of town was alight with dive bars, quick in and out eateries and liquor stores. He recalled visiting a hot dog shop around there early one morning and regretted the decision. He spent the rest of that weekend sitting on the toilet.

There was one locale in particular that truly stood out in the area, with its warm neon lit sign, beckoning each passerby. He could vividly recall that sign lit up in pink and blue.

Sexothèque

He also remembered the sound of music, which flowed out onto the street outside, each time the door opened. It acted as a siren song. Sydney was never really fussy on the music that played there though. A smile broke across his face when he remembered Albert bobbing his head along to the beat as he sat to the bar. "I wonder how the old place is holding up..." he said as he slowly swerved avoiding another large pothole.

He stopped at an intersection and looked over at a street sign. He had to squint to make it out under the dimming street light above. *Lavrenti Boulevard...this is it. It's been a long long time.* He turned down the dark road and began looking ahead for the warm neon lit glow of the entrance. He was thankful that the weather hadn't worsened. There were still flashes of lightning which illuminated the road briefly but they were becoming less frequent. He lowered his window and felt the breeze blow through his hair. A moment later he heard a low growl of thunder over the steady hum of the motor.

He reached a part of the street that felt familiar to him and pulled next to the decaying sidewalk and killed the engine. There was one lone street light across the road. He exited the car and felt he was in the right place when he noticed a familiar entrance concealed by a large tree. It's branches were full of orange leaves which partly obscured the view from the street. *This looks like the place but it's pretty quiet for a Saturday night. The place is usually jumping.* He slowly approached the entrance and in the shadows he saw an unexpected sight. The entrance was completely boarded up with large pieces of plywood and a thick steel chain was wrapped around the door handles held firmly in place by a huge lock. Pasted upon one of the pieces of plywood over the doors was a sign.

CONDEMNED BY ORDER OF THE CITY OF LANDO, ALABAMA
NO TRESPASSING

Sydney couldn't believe his eyes. He noticed that the once brightly lit entrance was missing all of its neon signs. The most impressive one, which hung across the outer frame of the building, had been totally dismantled. The fixtures that once held it in place were all that remained. "Oh, shit the time goes by," Sydney sighed.

Why am I even here? What was I hoping to gain by coming to this place? Lord knows I should have never ventured here in the first place, he thought as he continued staring in disbelief at the derelict building that was once the Sexothèque. *I guess I just needed to see the place one last time.* He looked at his watch and saw that it was after seven. *Alright, I've killed enough time here. Vicky should be home by now.*

He continued staring at the boarded up entrance when a hand came upon his shoulder and grabbed hold of him. "Any spare change, mister?" Sydney quickly jerked out of the grip upon him. In the shadows a man stood in dingy clothes. He had a thick beard and from the smell Sydney figured he hadn't bathed in quite some time.

"Um, sure thing. Here's a twenty. Hope it helps." Sydney handed the man a twenty dollar bill and smiled.

"Thank you so much, sir. You're a kind man. I can tell."

"No...not really. I'm not that great."

"You made my night. What's your name?"

"Sydney."

"Well, Sydney, how's about I draw something for you?" the man said, shaking off a black backpack from one of his shoulders. He reached into it and produced a large sketchbook. "I want to give you something to repay your kindness. What would you like?"

Sydney smiled, "You really can draw me anything I want?"

"That's right! Just tell me and I'll draw it for ya."

Sydney thought a moment and remembered the beautiful mural on the back wall within Q.L.'s. "Alright, I've got something for you." He described the mural in great detail to the man. As he described it the man's hand quickly began to move about the blank page. Sydney watched in astonishment as the mural took shape.

A few minutes later the man stopped and said, "How's this?", and handed Sydney his work.

"This...is amazing! It looks just like the mural in Q.L.'s!" The man packed away his supplies and smiled brightly. "You have a real gift...Oh, I never got your name!"

"Call me Jim."

"Alright, Jim. You should be doing this for a living, man." Sydney said, still staring at the exact duplicate of the mural.

"Well, once upon a time I was...until my wife passed away. I found myself drifting about with no real direction. We never had kids so it was just the two of us. She was all I had...She's been gone now about six months. Ever since I haven't been able to do anything productive. I haven't even been able to wash myself...sorry about the smell."

"I see...but you just made a piece of art again tonight, Jim."

Jim's eyes widened, "I suppose I have...no one usually gives me the time of day anymore. When I saw you across the street looking at this run down building it reminded me of myself. You had a haunted look on your face."

"Did I? I was just visiting some old ghosts here."

"I understand that one..."

"Jim, thanks for the art. I really must be going though. There's someone I need to talk to before it's too late. You should seriously consider returning to your work. I'm sure your wife would rather see you doing that than roaming these darkened city streets..."

"You may be right about that. Take care, Sydney..."

"Syd...call me Syd."

He entered his Miata and placed Jim's art upon the passenger seat for safe keeping. He then headed away from this darkened nook of downtown and its many ghosts.

Sydney tried calling Victoria once again as he drove along toward uptown Lando. The line rang and rang but no one answered. "Damn it. She's gotta be back by now." He came to a stop at a traffic light and the sky lit up with another impressive display of forked lightning. *I thought this shit had passed over*, as that thought left his mind the sky opened up and a torrential downpour began.

He continued onward down Broadway, turning his wipers on as fast as they could go, but the rain proved to be a bit too much. He slowed his car and pulled over into a parking space along the side of the road. As he sat waiting for the rain to slacken up, he noticed something glowing up the street a bit. As the wipers quickly swiped across the glass he made out what it was. "A phone booth! Maybe Vicky will

Some Things Last...

answer the phone if she doesn't know it's me? Worth a shot!"

Sydney quickly hopped out of the car and ran over to the phone booth. He swung the door aside, entered and quickly shut it behind him. He stood a moment, the cold rain dripping off of him forming a small pool beneath him, and eyeballed the phone. The rain pounded against the sides of the glass enclosure in steady sheets. He grabbed the receiver, slipped a few coins into the slot and began dialing. It rang four times and just as he was about to give it up a voice came upon the other end.

"Hello?"

"Vicky?" Sydney spoke cautiously.

"Syd? Where are you calling from? It's a weird number."

"I'm in a phone booth uptown...I've been trying to reach you all day."

There was a pause. "Yeah...I know. I haven't been up to talking. I just got back in from my parents with Vivian...What are you doing out in this weather?"

"I was out for a drive...I came by earlier but you were gone."

"Syd...please don't come over."

"Why not, Vicky?"

"Why? You lied to me," she said. Sydney could hear the tears in her voice. "You've looked me dead in the eyes and lied to me for years. I don't know if I can ever trust you again."

"That's why I want to come and speak to you. I know we can talk this through. I can't lose you and Vivvy." Sydney began to cry too as he continued, "I love you, Vicky. I'll do anything to fix this. I know your parents must hate me. I'm sure everyone does...but I'll talk to all of them and ask them to forgive me...and if they don't that's alright because I'm not letting you go."

"Syd, is there anything else you want to tell me?" Sydney thought a moment. "There shouldn't be any silence for you to think, Syd. Yes, or no?"

"No, I told you everything that happened."

"Really? You just lied to me again. I know what you did the other day with Vivian. You took her to that girl's grave. Why would you take our daughter to a place like that? Why would you involve her in that?" Sydney stood, unable to answer. "You talk big but your silence truly speaks to me. If you're not going to say anything then I've got to get Vivian ready for bed. She's had so many questions about what's going on. I told her you'll be home soon…but I just don't know."

"Vicky, wait! Please, let me come home."

"Syd, don't call me anymore from this number."

Victoria slammed the phone down and the line went quiet. He stood in silence a moment then hung the receiver up, defeated. He closed his eyes and a deafening roar of thunder came from overhead which made the phone booth shake. The storm showed no signs of slackening up. Even if Sydney could he'd never make it home in weather like this. As he stood in the foggy phone booth, a warm light erupted into life across the street. Sydney rubbed his hand across the fog covered glass and saw a neon sign glowing. The lime green light it emitted illuminated the falling rain.

RUTHERFORD'S

The sign beckoned him. From what Sydney could see it looked to be a bar. *Why not check it out. Not getting anywhere else tonight with Vicky…* He opened the door and ran out into the falling rain and darted across the street. He reached the establishment's door a few moments later and entered into the warm light within.

The door closed behind him and he surveyed the bar. It certainly had a relaxing ambience. There were several chandeliers hanging from the ceiling throughout the place that cast a soft light throughout. He noticed several booths covered in supple dark brown leather. In the back corner he saw a lovely baby grand piano. *This place sure is nice...but where is everybody?*

Sydney decided to take a seat to the bar upon one of the leather bound bar stools, which matched the supple leather of the booths. Other than himself, the bar was a ghost town. It made him feel a bit uneasy. *Place reminds me of something outta my dreams...I feel like any minute some specter's gonna appear.* He began eyeballing the many bottles of booze, brightly lit behind the bar, when a door swung aside and out walked the barkeep.

"Good evening, sir. I apologize for the - S-Syd?!"

Sydney averted his gaze from the bottles and noticed a familiar weathered face that he'd not seen in years. "Joe?! Wow, is that you!"

"In the flesh! Sydney Lee...how long's it been? Six, seven years now?"

"That's right...I was not expecting to run into you. I've been running into familiar faces from the past here lately...I wonder who'll be next...?" Sydney said, smiling.

Even though he was smiling, his eyes told a different story and Joe could see this. Joe stepped up to the bar and grabbed a glass and began to polish it with a clean rag he had retrieved from the back room. "Care for a drink, Syd? Don't tell me...sake served cold."

Sydney looked into Joe's tired eyes and smiled, "That's pretty impressive that you remember that. I haven't touched the stuff though in a *very* long time."

"So...you're not drinking tonight? Never thought I'd see the day...if you don't mind me saying so, Syd."

Sydney began to laugh, "I did raise some hell back at the Sexothèque didn't I?"

Joe continued polishing the bar glass, it gleamed in the soft light of the room. "You said you've run into some familiar faces from back then. Who did you run into?"

"Yeah…I ran into Olivia at the mall. She owns a pet shop…Olivia's Pet Shop Birdie Birds…what a name," Sydney said, laughing.

"That's wonderful news. I haven't seen her since she left the club. I'll have to go pay her a visit sometime."

"She'd enjoy that I think…" Sydney said, eyeballing a square teal colored bottle on the bottom shelf of the booze display.

Joe stopped polishing the glass and laid it upon the immaculately maintained surface of the bar. "I see you've noticed it. What's interesting is this is an imported bottle. I ordered it in last month on a whim. Normally, my clientele don't go for this stuff but I felt someone would come in and order it…and now lo and behold you've shown up."

Sydney smiled, "You were always a helluva barkeep, Joe. I always liked ya." Sydney reached over and tapped the empty glass. "Hit me, Joe."

"Right away, sir." Joe wrapped his hand around the stem of the bottle and placed it upon the bar. He leaned down and dished out a few cubes of ice into the glass. They tinkled against the sides, settled and Joe washed the sake over them. He grabbed a coaster and placed the drink before Sydney and smiled.

"Would ya look at that…takes me back."

"Me too, Syd. Enjoy."

Sydney eyeballed the drink sat before him. He thought back to the last time he'd had a drink. Images of Sharon flashed in his mind, her wrapped around him in the booth at Akane Dragon, him drunk off his ass without a care in the world while Albert sat across from him full of immense sadness. The guilt hung heavily upon his shoulders as he sat

Some Things Last...

there looking at the clear liquid held within the spotless glass.

He was tired. Tired of feeling guilty...tired of feeling responsible for everything that happened...and he was just plain tired of being tired. He reached for the drink and slowly brought it to his lips and began to drink. The old familiar taste of alcohol hit the back of his mouth and cooled his throat initially and quickly warmed it on the way down. "Ah, been too long, Joey my boy." He quickly tapped the glass and Joe filled it once more.

Sydney embraced the muddled feeling within his head. He prayed that he could get away from himself for a while. He so longed to be carefree once again.

He found himself downing almost the entire contents of the teal bottle but instead of feeling carefree he felt quite the opposite.

"Care for another, Syd?"

Sydney smiled and tapped the glass. "I hear bells a ringin', Joey my boy. An angel must've gotten it's wings." Joe replenished the ice cubes and poured another bit of sake in. "You know I ended up getting married, Joe..."

"Is that right?"

"Oh, yes...Me and her known each other since we were kids...been together seventeen years on Monday. We've got the cutest little girl you could imagine. I know what you're thinkin'. What was I doin' down at the club when I had her back home...no, no...not *her!* She's got a name, damn it! Victoria...oh, Vicky...what have I done? What would you think of me now? Lord...everyone would be better off without me." Sydney rested his head on the bar and began laughing. "Now's not the time time to cry! Now is the time to laugh! For if you laugh the world laughs with you. If you weep. You weep alone."

Joe placed his hand upon Sydney's shoulder, "Syd, I don't judge people. Nobodies perfect. We all make mistakes.

We all have pasts…sometimes memories have a bad habit of creeping up on you when you least expect them."

"Tell me about it. You're a good man, Joe. Thanks for helping her."

"Who do you mean, Syd?"

Sydney looked down at his drink. A lone ice cube floated upon the surface. "Sharon. Her last night on stage…she froze up. She's gone Joe…gone."

"Yeah, I heard about that. Such a tragedy."

"…I think it's about time I hit the old dusty trail," Sydney said, standing up and stretching. He quickly fell to the floor. "Whoa, got the rubber legs. Happens to the best of us…" He climbed to his feet and reached in his pocket for his keys.

Joe grabbed them from his hands and placed them behind the bar. "I can't in good conscious let you drive tonight, Syd."

Sydney noticed that the room was moving all over. Had he really had that much to drink? "Yeah, you're right…I'd end up getting my fool self killed or kill someone else. Maybe the former wouldn't be such a bad thing though."

"Hey, how about I play you a song on the piano? Liven things up in here. Usually, my cousin Tony plays but he didn't come in due to the storm tonight."

Sydney eyeballed the baby grand and smiled, "Yeah, play me a song, Joe. Maybe it'll perk me up a bit." Joe came out from behind the bar and walked over to the piano and adjusted the bench. A moment later he began to play. Sydney listened intently and closed his eyes as Joe's playing moved him deeply. He laid his head down upon the bar and began to weep as the events of the past week finally caught up with him.

"He plays beautifully doesn't he?" Sydney's eyes slowly opened as he looked over and saw a man sat next to him. He was dressed in a black pin striped zoot suit and had a thick moustache upon his weathered face.

"Where'd you come from?" Sydney said, eyeballing the mysterious stranger.

"Oh, you know...a place past Pluto...took a bit of a shortcut though around Saturn."

"Right..." Sydney said, smiling as he laid his head back down.

"Is everything alright? You seem to be sad," the man asked.

Sydney kept his head down and responded, "You could say that...I'm having a pretty bad day."

"Why not talk to me about it? I can sense your sadness."

Sydney sat up and looked at the man. His eyes were full of sincerity. "Alright. What's your name?"

"Call me John."

"Where do I even begin, John?"

"Wherever you like..."

Sydney began unburdening himself to the mysterious zoot suit clad gentleman. Every sordid detail came flooding out of his mouth but the man sat unmoving, his eyes welcoming. Soon, Sydney caught the man up on his entire life story, he felt.

He smiled at Sydney and finally spoke, "I knew before I arrived that you had a profound sadness within you. I just wasn't aware of the extent of it...You've been through so much. What if I told you that I could take you somewhere, far away but close at the same time, where you'll never have to worry about anything again?"

Sydney stared at the man a moment. The man's eyes were just as warm and sincere as ever. "I'd say that sounds like a beautiful thought, John...too bad it ain't that easy."

"It can be. Would you want to go? The sadness is emanating off of you in waves. I truly want you to feel the happiness that I do. You can leave all of that sadness behind you."

Sydney thought a moment. What if he really did leave? After everything that he'd done how could he ever make amends for it? Victoria would never trust him again and Vivian would grow up ashamed of him. No one would ever look at him the same. He'd forever be tainted.

"Yeah, John. I'll go," he said, placing his head back down upon the bar.

John smiled, brightly, "That's good. I'll see you soon, Sydney."

Sydney quickly looked up, "Hey, I never told you my name," but John was gone. Sydney scanned over the entire bar and saw no trace of him. *Maybe John hit the john?* Sydney thought laughing to himself.

Sydney noticed that Joe was still sat to the piano playing. *Damn, how long has he been playing? I feel like I've been sitting here for hours...It's odd though...he's still playing the same tune.* Sydney looked over and noticed the clock on the wall, 9:33. *I thought it'd be after midnight or something. I've only been here about two hours!*

He began listening to Joe's playing again and he felt the sadness well up in him once more. *I can't take it anymore. I gotta get outta here.* Sydney rose from his bench and nearly fell again but caught himself. He made his way to the door and re-entered the cool autumn air permeating outside.

The raging storm from earlier had finally passed. The gutters of the streets were still swollen with raging water. Sydney passed by a large storm drain and listened as thousands of gallons of water rapidly rushed through the pitch black pipes below. Over the sound of the rushing water, Sydney could faintly here Joe reaching what must be the crescendo of the piece.

Under the glow of the neon sign above, Sydney began to walk down the sidewalk. As he was walking he began

Some Things Last...

thinking about the mysterious zoot suit clad stranger, John. He thought of how he had briefly made him feel better. *Maybe that place he was talking about really does exist...* Sydney began to laugh. *Yeah...right.* Sydney reached into his jacket pocket and pulled out his cellphone. *Maybe I can get a cab?* He flipped it open only to be greeted by a black screen. *Dead...of course. Why am I not surprised.*

Sydney stumbled aimlessly unable to get his barrings. Soon, he found himself on the lakefront board walk, enveloped in a thick fog that had rolled in. In the silence of the night, he could barely hear the shallow waves of Lake Lethe crash upon the shoreline below. He continued up the boardwalk and stumbled off of it and down another residential street.

Sydney continued to press onward, unknowing of where he was. As he turned down another street, he could hear several dogs barking close by. *Last thing I need is to try to outrun some dog in the fog...* He picked up speed hoping the barking dogs in the distance were all bark.

His head began spinning and he felt like he was going to barf. *Pushed myself too much...it's all catching up with me.* Sure enough a moment later he hurled onto the sidewalk.

"Whoa, someone's been partying hardy." Sydney looked up and saw four people in various costumes. One was dressed as a king, complete with a jewel encrusted crown and sash. He had his arm around a woman, dressed as a queen. The other two were a knight and jester. They all began to laugh at him.

"Did you come here to lead the fool's parade?" the jester spoke, smugly. Sydney began to walk away, he was in no mood to be heckled.

The knight caught up with him and said, "Please, excuse them. We just left a costume party."

Sydney looked up and noticed it was a woman in the armor. "Nice costume...you wouldn't happen to know where Duke Avenue is would you?"

"Yeah! You're not too far! It's two blocks over. Just go straight and take two rights and you'll be there," the armor clad woman happily replied.

"Thanks...enjoy the fog."

Sydney followed the directions given to him. He was a bit skeptical of them but he had a feeling he could trust the knight. Sure enough, the old neighborhood started looking familiar to his bloodshot eyes. He walked up the sidewalk and soon his home came into view. It broke through the fog like a beacon, even though only one light shone through. He could see it clearly shining through the diamond shaped window on the door.

He tried picking up his pace and stumbled upon the wet grass of the front yard. He brushed himself off and continued closer. He gingerly made his way up the steps onto the porch and peeped through the window. There was a lone lamp on next to the window which was casting a warm glow into the living room. He saw no one sat upon the couch. *Surely they've all gone to bed...what am I even doing here? Vicky isn't just gonna let me in...but I'm so tired. I can't leave now.* He reached into his pocket for his keys and realized he never got them back from Joe. "Damn it! How am I gonna get in now?" He took a seat upon the wooden bench on the porch and began to think...he thought and he thought...his eyes growing ever more heavy until he drifted off to sleep.

An incredible sensation came over him. Within the darkness all around him, he felt as if he were flying forward at an incredible speed. Suddenly, the darkness broke as he flew over the edge of a dark cliff and he looked ahead of himself to see a city below him. The city was cloaked in fog but bright lights of various colors shone through. As he continued flying forward he recognized the city. It was Lando...his home, but somehow it felt foreign to him. Through the fog a light shone especially bright. It was brighter than the others. He felt himself slowly growing closer to it.

"Daddy? Wake up, Daddy. Come inside." Sydney's eyes opened and he looked around, unable to comprehend what was happening. "Daddy? What's wrong? What are you looking at?"

Sydney averted his eyes from the fog surrounding his home and noticed Vivian standing beside him. The front door stood open and cast it's warm light out upon the porch. "Viv-Vivvy?"

"Yes, Daddy. Come on in..." she said, taking his hand in her's and leading him inside. He slowly rose from the wooden bench and entered the warm living room. Vivian closed the door behind them and Sydney took one step forward and fell onto the couch causing a loud thump.

"Careful, Daddy...Don't wake Mommy...She's had a long day. She was very sad today...even though she tried hiding it from me. I don't know why though. I hope it wasn't something I did..."

Sydney tried raising his head from the couch, to tell her it wasn't her fault in any way but he was just so damn tired. The soft couch beckoned him to drift off again to sleep. He fought the embrace of it though, keeping his eyes halfway open. The world faded in and out of focus as he saw Vivian approach him with a blanket. It was her Celeste The Unicorn throw blanket. She placed it over him and tucked him in much like he had done for her many times.

"Don't want you to get cold. Celeste will keep you warm." She leaned over and kissed his forehead. "Goodnight, Daddy. I love you," she whispered and left him alone. Sydney could fight the temptation no longer. He became wrapped in the welcoming embrace of sleep.

He saw that beacon of light once again. It was as if he slipped right back in where he left off. He drew closer, the city growing in detail. As he approached the beacon, it began to dim and Sydney noticed he was outside of his home. The warm glow of the lamp shone through the diamond shaped window...and in the distance lying upon the couch was...

He awoke and sat up on the couch. He sat a moment, waking himself up. The living room was filled with a bright light. It appeared he had slept through the entire night and into the day. He threw his legs over onto the floor and noticed his shoes were still on. "Man, what a dream. What time is it? It's pretty bright outside," he said looking at his watch and was astonished. "That can't be right...after three in the morning?!"

He stood up and began to notice there was something *off* with this light. As he looked over through the diamond shaped window he began to feel warm inside. It was as if the light was calling him. He walked over to the front door and opened it. The light cascaded over him, enveloping him entirely. Through the blinding light, he felt nothing but love. He stood in the doorway a moment when he began to hear a voice.

Come to me, Syd, the voice spoke. Sydney stepped out into the light and walked down the steps into the yard. His body began to feel lighter and he felt as if he were floating upwards into that blinding light.

We'll be together again soon, babe. Just close your eyes...

He obeyed, completely handing himself over to this incredible feeling. He felt as if he were leaving everything behind. All of his guilt, self loathing, anger and sadness all seemed to be going away.

In that place behind him, which felt so far away, he thought for a split second that he heard, "Daddy!" By then, he was already gone.

SECOND INTERLUDE

I'M FLOATING

"Syd, we're here. Syd?"

He opened his eyes slowly and a blinding light shown right in his face. A moment later the light faded. "Damn car...what's it doing driving around with it's high beams?" Sydney said, turning around and glaring at a passing mini van continue up the street and out of sight.

"If you'd have been awake that wouldn't have happened."

Sydney hung his head a moment and replied, "Yeah, I'm sorry, Vicky. There's just something about being in the car that puts me out."

"I don't understand that. You slept as long as I did and I'm not falling over."

Sydney looked out of the passenger window at the beckoning entrance of John's Restaurant. He could already smell the delectable scent of freshly cooked steak. John's was in uptown Lando and had become a place of theirs that they liked frequenting on their date nights.

He could tell that Victoria was pissed off at him. He needed to smooth things over and fast. He reached over and placed his hand upon her leg and began to rub it. "Vicky, are you hungry? Raise your window down a tad and take a whiff."

Victoria raised her window down and breathed deep. "That steak smells so good...let's head in. I expect a cheese cake afterwards...and you can't have any," she said, sticking her tongue out at him.

"Aw, come on, Vicky. Just one little piece?"

"Nope. All for me!"

Sydney hopped out and ran over to her door and opened it for her. She stepped out and smiled. *Crisis averted...* he thought as they entered into the warmly lit interior.

As they waited to be seated, Sydney noticed that the place was in the process of being redecorated for Christmas. A few of the waitstaff were hanging some garland around the frames of several booths.

"You ready for Christmas, baby?" Sydney asked.

"Nope. I have some ideas though for your gifts..."

"Oh, really? Like what?"

"Not tellin'."

"Damn...Oh, come on just a hint."

"Nope." A young waitress approached the two and directed them to one of the freshly decorated restaurant booths.

After their meal, Sydney leaned back in his chair and placed his hands upon his stomach. "Man, that was great. John never ceases to amaze."

"I know, Syd. I feel like we keep coming here I'm gonna get fat."

Sydney chuckled, "Thanks for giving me a piece of cheese cake, sweetheart."

"Well, even though you fell asleep *again* after I've told you countless times not too...I had a great time out tonight. It just sucks that we might not get to come out here for a while."

"Yeah, but it'll all be worth it in the end..."

Sydney leaned back and thought about how he and Victoria hadn't been able to spend as much time together lately. She was in her first year at King City University, studying to become an English teacher. This year had seen the two of them separated a good bit of the time, especially during the current semester. Sydney knew that it was going to get worse towards the end of it. Finals were looming and he knew Victoria would be studying like mad.

"Everything alright?" Victoria asked.

Some Things Last...

"Huh?" Sydney was brought out of his reflections.

"You had a serious look on your face. Your brow was all furrowed."

"Oh, I was thinking about how I'm not gonna get to see you as much when the semester starts back from the Thanksgiving holidays."

Victoria frowned, "Yeah, finals are creeping up in a few weeks...I'm sorry that I've been leaving you alone at the apartment so much."

"No, I understand. I'm just glad you don't have to drive home exhausted...I'd come and get you if it wasn't for work...at least John and Alexis live nearby and they have a spare room for you to crash in."

"Yeah, I just wish you were there...it sucks sleeping alone."

"Maybe you should get a body pillow and pretend it's me..."

"It wouldn't be the same. A body pillow doesn't have what you have..."

Sydney's brow raised, "Oh, yeah? What do I have?"

Victoria blushed slightly, "A dick," she said, with a cheeky grin.

"OH, so that's *all* I am to you, eh?"

Victoria began to laugh. "Syd, go and pay the bill. I'd like to get home...and use what you have..."

Sydney hopped up from the table and grabbed the check. "Sounds great to me, baby!"

"I'll meet you in the car," she said, with a wink.

Sydney approached the counter and waited behind a tall, thin guy who was paying his bill. The guy finished paying and turned around and stopped. A look of surprise was on his face as he eyeballed Sydney.

"Is that you, Syd?"

Sydney returned the guy's look of surprise. "Do I know you, fella?"

The guy looked a little hurt by Sydney's response. "I know I look different but I hope so...has it really been that long that you don't recognize one of your old buddies?"

Sydney's eyes widened. "Wait a second...*ROLAND?! Roland Torfilio*?! Oh, my God! I haven't seen you in what?"

"Been about...eight years now."

"Wow...yeah, that's right. So, what are you up to these days?"

"Well, right now I'm back in town visiting my old man for Thanksgiving. What about you?"

"I was just out here on a date with Vicky...you remember Vicky, right?"

"Wait, you guys are *still* together? Wow, that's crazy."

"Almost ten years now."

"Hey, how about we meet up tomorrow evening and catch up?"

"Well, Vicky will probably be busy...but I'll be free."

"Even better...men's night out! Let me give you my number, bro." Roland grabbed a pen from the counter and scribbled his number on the back of his receipt. "Here you go. Call me tomorrow afternoon...I gotta be getting on. I got some pressing business to attend to downtown," Roland said with a grin. Sydney eyeballed his number for a moment and placed it in his jacket pocket.

Sydney returned to the car and noticed Victoria was in the passenger seat. He slid into the driver's seat and closed the door.

"That took a while. What was the hold up?" Victoria asked.

"You'll never guess who I ran into while paying the bill...Do you remember Roland?"

"What? Roland?! *Middle school Roland?*"

"The very same. He invited us out to catch up tomorrow."

Some Things Last...

"I won't be able to make it, Syd...I have to finish up a project in one of my classes...but you can go! I'm sure you'll have a lot of catching up to do."

"You're telling me...I'm just curious why he disappeared after seventh grade."

"Well, ask him tomorrow...Syd...remember what I told you to the table?"

"Oh, baby! Do I!" Sydney started Victoria's car and stepped on the gas. Roland quickly left his mind, at least until the following day.

The following afternoon saw Sydney and Victoria at their apartment. The two had spent the first quarter of their day together, as they usually did, watching movies. The two had decided to have a marathon of The Godfather films. While watching the first film, Sydney couldn't help but be reminded of an old memory from middle school.

"Did I ever tell you about the time I told Roland about the thunderbolt?" he said, smiling.

Victoria looked over at him. She was sitting on the recliner as he lay upon their navy blue couch. "The thunderbolt?"

"Yeah, Vicky. It was actually the day I met you...right before we met in the hallway outside the bathrooms. Kinda funny how we decided to watch this today...I haven't thought about that time in years..."

Victoria stood up and came over to Sydney. He moved back on the couch and made room for her. As she lie next to him she took his hand into hers and smiled. "I'm your thunderbolt?"

Sydney squeezed her hand. "You sure are, Vicky."

"Syd, do you ever think you'll feel like you're missing out on anything?" Victoria said, with a serious look on her face.

"What do you mean?"

"Like, I'm the only girl you've ever been with..."

I'm Floating

Sydney looked her in the eye and answered, "No. I've never thought that..." He pulled her close and kissed her. They continued watching the movie together, Victoria closely lay next to him upon the couch. As he held her he couldn't help but toss her words about in his mind.

As the movie finished, Victoria noticed the time. "Alright, Syd, I've gotta get started on the finishing touches of my project. Roland might be waiting for your call."

"Ah, he'll be alright. We've waited this long...I suppose I'll call him though." Sydney retrieved the number from his jacket pocket and then placed the call. The line rang two times before a familiar voice answered, "Hello?"

"Yo, Roland?"

"Hey, Syd, that you? You about ready to hit the town, bro?"

"Yeah, looking forward to catching up...what exactly are we gonna do though?"

Roland thought for a moment and answered, "Hmm, well, how about we hit up John's again? I'm in the mood for some surf n' turf and a few brewskis."

"Sounds good..."

"Alright! I'll meet you out there in about thirty minutes. Bye, Syd." Roland quickly hung up before Sydney could return the sentiment.

Sydney found Victoria, with all of her work laid out in front of her, sitting to the dining room table. She looked up from her papers at him and asked, "Did you get hold of Roland?"

"Yeah, we're going out to John's again. Didn't think I'd be going back so soon but that's fine with me."

"Aw, I don't think you've ever been there without me."

"Very true. It'll be strange...but I'll be thinking about you."

Some Things Last...

Victoria smiled at that. "You better head on out then. I'll probably order in something later since you two might be a while."

"Alright, sweetheart." He leaned over and kissed her goodbye.

"Be careful. Watch out for the crazy people..." Sydney grabbed his keys and waved bye to her.

He arrived ten minutes later and pulled into a parking space behind the building. It was a bit more crowded at John's than he'd expected. Normally, he and Victoria would park in front of the restaurant but tonight all the spots were full. He had hoped to see Roland somewhere out front but had no luck as he passed by.

He entered through the back entrance and proceeded down a hallway illuminated with bright multicolored Christmas lights which were blinking off and on every few seconds. He turned a corner and came to a podium where the same young waitress who had seated him the previous night stood smiling.

"Hello again. You must really like it here to come two nights in a row," she said, with a laugh.

"Yeah, um, I'm supposed to be meeting a friend of mine here. Tall guy, black hair?"

"Oh, I know who you mean. Right this way." Sydney followed closely behind as she lead him to the bar.

"Yo, Syd! I see you found me! Pull up a seat!"

"Huh, I wasn't aware John's had a bar," Sydney said as he took a seat upon a brown leather stool.

He noticed that Roland already had a bar glass sitting in front of him. It was full of a dark brown liquid. "What ya got there, Roland?"

He looked down at his drink and replied, "What this? Just a little warm up of things to come..."

"Things to come? You planning on getting wasted tonight?"

I'm Floating

"Always, Syd!"

Sydney laughed. "Well, damn. I wasn't prepared for this. How's about we catch up a bit, man. We don't need to get wasted..."

Roland raised his glass and smiled. "Of course. I was only joking..."

"Really? Didn't sound like it..."

Roland let out a laugh, "Eh, well, anyway. Let's catch up...Sydney Fuckin' Lee, how the hell have ya been?"

"Never mind how I've been. There's something that's been bugging me for a long time. You disappeared after seventh grade, man. What the hell happened to you?"

Roland chuckled and took a sip of his drink. "You don't waste any time do ya? I can imagine you wondered about that one. Allow me to explain. Well, my folks split right after seventh grade ended...My old man wasn't the greatest of guys. He had a bit of a drinking problem...The straw that broke the camel's back was that final day of seventh grade. You remember the awards ceremony?"

Sydney shook his head, "Yeah, man. I remember I was awarded the "Most Improved" award by Mrs. Stuermer."

A big smile grew across Roland's face. "Ahhh, Mrs. Stuermer! Damn, that woman was a fox. I haven't thought about *her* in a while...I wonder if she's still married..."

"Lord, Roland, that woman probably has kids by now."

"That's alright. I can be the daddy...in more ways than one..."

Sydney began laughing. "Oh, man. Feels like old times...too bad Al's not here."

"Eh, I'm glad he isn't. He'd probably just roll his eyes and sit with a scowl on his face. He was always a real buzzkill," Roland scoffed.

Sydney laughed even more. "You're probably right about that...still though Al's a great guy."

"What the hell is he up too these days?"

"Not much. Still living with his mom…still single."

"Poor bastard. I wonder if he's aware how bad he's got it," Roland said, taking another drink.

"He seems to be alright with things. I just saw him two days ago for Thanksgiving."

"Well, enough about ole Al. I didn't finish my story. The awards ceremony…you wonder why I never made it to school that day?"

"Yeah…of course. You were supposed to collect an award from Mrs. Stuermer too I believe."

"Yeah, opposite of your reward…top of the class. That woman *really* made me *love* math."

"Yeah, I remember…Go on."

"Right. Well, my old man showed his ass. Told my mom not to leave the house that day. He said he felt something bad was gonna happen…complete bullshit." Roland tossed back the rest of his drink and slammed the glass down. "Later that night my old man passed out and my mom took me and we left on a bus for my aunt's place up north in Michigan. We ended up staying and I enrolled in school there. Never met anyone like you guys though. Ah, I never even got to say goodbye. That's really stuck with me all these years."

"You talking about me or Mrs. Stuermer?"

Roland smiled and laughed, "*YOU* of course!"

Sydney rolled his eyes, "Right. I bet."

"Hey, now…don't roll your eyes…that's Al's job. I'm sure that motherfucker's eyes must have rolled back in his head by now and stayed there….AH! I need another drink. Care to join me?"

"What *I'd* like is a menu…why haven't they come back by yet?"

"It's all good…I already ordered for us…it's on me, man. The meal anyway…if you want some booze that's you."

"What did you order me?"

I'm Floating

"Got ya a juicy steak...*AND* a lobster tail. Sound good?"

Sydney shook his head. Boy, did it ever. He eyeballed the liquor selection behind the bar. "Hmm, maybe I *will* have a little drink...just one."

"That's the spirit! Barkeep? My friend needs a drink! What do ya want, bro?"

Sydney noticed a black bottle of sake perched atop one of the shelves. "How's about some sake? Been a good long time."

"Right on, man. Sounds good to me!"

Sydney finished off his supper and took another sip of sake. "Man, that was some good stuff..."

"Yeah, it was. I'm glad my old man suggested this place to me...if not we wouldn't have crossed paths again. For once in his life he did the right thing," Roland said, dryly.

"So, Syd, when are you and Vicky gonna get hitched?"

"We haven't really discussed anything definitive yet...I imagine though it'll probably be in a few years, sometime after she finishes up with her degree."

"So, she's really doing it, eh? Good for her...She's not the only one who's gonna have a degree."

"Wait...you're after a degree too?"

"Yep, sure am...trying to get into law school at the moment, man. The future looks bright too."

"Wait...*YOU* a *LAWYER*?"

"Why do you sound so surprised?"

"Sorry, Roland. No offense. It's just I wasn't aware you were interested in law."

"None taken. Believe me...my old man was shocked too but you should have seen him. He sure was proud to hear it..."

"I bet he was. Well, good luck, man. If I ever need some law advice or if I happen to chop Vicky up into little bits and need council I'll call ya."

Some Things Last...

Roland broke into a loud laugh, "I'll beat the rap, Syd. You can count on it."

Sydney raised his glass and threw back the last mouth full of sake. "And on that note...I think we should wrap up this evenings affair. Vicky's gonna be wondering where I'm to," Sydney said, eyeballing his watch.

"Oh, no...but it's still early yet, bro," Roland said, visibly upset.

"It's nine forty five, man. John's closed up like fifteen minutes ago."

"That's alright. I know a place we can go that stays open all night...what do ya say we take this reunion to the second act?"

Sydney looked away from Roland and replied, "I don't know, man...I'm sure Vicky's wondering about me already."

"I'm sorry, Syd. I wasn't aware she had you on such a short leash."

Sydney looked over at Roland, annoyed. "Hey, I'm not on a fuckin' leash, Roland. You see a collar around my neck?"

"I sure do...you apparently can't see it since it's been there so long...ten years is a long time."

"Fuck you. I just want to respect her. What's wrong with that?"

"Nothing...but she should respect you too and let you spend some time with your old buddy. When the hell are we gonna get to go out again?" Sydney thought a moment. "Exactly. You don't know. Who knows when the hell I'll be back in Lando! So, let's enjoy this night while we can!"

Sydney looked down into his empty glass, a lone ice cube sat in the bottom, melting. "Alright, but let me call her at least and tell her I'll be getting in later."

"Right on, Syd!! Let's go outside. I need some air...bit stuffy in here."

I'm Floating

The two proceeded to the back of the restaurant and entered into the brisk night air. "Ahhh, I feel alive again, Syd! Hurry up with that phone call. The night beckons," Roland said, taking out a cigarette from his jacket pocket and lighting it up. He held the box out offering Sydney one but he politely turned him down with a wave as he held his cellphone up to his ear.

The line rang twice when Victoria answered.

"Hello?"

"Hey, sweetheart, I just got finished eating but Roland wanted to go hang out a bit longer."

"OK, well, where are you guys headed?"

"I'm not sure yet. He said he knew a place open all night…a diner close by I suppose."

"Well, I guess so…I was hoping to climb into bed with you soon but that's alright. Tell him I said hello and I was sorry I couldn't make it."

"I will, baby. He understands. I miss you."

"Miss you too. Love you, Syd. Bye."

"Love you too, Vicky. Bye bye." Sydney closed his phone and ended the call.

Roland started to chuckle. "Something funny, Roland?"

"Nah, not a thing. So, you ready to go lover boy?"

"Yeah…and don't call me that," Sydney said, giving Roland a shove. "We going in yours or mine?" Sydney inquired.

"Um, yours unless you wanna hop on my back, bro. I took a cab here."

"Ah, I see. Well, right this way. Our chariot awaits." Sydney lead Roland to his car and held his arms out, "Here she is."

"You own a Miata? How do ya get in this thing?"

"You open the door and kinda fall back into it."

Roland laughed and asked, "So, why a Miata?"

"You say that like I did something wrong. Why NOT a Miata is the better question," Sydney answered, defensively.

"Bit small ain't it?"

"Well ya know what they say about guys with big trucks and shit. My Miata might be small but I'm not…"

Roland burst into a fit of laughter, filling the parking lot. "Right on, Syd. Alright, she's a nice ride. Got a nice shine to her."

Sydney smiled and entered the car, leaned over and opened Roland's door. Roland leaned down and fell onto the tan leather seat. "Ah, damn. Not used to being so low to the ground. Hey, you wanna let the top down, bro?"

A smile broke out across Sydney's face. "Of course! I was just about to do that." Sydney lowered the top and started the engine. "So…where we headed, Roland?"

"I'll tell ya how to get there…just follow my directions."

A curious look developed upon Sydney's face. "Rather cryptic…you can't tell me?"

"Don't worry about it. It's a surprise."

"Alright…Lead the way."

A few minutes later they were driving along through downtown Lando.

"Take a right, here," Roland said.

"Are we almost there?"

Roland grinned and replied, "A little further. Take a left."

Sydney turned down yet another street he'd never been down before and cruised along slowly. He looked into the sky a moment at the moon hung brightly above when Roland said, "OK, we're here, bro…pull up behind this bright green Jeep."

He parked the Miata and looked over at the bright glow above them. Emblazoned in neon letters was a large bright sign hanging above the entrance.

Sexothèque

I'm Floating

Its pink and blue letters cast a warm glow into the interior of his Miata.

"What the hell is this place?" Sydney could hear the thumping of what sounded like music coming from within the establishment.

"This, my friend, is the Shangri-La of Lando...where the honey flows and the beautiful ladies take you by the hand."

"Beautiful ladies? Drinks? Is this a titty bar, Roland?!"

Roland laughed, "I prefer the term "gentleman's club." I stumbled across this place a few days ago...I thought you and I could *really* unwind here...get a bit crazy...*live* a little in your case...unless of course that leash is shorter than I thought...maybe she has you by the dick instead?" Sydney looked over at Roland with a piercing gaze. "You can give me the stink eye all ya want. You've been with Vicky for all these years, right? You never cheated on her once?"

"No, I haven't."

"You never thought about other women?"

"No."

"Really? You sure about that, bro? I saw the way you eyeballed that waitress's ass at John's. With that little apron tied around her waist...I saw the gears turning. You had the same look as me...and about every other guy in the place." Sydney shamefully looked away from Roland across the street. He didn't want to admit it but he was right. "Syd, it's nothing to be ashamed about. So what you looked at her ass? Big fuckin' deal! There's nothing wrong with looking. Listen...you're not gonna be fucking the women here tonight...you'll be doing the same thing you did back there. Except this time the women will be *naked*!" Sydney remained quiet.

Roland exited the car and closed his door. He turned around and leaned down on the window sill. "Come on, man...live a little. We'll just talk a bit and have a few drinks. I tell ya what...the drinks are on me even! We won't stay too long…I promise I'll get ya home safe to Vicky. What do ya say?"

Sydney thought a moment about what Victoria had mentioned earlier that day. Her words echoed in his mind. *Syd, do you ever think you'll feel like you're missing out on anything?* Sydney took a deep breath and finally looked over at Roland. "OK, let's go."

Roland smiled brightly and yelled out, "Hell yeah! That's what I wanted to hear!" Sydney quickly hopped out of the Miata and followed closely behind Roland.

The two pushed the doors aside and Sydney immediately felt as if he'd been transported to another time. The floor was covered with a bright red carpet and the walls were adorned with bright golden fixtures. Within the center of the room was a wooden stage with a metallic pole in the middle. Above the stage was a large disco ball.

Shangri-La, huh? Whatever… Sydney noticed there was a DJ across the room. He was stood in front of a turn table flipping through a box of records. It looked like he was in the middle of sorting out his set list for the evening.

"Let's get some drinks set up, Syd. What do ya, want?"

"I don't know…surprise me."

"You got it, bro. Why don't you go grab us a seat and I'll bring the drinks."

Sydney walked over to a booth next to the stage and slid onto the cool, red vinyl seat. He leaned back and stretched a moment. *I guess there's nothing wrong with expanding your horizons sometimes…nothing wrong with a little drink and a look…just a look…*

"Here ya go, bro." Roland placed a large glass in front of Sydney with a bright red straw sticking out of it. The liquid within was honey colored.

"What did you order me, man? I just wanted a little drink…I already had that sake earlier."

I'm Floating

"Oh, come on, Syd. This is good shit. This elixir will make ya feel good. Give it a taste."

Sydney grabbed the straw and took a sip. "Pretty good…what is it?"

"Long Island iced tea."

"I've heard about these…never tried 'em."

"Now's your chance. Hold on I'll be back. I gotta take a leak…looks like the show might be starting up soon…hope I don't miss the opening act…"

Sydney continued to sip upon his drink as the lights began to dim and the DJ finally hopped onto the mic. "Good evening gentlemen and welcome to the Sexothèque!! I'm D.B. your *D.J.* and curator of all the hot tunes to match the smokin' hot talent we've got here tonight. First off let me welcome to the stage the delightfully lovely and stunning….Miss Moon…" A moment later D.B. dropped the needle down upon a record filling the room with a loud thumping bass line.

One of the lights from the front of the stage lit up and shone upon the disco ball, casting shards of light in every direction. It was then that a beautiful woman slowly walked out of the shadows from behind the stage. She had lightly tanned skin and short black hair. Other than a cheeky grin upon her crimson lips she was completely nude.

The woman quickly approached the pole within the center of the stage and wrapped her body around it. Sydney stared at her unable to look away. She twirled about several times clasping the pole between her legs and leaning back staring out into the audience…he felt she was staring out at him specifically.

Their eyes met for a moment and under the flashing lights above he became captivated by her stare. An old familiar feeling came over him. He was reminded of the old thunderbolt once again. He couldn't understand it but it was a feeling he very much welcomed. He felt himself being drawn in by her. She began to smile and slid down the pole onto the floor, standing up seductively away from Sydney. She had two dimples staring out at him above her plump behind.

"Whoa! Look at the ass on that one!" Roland yelled out above the loud music. Sydney quickly looked at the disco ball rotating and took a big sip of his drink from his straw as his mouth had become quite dry. "You alright, Syd? You just downed half of your drink in one go!"

He looked down and saw his glass was empty. "Ya mind getting me another, Roland?"

Roland beamed, "Not at all, bro! I'll set ya right up!" He didn't really want another drink but he wanted Roland out of there. Sydney's head felt a little cloudy but he felt good. He looked up and saw the woman was still hanging onto the pole. She held onto it closely as she moved it up and down between her breasts. He smiled and began to laugh to himself. *Damn this girl is somethin' else...*

The music slowly faded as she turned around and cast a seductive look over her shoulder at Sydney. "Here's your drink, Syd," Roland said, placing another tall glass of Long Island iced tea in front him. "Syd...that girl was totally checking you out...and I saw *you* checking her out too...you two were practically *fucking* right in front of me."

Sydney's eyes widened, "You're a funny guy, Roland. I was just watching the show..."

Roland smiled smugly and replied, "Right...So, nothing was going on there?"

Sydney leaned back in the booth and replied, "Not at all."

"So, you wouldn't mind if I invited her over to the table for a bit would you?"

Sydney played it cool, "Go right ahead, bro...we're here for a good time, right? She's all yours." Roland scurried off and left Sydney alone once again. *Why am I feeling nervous*

I'm Floating

right now? The fuck's my problem? Damn it... He quickly downed another big gulp of his drink. He could tell the room was beginning to spin a bit.

"Yo, Syd. I'm back and I have a guest..." Sydney looked up at Roland and standing next to him was..."Syd, allow me to introduce Miss Sharon Moon."

Sydney looked over at her, she was still completely nude. Seeing her up close, Sydney could see all of the freckles upon her shoulders. She gave him the same seductive smile as before. He returned the gesture, smiling brightly and replied, "Hello, Sharon. I'm Sydney Lee..."

Blurs. Blurs of laughter and drink after drink. He stumbled to his feet.

"Looks like you're going home, bro. She'll take good care of you," Roland said, laughing.

In and out of darkness, he felt himself moving but didn't know how.

"Why is it so damn hot?!" he yelled.

"Here, let me get you out of those clothes, Syd."

Sydney laughed and fell back onto a softness. He didn't know how but it felt like a bed. *So tired. Sleepy time,* he thought and smiled. He opened his eyes one more time. It was Victoria he saw, smiling at him. "Goodnight, baby," he said.

"Goodnight, babe."

Sydney's eyes slowly opened and in the glare of cold and truthful sunlight he sat up in bed. His head erupted in a flash of pain. "Christ on a bike!" Sydney's head pounded to the steady beat of his heart. It felt like he'd just gone ten rounds with a mutant alligator. "Too many drinks...they went down easy but man did they ever fuck me up." He tried shaking off the pain and kicked the heavy comforter from his legs, throwing his feet onto the floor.

He began to notice the smell of bacon wafting in the air. The thought of Victoria cooking breakfast made him smile.

She must not be mad at me for coming in drunk last night. At least I got that goin' for me. He tossed the sheets aside and noticed he was completely naked. "Damn, I don't remember getting undressed. What the fuck happened last night...?"

He looked around the room and realized that he wasn't in his bedroom at all. Across the room, under the window, were many stuffed animals of all shapes and sizes. They gazed at him with their accusing eyes. He grabbed a sheet and pulled it over himself. *Just what the fuck happened last night!?*

He got up from the bed and with the sheet still firmly wrapped around himself, slowly opened the door. Thankfully, it opened silently and he began to hear the sound of someone humming a song. He slowly crept down the hallway towards the sound and came to a corner. He ever so slightly peeped his head around it and saw a sight that got his heart racing. Stood in front of the stove was a woman wearing a small white apron. The bow was tied over the two dimples of her behind. As he stood there a board beneath him creaked and she quickly turned around. Their eyes locked and she gave him a grin.

"Good morning. I hope you like your eggs scrambled."

He remained silent a moment and then spoke, "You're Sharon, right?"

"That's right. I'm glad you remembered."

Sydney felt the sheet beginning to slip out from around him. He quickly tightened his grip.

"No need to be bashful around me. I saw everything last night...everything. That makes us even, huh?" she said, turning around and removing the pan from the stove. She quickly plated the food and took the two plates to a table across from the kitchen which sat in front of a dark brown couch. "I've made a strong pot of coffee. That should help your head. I can tell you're in pain, please take a seat."

I'm Floating

Sydney obeyed and slipped onto the couch. He kept the sheet firmly around him. He eyeballed the plate of food. The eggs were fluffy and yellow. Beside the eggs were two crispy pieces of bacon. Sydney had never been fussy on bacon but in that moment they smelled heavenly. Sharon quickly placed a large mug of pitch black coffee next to him. Steam billowed from the top of it and soothed him.

"Make sure you drink all of that and eat your food. I guarantee you'll feel much better."

"Thanks...why aren't you hungover?" Sharon fell onto the empty seat next to Sydney on the couch. He couldn't help but notice her breasts bounce as she did so.

She smiled at him, knowing full well he had checked her out. "Well, we girls can't go overindulging now can we? A lot of bad things can happen that way. A lot worse compared to a guy doing it. I've seen some girls have a few too many. They ended up making spectacles of themselves and getting fired."

"I swear I remember you drinking with me last night..."

"Oh, I was. Just one drink. A virgin piña colada."

Sydney leaned back and let out a laugh. "I see. Maybe I should have had one of those too...then I wouldn't..." His eyes went wide with realization. "What time is it? I should have been home last night! Oh, my God..."

"It's one o'clock and time for lunch...or a late breakfast in our case. Did you have someone waiting for you last night? Was it the girl from your wallet?"

Sydney turned to her slowly. "What were you doing in my wallet?"

"Your buddy Roland and I were checking your pockets for your car keys. I found your wallet and got curious. I saw the photos of you and her. After we found your keys I drove us here."

Sydney stared at the floor a moment. "I need to make a call."

Some Things Last...

"Sure. Go ahead. Your cell phone should be with your clothes in the bedroom."

He felt fear in the pit of his stomach. What was he going to say? How would he explain himself not coming home? He slowly rose from the couch and returned to the bedroom. Sure enough he found his clothes bunched up in a pile by the closet. His phone was in his pants pocket. He punched in the number slowly. Each number hit his ear like a hammer. The line began to ring and after a few moments he heard the receiver being picked up.

"Hello?"

"Vicky? Hey, it's me."

"Syd? Where are you? I've been worried about you!"

He hesitated a moment and answered, "Roland's dad's. Yeah, I'm over at his old man's place! I'm *so* sorry! We got out of that diner *super* late and I didn't want to wake you! So, I crashed here. I just woke up."

The line was silent a moment. "Syd, I was really worried something happened to you. I understand you haven't seen Roland in years but that doesn't excuse you leaving me alone without a word all day! You should have called! ...I don't have time to deal with this. I'm finishing up my project and I'm taking off for King City in a few minutes. I'm gonna spend the night with Alexis and John for my morning class at eight tomorrow. I was hoping we could go in the Miata and put the top down. It's such a lovely day...so much for that. Maybe I'll go and not call *you*. See how you like it."

"Vicky...I'm sorry."

"Sorry isn't a cure all, Syd. I gotta go. We'll talk later..." The call ended and Sydney was left alone in the silence of the bedroom.

He returned to the living room and sat down, his head pounding even harder.

"Is everything alright?" Sharon asked, coming close and placing her hand upon his head. He could smell the faint hint of coconut upon her skin.

"Eh, not really but it could be worse I suppose." He grabbed onto the warm mug of coffee and began to slowly drink it. It was some potent stuff. It gave his system a much needed kick in the ass. "Ah, damn good coffee!"

"Glad you like it. Now, how 'bout those bacon and eggs?"

"Alright!" Sydney said giving her a thumbs up.

"You're pretty cute. You know?" she said with a smile. "You don't have to say it. I know you were watching me last night at the club…"

Sydney finished off his eggs and turned to her. "Well, don't guys check you out all the time? It's kinda your job, right?"

Sharon frowned, "Yeah, but you make it sound dirty when you put it like that. There was just…something special about you."

Sydney began sipping on his coffee again. "Sharon…I…"

"Don't say anything," she said cutting him off, "I know you're involved with someone else. It's a bit silly…but I like you."

Sydney placed his warm coffee mug down onto the table and replied, "You're a nice girl, Sharon. Thanks for the breakfast."

Sharon smiled. "Thanks. I'm quite the chef you know. Don't be fooled by the basic breakfast. I can make breakfast tacos, biscuits, pancakes…all kinds of things. I can also make a mean egg sandwich. Maybe you can try them all sometime?"

Sydney smiled. "Yeah, maybe…"

"Do you need to go? You seem a bit fidgety."

Some Things Last…

"It's just that…you're only wearing an apron…and a tiny one at that. It's a bit…you know."

Sharon looked down and laughed. "I kind of forgot that you were so drunk last night you don't remember these," she said, pointing to her chest.

Sydney laughed and said, "Yeah, I was pretty wasted. I haven't been like that in a *long* time."

"Nothing wrong with having a drink every now and then…especially to loosen up."

"Yeah, I guess so." Sydney leaned back and stretched a moment. "Well, Sharon, I should probably be going."

The light from her eyes began to fade. "Oh, so you *do* need to go? I guess that's to be expected."

Sydney looked at her and saw she looked quite forlorn. "Hey, don't look that way…I…don't actually have to go home for a while yet."

Sharon perked up and slowly smiled. "Really? Then how about we go out? There's this lovely park around the corner from here. They have these ducks that I sometimes go to feed…"

Sydney smiled, "Sure. But we gotta get dressed first. As much as the ducks might like your apron full of bread the police might frown upon it." Sharon laughed and they both got up from the couch.

Sydney threw on his wrinkled set of clothes from the night before. His clothes certainly matched the way he felt, although his head had finally stopped pounding. He exited her bathroom and found Sharon standing by the door. She was wearing a black cardigan with a white t-shirt underneath and a bright red pair of pants.

"Are you ready? Follow me!" she said, excitedly. It was a bit strange seeing Sharon fully clothed. He felt the two of them had done things backwards. He had seen her naked first and then clothed.

I'm Floating

He followed behind her into the cool, hallway outside of her apartment, turning around he saw the bronze numbers '710' upon her door. A low hum filled the air outside of her apartment. It was a bit unsettling. She lead him down the hall to the elevator and she pressed the call button. A moment later the doors opened and they both hopped on. She quickly pressed 1 and the elevator slowly descended the building.

"You're pretty high up. I never bothered looking out the windows."

"Yep, I like it up there. I have a lovely view. Especially of the sunrise."

The elevator came to a halt and slowly opened again. Sydney stepped out onto the reflective linoleum surface of the apartment's lobby. His footsteps echoed along with her's as they exited the building and into the warm afternoon air which permeated outside.

Sydney followed Sharon around the block to a lovely park with a small pond in the center. Along the border of the park was a walking track and several benches and a set of swings. They took a seat upon one of the wooden benches.

"Watch this…" she said, producing a few pieces of bread from the purse hanging from her shoulder. Sydney could see three brown ducks on the opposite side of the pond floating about, minding their business.

As soon as she dropped the pieces of bread the ducks quickly came flying over to them. They eagerly ate up the pieces and eyeballed Sharon for more.

"Looks like they remember you," he said, smiling.

"Oh, yes. They certainly do. Here, throw them some!" Sharon handed Sydney a few pieces of bread and he tore them into smaller pieces. He tossed them out to the ravenous ducks and they quickly devoured each piece. They eyeballed the two of them wanting more. Sydney held his hands up to signify he had nothing left. After a few moments they waddled back to the pond and left the two alone.

"Hungry little guys, huh?" Sydney said, laughing. "This is a nice little park. Great to have it so close to your apartment too."

"I like to come here to think."

Sydney looked ahead of them at the pond. Several trees had grown on the banks of the pond and their roots were springing up out of the water. A light breeze began to jostle the leaves overhead causing a few brilliantly colored leaves to come gently floating down. One of them landed right at their feet. Sharon reached down and picked it up. She stared at it a moment and smiled.

"How lovely. Autumn is definitely my favorite time of the year. What about you, Syd?"

Sydney looked at the bright red leaf in her hands and nodded, "I don't know…I think summer might be mine."

"Summer?" Sharon said, scrunching up her nose, "I hate summer. I hate the heat and feeling the sun beating down on me. I'm already tan enough…I hate my skin. I wish I were paler…"

Sydney frowned, "There's nothing wrong with your skin. I like it."

Sharon looked away, smiling. Sydney could see she was blushing a bit.

"So…what's up with all the stuffed animals in your bedroom?" he asked, wanting to change the subject.

Sharon smiled, "Aren't they the cutest babies you've ever seen? I've been collecting them since I was a child. The oldest one I have is Chomper. The little purple dinosaur. Did you see him?"

Sydney thought a moment and replied, "Yeah, I believe I did. When I woke up I saw all of those eyes staring back at me and I'll admit I wasn't expecting all of these things to see me naked."

I'm Floating

"They're BABIES! Not *things*!"

"Right...I'm sorry," Sydney said, surprised at her outburst.

"You don't think I'm immature do you? For still having my babies?"

"No, of course not. It's nice to have sentimental attachments...they're cute," Sydney replied.

"I'll have to introduce you to them all," Sharon beamed.

"I'd like that," he added with a smile. "Care to go for a walk around the pond?" Sydney asked.

"Sure, it really is nice out today. It feels so warm but the trees have ignited in a burst of color. You never get that with summer. Just green. It gets to be a bit boring. I love the yellow leaves."

"Oh, really? Why's that?"

"Because yellow's my favorite color."

"Makes sense," Sydney said keeping pace beside her as they traversed the walking path around the pond.

"So, how did you enjoy your Thanksgiving?" Sydney asked.

"It was alright. I visited my family in King City. We usually meet at my grandmother's house and have the usual. I'm a bit of a picky eater so I just have turkey and mashed potatoes. Oh, but the rolls are my favorite part...especially fresh out of the oven."

Sydney couldn't deny that. "Oh, yeah...rolls are my favorite too."

"So, what did *you* do for Thanksgiving?"

"I went over to my aunt's house and had supper with my folks and my cousin Al."

"What about the girl from your wallet? She was there too, right?" Sydney turned and looked out at the pond. He could see the ducks floating along on the opposite shore. "Maybe, I shouldn't have asked about her."

Some Things Last...

Sydney quickly looked over at Sharon and replied, "It's alright. Yeah, she was there too."

"I figured...Is your cousin like you? Does he like to party?"

Sydney burst into a fit of laughter, "*Al? Party?* Now, that's funny. Those two just sound out of place in the same sentence. He's about as far away from that as you can get really."

The two of them continued around the park talking and getting to know one another a bit and time quickly passed as it does. Before they realized it, the sun was setting and the parks lights began to spring to life.

"Looks like the night is upon us," Sharon said.

"Yeah, I guess so..."

They retraced their steps in the gathering gloom back to the front entrance of Sharon's apartment complex.

"Well, this is me...and this is me," she said, pointing to herself and forcing a laugh. "The parking lot is around the corner there. You'll find your car in the middle of it..."

"Thanks, Sharon...I had a nice time today. You're a neat girl."

Sharon smiled and replied, "Sydney, I was wondering...How early would you tell someone you cared about them? If someone said they loved you after a first date would you say it back?"

Sydney thought a moment, "Well, I think it'd be a bit too soon to say something like that after a first date..."

Sharon looked at Sydney a moment with a slight smile, "Well, I love you, Syd."

Sydney was taken aback by this. He remained quiet a second and replied, "I...love you too, Sharon."

She lit up and ran for the front door. Before she disappeared inside she turned the same way she did onstage and tossed him a cheeky grin. After that she was gone and Sydney was left with the words still hanging on his lips.

I'm Floating

He sauntered back to his car and slipped inside still in shock of the words that had departed his lips. He sat a moment staring up at the thin crescent moon hung in the sky. *I can't believe she said that...and I said it back...* He started up the engine and took off a moment later.

As he pulled out onto the street beside Sharon's apartment he drove along and slowly recognized where he was in Lando. It came as a bit of a shock to him when he realized that he wasn't very far from his own apartment complex. A few minutes later he pulled into the parking lot of his apartment and parked his car. Victoria's bright yellow Cavalier was nowhere in sight. *Looks like she took off like she said she would...I don't feel like going up to the apartment just yet...think I'll go for a little walk. Clear my mind.*

As he hit the streets, a cool breeze jostled his hair and chilled him a bit. He buttoned up the black blazer he had been wearing and already felt warmer. By now, the sun had long since set and Sydney noticed the stars hanging high overhead. A few thin clouds slowly passed in front of the crescent moon.

He continued onward down the block becoming lost in his thoughts. He tried piecing together what had occurred the night before but became frustrated when he could only recall bits and pieces. *How could I let myself become like that? Damn that Roland...if it wasn't for him I wouldn't be in this mess with...Sharon.* He found himself thinking about her face. He imagined each detail, slowly recreating her within his mind. Her eyes stared back at him with that seductive look.

His cellphone began to ring within his pants pocket, pulling him out of his thoughts. He quickly brought it out and answered it.

"Hello?"

"Syd? It's me."

"Vicky? Hey, I'm glad you called."

"Yeah, I wanted to call before it got too late. I know you have work in the morning…Where are you? Are you outside?"

"Yeah…I decided to go for a little walk."

"Be careful out there. You should be getting back. It's a little chilly tonight."

"I've got a jacket on. I was gonna turn back anyway…I hope you had a safe trip. Sorry again about last night. I'll make it up to you. When are you coming back?"

"I'll be back on Friday, Syd…I really wish we could have had a proper send off. Eh, well, you'll just have to wait for me as punishment…"

"Oh, Vicky…alright. I'll wait then."

"Good. I'm not gonna wait for you though. In fact I have something here to keep me company tonight."

Sydney could hear a buzzing in the background. "Ah, damn it. Don't do me like this, Vicky!"

"You did it to yourself. Goodnight, Syd…be careful getting home. Love you."

"Love you too, Vicky." The call ended and Sydney felt the old familiar tension building within him. He took a deep breath and lightly cursed himself. "This has been some day…"

He turned around and began walking home, trying to distract himself from the thoughts of what Victoria was up too in that moment. He found his thoughts drifting back to Sharon and their parting words once again. *I love you too…I wonder what Sharon's up too tonight?* A moment later his apartment complex came into view and he quickly dismissed the thought. He hurried along and the wind began to pick up. He could feel rain in the air.

The week trekked onward as Sydney went to work and came home to his empty apartment. He tried keeping his mind preoccupied as best he could. He had promised Victoria that he would wait for her to come home on Friday.

I'm Floating

He had a penance to pay which was nothing compared to what it would be if Victoria knew the truth of where he had been that night. He tried not to think about Sharon and their lovely afternoon together, pushing it out of his mind. He found it wasn't so hard at first but Wednesday night came and his cellphone rang again.

"Hello?"

"Hey, baby...you miss me?" Victoria said, seductively into the phone. From the sound of things she was in the middle of what she'd been up too before.

"Vicky...why are you calling me like this? This is torture for me you know that?"

"Ohh, really? I know it is. I bet you want to touch yourself don't you? You better not...you have to wait until Friday," Victoria moaned.

Sydney moved the phone away from his ear and sighed. He could hear her continuing to moan. She was really putting on a show...that made Sydney think of someone else who might be putting on a show tonight. He couldn't listen to this anymore.

"Vicky...I need to go. I haven't been feeling well tonight. I went out earlier for some Mexican food and it's really messed me up..."

Victoria went quiet. "You should have told me right away, Syd. I understand. Hope you get to feeling better..."

"Yeah, me too. Have fun, Vicky. I'll be better by Friday..."

"Yeah...I know. I love you, Syd."

"Love you too, Vicky." He hung up and was left alone wanting to go somewhere but not sure where. He looked at his watch, 9:30 PM. "Fuck it...I gotta get outta here. Think I'll go for a drive."

He ran out to his Miata and hopped in, throwing the top back and feeling the brisk winter night air flow through his

Some Things Last...

hair. He didn't know exactly where he was headed. He drove aimlessly through the city streets.

After a while, he found himself on a familiar street downtown illuminated by the warm neon lights above. They called out to him. *Maybe a drink will help settle my nerves? Just a little drinkie poo and a show...I'm sure Sharon's not even here tonight...* He hopped out of his car and entered into the wall of sound waiting for him as he pushed the doors aside.

When he entered his eyes gravitated toward the stage but Sharon was nowhere in sight, instead a woman with dark ebony skin and an Afro was slowly walking off stage. He headed for the bar and took a seat.

The bartender approached him and asked, "Hey, there. You were in here this past weekend, right? Nice to see you back again."

Sydney smiled, "Yeah, nice place ya got here, uh?"

"Joe, nice to meet ya," he said extending his hand across the bar.

Sydney grasped it firmly. "Sydney. Nice to meet you too, Joe."

"Well, Sydney. What'll it be? Another Long Island iced tea?"

Sydney remembered what happened last weekend and shuddered. "No thanks. How about a...Moscow Mule?"

"Coming right up."

Sydney waited for his drink when someone sat next to him to the bar.

"Hey, sugar. Welcome back."

Sydney turned and saw it was the woman from the stage he'd seen earlier. She was completely nude and sitting with her legs crossed, smiling at him.

"Have we met?" he asked.

"You forget me already, sugar?"

I'm Floating

Sydney began to laugh, "You'll have to excuse me. I was a bit, uh, *fucked up* the other night. Let's pretend I'm *just* meeting you now."

The woman laughed, "Yeah, you certainly were. Sharon and your buddy had to almost carry you outta here. I'm Olivia by the way…and *you* are Sydney."

"I don't remember any of that. Nice to truly meet you Olivia…so, what's Sharon been up too?"

A big smile broke across Olivia's face, "Did you come back for round two? She told me about you guys' date at the park." Joe walked over and placed Sydney's drink in front of him. "Ah, I see…you ARE here for round two."

Sydney laughed, "Maybe…" he replied, playing it cool.

"Well, Syd…you care for a dance?"

Sydney looked over at Olivia and smiled. "Nah, that's OK. Think I'm gonna sip on my mule here for a bit. Take things slow."

"I had to ask, Syd. Joe *is* the boss after all." Olivia tossed a wink at Joe and he smiled in return. "Maybe I'll catch ya later…You've been captured by another girl's wiles." Sydney raised his glass to her and took another sip.

"I couldn't help but overhear you're here for one girl in particular. Sharon will be on in a few minutes if you want to get a seat by the stage."

Sydney smiled, "Thanks for the heads up, Joe. Here's a little something for you." He slipped a $20 bill across the bar.

"Thank you, sir. Please, go ahead." Sydney did just that. Grasping his drink he walked across the club to an open booth beside the stage and slipped into it.

He took another sip on his drink as the lights dimmed and a funky beat filled the air. After another enthusiastic introduction from D.B., Sharon slowly walked out on stage. Sydney sat captivated by her as she did her routine. He hoped their eyes would lock again but he felt she failed to notice him. He finished his drink as he watched her walk off stage and decided to head for the restroom.

I shouldn't be here. This is crazy...I should go home and go to bed. I got work in the morning, he thought, finishing up relieving himself. He washed his hands then decided to head back to his car. He exited the old, white tiled restroom and proceeded to the exit. As he was pushing the door aside, a familiar voice called out to him, "Syd! You're not gonna say hello?"

Sydney turned around to see Sharon standing before him, wearing a smile and nothing more than a pair of red heels.

He returned the smile. "Hey, I didn't think you saw me..."

"Oh, I saw you. It's called playing hard to get. I thought you'd have picked up on that. Instead you were about to leave? Do you have some place to be?"

Sydney waited a second and replied, "No. Nowhere at all."

"How about we have a drink together then?"

The night passed. He spent most of it chatting with Sharon and having a laugh. She stayed by his side the entire time only leaving him to go up on stage a few times for her routine. He ordered a few drinks but eased off the hard stuff. He didn't want to get into the same state he was in before. As he sat, all concept of time was lost. It wasn't until D.B. signed off and the club went quiet that Sydney realized what time it was. He checked his watch and saw it was after five in the morning.

"Holy shit. Where did the time go?"

"Time flies when you're having fun as they say," Sharon said, laughing.

"Guess I gotta hit the road, huh?"

"Well, yes...but why don't you come over to my house...please. We can have some breakfast."

I'm Floating

Sydney thought a moment. *I gotta be at work at eight...I should have enough time.* "Yeah, sure, that sounds good."

"Alright!" Sharon said as she leapt up and ran for the back room.

Sharon emerged about twenty minutes later dressed in a stylish brown leather jacket. "Will you be driving, Syd?"

Sydney laughed and replied, "Yeah, I'm not gonna be passed out in the passenger seat this time. I think I remember how to get to your place from here."

Sydney lead Sharon outside to his car and opened the passenger door for her.

"Thank you," she said slipping onto the passenger seat. He went around and reached for the top, beginning to raise it. "Leave the top down, Syd. I want to feel the wind in my hair." Sydney smiled and obeyed her request. He started the engine and turned the heater on. He could tell Sharon appreciated the gesture. He then quickly took off up the street.

The cockpit of the Miata became quite toasty as they sped through town, heading for Sharon's apartment. The sky became a lovely hue of bluish pink as the sun gradually rose over the horizon. Sydney glanced over at Sharon and saw that her eyes were closed.

"You awake over there?"

Her eyes slowly opened and she smiled at him. "Oh, yeah. I'm not tired. I was just enjoying the ride. I really love your car, Syd. It's very cozy in here."

"That's a nice way of calling it cramped," he said, laughing.

"No, I seriously like it. It's nice being close like this."

He turned into her apartments parking lot and pulled into the same space she had used previously. He killed the engine and Sharon immediately hopped out of the car.

"Brr. It's chilly out this morning. I never really noticed with your heater on."

Some Things Last...

Sydney got out and raised the top, locking it into place. "Yep, once you get driving you get a bit of a bubble going on inside."

Sharon nodded and smiled. "Well, how about that breakfast, mister?"

"Sounds good..."

The two traversed the elevator and stepped out onto the carpeted hallway leading to her apartment. The hallway was bone chillingly cold. Sharon fumbled for her keys in the warm lighting and opened the door. The two slipped inside the dark apartment as Sharon flipped the light switch.

"It'll take a bit for it to warm up in here...let me turn the heat up." Sharon walked down the hallway and moved the dial on the thermostat. Sydney exhaled and could see his breath a bit. He took a seat upon the couch and stretched. He heard a few of his joints pop as he did so.

"I think I might hop in the shower before that breakfast. You can turn on the television if you'd like," she said. Sydney watched as Sharon slowly unzipped her jacket and tossed it next to him on the couch. She turned around and walked up the hallway to the bathroom.

Sydney wasn't very interested in watching television but he turned the old set on. It reminded him of the one he had back in his apartment. This one was slightly larger though. The early morning news was on and weather man had the five day outlook onscreen. Looks like clear skies the rest of the week.

He slowly crept over to the corner and peeped around it. Along the floor leading towards the bathroom door was a trail of clothes. He could hear the water running and steam was slowly billowing out of the slightly open door. He lowered the volume and could hear her singing. He didn't recognize the tune but she sounded lovely.

He stood up and decided to take a peek out of her living room window. Parting the billowy red curtains, he gazed

I'm Floating

out upon the city below. *She wasn't lying. She sure does have a hell of a view from up here.*

"Enjoying the view, Syd?" Sydney quickly turned around and saw Sharon sitting on the arm of the couch, a black towel wrapped around her still glistening body. Sydney's heart couldn't help but skip a beat.

"Uh, yeah. It's quite a view."

Sharon smiled, her brow raising, "You know what else is quite a view?" She stood up and her towel opened, falling gently to her ankles. "How do you like *this* view, Syd?"

Although Sydney had already seen her nude, there was something different about this. There was an electricity in the air. She slowly crossed the room and took his hand. "I know you want me, Syd. Feel how warm I am? My body feels like it's on fire...*Touch* me!..*Feel* me!"

Sydney placed his hand upon her breast and squeezed it softly. She moaned softly in his ear, "Keep going...your touch is driving me crazy." He kept going. Running his hands up to her neck and along her collarbone. "Kiss me..." she pleaded in his ear. Sydney kissed her neck and began to lightly bite her.

"Oh, Syd...Come with me..." she said, stopping him. She grabbed his hand and lead him to her bedroom. Sydney stopped outside of her door.

"I need to use the bathroom real quick."

Sharon kissed his lips lips softly and said, "OK, I'll be waiting..."

He entered the bathroom. His shoes lightly echoed on the hard white tile beneath his feet. He approached the mirror, wiped away some of the fog then looked at himself. *I can't believe this is happening! I should be at home in bed...waiting for my alarm to go off in a bit. Instead I'm here...about to cross a* **huge** *fucking line. Christ, I crossed the line a while back but* this *one...!*

"Syd?! You alright in there?" Sharon yelled out.

"Be right out!"

"Hurry up! I'm waiting…"

I can't do this to Vicky…can I? Victoria's words rung in his mind once again. *Maybe if I do this it'll make me appreciate her more? No, that's just stupid…damn it! I should go…*

A knock came upon the bathroom door. KNOCK KNOCK "Syd? Did you fall in? Do I need to call for the jaws of life?"

Sydney reached over and flushed the toilet and ran the sink a few seconds. He could see her shadow beneath the door. He took a deep breath and opened it.

"Took you long enough. Is everything alright?"

"Yeah, it is…Sharon, I…"

She quickly wrapped her arms around him and kissed him deeply. She pulled him by the arm into her bedroom and shoved him onto her bed. Sydney was taken aback by her forcefulness. She leapt onto him like a feral cat and began to undress him. Sydney found himself going along for the ride and thoughts of Victoria floated away.

Hours later, Sydney awoke to the sound of his cellphone ringing. He found Sharon nestled close to him under the sheets. His arm was around her. Everything came rushing back to him. What he'd done. His phone continued to ring.

Fuck me! What if this is Vicky? Did she come home? Is she looking for me? What time is it? What day is it? He leaned over and reached for his pants beside the bed and retrieved his phone from his pocket. He answered it and brought it to his ear.

"Hello?"

"Syd? Where are you, my son? It's bloody lunch time and you never showed up!"

It was Waylon! Sydney had forgotten all about going to work.

I'm Floating

"Waylon, oh, I'm so sorry. I...was ill last night. Food poisoning...was hoping it was gonna pass off but no such luck yet."

"Oh, damn. Where'd you pick that up to?"

"That new Mexican place in town."

"Right on...I'll have to avoid that place. Should have just gone down to Q.L.'s and ordered a dinner all legs!" Waylon said, laughing.

"Yeah...I wish I would have now. I don't even wanna think about food right now. In fact I think I gotta let ya go. Feeling another wave coming on."

"Alright, Syd. Get to feeling better. If you're still fucked by tomorrow, call and let me know would ya?"

"Will do, Waylon. See ya." He quickly hung up and dropped the phone onto the carpet below.

"Food poisoning, babe?" Sydney turned and saw Sharon grinning at him.

"Yeah...I forgot all about work this morning. I was supposed to be there at eight."

"Are you in trouble?"

"Nah, it's all good."

"Hm, most places you could lose your job over doing that. What is it that you do exactly?"

"I'm a carpenter."

"Still, it seems like you'd get in trouble for not going in and not calling."

"Well, it helps that my boss' sister is my girlfriend."

"Oh...I understand now," Sharon said, growing quiet. Sydney sat up and began to reach for his clothes scattered around the bed.

"Syd? You don't regret what we did do you?"

Sydney slipped his shirt on and began to button it. "...You know I'd never been with anyone besides Vicky before. You're the only other girl I've been with."

"OK, but do you regret it? I know I was a bit forceful. I just feel this connection to you. I can't explain it."

Sydney sat on the edge of the bed. "No, you didn't force me to do anything. I made that choice. I felt something too…and I didn't regret it."

Sharon leaned across the bed and wrapped her arms around Sydney. "Good. I'm glad. Since you don't have to worry about work today, why not stay for lunch? I'll make us some chicken alfredo."

"I could go for a bite to eat. Can I help?"

"Sure! Let's do it!"

After lunch Sydney said his goodbyes to Sharon. She hugged him tightly as he left. When he made it back home he felt as if he'd been gone for a week or more. The place was exactly how he'd left it. It was dark and the apartment was silent. A part of him wished Victoria had come home a day early. He wouldn't be seeing her until the following day though.

"So what next?" he spoke, shattering the silence. Sydney walked over to his old television set and pulled the power knob. The screen remained black. "Oh, come on." He pushed it back in and tried again. Still nothing. He checked the power cord and saw that it was firmly plugged into the wall. He began to slap the sides of it in frustration, gradually hitting it harder.

"Damn it! You've got to be joking. Looks like this thing finally shit out on me…" He took a seat and looked at the old TV and a melancholic feeling overtook him.

He thought about all the good memories attached to the TV, all the movies he and his buddies had watched on it over the years. The last memory he had of it struck him the hardest. He was here with Victoria watching The Godfather. Tears began to fill his eyes. He wiped them away and fell onto his side on the couch, turning inward away from the TV. He drifted off to sleep and slipped into a dream.

In the dream he was lying on the couch watching a movie. Someone was behind him, holding him tightly. He felt it was Victoria but he didn't look behind him. His eyes remained on the screen. On the screen he saw someone driving through empty city streets. He felt his hand being squeezed tightly. "That's a good idea. Let's go for a ride," Victoria said behind him.

He found himself inside the car. It was his Miata. He turned to his left and saw Sharon smiling. She was completely naked. He looked down and saw he was as well. "It's so warm in here. My body feels like it's on fire..." Sydney leaned over and kissed her. He felt like he was on fire too. He felt like they were driving faster and faster. He looked down at the speedometer. The needle was on 100 and rising.

"Slow down, Syd! Are you trying to kill us?!" He looked over. Victoria was beside him. She wasn't naked instead she wore her pajamas.

"Hey, I bought the whole speedometer and I'm gonna damn well use it!" he yelled over the wind. She leaned over and slapped him.

He looked back and saw Sharon sitting in the passenger seat again, laughing. "Oh, God, Syd. Don't slow down. God, YES!!" She yelled out as did he as the Miata burst into flames.

"Syd? Syd!? Wake up!"

His eyes flew open and he was thrust into the here and now. He began to cough and fell off of the couch.

"V-Vicky!? What-what are you doing here!?"

Victoria helped him to his feet. "I live here last time I checked! I just got back and saw you kicking and screaming in your sleep. What the hell were you dreaming?"

Sydney calmed himself and realized it had gotten dark outside. "Now, it's dark...when did that happen? What day is it?"

"It's Thursday night. It's after seven. I came home early, Syd. I missed you. I wasn't expecting to find you like this. That Mexican *really* fucked you up."

"Yeah...I feel terrible. I'm burning up. Why is it SO HOT!?" Sydney yelled, ripping his shirt off.

"Come along, Syd...you need to get into bed. My God you *are* burning up!" She tucked him into bed and he gradually fell back to sleep. Mercifully, he didn't dream anything else.

The weeks of December ticked on by. Sydney continued to visit Sharon at the Sexothèque every opportunity he got. He began to develop a fine balance between his two lives. Monday through Wednesday night he'd be with Sharon and each morning he'd clean himself up and drag his ass to work. It caught up with him a few times. Most notably when he gave his thumbs a good whacking with a hammer. He'd take naps on his lunch breaks some days. He began to wonder how long he could juggle the two. What was interesting was Sharon knew full well that Sydney had a girlfriend. At first it seemed she didn't mind it...but when Victoria finally wrapped up her finals for the semester, Sydney couldn't exactly visit her as he had done during the previous weeks.

He drove to King City to pick up Victoria at John and Alexis's apartment and ended up staying at their place for an entire weekend. Monday arrived and they left bright and early. On the drive back to Lando, Victoria surprised him by revealing she had booked a hotel room as an early Christmas gift to him.

"I want us to make up for lost time, Syd. Those finals really got me pent up. We hadn't had much luck these past few weekends, huh? What with you getting the flu and me stressed out over my finals. ...I really want you to give it to me...I want you."

You would think Sydney would have felt the same...the problem was he wasn't exactly pent up. The past few weeks sex had flowed like the alcohol he'd been imbibing.

As soon as they entered the room, Victoria slipped out of her clothes and beckoned him to the bed. She took great

I'm Floating

pleasure in teasing him believing that he'd been totally celibate. Even though he had far been celibate, it had been since Thursday morning that he'd bid farewell to Sharon. Victoria had no idea about Sydney's escapades. He played the role of the tortured to a T.

After their marathon love making session came to an end, Sydney stepped out to get some ice as Victoria ordered room service. He made it to the ice machine and placed the dark brown, plastic container under the dispenser. Before he pressed the button, however, he wanted to place a quick phone call. He slid his cellphone out of his pocket and input the numbers for Sharon's apartment. He noticed it was after noon and figured she should be awake.

"Hello?" Sharon spoke softly into the phone.

"Hey, babe. Long time no hear," he said forcing a laugh.

"Syd? I wasn't expecting you to call. Where are you? Why don't you come over?"

"I can't do that today, Sharon…"

"Why not? Are you working?"

"No…I'm out."

"Out?" The line went quiet. "You're still with her? I thought you said you would be free today."

"I thought I was going to be. She surprised me with a trip to a hotel in town."

"A hotel? Must be nice…I'd like to be taken to a hotel. Taken *anywhere* really! It feels like the only place I see you is down at the club or here in my apartment!"

"Sharon…"

"I was waiting for today. You said you'd take me out for a drive this afternoon! Was that just talk?"

"No, it wasn't."

"Did you fuck her, Syd?" He remained silent. "You don't have to say it. I know you did. I'm going. Enjoy your Christmas."

"Wait!"

"Don't call me back. I'm going to my families place in King City for the week. Bye." She hung up and the line disconnected.

He stood in the small room for a moment contemplating calling her back but instead deleted the call log and filled the container to the top with glistening ice cubes.

When he returned to the room Victoria questioned him on why it took so long. "There was a bit of a line. I had to wait for like three people to get ice." She shrugged it off and Sydney saw that their food had arrived while he was out. He sat down across from her and smiled not missing a beat.

Christmas passed and Sydney heard nothing from Sharon. He could have cut her loose but those eyes of her's kept piercing his thoughts. He had it bad for her. He decided he'd pay her a little visit on New Years Eve. Bring her some flowers and chocolates. It felt a bit cliché but he thought she'd see he felt sincerely bad for being absent for so long. The problem was how was he going to get away from Victoria long enough to do it?

The sun had quickly disappeared outside of their apartment window. Sydney could already hear pops and explosions in the distance from people setting off fireworks. He lied back on the couch watching the brand new television set his parents had given he and Victoria as a Christmas gift.

"Man, I don't think I could ever go back to that other TV of yours, Syd," Victoria said, as a commercial came on the screen for a local campground.

"Come on down to Spud's Cabins by the Lake for a picturesque experience. Located on the scenic banks of Lake Lethe. Enjoy breathtaking sunsets and sunrises right from the comfort of your centrally heated and cooled cabin," the man on the screen said.

"Oh, maybe we can go down there in the spring, Syd? Looks like a nice getaway."

I'm Floating

Sydney smiled and nodded half paying attention to the annoying advertisement, when his cellphone began to ring.

"Ahoy hoy?"

"Hey, Syd. It's your Aunt Milly!"

"Hey, what's going on? You and Al ready for the New Year?"

She sighed and spoke, "Well, Alby hasn't been feeling too well these last few days. I was calling to ask if maybe you could swing by and cheer him up?"

"I'm sorry to hear that. Yeah, I can come over in a bit…" He eyeballed his old television set that he'd placed in the corner. The thing was dead but he thought that Albert might be able to fix it…plus this gave him the perfect opportunity to set his plan with Sharon into motion. "…in fact I have a little gift here for him. I'll bring it by too."

"Oh, you're a real sweetheart, Sydney. Victoria's a lucky lady."

"…Right. I'll see you soon, Aunt Milly."

"What's going on, Syd?" Victoria asked, concerned.

"Oh, it's Al. His mom called and asked if I could drop by for a while. I'm gonna grab my old TV and bring it over to him…he's got all kinds of books over there. Maybe he can breath new life into it…"

"OK, Syd. Just make sure you get back before it gets late. I wanna watch the ball drop with you."

"I wouldn't miss it for the world, honey." He walked across the room and gave her a kiss then picked up the heavy TV and carried it in his arms to the door. Smiling, he entered into the chilly evening air outside his apartment door and minutes later was heading for Albert's house.

Wrapping up his brief visit with Albert, Sydney stopped off by Food Paradise and snagged a box of chocolates and a bouquet of flowers. He then rushed over to the Sexothèque and could hear the place thumping before he pulled up. It sounded like a rager of a party inside already and it was only seven o'clock.

He exited his car, chocolates and flowers in tow. He felt a little embarrassed bringing this stuff in with him but he pushed the doors aside and entered into the humid atmosphere of the club. Looking around he didn't see Sharon.

He approached the bar and Joe sauntered up with a grin.

"Evenin', Syd. Lookin' for Sharon?"

"Yeah, Joe. You know it. Where's she at?"

"She took the night off. Said she wasn't feeling too well. Think it's this flu bug going around."

"Oh, yeah...I picked that shit up myself a few weeks back. Think I'll head over and check on her. Thanks, Joe...and happy New Year." Syd slid a $20 bill across the bar with a smile. Joe winked at him and began prepping a drink for a thirsty looking guy at the other end of the counter.

After a quick drive across town, Sydney found himself outside Sharon's apartment building. It was approaching 7:30. He didn't have a lot of time to devote to this so he jogged through the brisk evening air and raced for the elevator.

KNOCK KNOCK KNOCK He pounded upon her door. As he waited for her, he made sure to stand with the flowers and chocolates in each hand and a smile. A moment later the door slowly opened followed by several coughs.

"Syd?" Sharon peeped out at him from a crack in the door. "What are you doing here?" she asked as she slowly opened the door.

Her hair was a mess, her eyes puffy and red, one side of her nose was full of tissues and she was wearing a pair of baggy pajamas. Even in such a state, Sydney wanted to take her in his arms and hold her tightly. He held out his gifts to her, she smelled the flowers and seconds later sneezed all over them, shooting her tissue into the bouquet.

I'm Floating

"Sorry, Syd. I've been really run down today." She grabbed the flowers and placed them in an empty vase beside the kitchen sink. "Could you fill that with water? They're lovely…just wish I could smell them properly."

After watering the flowers, he followed Sharon to her bedroom. She fell onto the bed and coughed.

"I wasn't expecting you to drop by tonight."

"I stopped by the club…Joe said you weren't feeling well. I thought I'd check on you. Maybe make you feel a little better. I've been thinking about you, Sharon. I hope your Christmas went well."

"It was…OK. Christmas was never my favorite holiday. Easter has that honor."

"I'm sorry about last week…"

"Syd, let's not fight about that. I haven't the energy. Would you mind making me some chicken soup?"

"Sure, I'll heat up some."

"And crush the crackers really well too, please?"

"You got it…"

Sydney proceeded to the kitchen. He stepped onto the green and white diamond tiled floor and opened the door to the pantry puling out a can of chicken soup. He emptied the contents into a pan and turned the stove top on.

This wasn't the evening I was expecting, he thought to himself, looking out of the small window above the kitchen sink. The sky was dark but Sydney could make out a few stars. A moment later a large firework burst into life in the distance and gradually faded as it fell towards the ground.

What can I do to make her feel better? It's not like I can take her anywhere in the state she's in right now. I never take her anywhere anyway…that's what she said. He leaned over and dropped the sink plug over the drain then turned on the faucet. Water began pooling at the bottom of the sink. He watched it slowly rise, then an idea hit him. *Wait a minute.* He leaned over and cut the water off. *Holy shit! That's it!*

Some Things Last...

A few minutes later, Sydney returned to Sharon's bedroom. She was lying on her side facing away from him. He could hear her breathing heavily from her mouth.

"Sharon? I've got your soup here and some orange juice." He placed them both onto a small folding table beside her bed.

She slowly turned over and sat up, smiling at him.

"Thanks, Syd. You're very nice."

He shook his head. "No, not really. I feel terrible for not seeing you for so long. That's why I want to make it up to you."

Sharon blew on her soup and ate a mouthful. "Oh? How do you intend to do that?"

A big smile formed upon Sydney's face. "Oh, you know. How about I take you out to this nice campsite on the edge of town and rent us a cabin. It'll be just the two of us."

"Really? What about our jobs How can we both miss work? How will we be able to do that?"

"You can ask Joe for some time off…I'll pay for what you miss down at the club and I have some time I can use. Easy."

Sharon dropped her spoon into her soup and leapt over to Sydney giving him a tight hug. "Oh, Syd! When are we gonna do this?"

He thought a moment. "How about next week?"

"I can't wait! I'd kiss you but I don't want to get you sick too." she said, holding onto him tightly.

The happy moment was interrupted when Sydney's phone began to ring.

"Ah, who's this now? Hello?" he said, placing the phone to his ear.

"That's some way to answer your phone, Syd."

Sydney stepped away from Sharon, his stomach turning into knots. "Hey, Vicky. I wasn't expecting you to call."

I'm Floating

"Why not? It's nine o'clock and I'm over here waiting on you. What's the hold up?"

"Sorry, I lost track of time seeing Al. He's been ill and I wanted to cheer him up a bit."

"You've been over there a while. Is he really that bad?"

"Nah, not really. I just haven't seen him in a while."

"You saw him last week on Christmas, Syd."

"Oh, yeah. Feels longer than that. I'm about to head home. I'll be back soon."

"Alright, tell Albert I said hello. I hope he gets to feeling better."

"Will do. Bye for now, Vicky."

Sydney hung up and turned around seeing Sharon turned away from him once again.

"Sharon? You didn't finish your soup. It's going to get cold."

"I'll finish it…when you leave. You better get back to her, Syd. Wouldn't want to shatter the illusion."

Sydney walked over and kissed the top of her head. "I hope you get to feeling better. I promise we'll go out next week…"

"Yeah…OK," she said, softly.

"Happy New Year, Sharon." She remained quiet, the only sound in the room was her labored breathing. Sydney saw himself out and quickly headed home.

He rung in 1998 with Victoria but within his mind he imagined Sharon all alone and sick. He wished he could do more for her. As he kissed Victoria and made love to her later that night, the feelings of guilt began to fester within himself. The thought of taking Sharon out to that cabin by the lake brought him a feeling of shame but at the same time a slight bit of comfort as he drifted off to sleep.

The week went by at a leisurely pace as Sydney chipped away at planning his little getaway with Sharon. He was relieved to have Victoria going back to her classes the

Some Things Last...

following week. The spring semester had arrived and Sydney relished in the thought of being left alone as he had been weeks before.

As they sat to their dining room table having breakfast Sydney said, "Well, the winter break didn't last too long did it? At least we got to make up for that time after Thanksgiving."

"Yes, we did. I'm gonna miss spending as much time here...but after this semester I'll only have one year left. We can make it, right?"

Sydney reached over and took her hand.

"Of course we can," he said, squeezing it tightly.

"I was thinking, Syd...that maybe I could stay with John and Alexis during the week...I could come back here Friday and spend the weekend with you. Would that be too hard for you?"

Sydney sat a moment thinking of how that played out for him over the past month.

"Vicky, if that would be easier then I can wait for you."

Victoria walked over, kissed and hugged him tightly. "I thought you'd say that. You're the best, Syd." Sydney forced a smile and hugged her again.

She soon got dressed and after a bit of a tearful goodbye, headed off for King City.

So, there Sydney was...alone again in the apartment with a semester stretched out before him. He fell back onto the couch and started laughing.

Looks like I won't have any problem taking Sharon down to the cabin. I think we'll head out on Wednesday. He noticed the time and quickly hopped up. *Shit, gotta get to work. Today and tomorrow...then Wednesday is Sydney's time!*

Sydney awoke early on Wednesday morning. He'd already packed everything he'd needed the afternoon before and informed Sharon to be ready at eight because he'd be by to pick her up. He quickly showered, got dressed and took everything out to his Miata. Before hopping in he quickly threw the soft top back and then took off for Sharon's place.

A few minutes later he pulled into her apartment complex and found her waiting for him. It was a bright and unseasonably warm January morning.

He pulled up beside her and said, "Hey, baby, you wanna ride?"

She started laughing at him, "Yeah, you going out towards the lake?"

"It's your lucky day, honey. Hop in."

"Can you pop the trunk, Syd? I wanna put this stuff back there."

"What did you bring along, Sharon?"

"I brought us some food along for later."

Sydney reached over and opened the center console and pulled on the lever, opening the trunk. She quickly placed the bags she'd brought along inside and closed it. She hopped in and Sydney revved the engine.

"You ready to have some fun, babe?"

"Oh, yeah. Let's hit it, Syd!" Sydney sped off out of the parking lot as Sharon screamed in delight.

Driving along down the highway leading to the edge of town they passed through a tunnel cut through the side of Murphy Mountain which overlooked Lando. Sydney turned his lights on and the pop ups sprung to life. Sharon let out another scream which echoed in the tunnel. Sydney honked the horn several times before they passed through the tunnel and back into the daylight.

They pulled over at a rest stop overlooking the city and Sydney checked his map.

"How much further is it, babe? Aren't we supposed to be going towards the lake? The lake is over there!" Sharon, said pointing across the vantage point.

Some Things Last...

"Yeah...I think I took a wrong turn somewhere. Wait, this road here can get us back on track. It says it's a private road though."

"We're wasting our day, Syd! Let's take that road. It'll be fine." They hopped back in and took off up the road a piece and then turned left onto a bumpy unpaved road.

The road was rough to drive on and Sydney had to dodge large potholes but they continued onward.

"Stop the car, Syd!"

Sydney hit the breaks and came to a stop.

"What? What is it?"

Sharon hopped out of the car and ran over to the side of the road where Sydney saw several baby sheep. He parked the car and got out to join her.

"Aren't they just the sweetest things you've ever seen?" Sydney was amazed at how soft and fluffy they all looked. Their wool was so pristine and white. As she knelt down kissing one of the babies a larger gray sheep came running up.

"Wow, look at that big fella," Sydney said. This sheep began running around after the baby sheep. A few minutes later a few other larger sheep joined in the fun.

"You think that sheep are calm but they're not. They're playing just like dogs. Look at that!" Sharon said in amazement.

Sydney couldn't help but feel amazed watching them too as the larger ones jumped off of tree stumps and soared through the air. A few of the big sheep began head butting one another.

"Too bad we don't have any food for them," Sharon said, a bit sad.

"Yeah, maybe we can come back up here another day. Swing by the grocery store and pick up some carrots or something."

I'm Floating

Sharon smiled, "That sounds fun, Syd. Well…we better be heading on. We don't want our picnic lunch to spoil."

"Picnic lunch?" Sydney said, surprised.

"Yep, you'll just have to wait and see…"

They returned to the car and slowly took off. Sharon turned around watching as the sheep continued to play. Sydney watched too through the rear view mirror until they disappeared around a corner.

A few winding turns later upon the unpaved road and they were back to smooth driving again. After another short drive through the scenic outskirts of Lando, Sydney noticed the lake alongside of them. He was a bit relieved to see the entrance of the campground on the right and slipped down the road and into the shade the tall pine trees provided.

He pulled up to the main office, which looked like a combination of a general store and bait and tackle shop.

"I'll go and pay for the cabin. You wanna come in or wait out here?"

"I'll come in, Syd. Doesn't look like too many people are here today."

"No, thankfully it's the off season, babe."

Sydney hopped out of the car and ran over and let Sharon out. She smiled at him as she slowly rose from her seat.

He grabbed onto the cold handle of the glass door and a sticker upon its surface caught his eye.

KEEP IT WET

Oh, I certainly plan to… he thought as a mischievous grin formed upon his face.

"What are you smiling like that for?"

"Oh, nothin', babe."

"You look like you've got something on your mind."

Before Sydney could reply a loud voice cut through the quiet of the shop.

"Good mornin'! What can I do ya for?" a large man said from behind the counter. He was wearing a red flannel shirt and jeans. If he'd had a great big bushy beard Sydney would of taken him for a stereotypical lumberjack but alas his face was as smooth as a baby's bum.

"Hey, are you Spud?" Sydney asked.

"That I am! How can I help you?"

"Well, I wanted to rent one of your cabins."

"Ah, I hear ya, sir. A little getaway for you and your girlfriend here?"

"Yeah, that's right," Sydney said as he put his arm around Sharon. "Saw your commercial and it looked like a nice place to take her."

"Well, at least someone did! Maybe I'll get my money back on it yet." Spud reached under the counter and produced two sets of keys. "Here you two go. These keys open the front and back door. You'll be in cabin 14 which is our most popular one overlooking the lake. You're in for a great view this afternoon and tomorrow morning…if you're awake," Spud said, smiling.

Sydney sorted out the bill and met Sharon outside.

"Alright, we're good to go."

"So…I'm your girlfriend now?"

Sydney smiled. "What else could I call you? We're not married. You're not a booty call."

"Oh, really? I've felt that way a few times."

"Do you feel that way today?"

Sharon went quiet then answered, "No, I don't."

"Good. Let's enjoy the day, babe. You heard the man. We have the best cabin here. Although, I already have the best view right here."

Sharon leaned over and pushed, Sydney playfully. "Stop. You're crazy."

They drove along down the small two lane road which lead to several of the cabins until they came to a fork in the

I'm Floating

road with a sign. They turned left following the sign which pointed towards cabins 14-20. They continued and passed by several cabins and then found a road which lead to cabin 14.

"We're gonna be by ourselves out here," Sydney said.

"Good. I can kill you without any witnesses," Sharon said softly.

"What?"

"Nothing, babe. Oh, look there it is!"

Sydney approached a large cabin which certainly lived up to the hype Spud had given it. He parked in front of the place and killed the engine. He sat a moment looking up at the cozy place before him.

"Let's go inside!" Sharon said, excitedly.

He fumbled for the key and then brought it to the lock. Hearing the lock turn he pushed the door slowly and it opened with a soft creak. The inside of the bottom floor was bathed in early morning sunlight. Stepping into the great room, Sydney felt it was a good twenty degrees warmer inside. As his eyes adjusted to the bright light he could see all the amenities of home had been provided; a comfortable couch, small kitchen set up with a stove and sink, a fridge and even a small television set. Although, Sydney felt they wouldn't be having much use for the TV.

"Look here, babe!" Sharon said as she opened and looked inside of a door next to the kitchen area. "It's a little bathroom. We have nice little shower in here and a little window looking out on the banks of the lake."

Sydney entered the cramped bathroom and peeped out of the shower. Sharon was very close to him and he could smell her perfume. He couldn't help kissing her neck and nibbling on it a bit.

"Syd...later, OK? Then afterwards you can scrub my back in here...among other things."

Sydney smiled, "Alright, I'll wait. Let's take a look upstairs."

They entered the great room again and walked over to the stairs across from the couch.

"After you, babe," Sydney said.

"Syd…are you gonna eyeball my ass as I walk up the stairs?"

"What? I would never…In fact I'll wait here on the couch as you walk up first," he said, shocked.

"If you did I wouldn't mind…but alright you're loss."

Sydney's face dropped as she quickly traversed the stairs, stopping halfway up to stick her tongue out at him. *That little…damn, she's cute*, he thought.

He quickly followed behind her and discovered her sprawled like a giant starfish out on the large bed in the loft above.

"This bed is so comfy, Syd. Come join me."

He jumped onto it and quickly discovered it was a water bed.

"Whoa! What the hell? I wasn't expecting this!"

"I wasn't expecting you to jump onto the bed like a dog either! Calm down, Syd! I'm not even naked yet!"

A minute later the waves finally calmed and the two of them lie there together holding one another.

"This is nice," Sharon said, "We haven't gotten the chance to just lie next to one another and talk."

Sydney took a deep breath and exhaled. "Yeah, come to think of it…I don't know all that much about you, Sharon. Besides your name and where you live."

"No…I suppose you don't…I could say the same to you but I did look at your license. So, I know when your birthday is," she said, forcing a laugh. "What would you like to know?" she asked.

"Well, for starters…when's your birthday?"

"July 27th…1976."

"You're a little younger than me. Where are you from?"

I'm Floating

"Lando. My folks are originally from here...but I moved to King City to live with my grandmother when I was around five."

"Brothers and sisters?"

"Yeah, I've got an older sister."

"So..."

"Syd...I don't wanna get into my family too much right now. Hey! Let's go down and get our lunch! I made us a nice spread. We can go out beside the lake!"

Sharon quickly got up and raced down the steps leaving Sydney alone before he knew what was happening.

"Guess we're having lunch now...well, I am a bit hungry."

Sharon refused to tell Sydney what she had made until they reached the picnic table behind the cabin. It was positioned on a deck slightly above the lake. She told Sydney to close his eyes and when he opened them he saw that she had indeed brought along quite a spread. She had placed in the center an entire grilled chicken. Surrounding it were biscuits and some macaroni and cheese.

"Lunch is served!" she said with a big smile.

"Wow, this is amazing! You made all this yourself?"

She nodded and grinned.

"You're quite the chef!"

"Here you go, babe...you can have the legs."

Sydney laughed as he grabbed the plate from her.

"Well, let's dig in!"

Sydney slapped his stomach and exhaled loudly.

"Man, that was delicious, babe! You really did a great job."

Sharon giggled and answered, "One of my many talents. If you came 'round every night we could eat like this all the time."

Some Things Last...

"I'd get fat if I did that," he said, seeing Sharon's face drop. Sydney knew he said something wrong. "Sharon...would you like to see me eat a fork?"

"What?" she said, completely taken aback.

He held up one of the silver forks with his right hand and with his left hid it within his hands. It appeared as if he'd swallowed it. Sharon began to laugh at his foolishness.

"Hey, how about we go for a walk? I see a walking trail over there beside the water. Let's see where it leads!" she said.

Sharon walked off toward the head of the trail, skipping along as she went. Sydney could feel she was masking some sadness welling up with her. He left their paper plates on the table and thought they'd clean up when they returned. He quickly jogged to catch up with her.

The two walked along the dirt trail beside the glimmering water of Lake Lethe. The sun hung slightly overhead. Sydney looked upward through the jagged branches of the many pines above. The needles moved aimlessly in the light breeze which blew across the lake. Although the temperature was quite warm out for early January, the wind which blew from the lake held a hidden kiss of the wintry air that was sure to come.

"It really is nice out today. You couldn't have chosen a better day for us to be out here," she said.

Sydney smiled and put his arm around her.

"Syd, have you seen my sneakers? I got them especially for today."

He looked down at her fresh white sneakers and nodded.

"I like those shoes," he said.

As they continued along down the trail, birds chirped gleefully in the surrounding treetops.

"Listen, Syd. It's as if the birds are singing just for you and I," she said squeezing him tightly and kissing him.

I'm Floating

They returned to the cabin, slipping out of their clothes as they climbed the stairs to the loft. In the golden rays of the late afternoon sun, it was as if Sharon's body was glowing. Sydney smiled and ran the back of his fingers against her soft cheek. Her skin was on fire. He leaned in and kissed her, softly at first then more intensely.

He took Sharon and made love to her. Their bodies ignited in an explosion of passion he'd not quite felt before. For a brief moment he felt guilty. He'd been with Victoria many times but he'd never felt quite like this. This feeling that enveloped him was something new and wild. As quickly as it came, this feeling of guilt left him as he looked down upon Sharon. Her hazel eyes sparkled in the dimming sunlight just as the surface of the lake had. She had completely given herself to him and he to her. As they reached their climax together they each screamed out and then fell silent. Their bodies hot and wet with sweat. They held each other for a long while as the loft gradually grew darker.

"Syd? Wake up, babe."

Sydney's eyes slowly opened and he saw Sharon sitting beside him on the bed. She was wearing a blue robe with a towel wrapped around her head.

"Did we fall asleep?"

Sharon smiled, closing her eyes at him. "Yep, it's after nine."

"Oh…we should get up."

"Yeah, I took a shower. I thought of waking you but you looked so peaceful."

"Ah, I would have liked to join you."

"It's OK. I was singing anyway. I kinda like to do that alone."

"Oh, alight. I guess I'll hop in there then and maybe we can go for another stroll."

"That sounds fun!" Sharon said, all smiles.

After he cleaned himself up and got dressed he returned to the loft to find Sharon missing.

"Where'd you go, babe?"

He noticed a flicker of light outside of the window and approached it seeing Sharon out back beside a small fire in a pit. He exited the cabin and stepped into the cool night air outside.

"Hey, babe! I found some wood here and some matches inside and got this fire going while you were showering. I thought it'd be romantic. It's nice and warm around the fire." Sure enough it was pretty warm.

"This is nice. Are you ready for that stroll? You're still wearing your robe...I see you put your new sneakers back on though."

She smiled at him, "Yes, my robe is fine. The fire made me toasty...let's go, Syd."

They returned to the trail beside the lake and held each others hands tightly. The wind had picked up a bit from earlier but Sydney felt comfortable. The fire that Sharon had built had warmed him all over. The wind felt refreshing as it blew through their hair. They stopped at a bend in the trail which lead out onto a small beach.

"Let's check this secluded beach out, babe!" Sharon said, stepping off of the pathway onto the sandy shoal.

Sydney followed and stood next to her upon the banks. They stood in silence staring out at the quarter lit moon which hung low over the water. Its image became distorted upon the surface of the lake as the wind blew waves across it. Sydney jumped slightly as he heard an owl in the tall branches of a nearby tree call out into the night. Sharon began to laugh and moved closer to him. She began to hug him. He put his arm around her and kissed her head.

"I had a lonely childhood, Syd," Sharon spoke, shattering the silence. "My mother and father separated. He left my mother and moved out west. I haven't seen him since the day he left. I'm not even sure where he is."

Sydney listened closely. He felt she had more to say.

"My Mama was shattered when it happened. She entered into a great depression. That's why the three of us left here and went to King City. We went to my grandmother's to live because she couldn't cope being on her own with me...I was a very naughty little girl. I wasn't easy to deal with...my father could put me in my place but she never could figure out how to do it. Maybe, I helped put her in that state of mind...either way we moved in with my grandmother. I left all of my friends behind and knew no one. The school I went to was so BIG and no one wanted to deal with the spastic new girl...My sister is ten years older than me. She was already in high school. I tried making friends but it was so hard. Most of the kids just made fun of me...especially when they found out the state my mom was in."

Sharon continued looking down. Sydney could see tear drops reflected in the pale moonlight, falling onto the sand below.

"My mother...she never recovered from what happened. In the end she wasted away...unable to get up and do anything...I think my parents had me as a last ditch attempt at working things out...if that's true...I wish I'd never been brought into this world."

Sydney couldn't keep silent any longer.

"No, Sharon, that's wrong. You're a lovely girl...and despite all those hardships you still remain bright and cheerful. Your dad might have fucked off but damn it that's his loss. He's a coward."

Sharon began to sob. "My sister left me too. She graduated and entered the air force. I think she did it to get away from everything. I thought about that too...but I couldn't muster the courage...I somehow found myself coming across an ad in the King City News for a new club opening here. The pay was great. I just had to show some skin. I thought it'd be a great chance to make a new persona for myself. A confident and sexy one. I'm happy that I did it now…because I met you."

"Me too," Sydney said, softly.

"Would you ever leave me, Syd? I LOVE YOU SO MUCH! I'm lucky to have you, baby, and I'm so glad we met. Please stay with me forever. I want you. I need you. I love you!"

Sharon began to cry again. She sobbed onto Sydney's shoulder. He remained quiet as she let it all out. He could tell that this was something she had been carrying deep within herself for a long time.

He ended up carrying her back to the cabin. She cried so much that she hadn't the energy to walk back. He carried her upstairs and tucked her into bed. After kissing her head, he returned downstairs where he fell onto the couch and looked up at the ceiling fan above. The light was bright and warm.

He felt himself gradually slipping away and almost felt as if he were floating. "Daddy!" He thought he heard a voice call out but it was distant and wasn't that of Sharon's. He drifted off into a deep sleep. He happily let it take him away.

PART III

ILLUSION OF HAPPINESS

CHAPTER 15
Espers

He felt himself drifting through that blinding light for what felt like eons and no time at all. He felt carefree…It was a feeling that he'd not felt in such a long time. It felt quite foreign to him but the light persisted. He felt as if he weren't alone. Someone was with him guiding him to a better place.

"Here you go, babe. Get some rest. You'll need it for tomorrow."

He smiled and the light gradually began to fade to black. He blissfully slept until he found himself awoken to the cheerful chirping of birds. His eyes slowly opened and began to focus. He slowly raised his head from his pillow and a steady throbbing began to plague him.

"Ah, damn it…what's this pain I'm feeling?" he muttered as he returned his head to the billowy soft pillow. Bits and pieces began to slowly come to his mind. He recalled throwing back quite a few drinks the night before.

"Oh, yeah…I remember now. Guess I'm not a young man anymore…the hangover finally found me."

He felt a bit warm and kicked the comforter from his feet and realized he was still fully dressed.

"What the…wait a minute…where am I?"

He threw his feet over and rose from the bed. His head begged him to lie there still but he had to know what was going on. He grabbed the drapes and cast them open. Within the glare of the cool morning sun just creeping over the horizon he realized he was back in his bedroom…but Victoria was nowhere to be seen.

What the? Did she put me to bed? Christ...maybe she did. I was pretty fucked up last night...but why would she do that? Has she forgiven me? Is this her way of showing she missed me? If so why isn't she here? Oh, for God's sake...my head!!

He took a seat on the side of the bed and held his head within his hands. He sat there listening to the sounds of the birds outside his window. They all sounded so happy and excited. The sun was quickly rising and each passing moment Sydney noticed the room slowly filling with a cool blue glow.

I need some coffee. That'll kill this hangover, he thought as he took to his feet once more and headed for the kitchen.

He entered the kitchen and immediately noticed the coffee pot was missing from the faux wooden countertop.

Vicky must really want me to suffer...what about some headache pills? Time to hit the medicine cabinet. He checked the cabinet over the fridge and found it was completely barren. "What the hell is this? Vicky, I deserve this. I'll just have to endure the pain for you..."

Sydney decided to go into the living room and sit back in the recliner and watch a little TV. He had hoped to find Victoria out there waiting for him but he found the place devoid of life. *Where the hell is she? Did she take off somewhere? I hope she's not at her parents!* He looked out the window and saw that the driveway was empty. *No, no...what about Vivian!? Is she gone too?* He ran down the hall and opened her door to find her room as dark and empty as the rest of the house. He walked over and placed his hand upon Vivian's small twin bed. It was cold. He took a seat and felt overwhelmed.

A moment later he heard a knocking upon the front door. KNOCK KNOCK KNOCK Sydney rushed down the hall to see who it was. He looked out through the diamond shaped window to see a man standing there he didn't recognize. The man smiled and waved. His smile made Sydney feel slightly relieved and he quickly opened the door.

"Good morning, Sydney. I hope you slept well, my friend," the man spoke with a bright smile. He wore a crisp, blindingly white suit complete with matching fedora. He looked almost angelic to Sydney.

"Who…who the hell are you?" Sydney said, staring the gentleman down, suspiciously.

The man began to laugh, "Have you forgotten me that quickly, Syd? Well…I guess I can understand you were a bit inebriated the last time we spoke."

Sydney eyeballed the man a few moments longer and then spoke, "Wait…I remember you now. You were at Joe's last night!"

"I sure was. Lovely place I must say. I really dig the atmosphere there."

"John…right? So…was it you who brought me home last night? Is that why you're here? I mean how the hell else would you know where I live…" Sydney said, feeling a little uneasy.

"I didn't bring you home last night…at least not in the sense that you're thinking."

Sydney wasn't in the mood for riddles, in fact all of this was making his hangover even meaner. "Look I don't know what you're doing here, buddy, but it feels like I've got a room full of monkeys typing the greatest story ever told inside my skull…so…if you'll excuse me…"

Sydney went to close the door and John interjected, "You don't have any coffee, Syd? I was afraid I'd forget something…" Sydney angrily looked at John and said, "What are you getting on with? This is MY damn house. You've never even been here before. How could you forget anything?!"

"I apologize, Syd. May I come in? I can help you get some coffee and I guarantee you'll feel loads better real soon."

Sydney beckoned him inside and John entered, removing his white fedora.

John took a seat upon the recliner and spoke, "OK, Syd...this might sound a bit odd..."

Sydney laughed, "Oh, do go on...I'm used to you sounding a *bit odd* at this point."

"Right. I want you to imagine within your kitchen a coffee pot brewing up a fresh pot right now. Imagine that for me."

Sydney blinked slowly at John. "What good is *that* gonna do? I can't drink imaginary coffee, John!"

"If you imagine it...*will* it to be...it *will* be, Syd. Trust me."

Sydney began to laugh. As strange as it felt, Sydney knew John was being as sincere as ever. "I like you, John. There is no lying in you. Because of that...I'm gonna entertain your foolishness."

Sydney closed his eyes and began to imagine the coffee filling the pot. It streamed into the glass pot, as black as midnight on a moonless night. The best kind to cure this kind of hangover. An aroma began to fill the air. His eyes slowly opened and he looked at John.

"Do you smell something, Syd? Go to the kitchen and check it out," he smiled. Sydney looked suspiciously at John but rose to his feet and slowly followed his words.

As he grew closer to the kitchen the smell grew more potent. He slowly peeped around the corner and saw the coffee maker sitting where it should have been with a freshly made pot beckoning to him.

"What the *hell*? John! What is this?"

John entered the kitchen a moment later and looked at the pot. "Looks like some coffee, my friend." He walked past Sydney and retrieved a glass from the cupboard and filled it halfway with the dark elixir. Sydney watched him bring the cup to his lips and sip it lightly. "Oh, wow. That is delicious...Very good, Syd. Some people have trouble materializing their first time...you've done quite well. Bravo!" John said, clapping.

"Put your fuckin' hands down. What...what the hell *is* this?!"

John smiled, "It's your coffee, Syd. You made it. It's exactly how you imagined it. Go ahead try it," John said, handing him his glass. Sydney took it very gingerly and brought it to his lips. He sipped on it and as soon as it went down his throat he immediately felt better. By the time he finished the glass his hangover had disappeared.

"Feeling better, Syd?" John asked, with that same heartfelt grin.

Sydney laughed, "Yeah, I do! My head is really clear. Now...that that's out of the way...who are you? How...did *that* happen?"

John smiled, "Let's return to the living room and sit down...but first I'm gonna get me another cup of that delectable coffee. Really, well done, Syd."

They returned to the living room and this time Sydney claimed the recliner. He leaned back and said, "Alright, let's hear your story. Just who the hell are you?"

"I'm an emissary from another world tasked to bring lost souls to a better, happier place."

Sydney's eyes, widened. "Oh, God...I knew their was something about you. You really are an angel. I've died haven't I? That's why I'm here. I felt there was something 'off' about this house. Wait...is this Heaven or Hell? This must be Hell...I'm not saved! I remember all those Sunday services as a boy just sitting there when they called for people to get saved! What have I done?!" Sydney began to weep.

"Syd? Syd? Sydney!" Sydney looked up at John and John pet him softly on the knee. "You're not dead, my friend."

"You're just saying that to make me feel better."

John smiled and lightly chuckled, "No...I'm not. I cannot lie, Syd. You weren't wrong about that. We Espers don't understand how to do such things."

"...Espers?"

"That's right. My people have mastered the farthest reaches of our own minds and have in turn been able to reach out past ourselves to help other developing cultures across the cosmos."

"You mean...you're an alien?"

John laughed, heartily. "From my perspective, *you're* the alien, Syd...but for you, yes, I am."

Sydney sat dumbfounded for a spell. John leaned back and sipped on his coffee while Sydney's mind reeled.

"...So, where am I?" Sydney, finally spoke.

"You're within your own slowly developing world, Syd. I'm here to act as your *training wheels* if you will."

"My...my own world?! It just looks like my house to me."

"Yes, your mind constructed this place from your memories and experiences. As time progresses, more will materialize."

"Really? What else can I materialize then?"

"Your imagination is the limit."

"How about my wife and daughter?"

For the first time John frowned. "Materializing sentient objects is an advanced technique that you're not quite ready for, Syd."

"...OK. Well, what about my car then?"

"Hmm, I suppose you could give it a try. A vehicle is a bit of a large object but I have faith that you can materialize it here. Just lean back and focus your mind...think of as many details as possible...the exterior as well as the interior."

Sydney leaned back in the recliner and focused himself as John instructed. He imagined his bright red Miata, imagined its black, vinyl soft top, soft tan carpet and worn tan leather seats. He imagined it sitting outside in the driveway and the sound of its horn.

BEEP BEEP His eyes flew open and he leapt from the recliner and looked out the window. His car gleamed in the bright sunlight. It's headlights were up and Sydney could've sworn it was smiling at him. "Way to go, Sydney, my friend! That's quite the ride you have."

Sydney smiled brightly and then felt his head begin to spin. He fell and John quickly grabbed him. "Oh, I was afraid of this! Materializing such complex objects always exhausts beginner Espers."

"E-Exhausts?"

"Don't worry. You'll be as right as rain after you've had a nice rest." John helped Sydney walk to his bed and allowed him to fall onto it and remove his shoes. "Rest now, Syd. You've had a lot to process today. I'll return tomorrow to check in on you. If you ever need me...just think *JOHN!* real loud. I'll come running. Goodnight, my friend." Sydney closed his eyes and immediately fell into a deep sleep.

Within the depths of his subconscious, he became enveloped in that blinding light once again.

"I've been watching you, babe, for such a long time. Now, we can finally be together again."

"Together again? Who are you?"

"You know me, Syd. Listen to the sound of my voice..." Sydney knew who it was. He had known the moment that he heard the voice calling to him.

"Sharon...it's you. I thought you were lost forever."

"No, nothing is lost forever. Not here anyway. Now...I want you to think of me. Imagine everything about me. I know you remember me. I never left you."

Sydney began to imagine Sharon; her velvety dark hair and how it smelled when he delved his face into it, the sultry gaze of her hazel eyes, her lips and how they parted to reveal a lovely smile, the way that she laughed when he would tickle her sides…He imagined every intimate detail he could gather of her body and of her personality. It was true…she had never left him. For a moment he thought that he should feel guilty of this. "Don't feel guilty about that, babe. You've left all of that behind you. Now, it's just the two of us."

Through the light, he began to see a figure approaching him. As it drew closer the lines grew finer until…"I-It's you!" he said, in amazement.

"That's right! Here I am," Sharon said as she slowly approached him. She was naked with her arms stretching out waiting for him. She was just as he had imagined her. She looked the same as he had last seen her. She hadn't aged a day. Before she… "Let's not think about that, Syd. This is a place for happiness. No more tears."

"You're right. I'm so happy to see you…I never thought I would again."

"Here I am, Syd. Come here."

He approached her and wrapped his arms around her. Her soft breasts pressed into his chest and she began to laugh.

"My God…you're so warm!"

"Did you expect me to be cold, Syd? No, I'm just as I was every time you ever touched me."

Indeed she was. He buried his face in her neck. He could almost feel her pulse as he sunk his teeth into her and began to kiss her. She was alive! Within his arms! Not dead and buried in the ground underneath that red tree. This was real, tangible and hearing her moan his name into his ear pushed any and all doubt from his mind.

He looked over and saw his bed and threw her onto it. She smiled at him…flipped over and got onto her knees, presenting herself to him. Sydney admired the view for a

Some Things Last...

moment. "What are you waiting for? Don't tease me. I've waited far too long for this!"

A smile spread across his face. He felt powerful...in control. Something he hadn't felt since they had been together all those years before. He loved it and he loved teasing her...but more than anything, he wanted to be with her again. He began to make love to her. She screamed in ecstasy when each climax came to her. It was just as it had been back then. Making Sharon feel this way always made Sydney feel like a big man. It came so easily...

The two were a sweaty mess when all was said and done. They both fell onto the bed and breathed heavily...Sydney a bit more so than her. Time had sadly not halted for him.

"I love you, Syd," she said, as she leaned over and began to kiss his chest. "Round 2?" she asked, looking up at him.

He began to laugh, "Sharon...baby. I'm very very tired now. Let's lie here together, OK?" She smiled at him and slowly closed her eyes. He leaned in and placed two kisses upon her eyes.

"Alright, Syd. Let's get some sleep. I bet you *are* tired. You did quite a lot." She leaned over and placed her head upon his chest. "Your heart...it's so soothing..." Sydney closed his eyes and that blinding light faded away.

He awoke the following morning feeling more rested than he had ever felt in his entire life.

"Damn, what an amazing dream," he spoke aloud, looking over to the empty place in bed beside him. "It felt so real..." He leaned over and felt the bed. *Cold...just as I thought. A dream and nothing more.*

He got out of bed and entered the bathroom. He used the toilet and then hopped into the shower. Upon finishing his shower, he stepped out onto the dark brown rug and began to dry himself. He began to notice a delectable scent which was wafting in from under the door. He quickly returned to the bedroom and threw on a pair of boxers and pajama pants and quietly followed the smell to the kitchen.

He could hear the sizzle of meat upon a skillet and someone humming. He approached the corner and peeped around it and what he saw turned his face white. Sharon stood in front of the stove wearing nothing but an apron. She wiggled her behind and those dimples stared out at him. He quickly retreated to his bedroom and closed the door, locking it. He jumped into the bed and covered himself. In the darkness he felt slightly safer until a knock came upon the door. KNOCK KNOCK "Syd? Are you awake in there? Why's the door locked?"

Go away. Lord, just go away. This can't be happening. Silence…Sydney let out a loud breath of relief which was extremely short lived when the blanket was ripped from him and he was face to face with…

"Good morning, babe!" Sharon said, winking. "Did you lock the door by accident? I had to go get a knife and jimmy it open. You know I felt your eyes on me…" Sydney remained speechless. "What's wrong, Syd? Still worn out from last night?"

"Last night?"

"He speaks! Yes, last night. We had quite a reunion did we not?"

"It wasn't a dream?"

"Well, Syd…you tell me? Does *this* feel like a dream to you?" Sharon took his hand and placed it between her legs. He quickly took it back but not before feeling the warmth that emanated from between her silky smooth thighs.

"What the hell? How?"

"This is *your* world, Syd. You really want to question things? You're the king, baby, and I'm your queen."

"But John said I wasn't ready for this!"

"Clearly, he didn't take your feelings for me into account. Here I am. You brought me here, Syd, all by yourself."

Sydney remembered what John had told him the day before. *This better work...JOHN!* A moment later Sydney heard a knock upon the back door.

Sharon turned and looked. "Who could that be?"

"I think I know who it is..."

"Well, whoever it is don't take long, Syd...we have breakfast and round 2 has yet to commence..." Sydney smiled and leapt out of the bed. He ran out of the room and threw the back door open to find a familiar face smiling at him.

"Good morning, my friend. I heard you calling. Here I am. Quite the system, huh? So, what's going on?" Sydney stepped out onto the back deck and closed the door behind him. "Mmm, that smells delightful. Did you materialize that breakfast this morning?"

"John...something happened last night while I was asleep." John listened closely. "You said I wasn't ready to materialize sentient objects, right?"

John shook his head. "That's correct, Syd. I said that. You're not ready to undertake that just yet."

"Oh, really? Then how do you explain this?" Sydney opened the door to find Sharon leaning against it. She stumbled out onto the deck and into Sydney's arms.

"Hola!" she said, smiling and waving. She was still wearing her apron and nothing more.

John averted his eyes and blushed. "Good heavens. This is *extraordinary*! Normally, Espers can't manifest anything that's living until they've reached a certain maturity. Let alone something sentient. For you to have brought this girl..."

"The name's Sharon," she said, still smiling.

Illusion Of Happiness

"Right. For you to have brought Sharon here…wait she's the one you knew before. I recognize her…I saw her within that profound sadness emanating from you. I understand now…Sydney…it seems that her spirit was with you when I brought you here. She really must have cared for you to have attached herself to your spirit in this way. You've been given an incredible opportunity…granted a second chance if you will, to be with her again."

Sydney stood in silence for a moment. "Can you leave me and John for a moment, Sharon?"

Sharon turned to Sydney and replied, "OK, Syd…I've really missed you. Hurry inside. Remember what I said before." She turned around and Sydney watched as she slowly walked inside and shut the door behind her.

John cleared his throat. "Syd?"

Sydney quickly turned and looked at John. "I apologize, John. I always lose myself in those dimples…What can I say?"

"You wanted to ask me something?"

"Yes…why would I bring her here? John…she's dead. Gone…I visited her grave myself. This…isn't natural."

John smiled, "I can understand how you'd feel uneasy about seeing her. Things here are different though than back there on Earth. It's quite normal to see an Esper converse with someone who has forgone their initial body. You see we all have spirits. Sometimes, like in your case for example, spirits can become intertwined. Your spirit became intertwined with that of Sharon's. When you came here she called to you and you answered…from the sounds of it you two had *quite* an experience. I've heard such occurrences can be very powerful. This is my first time actually seeing it."

"What should I do, John?"

"Be happy, Syd. That's what I brought you here for. No more sadness. You wanted to leave all of that behind."

Some Things Last...

Sydney hung his head a moment, remembering why he'd left in the first place. "Right, I remember."

"Then go inside. Sharon's waiting with your breakfast."

"I will. Thanks, John."

"No problem, my friend. Enjoy her company. I'll come round for a visit soon. If you ever need me you know how to reach me!"

Sydney turned around to find John had disappeared. He looked out on the backyard a moment longer. A bluebird flew by in the distance, chirping happily. It made Sydney feel slightly more at ease as he turned around and entered the house.

He found Sharon sitting to the dining room table eating her bacon and eggs. They looked and smelled amazing. Across from her was his plate all ready for him to eat. "Take a seat, babe. The food's still warm." He sat down and grabbed one of the pieces of bacon upon his plate. It amazed him how hungry he suddenly felt. "Well, you haven't eaten since you got here you know."

"That's true. Wait a minute...how do you know that?"

Sharon began to giggle. "Didn't John tell you? We're connected you and I. I can sense your feelings. I also know what you said to him when I left. I don't want you to think about what you left behind. You don't need to worry about any of that. You're with me now and you can be *so* incredibly happy here. Alright, babe?"

"Yeah...alright," he said, biting into the scrumptious piece of bacon.

"How is it?"

He took a deep breath. "Same as I remember it...delicious."

Sharon beamed. "Good. Now, let's eat."

At first Sydney found it a bit difficult to shirk his feelings but Sharon persisted in showing him that his new life could be so much better and carefree. After their breakfast, Sharon wanted to go for a ride in Sydney's car. For a moment he forgot that he had manifested the Miata outside in the driveway. Before he realized it, Sharon was already out in the passenger seat honking the horn. He stepped out onto the front porch and looked at her and his jaw dropped. He also didn't realize that Sharon had run out to the car completely naked…sans apron this time.

"Jesus, Sharon! I can't take you around like that! What if I run into a cop!?"

Sharon rolled her eyes at him. "Unless you will one into existence, the only people that'll be on the road are gonna be me and you. Now…get over here. I want to feel the wind through my hair again."

Sydney ran over and hopped in and found the key in the ignition. He turned the key and she started like a dream. He backed up and pulled out onto the road. He admitted it was quite exciting looking over and seeing Sharon there baring all next to him.

"Keep your eyes on the road, mister. You can check me out later."

As he sped along through the neighborhood streets, he completely ignored stop signs. They became nothing but set decorations to him now that he was master of his domain.

"Faster, Syd!" Sharon yelled standing up. "God this feels amazing! The wind feels so invigorating on my skin…and the sun…I feel so alive, Syd! More than I ever did before! Faster!"

He found his way to the straightaway uptown. He zipped past the library and the small mom and pop shops. Sharon screamed out in excitement. Never did he think that he'd be doing 80 mph down this road without a cop chasing him ready to haul his ass in for reckless endangerment.

"Syd? Let's slow down. I wanna head over for a drive by the lake now."

Some Things Last...

He slowed down and traced his way to the scenic road she wanted to visit. A few minutes later they were cruising alongside of the lake. Sydney could see small waves crashing against the shoreline.

"Look up there, Syd. Do you remember when we drove out here that one time? Remember what I said?"

"I remember...you said you'd wondered what it was like to live in one of those houses up there on the cliffs overlooking the lake."

Sharon smiled, but her gaze never left the houses. "I bet those people never even appreciated it. I wouldn't have been like that. I'd have woken up every morning and been in awe of that view." Sydney felt a wave of sadness go through himself. "It's OK, babe. I'm happy that you remember that day. It was one of my favorite memories with you."

They returned home and Sharon streaked across the lawn inside. He quickly followed behind her and met her in the living room. Having her next to him that entire time while keeping his eyes on the road had taken a lot of will power to not stop and take her before now.

"Ready for round two, Syd?" Indeed he was.

Later that night, the two lie in bed much the same as they had the night before. Sharon passed out beside him, her breathing deep and even. Sydney was pretty tired but he couldn't help but remember what Sharon had said earlier about the cliff-side homes. He had once upon a time promised to build her a home of her own up there. Living here in Albert's old place didn't feel appropriate to him. There were too many memories here that he felt he needed to leave behind.

You're gonna get that home, babe...better late than never, he thought looking over at her blissfully sleeping next to him. A smile spread across her face. He felt she heard him. He closed his eyes and began to construct Sharon's home. He imagined a great room which overlook Lake Lethe and a large deck which stretched out offering an even more awe inspiring view. He imagined all kinds of furniture he thought she'd enjoy and just before he felt the last of his energy leave him he placed a street sign outside. He struggled to stay awake as he finished placing the letters upon the sign.

SHARON ROAD

"Syd? Get up, lazy." Sydney's eyes slowly opened and he was met with Sharon staring at him. She was standing beside the bed, surprisingly dressed this time, with a look of slight annoyance upon her face.

He smiled at her, "Hey, babe. Good morning."

Her face remained unchanged, "More like afternoon. It's 1:00! You slept a really long time."

"Yeah...I did. I guess you wore me out last night. It's not like we have anywhere to be though," Sydney said, then remembered what he'd done the night prior. "You in the mood for another drive?" he asked, with a smile, as he leaned over pulling Sharon on top of him.

"Syd! You know I always am. Got a destination in mind?" she said, finally smiling.

"You could say that..."

Sydney drove along the winding road climbing higher above his personal version of Lando. He was loving the sharp curves and the knowledge that no one was on the road except the two of them.

"Keep your eyes closed. I don't want the surprise spoiled."

Sharon sat next to him and had her hands tightly over her eyes. "Alright, Syd, but you know I hate surprises!"

"You'd make a terrible doctor."

"Why do you say that?"

"Because you don't have patience." Sydney chuckled a bit as Sharon groaned at his awful joke. "We're almost there. Just a bit further."

Sydney turned onto Sharon Road and a moment later the cliff side home from his imagination appeared before him. It was just as he had imagined it. He expected it to be but still...he'd not gotten used to being able to construct with his mind. He pulled into the driveway and stopped.

"We're here...open your eyes." Her hands slowly dropped followed immediately by her jaw. She stood speechless, momentarily, then began to scream in delight. "It's all yours, babe," Sydney said.

She wrapped her arms around him and squeezed him as tight as she could. "I love you, Syd!!"

He squeezed her and replied, "Ready to go inside?"

As they approached the door, Sydney picked Sharon up and carried her in his arms. She let out a surprised yelp and he laughed. They reached the door and she turned the knob. Pushing it aside, he carried her over the threshold into the dimly lit interior. Their footsteps echoed upon the floor as he let her down onto the reflective surface of the hardwood in the manors front vestibule.

"Oh, my God, Syd! It's beautiful. Everything is just gorgeous," she said, proceeding deeper within.

"That's nothing, babe. Why don't you step out onto the balcony."

She pushed the sliding glass door aside which lead out onto a large wooden balcony that wrapped around the back half of the mansion. Sharon approached the edge of the balcony and leaned forward, staring out with a look of wonderment upon her face. Sydney followed her and did much the same as he stood beside her. They stood in silence admiring the amazing view of the entire city below.

"You can see everything from up here. Hey, I think I can see Albert's place down there," he said, pointing.

"Thank you so much for this, Syd. I...never thought I'd be here. This is a world I used to dream of but could only watch from afar."

Sydney looked over at her and then back at the city before them. He put his arm around her and they stood there together for a long time just admiring the majesty of the scenery before them.

The worries that had plagued Sydney when he had arrived slowly began to disappear with the passing of the days. With each seamlessly passing day into the next, Sydney found himself busy with Sharon. They became inseparable, spending almost every waking moment together. They would wake in the morning and make love with one another, the sun peeking through their upstairs bedroom window gradually illuminating the entire room. Breakfast would follow along with a quick morning shower and most of the time a drive through town with the top down of course. The weather was always perfectly sunny and warm out. Usually, after their drive, they'd come back home and watch a movie and have supper. Sometimes, the movie would get interrupted by them fooling around again. Sharon had taken a liking to doing it out on the balcony at night. She enjoyed looking up into the clear night sky with all of its stars. Sydney couldn't help but feel a tinge of sadness when she had suggested it. He was perfectly happy to do it inside but she always had a way of getting what she wanted.

Life was good, each day ended just as happily as the day before it. Besides the brief tinge of sadness he'd felt regarding making love to Sharon beneath the stars, he had never felt happier. Things were going perfect. Sometimes before he'd drift off to sleep, with Sharon beside him softly breathing, he wondered if all of this was simply a dream. As he thought this, Sharon reached over and pinched him. "OW!" he yelled out.

"This is no dream, babe. Now, get some rest. We've got another fun day tomorrow."

Some Things Last...

The next day arrived just as all the others had. Not a care in the world was to be had. After their usual jaunt about town ended, they came home and closed the door behind them. A moment later a knock came upon it. KNOCK KNOCK. Sydney jumped a bit and turned around, staring at the door a moment. He had gotten so used to it just being the two of them that the thought of someone else there frightened him.

"You gonna answer it, Syd?"

"Sure, I was just surprised is all." He approached the peep hole and looked out. A smile spread across his face. "Well, well, well. Look who it is," he said as he swung the door aside.

"Good evening! Long time no see!" John stood on the welcome mat holding an unopened bottle of wine. He held it out with a smile. "For you, my friend! I see you've built a sizable love next for the two of you. Quite impressive I might add."

"Thanks, John. For the wine and the kind words. Care to take the tour?"

"I thought you'd never ask."

After the grand tour Sydney showed John to the deck and they all took a seat, looking out upon the city below. City lights in the distance were quickly igniting into life as the night was slowly creeping in.

"Quite the view from up here," John said in awe.

"Oh, yeah. It sure is nice. So, tell me, what brings you by? It feels like a few weeks have passed since I saw you last."

"Yeah, it's been about that long here I suppose. I reckon it gets kinda hard to keep track of time when everything is as perfect as it is here! I just thought I'd check in on you since you haven't called for me. I thought maybe...the two of you would be interested in a trip into the city?"

"The city? Well, sure, but I only have a two seater." John laughed and said, "I didn't mean *this* city. I thought I'd invite you to check out the Espers capital. I know this really lovely bar I think the two of you would absolutely adore."

Sydney turned to Sharon and her face mirrored his own expression of surprise. "Why not? Just let us go inside and get ready!" Sharon said, excitedly.

Sharon quickly slipped into a new set of clothes as Sydney entered their bedroom. "This is gonna be so cool, Syd! I wonder what this city will look like?"

"I don't know…if everyone looks like John we'll stick out like a sore thumb."

Sharon began to laugh, "Why? Is it his suit? Maybe we can get John to show us where he buys them from. I think he looks *very* stylish. Alright, Syd. I'm all ready to go. Hurry up downstairs." Sydney watched as Sharon left the room in a flash.

He quickly picked out an outfit. He found his old jacket he'd arrived with hung up in the back of the closet. "It might be chilly out. Better to be safe than sorry." He tossed it onto the bed and grabbed a shirt and some pants, slipping into them as quick as he could. He pat his pockets and realized he didn't have his wallet. "Oh, yeah!" he said, running over to the bedside table. He slid the drawer open and in the back was his worn black leather wallet. He quickly dropped it into his pocket. *Might come in handy…you never know.*

He found John and Sharon sitting in the living room laughing. "Ah, there he is! All ready? Follow me. We'll be there in no time at all!" They followed behind John as he gripped the metal handle of the front door. A moment later he opened it. "Here we are, my friends. Just step on through."

Sydney's eyes grew wide. He didn't exactly know what to expect but John simply opening a door into another world was something that had caught him off guard a bit. He took Sharon's hand as they both stepped through into the inviting light on the other side.

Some Things Last...

"Holy shit..." Sydney couldn't help saying, softly to himself, as he began to look around. They had stepped out onto a warmly lit city street with a large ornate fountain in front of them.

"Well, allow me to welcome you to my homeland...Esperia," John said, holding his arms out as the large fountain shot a powerful stream of water high above them. It was almost as if he'd been waiting for it, for dramatic effect.

Within the sky Sydney could pick out an almost infinite amount of stars that were slowly appearing. He turned his head and almost lost his balance when he noticed what appeared to be a large planet in the sky. "Wh-what's that?!" he asked, John.

"Oh, that's Genight. Quite a difference from the night sky on Earth, eh?"

Sydney stared at Genight a minute, admiring the huge multicolored ring that encircled it. "It's kind of like Saturn, isn't it?" Sharon said, in awe.

"It is..." Sydney agreed. He averted his gaze back to the street in front of them. Warm street lights were springing into life as Sydney finally noticed dozens of creatures going about their evening, happily walking down the road without a care. Some of them astounded him at how alien they appeared to him. Somehow he could just *feel* that they were all happy. There was absolutely no fear or unease in the air.

"I'm sure you're both eager to see the city. Trust me, they'll be plenty of time for that later. We'll hit the bar first and get a bite to eat. They serve food there that you two will be familiar with. I'm quite partial to a few items there myself." John beckoned them to follow him and they set off down the street.

They turned a corner and John pointed to a bright pink neon sign glowing over a doorway. Sydney looked up at the sign.

Qube Lounge

"That's it there. See, not far at all. Hope you two are hungry because I am *famished*."

They proceeded through the ornate wooden door into a small vestibule that was warmly lit. "Where's the bar, John? All I see is a staircase," Sydney said.

"Indeed, the bar's on the roof. It's worth the trek. The view is exceptionally wonderful." John quickly darted forward and began to almost levitate up the stairs. Sydney approached the stairs and looked upwards. Floors and floors stretched out above him.

"Up we go, Syd," Sharon said, eagerly taking the steps two at a time.

This place better damn well be worth it.

"It is, my friend! Now come along! You'll be at the top before you know it!"

He began what he imagined was going to be quite a climb...but once he reached the top of the first flight of stairs he looked up to find John and Sharon standing under a smaller version of the sign that had been illuminated outside.

Sydney smiled, "You never cease to amaze, John."

John let out a laugh, "I told you that you'd be there before you knew it. Now, let's head inside!"

He entered the establishment half expecting to see a slew of creatures much like he had witnessed on the street below but to his surprise he found most of the clientele were human.

"I didn't want to overload you two on your first trip to Esperia. So, I decided to show you guys to one of my favorite spots I knew wouldn't be too much to process."

"That might have been for the best. Seeing some of the creatures down below was a bit wild for me," Sydney said.

"Right. You could feel them though, right? Their happiness?"

Some Things Last...

"Yes, I certainly could. Enough of all that though. How about that drink?" Sydney said, happily.

The trio took a seat to the immaculately maintained bar. "Joe would be jealous of this place," Sydney said, with a chuckle. He grabbed a menu that was sitting in front of him and flipped through it. "Hmm, let's see."

"That's the burger and fries combo I mentioned," John said, pointing at one of the listings.

"The QB Burger with truffle fries? I'll take your word for it, John. I'll order that along with…a Long Island iced tea."

"Oh, I remember the last time you had one of those. In fact it was the night I met you."

"So it was…" Sydney said, reflecting a moment on that night and how long ago it truly felt. "This time I don't intend on you driving me passed out back to your place though." The two of them laughed as Sydney reached over and placed his arm around Sharon.

They placed their orders and decided to take a seat out in the open air lounge. Genight had really come into full view above them along with a blanket of stars. Sydney had this incredible sensation. He wasn't used to such a large object looming above him. When he looked back down, relief washed over him when he found that his Long Island was waiting for him. He happily brought the straw to his parched lips and began to imbibe of the strong cocktail within the tall glass. Halfway through the first glass he found the unease of looking at Genight had faded.

John had been as true to his word as ever. Sydney never had tasted a better burger in all of his life and the fries were the perfect compliment to it. By the time Sydney had finished his meal he was already two Long Islands deep and feeling no pain…not that he had been feeling any beforehand.

"I think I'll leave you two kids alone for a while. I'm going to step inside. When you're ready let me know." Sydney raised his glass to him and smiled.

Two drinks and an hour later..."You look a bit out of it, Syd."

"I'm feelin' fine, Sharon. Have you felt these chairs? They're so *soft*! Although, if you'll excuse me. I've got to use the fo-cilities!" Sydney stood up and walked over to the corner.

"Whoa, not there, Syd! The restrooms are by the entrance to the bar!"

"Oh? Woops! Thanks, babe. I'll be back."

Sydney stumbled inside and found John sat to the bar with a glass of wine in front of him. "Johnny boy! There he be!"

"Hello, Syd! Ready to go? I was enjoying this lovely plum wine."

"Oh, looks tasty. Here..." Sydney reached into his pocket and fumbled for his wallet. He brought it out and practically threw it at John. It hit his chest and landed on the floor. "Damn, I didn't mean to do that. I wanted to pay our share of the bill."

John reached down and picked up Sydney's wallet, chuckling to himself. "Your money's no good here, Sydney. Put this away." Sydney took his wallet back and dropped it back into his pocket. "Oh, wait a second...something fell out." John reached back down and picked up a folded piece of lined notebook paper. He passed it to Sydney.

"Anything you say, Johnny boy! Forgive me. I'm about to burst here," Sydney said as he ran off to the restroom.

He stepped out of the stall and exhaled. His head had began to spin a bit as he walked forward and stood in front of a mirror. He noticed he had something in his hand. *What's this? Oh, yeah...John handed me this. Fell outta my damn wallet.*

He slowly unfolded the notebook paper and stood a moment looking at a red blotch upon the paper. It took him a moment to remember just what it was he was looking at. "Wait! This is!……That's…That's me! " He stumbled backward and leaned against the wall holding the paper with both hands. Tears began to stream from his eyes.

He remembered the night he had been given this paper. It was a crude drawing of him in red crayon holding a chicken leg. "Vivian! I remember your little hand giving this to me… How could I leave you behind? How could I let myself forget about you and…Vicky! I just gave up. I shouldn't have left….it's all been so easy here for me…" As he stood there reeling, his head quickly began to spin faster. "No, not now. Damn it! I gotta keep it together. This can't happen tonight."

He left the bathroom, slipping the drawing into his jacket pocket. He breathed deep, trying to keep himself together. He found John still sitting to the bar, throwing the last of his wine back in a final gulp. Seeing John take that final sip did nothing for Sydney's fragile state. "Syd? Is everything alright? You appear to be ill!"

"I need to go home, John. I…my head…it's…"

"Is everything alright, Syd?" Sharon called out. She ran up next to Sydney and placed her hand upon his shoulder. He could feel the warmth of her hand through his shirt. It made him reel even further. He couldn't take anymore. A moment later he ran back outside to the open air lounge, leaned over the balcony and began to retch. A few minutes later he looked at the city of light stretched before him. It looked so warm and welcoming, yet he felt cold inside.

The nights festivities came to an abrupt end. Due to Sydney's ill state of being, John decided to escort the both of them back home. Sydney could tell that Sharon was disappointed but he was relieved to find out that due to his clouded mind it appeared that she hadn't been able to discover what had sent him into such a tailspin. Both Sharon and John assisted Sydney down the stairs back to street level and just around the corner they entered a doorway and found themselves back in their cliff-side home overlooking Lando.

Sydney quickly thanked John and apologized for his embarrassing behavior. John simply smiled. "It's OK, Syd. I should have watched after you better. You're my responsibility. Get some rest," John said and wished them both a good night. Somehow Sydney felt that sleep wouldn't come easy this night. Not easy at all.

CHAPTER 16
Embracing The Truth

Walking onto the balcony, Sydney closed the glass door behind him. He wanted to be alone. His head was pounding fiercely. He deserved the pain, he felt. He fell into a soft wicker chair and stared out onto the glowing city before him. *It's all fake*, he thought with a straight face, *All of it...none of this matters.*

Sydney continued staring forward, his gaze unmoving as he heard the glass door open behind him. "Syd? Is everything alright?" Sydney remained silent but closed his eyes. "Are you asleep? Come on. Get up. Let's go to bed." Sharon leaned down and grabbed onto Sydney's arms.

He shook her off and opened his eyes. "I'm awake...I wanna stay here for a while. Would you mind giving me some time alone?"

Sharon looked incredibly hurt by this. "Alone? Why? What's there to do alone that you can't do with me? Something's wrong...I don't know what. Everything is all muddled in your mind. I can't pick it out. Something happened earlier didn't it? You were fine when we were sitting at the table outside...What happened when you went to the restroom? Syd, talk to me, please."

He sat a moment in silence and then replied, "Sharon, I'm just feeling really...sad."

Sharon stood a moment, surprised by Sydney's response. "Sad? I don't get it, Syd. You got it made here. You don't have *ANY* responsibilities; no work, no bills, free food. You have a cliff-side mansion with a breathtaking view...and let's not forget you have *ME*! All my love and attention with all the sex you could possibly want. What MORE could you possibly want?"

He could fight it no longer and the tears began to stream down his cheeks. "I want Vicky and Vivian, Sharon!" He began to sob uncontrollably. The truth had been released. He had no idea how she was going to respond but he felt a sense of relief wash over him, despite the relief though, he continued to sob knowing it was wrong of him to tell her this.

"You can be so happy here, Syd. I know it's only been a few weeks since you've been here but I know in time-"

"Time isn't gonna make this go away. I know it. I left them behind, Sharon. I ran away," he interrupted her.

"What will you do then?" Sharon asked, flatly.

"I should go. It was never right of me to simply vanish. I'm sorry..."

Sharon stepped away from him. "I see...no matter what I do the outcome will always be the same. You'll always want to go back to her...to that life. No matter how much pain it might cause you...or me," she finished saying as she ran back into the house. He looked up, tears blurring his vision. He hung his head and tears began to fall at his feet.

Sydney could feel the wind beginning to pick up around him. It caressed his cheeks at first, drying his tears, then quickly grew to a strong gust nearly blowing him out of his chair. He looked out across at the sky above the city as a bolt of lightning forked above it, startling him. He watched the sky as it turned to black with furious clouds.

He ran inside and a torrential downpour began to batter the mansion. Sydney could feel the wind shaking the very foundation of the place. "Sharon?! Where are you? We gotta get outta here!" He ran upstairs to their bedroom and found no trace of her. He continued to call out to her as the lights went out and Sydney ran for the front door, behind him he heard a loud explosion of glass. He thought it might be the balconies entrance but he didn't dare go back to check. He felt this cliff-side home was dangerously close to tumbling down.

Casting the door aside, Sydney had hoped that he'd fall onto the warm city street of Esperia but no such luck. He fell forward and entered back into the storm outside. The wind ripped at his jacket, nearly tearing it off of him. He looked up and saw his Miata sitting there, its pop ups raised. It looked about as frightened as he felt. He beat his way through the stinging rain and wind to the driver's door and forced it open against the wind.

He slipped inside and looked up at the house. It was quite literally swaying in the wind. He felt any second the place was gonna give way. He started the engine and quickly backed away right before the place began falling into the darkness.

From the street, Sydney watched in horror as the mansion fell. As it was falling, everything went eerily quiet. There were no great snaps of lumber or crashes of any kind. In fact, the storm itself disappeared as quickly as it had appeared. It was like someone simply flipped a switch. He cautiously exited the vehicle and approached the edge of the property. A few minutes prior Sharon's dream home had been there, what lay before him now was an immense chasm. He could see nothing through the darkness.

"Sharon!! Where are you?!" he yelled into the abyss. "She can't be gone...not again." *JOHN!? WHERE ARE YOU!?* He waited, hoping that John would magically step out of the darkness, a beacon of hope. He felt he'd make everything right. Minutes passed and Sydney continued to call for John but he didn't come.

He ran back to the Miata sat a moment. "Looks like John isn't coming...no use staying here. There's gotta be a way out of here. I need a doorway...some way to leave..." He tried to calm himself, to imagine a door in front of him. He imagined one, every detail he could possibly muster. He opened his eyes expecting to see it in front of him but was greeted with darkness. "This isn't right. I gotta find a way outta here!" He took off forward into the darkness. He wasn't sure where to go but he felt out there somewhere was the answer.

He noticed the darkness was all encompassing around him. There were no stars or lights of any kind around. He felt it was getting worse the farther he went along. He switched his brights on and saw almost no difference. He managed to leave the curvy mountain roads behind him and found himself heading back towards town. "I don't know where to go...what can I do?" He asked to the empty cabin of the Miata.

The radio sprung to life, it's ghostly glow surprising Sydney. He came to a stop. "Syd, I'm here. Where are you? Come to me. Do you hate me? I'm waiting nearby...on the roof. Please, come, Syd. Are you lost? Syd? Syd!"

"That voice! Sh-Sharon!?" He listened closely as Sharon's pleas grew silent and were replaced with static. "The roof? Of all the places...not there again!" He knew she wasn't going to say anything else. He had his destination. Truly, it didn't surprise him much. That roof had taken on an almost mythical feel to him in the years since he'd last trekked upon it. He was going back...back to where it all began...

He arrived outside of the apartment complex after speeding through the darkened streets. He was a bit surprised he'd made it there but he was guided by a strange feeling he couldn't explain. Somehow, it had lead him to the front entrance of the complex. He parked his Miata and stepped out onto the street. He half expected some sort of abomination to come leaping at him out of the darkness but thankfully the air remained still and quiet. He gazed upwards, along the face of the building, trying to see the rooftop but the top was cloaked in shadow. *Looks like this is the end of the road for you, old friend...* he thought as he placed his hand upon the convertible top. The pop up lights retracted and the engine shut off. Sydney gave the roof two pats and turned toward the front door. He was surprised to see a bright light emanating from within the interior. It beckoned him forward. He steeled himself for whatever fresh hell lie inside and ran for the door.

Pushing the antique doors aside, Sydney's steps echoed upon the walls of the frigid lobby. The light within was warm but the air was like that of the grave. He took a deep breath and exhaled, releasing a cloud of steam. He slowly walked across the lobby towards the elevator but stopped when he noticed a sign across the entrance.

OUT OF ORDER - Take the stairs

"Why am I not surprised? This reminds me of that night all over again..." Flashes of the last time he'd set foot here came back to momentarily haunt him but he cast them aside. "Now is not the time. I gotta start climbing. Only one way to go now," his words echoed ghostly through the still air.

He had hoped that maybe the flights of stairs would act similar to the ones present within the bar he'd visited earlier that night...Christ, had it been such a short time ago? It felt like so much more time had passed. These stairs weren't helping in that department. In many ways it felt as if he'd been traversing them for hours. Each floor slowly passed and Sydney steadily continued to climb.

He reached the seventh floor and stopped. "Sharon's apartment is on this floor..." He approached a small window and peeped through it. The view offered little to see, other than a drab grayish green wall, so he slowly opened the door. The handle was bone-chillingly cold to the touch. He stepped out into the dimly lit hallway, his footsteps muffled by the soft gray carpet beneath his feet. A steady low hum menacingly filled the air. He looked to his left and thought, *Right around that corner there is her place.*

He slowly turned the corner and saw a familiar off white wooden door. Adorning it was a bronze plate with the number '717' emblazoned upon it. The lights flickered off for a brief moment and he was left standing in the darkness. Although, it had been only a second, Sydney felt a knot form in the pit of his stomach. Something wasn't right here. He eyeballed the door wondering if it would swing open, wondering if Sharon was looking at him through the peephole. The knot in his stomach pulled tighter. She said she was on the roof yet he felt pulled toward her apartment door. He approached it and wrapped his hand around the door knob. It matched the chilling cold of the stairwell exit. He pushed forward but the door remained firmly shut. A part of him was thankful for this.

I should go. She's not here, he thought stepping away. He began to hear sobbing then. Soft at first, then growing louder. It was coming from the opposite side of the door. He knocked on the door. "Sharon? Are you in there? I thought you were gone." The sobbing continued to grow louder as the lights flickered off again. This time though, they remained off. Sydney stood outside of Sharon's door as the sobbing continued to grow to a deafening roar. He banged on the door and yelled, "Sharon! Stop crying! Open the door! Let me in!"

The roar abruptly came to a stop and the lights graciously came back to life. Sydney jumped back in surprise as the door slowly opened, silently. The inside of the apartment was shrouded in total darkness. It was the same darkness he'd seen driving here. He felt if he stepped in there he wouldn't be coming back out. He slowly began to inch away from the door when it slammed shut and the deafening sobbing began again. He covered his ears but it did no good. The sobbing echoed within himself. He ran back to the stairwell and slammed against the door.

He fell onto the cold concrete steps and thanked God for the silence. He felt if he'd stayed a moment longer in that hallway he'd have gone mad. He turned and looked back at the window. The lights flickered off in the hallway and the glass began to crack. A moment later the glass shattered and the roar followed him into the stairwell. "Jesus Christ!" he yelled as he began to traverse the three remaining flights of stairs. The deafening roar grew quieter as he put distance between him and the seventh floor door. He made it to the eighth floor and heard a terrible sound directly below him. It sounded like a combination of splintering wood and metal. He nervously looked down over the side of the staircase and saw the darkness creeping below him. It was climbing upwards towards him. "Oh, God!" he yelled as he took off for the stairs again.

He felt the darkness gnawing at his heels, growing ever closer with each step. Floor nine passed in a blur. Sydney's lungs felt like they were about to burst but he pressed on for dear life. Floor ten mercifully flew by and Sydney's sides were on fire. He beat his way through the pain breathing heavily. He didn't look back but he could feel the cold blackness directly behind. He saw it then, a door labeled with bold black letters.

ROOF ACCESS

He flung himself at the door and fell forward onto the gravel floor of the roof. The door slammed behind him and he began to throw up for the second time of the night. He retched and struggled to catch his breath. He thanked God that he was still alive.

"Don't thank God just yet, Syd..." He rose to his feet and looked around. It took a moment for his eyes to adjust and see Sharon sitting on the edge of the roof.

"Sharon!"

"Stay right there, Syd. I've been waiting for you. I'm glad you managed to make it. You would have been better off not poking around my old apartment. Too many bad memories there…" He managed to bring himself to his feet and took a step forward. "I told you to stay THERE!" Sharon yelled. A bolt of lightning forked across the sky above them, illuminating the rooftop. Sydney could see she was wearing her old blue robe. It looked discolored though like it was stained with, "Blood? That's right, babe. I was wearing this the night I…died. I was in this exact spot when I…"

"Sharon! Enough of this! Come away from the damn edge! You don't need to do this…"

"Oh, really? You think you can order me around? Tell me what to do? What right do you have to tell me *anything*?!"

"I love you, Sharon. Don't do this!" Another bolt of lightning flashed as a clap of thunder followed it. In the flash of light Sydney could see that her face was covered in blood.

"*LOVE*?! ME?! You've only ever loved one person…*yourself*! Don't you *fucking* lie to me, Syd!" Sydney inched closer to her. "I told you to stay away! You really think you can save me? Where were you the night I was here all alone? I know where you were. You were tucked into bed. Dreaming your sweet dreams while I was going through hell! The moment you told me you wanted to go back to her was when all of those awful memories overtook me. No matter what I do you'll always leave me. Just like everyone else. Every single time. All of the pain and loneliness I felt back then came flooding back in waves. It's too much. I can't do this anymore, Syd!"

She looked over her shoulder at the drop behind her. "It would have been better if I could have remained up there among the stars. It's so much better there."

She slowly leaned back and Sydney sprinted forward with his arms reaching out. He grasped at her open robe. For a split second he felt it's soft surface touch his fingertips. Sharon smiled at him and for a moment he felt maybe everything was going to be alright. That he would save her and take her down off of the roof. That they could be happy. That moment slipped away just as she did through his fingers. In slow motion he watched as she fell down…down…to the end.

"Sharon? NO!!" He looked at her body on the concrete below. She lie motionless in a pool of ever-growing blood beneath her. He took a step backward and fell to his knees, looking down. "No…no, no, no. Not again, damn it. *NOT AGAIN GOD DAMN IT!!!*" He had no more tears left to shed.

Seeing her fall before his eyes, he felt something had snapped within himself. "I was weak. A beautiful young girl who immediately took a liking to me. I was addicted to the attention. The way you made me feel. The mystery surrounding you…but I already had someone. Someone who thought the world of me…and me of her…at least I did once upon a time. Can I really say that now? Those days when we were kids…oh, how I wish I could go back to that time. I shouldn't have gone there that night. That damn Roland…no, that's not true. It's not his fault. I can't blame anyone but myself. He didn't force me to go. I went because I WANTED to! If I'd have just gone home…you'd still be alive…Sharon. I was such a selfish fucking prick. I lied to her, to you, to myself. In the end I don't deserve to have anyone. Al was right…I should have told the truth. He knew it…and he's gone too because…of me…I don't care anymore. The darkness can take me too. It's taken everything else…"

Sydney could hear loud banging behind him. He knew it was coming from the doorway of the roof. He continued looking down. He expected it to be the darkness that he'd fled from up the stairs. He was tired of running. He was ready to atone for his sins. He climbed to his feet and turned around. As he did so, the door flew open and the shadows rushed him. Sydney closed his eyes and embraced whatever may come. A singular thought came to him as he was staring down the pitch black, the smiling face of his little girl Vivian.

Right as the darkness was about to engulf him, a blinding light cut through it to its very core. Sydney stood in awe as he watched the light rise above him and stop. "The weight you've barred has been a heavy one. You can't give up. You can't change the past but what you can do is prevent it from repeating itself. Syd, Vivian...she needs you. I saw her face and how precious she is. Don't let what happened to me happen to her."   "Sharon...I'm so sorry."

"I know. I truly feel that you are. Your mind is quite strong. It was never me who put you through all of these horrible things. You've persecuted yourself. I don't hold any ill feelings toward you. All I do now is simply watch over you. It was so good to see you again but you're needed elsewhere. So...I guess this is goodbye...at least for now. Know this...I'll always love you. Now, go back home, babe."

From behind Sydney a loud bang came once again. He quickly turned around, not sure what to expect. "Sydney! What's going on?!" It was John and his eyes were wide with shock. He stepped out onto the roof and began looking at the bright light which had quickly risen into the darkened sky above. A moment later it reached its peak and with an immense flash the sky erupted into a sea of stars. Sydney stood in utter shock when the sight of it all hearkened back to a memory of his. It was the very first time he looked into Vivian's eyes. They sparkled with the miracle of new life. She stared at him through those eyes, unblinking, as she knew something he didn't. The sky above him now looked just like her eyes on that day.

"John...I'd like to go home now, please."

"Well, of course. I don't blame you. We'll get you back to your cliff-side home in a jiff."

Sydney shook his head and smiled. "No, my real home...I want to go back to Vicky and Vivvy."

"What? Are you absolutely sure, Sydney?" He nodded, yes. "I'm terribly sorry, Sydney...for not making it here sooner. I was locked out. It very rarely happens but it is possible...you never cease to amaze me. ...But anyway, if you're absolutely positive on this I'll need to call in one of my associates."

John closed his eyes and smiled. "He'll be here in a moment." True enough the roofs door slowly opened again and out stepped a tall man around the same age as John. He had a salt and pepper colored beard and wore black tea shades with a black overcoat stretching below his knees. It seemed not all Espers shared the same style as John.

"John, so this is him," the tall man said.

John smiled and nodded. "Hello, Jean. Yes, Sydney here wants to be returned."

Jean remained quiet a moment, looking up at the explosion of stars above. "We can return you but I must advise you that things might have changed in your absence. We rarely get anyone who desires to return. I must ask you...are you absolutely certain, Mr. Lee?"

Without any hesitation Sydney responded, "Yes."

Jean nodded and placed his hand upon the door. The doorway around it glowed brightly. "Open this door. There's no turning back. Do you still want to enter?"

Sydney approached the two men. He extended his hand to John who firmly grasped it. "I'm terribly sad to see you go, Sydney. I know you can be happy here."

"I was...for a while but I need to wake up now." He approached the door and looked over at Jean.

"Very well then. Off you go, Mr. Lee...you'll be home before you realize it." Sydney grasped the knob and opened the door slowly. He closed his eyes and stepped into the unknown.

Sydney opened his eyes and was astonished to find he was standing in his front yard. Everything was cloaked in darkness but it appeared to be the way he'd left it. He didn't know what to expect from Jean's cryptic words but he shrugged them off as he ran for the front door. He knocked loudly upon the door and waited. He expected Vivian to swing the door open and give him a funny look, wondering why he'd stepped outside in the middle of the night. He was prepared to whisk her into his arms and hug her tightly. He banged louder and called out, "Vivvy? It's Daddy! Vicky? Let me in, please!!" He waited...and he waited...but no one came to the door.

He looked through the diamond shaped window to try and see anything. He couldn't make anything out through the darkness. *They must both be out like lights*, he thought as he stepped away from the door. *Wait! I know! I'll go tap on Vivvy's window. I don't wanna wake Vicky just yet...Vivvy will let me in for sure!*

He hopped off the porch and ran along the house until he reached Vivian's window. It was slightly above his head. He tapped on it, loudly. He saw that her drapes were open. He turned around and found an old chair discarded in the back yard. *Who the hell put this out here? Eh, whatever. Lemme get a look into her room.* He placed the chair beneath the window and stepped up onto it. Much like the living room it was hard to see inside.

He cupped his hands against the window and struggled to make anything out. It was then that he felt something being pressed into his lower back. "Hold it right there. You make any sudden moves and you're gonna get a shotgun suppository!" A gruff voice spoke. Sydney tensed up. A bright light shone behind him. It shone for a split second into the window revealing something Sydney couldn't begin to fathom. "Come on down from there you son of a bitch!" Sydney stepped down off of the chair. "Turn around, slowly." He obeyed. The light shone brightly onto Sydney's face, blinding him. "Alright, you're comin' with me."

"What? No…I gotta see my family."

"You ain't seein' nothin' except the back of a cop car. Now move it!" The man told Sydney to get walking. He felt frightened. Not because of the shotgun pressing into his back but by what he had caught a glimpse of through Vivian's window. He saw an empty room with tattered drapes adorning a dust covered window.

PART IV

ONE DAY AT A TIME

CHAPTER 17
Now, I'm Back Again

"Alright, get walkin'. We're goin' next door."

"What's next door?"

"My house. Now enough with the questions and get walkin'." Sydney slowly walked across the damp grass of the front yard. On the way, he began to notice three cats walking along beside him. One of them, a black one, looked up at him and let out a quiet meow. "Pay no mind to them. Those are my cats. They want their breakfast. I was in the middle of going to get their food when you interrupted me." Sydney pressed forward as the black cat continued meowing at both he and the man behind him.

Sydney noticed a bunch of Halloween decorations hung around the man's yard. A half dozen or so handmade ghosts from plastic bags hung from lawn furniture and bushes. They reached the front door of the man's home. "I've got to open the door. Don't get any wise ideas of taking off now. You won't get far. I'm a damn good shot." Sydney remained still as the man removed the shotgun from his lower back. He breathed a sigh of relief to not feel the cold metal of the barrel.

The front yard was cloaked in mist and shadows. A light breeze blew the plastic ghosts causing them to produce an spooky rustling out in the yard. A street light from across the way cast a pale peach colored light onto the street. In the dim light Sydney could see the black cat eye balling him, the glimmer of it's green eyes was all he could pick out of it's features.

One Day At A Time

Sydney didn't like the idea of going inside. For a moment he contemplated taking off into the night, but he didn't know whether the man was bluffing about being a good shot or not. For the sake of both Victoria and Vivian he didn't want to find out.

On a positive note, he thought perhaps the man might be able to tell him just what the hell he thought he'd seen through Vivian's window. He wasn't sure if it had been a trick of the eye. Certainly it had to have been. His family was close and they would be able to sort all this nonsense out. "OK," the man said, clearing his throat, "Get your ass inside." He turned around and pointed the shotgun at Sydney. *Now isn't the time for questions*, Sydney thought, *Once he's put the gun down, I'll get to the bottom of this shit.* He walked up the five wooden steps leading into a closed porch and entered through the doorway into the warm interior of the house.

The door was slammed behind him and firmly locked by deadbolt. "Take a seat." Sydney eased himself onto an weathered dining room chair and got his first actual look at the man who'd been ordering him around. He was an older man as far as he could tell. His hair was thick and black in color but pieces of salt and pepper were scattered through. He wore a gray hoodie, a pair of insulated pants and holding them up were tan suspenders. Below his pants were a well worn pair of black biker boots. His face was covered with a light beard which matched the color of his head. His eyes a dark green color, pierced through Sydney.

"You want a beer before you get hauled off? I got some Natty Light." Sydney winced at the mention of it. His old man had enjoyed throwing back a few brewskis during the weekend but Sydney had been more for liquor over beer. "I can tell by your face you're not interested. Suite yourself but it might be a while before you get to have another choice.

Guess it's time to make that call. I got more important shit to do than deal with prowlers."

"I'm not a prowler! I was trying to wake my family up. Usually, it doesn't take that much to get them out of bed…but they've been through a lot the past few days."

"Are you drunk? Did you get lost along the way home?"

Sydney looked at the man, annoyed. "No, I'm not drunk! That's my house! 402 Duke Avenue!"

"Really? I think you're fulla shit. You could easily see the house number and just say that…you ain't gettin' anything past me."

"I'm not trying to get anything past you. Look…I guess you never noticed me coming and going…I realize I'm not the best neighbor. I kind of stick with my family and don't branch out but you must have seen my wife and little girl out in the yard!"

The man grabbed a seat from the dining room table and pulled it across from Sydney. He sat down and gave Sydney a steely gaze. "Look, I've been living here for two years and that house has been empty the entire time I've been here. Vandals broke into it last year and were hole up in there a while. Ever since, I've been keepin' an eye on the place."

Sydney sat trying to process what he'd heard. *VANDALS?!* He was filled with anger and disgust all at once. He wanted to take to his heels and dash out of there across the street to check on his home, but he knew he wouldn't be getting too far.

"Yo, you alright? Look, you seem to be a bit out of it…like I said, I don't got time to deal with this shit. I got cats to feed and I gotta get to the store to buy them some food. Otherwise they're gonna wreck the house."

"So…you said no one lives there? If that's true then who owns the place?" Sydney asked.

"A woman by the name of Lolita Lee. She lives on the other side of town."

Sydney's eyes lit up and he jumped out of the chair. "That's my mom! Give her a call! She'll be able to back up what I've told you!"

The man shifted his eyes over to the phone beside the fridge. "I guess…it's a bit early but she might be awake."

"Yes, she'll be awake! She always wakes up early. Her and my old man have work to get to."

"Your old man?" the man asked, concerned.

"Yeah, Harry Lee. He's the store manager at Mickey's Glass."

"I thought they went outta business a few years back."

"What? No, must be another place."

"Alright, I'll give her a call. Grab some wood there, bub."

Sydney returned to his seat and listened as the man stepped into his living room and dialed the number. He heard the line ring, once, twice and finally upon the third ring someone answered. "Lolita, good morning this is…yep, that's right…Hope I didn't wake you…Good, well, I was calling to say I caught someone poking around your house over here…no, no. It's not those kids this time. Just one guy…I'm not sure. He looks about twenty something I guess…Right, he was banging on the front door and poking around at the bedroom window on the side of the house away from me…He looked like he was scoping the place out through the windows…Right, I snuck up behind him with my shotgun. Gave him the fright of his life. Ha,ha! Anyway, I got him here in my house and he said he used to live there…Yeah, weirdo. Get this though, he said you were his mother when I told him you owned the place. Said your husband was Harry Lee, worked somewhere called Mickey's Glass? Didn't that place close down? …Lolita? You there? You alright? What's wrong? …You wanna speak to him? Um…sure. Hold on a minute…"

The man's loud steps echoed through the quiet house as he approached Sydney. "Um, she wants to talk to you. Here," he said, holding out the phone for Sydney to grab.

Sydney took the phone and brought it to his ear. He immediately heard sobbing on the other end. "Mom? Is that you?"

"Oh, my God...Syd!! It *IS* you!! I...can't believe it!" She began to sob again.

"Why are you crying? All I wanted was to go home...to see Vicky and Vivian! Then I got a shotgun pressed into my back. What is going on here?!"

"Sydney, I...need to *see* you! I can't truly believe this until I actually *see* you!"

"Ummm...OK."

"Good! I'll be on my way over. Don't go anywhere! Stay right there! I'll see you soon! I love you, Sydney!!" The line disconnected and he was left with even more questions.

"My mom's on the way over here..." Sydney said.

"Alright, take a seat and we'll wait for her...if you're not who you say you are then God help you...and if you are...God help you too." Sydney didn't like the sound of that. *What the hell's going on here??* That singular thought rang out within his mind as he waited and watched the sky slowly grow brighter out of the window next to him.

The yard outside began to erupt into life as the cats the man had mentioned having to feed were waking up for the day. Sydney counted at least five of them outside the window. Some were simply stretching and walking around the yard. One of them, the black one he'd seen earlier following them home, was stretched out upon the man's dark brown car, an Oldsmobile...emphasis on old. From the looks of it, Sydney figured the car had been around for quite a while.

As he was checking the car out, another vehicle quickly pulled up next to it. It wasn't one Sydney recognized. A moment later a figure rushed across the window in a blur. A pounding came upon the front door next. "Hold on! Don't beat the door down!" the man yelled out, quickly walking over and opening the door. Sydney looked as his mother entered into the house, paying no mind to the man's presence. At first she stood there staring at him unmoving. Sydney looked back at her for a moment. It felt so good to see a familiar face after all of the things he'd been through...but there seemed something different about her.

"My God...it *IS* you!!!" She ran across the kitchen and wrapped her arms around Sydney tightly. He sat with his eyes wide and gave her a pat on the back.

"Mom, you're choking me." She released her grip on him and he breathed a sign of relief.

"You know this fellow?" They both turned and looked at the man who was standing with a perplexed look upon his face.

"I do, indeed. This is my son, Sydney..."

"Well, I'll be damned...you two have a lot to talk about."

"Yes, we do! Come on, Sydney...let's go home." His mom took his arm and lead him to the front door. Sydney remained silent as she opened the door and lead him down the steps of the porch past the hungry, mischievous eyes of the cats. The black one meowed softly at him as he passed by it and stood beside his mother's dark purple four door.

"Hey, Mom...that guy told me a bunch of strange stuff. He said some kids broke into the house last year...What a bunch of crap. Get this... he said that NO ONE lives there either! Well, the guy must have never seen me, Vicky or Vivvy out in the yard." His mother opened the driver's door and sat down, she then reached over and opened the passenger door a moment later. Sydney stood outside the car, looking across the road at his house. "I don't understand why he'd hold me at gun point. Ah, whatever...I just wanna go home. Let's go across the street. We can talk there."

His mother started the car and sat a moment in silence. "Don't pay any heed to what you heard in there. We're going back home, Sydney."

"Well, that's *my* home over there," he said pointing across the street. "I tried getting Vivian or Vicky to the door earlier…now that it's daylight out I can see her car isn't there…did she take Vivian over to her parent's place?" His mother remained silent. "Yo, Mom? You alright? I'm sorry if I scared you this morning. Everything is alright now."

"Don't apologize, Sydney. I'm just happy that you're home again."

Sydney was perplexed by her statement. "It's November 1st right?" His mother nodded. "You make it sound like I've been gone for ages. It's only been a night." His mother looked at him, her eyes wide and full of surprise, a moment before looking away from him.

"Hop in, Syd. I wanna get you back to *our* home. We'll go over there another time…today isn't the best day for that."

Sydney sighed, "Alright, let's just go…I don't wanna linger around here anymore…"He slid onto the passenger seat, immensely relieved to be leaving the confines of that house. Still, everything the man had said gnawed at him. Was he simply mistaken? Perhaps he had a few too many brews before Sydney had shown up? The man seemed pretty sober though. As his mother drove past his home, Sydney looked over at it. The front of the house was still shrouded in shadow and mist. Everything appeared to be alright…but he noticed something. All of the Halloween decorations were gone. *Did Vicky take them down in the middle of the night?*

His mother quickly drove through the city streets of Lando, slowly becoming bathed in golden early morning sunlight. As they drew closer to Sydney's childhood home, details began to catch his eye. There were changes he didn't recall; new restaurants he'd not heard of, buildings that had never existed in vacant lots and entire streets that were nothing but forest the last time Sydney had checked. Stuff like this didn't simply pop up overnight. Something was certainly wrong here.

He looked over at his mom. The light of the sun shone through the windshield upon her. The longer he looked at her, he began to notice she appeared a bit different. He had noticed it earlier but really could see it now. She appeared to be...older? Her eyes seemed more tired. They seemed to carry something within them that hadn't been present the last time he'd seen her.

It was time for some answers. "Mom?"

"Yes, Sydney?"

"Can you take me to see Vicky and Vivian, please?" His mother continued driving, ignoring his question. "Mom?!"

"Yes, Sydney?"

"Did you hear me? I need to see Vicky and Vivian!"

"I heard you."

"Then why didn't you say anything?"

"We're almost home. We'll talk there, OK?"

Sydney let out a sigh, "Alright...fine."

His mother pulled into the driveway and Sydney hopped out of the car. He looked at his old place. *Place still looks the same... Hmm, Dad's truck is gone...looks like he must have already took off for work. Just as well. I'm not quite ready to see him yet.* "Come on, Sydney. Let's go inside."

He followed his mother into the warm living room he knew so well. Childhood photos stared back at him behind glass which gleamed in the morning light. *That kid has no idea what lies ahead of him. I wonder if it would have been easier or harder if he knew?*

"Would you like some breakfast?" his mother called from the kitchen, pulling him out of his thoughts.

"Nah, I'm not in the mood to eat right now...besides, we've got more important things to think about." Silence followed. "Mom? You still with me?"

"Come in the kitchen, Syd. Have a seat. It's time we talked."

He entered the kitchen to find his mother sat to the table with her hands clasped tightly together. He could tell something was bothering her. He pulled out his favorite seat and sat upon it. The vinyl beneath him let out a hiss as the air slowly seeped out of its sides. He looked into her eyes and began. "Where are Vicky and Vivian, Mom? I want to see them! You have no idea the things I've been through..."

"I could say the same, Syd."

"What?"

"N-nothing. Just don't raise your voice, please."

"Oh, right...Aunt Milly...she's asleep still? Sorry, Mom."

She looked away from him, out the window into the back yard. "You came back on such a beautiful day, Syd. I was planning to bring you flowers this morning...then the phone rang. You've made me so very happy." Tears began to fall from her eyes onto her clasped hands.

"You're not making any sense. Flowers? The hell do I need flowers for?!"

"Syd, please...none of that matters now. The important thing is you've come home. You're not out there any longer."

She turned her head and looked at him. Her hands reached for his and squeezed them for a moment and let them go. "I'm sorry. I just had to see if you were real."

Sydney stood up from the table. "Alright, that's enough. Just what are you getting on about? You act like you've not seen me in years!" She stared at him. Her eyes boring into him. "Stop it. I don't like the way you're looking at me right now. I've...gotta use the bathroom real quick. I'll be back."

One Day At A Time

He quickly exited the kitchen and practically ran for the bathroom door up the hallway. He pushed it open and slammed it shut behind him. In the mirror he was half expecting to see something different there, but his familiar mug greeted him. There was nothing abnormal about his appearance. *When I get back in there. I'm not listening to anymore of this nonsense. She's telling me where Vicky and Vivian are, damn it!* He became startled when he noticed the shower curtain begin to sway slightly. He leaned over and pulled it aside and saw that the bathroom window had been left ajar. A cool breeze was blowing in from outside. Sydney reached over for the latch to close the window when he began to hear a sound floating upon the breeze. It echoed softly upon the slick tiled walls. *Bells? Church bells? Is today Sunday? That's strange...I thought today was Tuesday. If that's the case...why isn't dad home?*

He quickly exited the bathroom but the sound of the bells tolling in the distance continued. It seemed to grow louder with each passing second. He returned to the kitchen but his mother was nowhere to be seen. "Mom? Where are you?"

"In the den, Sydney. Come in here." He ran into the den and saw his mother sat upon the couch. She was flipping through an old photo album. As he approached he saw some old photos of his father holding him as a baby. "I miss those days," she said, running her finger over his father.

"Where's Dad? You hear the church bells ringing? It's Sunday, right? Shouldn't he be here at this hour?"

"Syd..." A tear fell onto the plastic cover over the photo she had been looking at. "Your father...he's gone."

"Alright, when's he coming back?" His mother sat silently. "Well?!"

She began to speak, "He's not coming back...Your father passed away two years ago..."

Some Things Last...

"Wh-what are you talkin' about?! I talked to him just the other day! You must be joking! I don't have time for this! I gotta get to Vicky and Vivian! Now tell me where they are!"

His mother began to weep. "Sydney! Do you have any idea how *long* you've been gone?! *Ten years!* They're gone, Syd! They left long ago!"

He stood a moment, reeling. "That's not possible. I was here just last night…" He stumbled backward and slammed into the wall behind him sending several photos down onto the floor, shattering the glass. *Ten years? Ten…years?* The sound of the bells was maddening. He felt himself slipping away. He couldn't take it. He slid down the wall and crumpled up within himself. As the world around him went dark the bells tolled on.

He awoke several hours later lying upon the sofa. His eyes slowly opened and he saw his mother sat beside him with a damp cloth. "You're finally awake."

Sydney slowly sat up and leaned back on the couch. "What the hell happened?" he asked.

"You passed out, Sydney. Maybe telling you all of that at once wasn't the best decision."

Sydney's eyes grew wide when he remembered what she had told him before it all went dark. "Mom…how long have I been gone?"

"Last night was ten years…I never gave up hope that you'd come home. They said you fell into the lake…drowned because you were drunk."

"Who said that?"

"The police and some eye witness reports. They found your car parked uptown across from a bar. The owner said you'd been in for a few drinks and then disappeared into the night. Some other people said they saw you stumbling around close to the lake in the fog…"

"I see…well, as you can tell I didn't drown."

One Day At A Time

"You know Vivian said she saw you the night you disappeared. She said you'd come home that night and she tucked you in on the couch...No one believed her though. They thought she dreamed the entire thing."

"Is that so? What did she say exactly?"

"Well, it was everything after she tucked you in that made people feel that way. She said late that night she awoke to a bright light outside...brighter than the sun, she described it. She walked out to the living room and noticed you were gone. The door was open and she saw you floating upwards into the light! The light faded upwards into the sky and you were gone. Amazing how she came up with that, huh?"

"Yeah...amazing."

"I don't want to press you about where you've been. You can tell me in your own time. I'm just so happy that you're home...I so wish your father were here to see you too."

Sydney looked at her, unblinking and responded, "What happened to him?"

"Lung cancer...we found out around six years ago...the both of us believed you were out there somewhere. He tried holding on as long as he could. He wanted to give you another smack across the back of your head for...everything that happened."

Sydney grinned, "Is that so? I can imagine."

He leaned forward and looked out of the living room window at the street outside. By the looks of it the afternoon had come. He couldn't believe that his father was truly gone. There was just so much to process but he had to ask the all important question. "So...you said Vicky & Vivvy have gone? Just where have they gone off too? I need to know."

"It was around three years ago that you were pronounced legally dead. Victoria received the news. She took it very hard...she hoped that one day you'd show up somewhere..."

"Sounds familiar..."

"What?"

"With Al and all...sounds like she fell into my old habits. I ended up replacing Al. How ironic...."

His mother continued, "She waited for you. Vivian held onto the idea that you were among the stars on a grand adventure." Sydney smiled at this. "Then the news arrived that you were legally dead. Victoria quickly made plans to move away with Vivian. She couldn't take being here any longer. Everyone was sad to see her go but we all understood."

"Where did she go, Mom?"

"She packed up and headed off to Paris."

Sydney sat upon the couch, breathing deeply. His mother sat waiting for him to say something. "So...she finally did it, eh? She always wanted to go to Paris. We'd have gone ages ago...together. If only I could have left this town behind me."

"You two were planning to move away?"

"We had discussed it...it was one of her childhood dreams."

Sydney stood up and headed for the door. "Wait! Where are you going?"

"To Paris...I've gotta find them."

"Sydney, how do you intend to get there?"

"With money obviously!"

"How much do you have?"

"I've got tons in the bank! I just need to get to the airport!"

"That money is with Victoria now." Sydney realized she was right. He took his wallet out of his pocket and opened it. He counted two hundred dollars, in small bills, folded up tightly with a handful of spare change. He might could get

One Day At A Time

to Paris, Texas on two hundred dollars but certainly not Paris, France.

"Sydney, come here and sit down, please. There's no need for you to run off again. You're welcome to stay here as long as you want."

Sydney looked around the living room. "And sleep on the couch? No thanks. I'd rather not be a burden."

"You can sleep in your old room."

"What about Aunt Milly?"

"…Your Aunt Milly isn't here anymore."

"Don't tell me she passed away too?!"

"No! I'm so sorry! I didn't mean it that way! She doesn't live here any more. When your father got ill, it became quite difficult to look after the both of them. I had a word with the place she used to work and they agreed to take her in and watch after her."

"Duke's End took her in?"

"Yes. She's been there a few years now. I go visit her every week. You should come with me next time. She'd be so surprised to see you."

"So…she never came out of it, huh?"

His mother's eyes began to tear up. "No, she hasn't."

"I tell you what! How about I make you up some tasty chicken legs for supper. We don't need to think about all those sad things. We should celebrate your homecoming, Sydney!" His mother walked over and hugged him tightly.

He hugged her back. "Sounds good, Mom…" he said, forcing a smile. She released him and walked towards the kitchen wiping the corners of her eyes with the cuffs of her shirt.

Sydney took a seat upon the couch and reached for the remote. He sat a moment, in surprise, looking at the large rectangular set before him. What surprised him was the fact the set was so thin. *Televisions have certainly slimmed down while I've been away*, he thought. He flicked the television on

Some Things Last...

and was amazed at how clear the picture was. *Wow, quite the improvement over the TV we used to have.* He began to flip through the channels. He noticed a lot of shows and movies that he didn't recognize.

He continued channel surfing until he came across an old movie he remembered watching long ago one night with Albert. They were both in high school at the time and rented movies each Friday night. It had become a tradition from their middle school days that stretched all the way until around the ending of high school. That particular night they had both chosen a film titled, 'Electric Fantasies'. Sydney remembered he wanted to rent it for the title alone. He expected it to be full of erotica. Albert on the other hand, he recalled, wanted to rent it for the blurb on the back. A woman discovers a gateway to another world through her television set. Sydney smiled to himself remembering his juvenile thoughts and expecting the woman, who was a real babe, to show some skin in several parts but no such luck. At the end of the film, they were both disappointed for different reasons. Sydney leaned back and began watching the film again. He was lucky enough to catch it right as the opening credits were wrapping up.

As the film reached its end, Sydney began to smell the delectable aroma of his mother's signature chicken fill the air. "Sydney? Supper's almost ready." His mother poked her head around the corner into the living room. "What are you watching?" she asked with a smile.

"Oh, just an old early 90s movie me and Al rented eons ago..."

"Oh..." she said, her eyes looking down. "Well, I'm about to take the legs out and we have some mashed potatoes and gravy."

"Alright, Mom...this is about over."

The final scene faded to black and Sydney sat a moment with an incredible feeling of melancholy. The credits rolled

One Day At A Time

and he saw his distorted reflection staring back at him upon the screen. He turned the television off and thought about Albert for a moment. *I wonder if what happened to me happened to Al too. Where the hell else could he have gone? Wouldn't that make perfect sense? He was so sad back in those days. Damn it...I should have helped him.*

"Sydney?" his mother said from the kitchen doorway.

"I'm comin', Mom."

Sydney took a seat to the table and sat in awe a moment at the spread before him. "Eat up, Sydney."

"Thanks, Mom. It looks delicious." He grabbed one of the chicken legs piled onto the plate and took a bite. It was as good as ever. "Fantastic," he simply said. His mother smiled brightly and began to eat as well.

"Syd?"

"Yeah, Mom?"

"You looked like you were in deep thought out there."

Sydney finished off his first leg and grabbed another one. "Yeah, I suppose I was...just thinking about old memories."

"Thinking about Albert again?"

"Yeah...I miss him. I just wish I could have helped him that night." Sydney left his second leg buried in the mound of potatoes before him.

"It's not your fault. Your cousin hadn't taken his medication like he was supposed too. If he had, he wouldn't have become like that..."

Sydney closed his eyes and took a deep breath. "I'm not blameless...I wasn't out that night with Vicky...don't you remember? She told you and Dad what I did."

"Sydney, we don't need to drag up the past..."

As he tried to continue eating another thought came to his mind, "Mom? Where are Vicky's family now? They're still here in Lando, right?" His mom didn't answer. That wasn't a good sign. "Mom? What happened to them?"

"Well, her grandparents both passed on...Her grandfather passed around four years after you'd gone. Her grandmother followed him four years later." This really upset Sydney but he motioned for her to keep going. He had to hear everything. "As for her parents...they're fine. Waylon ended up moving his business to King City about a year before their grandfather passed. He's doing really well out there last I heard."

"Last you heard?"

"Yes. I don't hear much from them these days. Wayne and Greta ended up selling both houses on the hill...Victoria's grandparents place and her parents. They decided to move closer to Waylon in King City. Apparently, he built them a home next door to his."

"Sounds like something he'd do," Sydney said, flatly. "So...all that happened while I was away." His mother shook her head, lightly.

"Do you have her folks number?"

"Yes, I do...you can call them if you want...I've not told anyone you're back. Maybe you should wait until tomorrow? It's a bit late for a call like that."

Sydney forced a smile, "Yeah, that's true...What about Vicky's number?"

"I haven't heard from her or Vivian since Christmas last year. Victoria used a calling card so the number's no good. I don't know their actual number..." Sydney sat a moment, he had other questions but he couldn't bring himself to ask anything else. He sat and ate the rest of his legs in silence even though his appetite had left him.

He took a long shower after supper, losing himself in the tortuous thoughts of what he could've done...should've done. This wasn't the first time he'd stood in the shower lost in these thoughts...or the second time or the twentieth. He'd lost count ages ago of the amount of time he'd lived his life haunted by the memories of days gone by. He always felt in some way that he very much had one foot in the present and one firmly planted within the past.

A knock came upon the door, pulling him all the way back to the present moment. "You alright in there, Sydney?"

"Yeah, Mom...I'll be out soon."

"Take your time...I was just checking on you." *She's been too good to me. Gone for ten years and everyone thinks I'm dead...She hears I'm alive and comes running...I wonder if Vicky would do the same? Would she even care?* Sydney reached for the faucet and turned the water off. He stood a moment listening to water fall from his body onto the tub. He felt the drops splash onto his feet. He reached for the handle of the window above him and opened it a crack. A gust of cool air blasted against his body, momentarily giving him goosebumps. "Think I might try to get some shut eye...I'm feeling pretty damn tired."

Sydney exited the bathroom and heard the television set up the hallway in the living room. He walked across the hall to his old bedroom and placed his hand upon the cold golden door knob and slowly turned it. The room was cloaked in shadow and Sydney couldn't make out what it looked like within. His Aunt Milly's face flashed in his mind and he stepped backward a moment. *She's not here anymore. Turn on the damn light,* he thought and reached in and felt for the light switch on the right of the door frame.

He found it a moment later and the room was finally revealed to him. It looked about the same as it had when his aunt had stayed there. He saw a folded pair of pajamas set upon the bed. "I hope you don't mind wearing some of your father's pj's. I have some of your clothes packed away in the shed outside. I think I'll take a personal day off work tomorrow to help you find what's out there and to just spend the day with you...how does that sound?"

"Sounds alright, Mom...thanks. But why do you have some of my clothes?"

Some Things Last...

His mother began to rub her hands together. "Victoria gave them to me...before she left."

"Oh, I see...I'm gonna get some rest now. We'll sort that out tomorrow." She smiled and nodded, leaving him alone.

He closed the door behind him and walked over to the bed. He fell forward upon it and turned over onto his back. He closed his eyes and thought about Victoria's grandparents. *Christ, I can't believe they're both gone now. Pop...he seemed liked he'd live forever.* He opened his eyes and held his hand up above him. He imaged Pop's handshake and could feel the phantom pain of it gripping his hand tightly. For a brief moment he'd hoped that the power he'd developed upon Esperia had followed him home...that he could bring Pop back somehow. *I'm home now. Esperia is a long long way from all of this.*

He got up and slipped into his father's rather roomy pajamas. *Seems like the old man put on a bit of weight before he passed...* As soon as the sentence left his mind he regretted thinking it. "Dad...I'm sorry. I shouldn't have left. I should have stayed and been a man. Faced up to my mistakes...now it's too late. Why the hell did I take the easy way out?" He looked over at his bed and his stomach began to hurt. He fell onto it and breathed deeply, trying to combat the sudden ill feelings he felt. After a short while, the cramps subsided and sleep found him once again.

Throughout the night, Sydney was greeted with the warped images of the days events all jumbled together within his subconscious. He found himself back in the hallway of Sharon's apartment. He entered room after room to find himself entering into familiar places at first but everything quickly went wrong. He ran from one room to the next in a desperate attempt to find someone that he couldn't quite remember. He finally found himself in a room with one lone chair inside of it sat across from a large window. It was pitch black outside except for a crescent moon hung low in the sky. He took a seat and tried to remember what he was doing. He heard a knocking upon the door behind him. He rose from the chair and approached the door, cautiously. As he reached for the door knob it quickly opened by itself and a blinding white light cascaded over him. He stood before the light contemplating whether to enter it or turn around.

He looked over at the window and saw himself reflected upon its surface. Staring at his reflection, it slowly faded into the darkness. He shut the door and ran over to the window, pressing his hands against the glass hoping to see something. For a moment he saw tattered curtains and fell backward in surprise. He looked up at the ceiling at the lonesome light hanging down. He could hear the steady hum of electricity in the air growing louder. The sound grew to a maddening decibel and he reached for the legs of the chair. He took the front legs in each hand and raised it over his body and threw it at the window shattering the glass in an awesome explosion. The pitch blackness from outside the room began to creep inside and slowly overtook him. A moment later, the door burst open and the blinding light pushed the darkness back outside. Sydney rose to his feet and stumbled into the light.

"Sydney?" His eyes slowly opened and he looked around for a moment unsure where he was. "You OK?" It was his mother talking to him outside of his door. It all came back to him.

"Yeah, I'm alright."

"Are you gonna sleep all day? It's lunch time..."

"Lunch?"

"Yeah, I made us some soup and sandwiches."

"I'll be out in a minute." Sydney turned over onto his back and stared up at his ceiling. His room was filled with bright afternoon sunlight. He lie there a minute trying to remember the dream he felt he had just had. *Was I looking for someone? Vicky perhaps?* He smiled for a second then frowned. *Vicky...another day. My first real day back.*

Sydney tried putting her out of his mind as he hopped out of bed and started the day. After he and his mother had eaten their lunch she took him out back to their garden shed. Sydney entered into the shadowy interior to find boxes stacked seven feet high in some places. His mother pointed to a stack of two boxes toward the back with his name written upon them. He approached them and grabbed them under each arm. There were only two of them. All of Sydney's possessions were condensed into two boxes. He was curious what was packed away in them. One of them felt a bit heavier than the other.

He took the boxes back to his bedroom and placed them on the floor in front of his bed. He eyeballed them for a few minutes, putting off seeing what was inside. After he'd paced about the room a few times and went to the toilet to relieve himself he'd decided he couldn't put it off any longer. He grabbed one of the folded edges of one of the boxes and lifted it upwards. He did the same for the other side. He was careful not to look down into the box. Once the edges had been separated the first box lie open. He finally looked into it and saw it contained the countless articles of clothing his mother had mentioned. He immediately recognized the way they had been folded. *Vicky folded these...she put these in here. So...she really did clean out my clothes...*

Sydney removed and meticulously inspected each piece of clothing within the box. He was absolutely in no rush and took his dear sweet time looking over everything. When it was all said and done, Sydney found one of his favorite jackets at the very bottom of the box folded up tightly. It was a black wool blazer with white lines scattered all throughout the material. He took the blazer and slipped it on, despite the fact that it was quite warm within his room. The jacket felt like a hug embracing him and for a brief moment his anxiety let up...that is until he noticed the other box again. *I wonder what's inside of this one...more clothes?* He looked at his bed at the piles of clothes he had. He thanked his lucky stars to have some of his clothes back. Now, it was time to see what lie within the second box.

He treated the second one much like the first...drawing out opening it. When he finally did what lie inside was something he couldn't fathom. "What the...?" He reached inside and found two VHS tapes. He picked one up and read the white label across the front.

Vivian's First Christmas

He quickly reached for the other and saw it had no label. *Why did she leave these behind? I wonder what's on the other tape?* Beneath the tapes were several photo albums stacked upon each other. He reached in and took one out. The cover of it was wrapped in a thick, black binding which gleamed in the light overhead. He flipped it open and remembered the album. It was the one that he'd slipped Sharon's letter into all those years before.

He tossed the photo album upon his bed and several photos of Albert stared back at him. One of the photos just so happened to be taken here one Friday night during his middle school days. Roland stared back at him within the photo, a wide grin across his pudgy face. Sydney slammed the photo album shut and didn't dare touch the others at the bottom of the box. They contained more of the same, better times with Albert...and Victoria. Times that he couldn't bare looking through.

His door swung open and his mom stood silent a moment. "Sydney? Did you find your clothes?"

"...Yeah, Mom. Thanks..."

"OK, sweetie. It's almost seven. I was gonna order us a pizza tonight. How would you like it?"

Sydney let out a sigh, "I'm not hungry, Mom. You can order what you want...I'm just gonna put these clothes away..."

"Were there clothes in both boxes, Sydney?" He looked at the second box a moment and said, "Well, there were some old photo albums I had of Al...along with two video tapes..."

"Oh...I remember those albums now. I bet they have some really nice photos in them. Maybe we can look through them together?"

"Do we have a VCR around here?"

"The one we used to have played out a long time ago. There's a DVD player here now..."

Sydney frowned and replied, "That doesn't do me any good. Thanks anyway, Mom. I'm gonna get some rest now. Goodnight."

He closed the door and heard her slowly walk back up the hall towards the living room. He stood at the door a moment, his eyes closed, feeling cold. He buttoned his jacket but it made no difference. He turned around and placed the old photo album back into the box with the VHS tapes and closed it up. He then moved all of his clothes off the bed and back into the empty box and fell forward onto the soft mattress. He slipped out of his jacket and tossed it into the box as well and turned his light off.

He looked across his room at the window. The moon was almost halfway full in the dark sky. Across from it glowed a bright star. He turned away from his window and slipped beneath the sheets, covering his head. He lie still for a while, thoughts of the past flashing before him. This wasn't anything new for him, but all the previous times Victoria had been there lying next to him. Her warm body next to his was a presence which brought great comfort to him. For the first time in a long while he found himself totally alone with his thoughts.

The following day passed in much the same fashion. Sydney awoke after a restless slumber and shuffled about his old home trying to keep his mind busy. His mother had decided to take the entire week off to spend with him. Sydney wasn't exactly happy about this. She always hovered over him. He assumed this was because she expected him to disappear back to wherever he'd been for all the years gone by. *Maybe that wouldn't be such a bad idea,* he thought glumly as he sat upon the couch.

The night came once again and Sydney found himself pacing back and forth in his room. As the day had gone by he had become increasingly more fixated on what his "neighbor" had told him. His home had been empty for years...vandals had broken into it. He felt the anger well up inside of him again.

KNOCK KNOCK KNOCK He stopped pacing and stared at his door a moment. "Sydney? You alright in there? You've been in there for hours now."

"Yeah, I'm alright..."

"OK...You wanna watch a movie or something?"

"That's alright. You go ahead." He heard her footsteps disappear up the hallway then.

How could Mom let that house sit empty like that? What about Al? They never gave up on me coming home but it seems like everyone gave up on him long long ago...What if he came back home? No one's even there to greet him... As he continued to pace from one side of the room to the next the thought took on a maddening tone.

He longed for things to be the way they were before. Those carefree Sundays he'd had with Victoria and Vivian felt like they would be gone forever now. He closed his eyes and found himself lost in the memory of them. He thought of his old place across town, Albert's home, and of all the memories he'd made there. *This isn't where I need to be. My home is across town. It's waiting for me to come back...even if Vicky and Vivvy aren't there...I need to get my shit together. I'm going to see them again!*

He walked out to the living room and found his mother flipping through the channels on the television. "Hey,

Sydney! So, did you decide to join me for that movie after all?"

He shook his head, "No, Mom. I'm not out here for that. I want to go back home…To Al's old place. I don't want to stay here anymore."

His mother turned the television off and looked at him with tears forming in her eyes. "You what? What do you mean?"

"I want to go home. I appreciate everything you've done looking after me but I need to be alone to sort things out." She began to cry and Sydney walked over and sat beside her. "Don't cry. I won't be far away. I need to do this…for myself. I've had…*A LOT* on my mind."

His mother stifled her crying and said, "I can't begin to understand what you're going through. If you feel you need to go back over there for a while then I'll help."

"Thanks, Mom…I feel the answers to what I need to do are waiting for me there."

She smiled at him through the tears, "I hope so, Syd. I hope so."

CHAPTER 18
Vivre Mon Rêve

He sat listlessly in the back seat of his mother's car, staring out the window at the blur of passing streets. "Did you enjoy your breakfast, Syd?"

"Yeah, Mom, I appreciate you cooking us up some something...sorry if I was a bit...quiet. I'm just thinking about getting back home." It was true. He had barely gotten a wink of sleep. In the silence of the night, his thoughts kept him wide awake. He had tried to quiet those restless serpentine thoughts constricting him but no such luck. As his mother drove along over a particularly bumpy patch of road, Sydney had to grab onto the two boxes stacked up next to him full of his belongings. It seemed his entire life, almost, had been condensed into two cardboard boxes. He thought to himself, *I just need some time to sort things out...I'm gonna get you back, Vicky. Maybe then I can rest...*

The car came to a stop and Sydney realized they had finally arrived. "OK, Syd. Here we are. I'll help you grab your things." Before he could reject her kind offer, his mother had already gotten out and opened the left passenger door and had one of his boxes in her arms. He grabbed the second one and followed her up the walking path he'd walked so many times before.

Walking up the small set of stairs, he stepped onto the wooden deck out in front of the house and set his box on top of the one his mother had carried up. "Here are the keys," she said, holding them out for him to grab. He held his hand out and she gently placed them in the center of his palm. "I hope you find what you're looking for," she said, wrapping

Some Things Last...

her arms around him. He remained silent as she relinquished her grip and stepped away.

"The power will be on later today. I'll be back by later on this evening to check on you."

"That's not necessary, Mom. I got some sandwich meat and bread to tide me over for a bit. I'm here to do some thinking...some readjusting to reality."

"I understand, Syd. Still, I hate to leave you alone."

"Don't worry. I'll get Vicky and Vivian back and things can go back to the way they were before."

"Alright, Sydney. I love you. Be safe," she turned away from him and walked back to her car. Before she entered it, she waved goodbye and then slipped inside. A brisk breeze blew through the branches of the large tree in front of the house. A few of the brilliantly colored leaves above gently floated down onto the lawn below. A cold chill went down Sydney's back that he couldn't explain. He looked down at the keys in his left hand and wondered why there were two of them. *Maybe one's a spare?* he contemplated as he slid the duller of the two keys into the lock. The last time he'd opened this door his life was so much different. He longed to step through the door and be taken back to that moment. He closed his eyes and turned the key...and opened the door.

For a brief shining moment as he opened his eyes he believed he'd done it. He walked over to check the clock on the wall beside the couch. It's arms remained firmly planted upon 3:15. It appeared that the clock had long since stopped ticking. He stepped across the room to inspect the fireplace and found there were still coals there yet to be ignited. Still, everything seemed to be as he'd left it. It was quite perplexing to him. He then remembered what he'd seen through Vivian's bedroom window. He just had to know if what he'd saw that night was real or some kind of trick of the eye.

One Day At A Time

He quickly walked up the hallway, noticing that the storage room had a large bronze padlock securing the door. *That's new...must be what this bronze key goes to.* He decided to check that out later and walked on reaching the door to the bedroom. He placed his hand upon the cold doorknob and opened it, slowly. It took a moment for Sydney's eyes to adjust to the warm light cascading into the room. When they finally adjusted, he wasn't quite prepared for what he saw. There was nothing there within the room except for the tattered curtain adorning the cracked window that Sydney had looked into. He stepped back and slid down the wall until he sat upon the dingy tan carpet beneath him.

"So, it wasn't an illusion. It looks like those punks made quite a mess of Vivvy's room...Little bastards. How dare they!" Sydney yelled and slammed his fist down onto the carpet. He felt a sting of pain creep into it a moment later. His anger was quickly followed by sadness. For a brief moment he had hoped that when he'd opened that door that Vivian might be in here fast asleep. He wanted to wake her up. Take her anywhere she wanted to go. Get mommy and go feed Perkins some carrots. What he'd give if only that were true. If only he could go back. If only.

He sat against the wall for a while listening to the birds sing a cheerful tune outside in the trees, when a knock came upon the screen door. "Hello? Anyone home in there?" Sydney looked down the hall and realized he'd left the front door open. A moment later the screen door opened and in peeked a familiar face. "Hey, you alright, man?" It was his neighbor. *Oh, boy...here we go again*, Sydney thought as he stood up and walked to the front door.

"Yeah, I'm fine. Is there something I can help you with?"

"Help me? Nah, I was just driving by and noticed the door was open. I came over to check if everything was OK...You gonna be staying out here now?"

"That's the plan. This *is* my home. Like I said the other night…"

"Right…" the man, stepped back out onto the porch and Sydney proceeded to close the door when he spoke up once again, "Hey, listen…I feel bad about what happened the other night. How I treated ya and all. Not a very good welcome home…I know all about those…You wanna come next door for a cup of coffee and some strudel I picked up this mornin'? Just as a way of me saying sorry."

Sydney forced a smile, "I'll think about it."

"Well, don't think too long or the coffee will get cold. Oh, and don't forget your boxes out here. We're supposed to be getting a bit of rain tonight. I'll see ya," the man said, with a laugh and walked back towards his house.

Sydney brought his boxes into the house and placed them on the couch. He closed the door and laughed to himself. "Go next door? After putting a shotgun in my back? He thinks coffee is gonna make up for that? Maybe if it were some of that arabica with almost hallucinogenic properties…" Sydney turned around and sighed. "Who the hell am I even talking too? I don't think I've ever been alone here in this house…wait, no, that's not true. There was that one time…"

Sydney remembered rushing over here to find Albert, the night he disappeared. That night felt like an eternity ago. He shook the memory from his mind and went to take a seat upon the couch. He fell onto it and a fine layer of dust danced within a thin shaft of sunlight shining through the diamond window of the front door.

In front of him was the entertainment center, minus the entertainment. The television and everything else had been removed long ago. He wondered just where everything could be. He remembered the padlock on the door up the hallway and decided to check it out. He approached the door and grabbed the lock in his hand. It had some heft to it.

One Day At A Time

Whatever was in there must be valuable. *How the hell do I open this now? Oh, yeah. That other key...* he thought as he reached into his pocket. He brought the bronze key to the lock and began to push it through. He turned the key and the thick latch separated. Sydney removed the weighty lock and opened the door.

Inside, it was dark. He saw sunlight peeping in from beneath what appeared to be a curtain on the opposite side of the room. He slowly approached the window and his foot came in contact with something big and heavy. He was thankful that he still had his shoes on or else he'd have stubbed the hell out of his toe.

He navigated around the obstruction and approached the window. He grasped the curtain and moved it aside then raised the blinds and the room became fully illuminated by warm sunlight. He turned around and discovered just what he'd walked into. Three rows of boxes stacked waist high stood before him and in the corner of the room he noticed two box springs and mattresses stacked next to one another. He approached the boxes and opened one of them in the middle. "Ah, some DVDs! Maybe the TV is buried in here too?" He dug through several boxes and sure enough, he found his television set tucked into one of the boxes on the floor.

The other boxes contained various miscellaneous items such as silverware, cookware and decorative items. Although, one of the boxes contained an old album with various Polaroid photographs. Sydney barely recalled some of the faded photos within the pages. Some of them had been taken during his early high school days. As he flipped through each page, he discovered some of the photos had brief sentences written next to them in Victoria's lovely curvy handwriting. One of the sentences was beside a photo of the two of them out for a walk in the park nearby. The caption beside the photo read, *'Better Times'*. It appeared that

Victoria, perhaps, had decided to compile these photos into an album at some point after he had gone.

The final photo of the album was one that Sydney had recalled snapping not long ago. Yes, it was a candid photo he had taken of Victoria as she gazed out of the kitchen window of her grandparent's home while calling her parents to come over on the cordless house phone. She looked so beautiful standing there he couldn't resist capturing the moment. He removed the photo from it's spot in the album and gazed at it a moment longer, reliving the moment that he realized was over ten years ago now...For him it was only a few short weeks ago but for everyone else, time had marched on much faster. He looked away from the photo and tried to compose himself. *Now's not the time to get all misty eyed. I've got other things to do*, he thought as he slipped the photo into his jacket pocket for safe keeping.

The kitchen had been stripped of almost everything. Nothing lie in any of the cupboards. The pots, pans and plates were all packed away. Sydney knew he'd have to unpack everything soon, but not at the moment.

Upon entering the main bedroom, he already knew what to expect. An empty bed frame lie before him and across from it a familiar white set of drawers. He was a bit disappointed that he couldn't fall onto the bed and lie there for a while. It was still pretty early but he was already quite overwhelmed and ready for the day to end. He remembered the state of the couch in the living room, layers of dust floating upwards as he sat down upon it, and actually was relieved the mattress had been stored away. At least when he fell upon the bed he wouldn't be breathing in years of dust. He was desperately trying to look at things on the positive side.

He walked into the bathroom and stared into the mirror for a moment. He closed his eyes and took a deep breath and heard someone yelling from outside. He recognized the voice as his neighbor's. *What's that guy yelling about out there? Ah, hell. Who knows...*

He opened his eyes again and walked back out to the living room. He took a seat upon the recliner but only upon its edge. The house was quiet. Sydney hated it. Some might find the quiet peaceful but he found peace in the daily chaos he'd grown accustomed too. He longed to hear Vivian's footsteps running up the hallway, to hear Victoria's laughter. The silence was pressing in on him. He needed to get out for a bit. "I wonder if that coffee is ready. Think I'll take him up on that offer after all. What the hell else can I do today? Got no power...got to set up my bed..." He took to his heels and stepped outside, locking the door behind him. He eyeballed the house next door for a brief moment, then proceeded over.

Arriving next door, he saw two cats passed out on the hood of his neighbor's car. As he entered the yard, the cats eyes bolted open wide and watched him, cautiously. One of them, a fluffy gray/brown one, took off running into a fenced in area of the yard next to the car. The other cat, a jet black one with green eyes, ignored Sydney and went back to sleep. He recognized the cat from the other night. It had followed him and his neighbor in the darkness. He approached the car and pet the cat's head softly. It stretched it's legs out and yawned and let out a soft meow. It got up and began to bat at Sydney's hand. "You want some more, bud?" he said as he continued to pet the cat's soft, shiny coat. After a minute Sydney said, "Alright, I gotta go now. Can't spend the whole day petting you, fella." The cat meowed at him as if to say, "Sure you can!"

Sydney laughed and walked up the steps to the front door and took notice of the radio playing in the enclosed porch area. It was blaring a typical classic rock song that Sydney had heard countless times before. This particular track did nothing for him. He began to knock on the door when he heard a voice from outside call out, "I'm out here! Who's there?"

"Um, it's your neighbor...you invited me over for some coffee!"

"Hey, man! Come out of the porch and take a left behind my privacy fence."

He followed the man's directions and saw that he was directing him to where the cat had run earlier. He entered into a small "room" with a blue tarp roof and continued forward a few feet to find an open air area where his neighbor was sitting, wrapped in a warm jacket and ski cap. "Glad you decided to join me. I wasn't sure you would after...well you remember what happened. I apologize again for that misunderstanding. I saw you creepin' around and I grabbed Sweetie Pie and ran over there..."

"Sweetie Pie?"

"Yeah, my shotgun. Her name's Sweetie Pie. Haha! Take a seat, man. I'll run in and get a cup of coffee. How do you like it?"

"A bit of milk and sugar, please."

"Ah, that's how I like mine too. I'll be back in a minute."

He took a seat on a well worn lawn chair and began to take in the distinctive scenery. The lawn chair sat upon a cracked concrete floor which was littered with a number of small leaves. Next to him was a round table covered with a purple tablecloth adorned with skeletons wearing beachwear and pumpkins as beach balls. Across from him, several other lawn chairs were folded up against the wooden privacy fence along with a ladder which hung horizontal across said fence. A small grill sat across from him as well with an old heavy chain wrapped around the top of its legs. A light breeze rustled the leaves of the tree which had taken root outside of the fence. It was a lovely morning but he couldn't help feeling incredibly melancholic as he sat watching the branches of the trees sway too and fro. *I wonder how the branches look this time of year in Paris? Could Vicky be looking at the golden leaves right now too?*

A moment later he heard the man making his way back. He dismissed the thoughts he was having. "OK, here's your coffee. Nice and hot. Don't burn yourself. You might wanna let it cool a minute." He placed a mug, which had a family of snowmen on it, upon the table in between the two lawn chairs. The man eased back into his chair and took a sip of his coffee. "You like classic rock, man?"

Sydney grabbed his mug and blew on it. "Yeah, I haven't really listened to much music in a bit but I remember my old man was a big Kiss fan," Sydney said.

"No shit? Well, hell yeah. The Stones are my favorite! Best damn rock group ever. Kiss are right after 'em."

Sydney took a sip of his coffee and said, "Nice coffee."

"I had some of that strudel out earlier but one of the cats got into it so I had to toss it. Sorry about that."

"Don't worry about it." As Sydney finished his sentence the black cat came walking into the patio.

"Hey, Mr. Green! Finally wake up from sleepin' on my hood!" Mr. Green was plucked up into the man's arms and he held him for a minute petting him. "Yes, Mr. Green. It's nice and warm up here. He loves hopping up and climbin' inside my jacket some days. I don't mind it as long as he doesn't take a shit in there." Sydney laughed and watched the man continue petting Mr. Green until he fell asleep on his lap.

As the two of them sat sipping their coffee, Sydney's neighbor spoke up, "Think I might have a drink here soon. Some tequila with lemons. I sit out here in nature I'm gonna act like I'm fresh outta Mexico. You drink tequila?"

"It's been a while but I've had a bit of it, yeah."

"Well, damn. You wanna have a shot? I got a bottle I picked up yesterday evenin' and some shot glasses in the house. That would really make up for our little run in the other night wouldn't ya say?"

Sydney thought about it for a minute. "Why not. Set 'em up."

A few minutes later a fair sized bottle of gold tequila was placed proudly upon the purple tablecloth along with a hefty bright yellow lemon and a shaker of salt. "I only buy the best tequila in the world, man. Jose is my best friend sometimes."

"Right on. I'm not sure if I've had Jose before...like I said it's been a while. Last drink I had was a Long Island."

"Long Island! Those have got several liquors in them right?"

"Indeed they do. Tequila is one them."

"Well, we're cutting out all the others for the best right now," the man said, unscrewing the cap from the bottle and setting up two shots. After the shots were poured, he chopped the lemon up into sections. "What can we toast too? I know! Here's to new beginnings."

"Yeah...new beginnings." Sydney raised his glass and then sipped the entire shot. It caught him off guard a bit. It was some strong stuff. The warm feeling traveled all the way down his throat and into his stomach. He took a deep breath and grabbed a lemon slice and sprinkled it with a dash of salt then began to suck on it. The lemon certainly helped to ease the bite of the tequila.

"Good stuff, eh? Hey, you wanna have a little smoke?"

"Nah, I don't smoke."

"I mean weed, man, not cigarettes. I got some in the house if you wanna have a toke..."

"Oh, wow. I mean...I've got nothin' else to do right now. Sure."

Sydney eased back into the chair as he listened to the man tell stories from his glory days of the past. A song came on the radio and he went off talking about his younger days back in the mid 70s going to all sorts of concerts held in King City. Sydney listened but he gradually began to tune out what he was hearing. After several shots and tokes on a corn cob pipe loaded with marijuana he felt himself gradually slip further away. His worries began to fade until he found himself laughing at one of the cats sleeping on the back gate of the patio. It had it's legs tucked underneath it and looked quite comical to Sydney in his inebriated state. He thought the cat looked like it was on a monorail track or that it would slowly slide away like a giant snail.

"I need to use your restroom. Where's it at?"

"I got a homemade urinal over there by the way you came in. Look for the plastic jug cut open and aim for that. The piss goes into the pine straw outside the fence…pretty nifty, eh?"

"Yeah, lemme go check it out…" Sydney stood up and immediately felt a bit wobbly. "Whoa, here we go," he said, taking several steps and feeling out of it. He found the "urinal" and relieved himself, exhaling loudly. He walked back out to find the man had shed his jacket and had on a pair of black suspenders, over a gray thermal shirt, stirring two cups of coffee. "I feel kinda…out of it right now," Sydney said.

"Well, OK. Have a seat enjoy it."

"I'm good when I'm sittin' down it's just when I walk…"

"Shit happens when you do drugs," the man said, with a laugh.

After sipping on his newly poured cup of coffee and 'feelin' fine' as he liked to describe it, Sydney began to notice that the sun was setting. "Christ, what time is it?"

"Hmm, judging by the sun I'd say it's around five…Hey, you know what that means. Time for another shot. You want another one? I can keep goin' but this ain't no competition."

"Sure, I'll have another one. You know it's a bit fucked to say but I never got your name…"

Some Things Last...

"My name's Root Beer."

Sydney began to laugh, "Alright, Root Beer...Let's have another go around."

"Alright, you know what? I think I'll light a fire up tonight in my little grill here. Keep us a bit warmer while we sit out here."

A half hour later, Sydney found himself sitting beside a roaring fire. He starred into it as the flames danced wildly. Root Beer stood beside it warming his hands. "That fire looks so damn good! I wish I'd have bought some marshmallows and hot dogs. If I'd have thought about having a damn fire tonight. It'd be perfect."

Sydney thought about eating some marshmallows but the thought was a bit sickening to him. He took a deep breath and said, "I think I'm gonna call it for tonight. I'm not feeling so good."

"Too much of a good thing, eh? That's alright. At least you don't have far to go. Hey, if you wanna come over again sometime let me know. I don't have too many people to drink with anymore. Most of my friends are in the cemetery in town." Sydney felt a bit sad to hear that but his stomach prevented him from dwelling on it for long.

He walked across the street looking forward to getting home. It took a bit of concentration to keep walking straight. The world was spinning round and round. Somehow, he made it safely up the steps onto the porch and fumbled for his keys and unlocked the door. It was pitch black inside the house. He hoped what his mother had told him earlier was true and he flipped the light switch on. The room burst into light and he was both relieved and upset at the same time. He was happy to have the power back on but damn did the light hurt his eyes. He stumbled over to the recliner and fell onto it and closed his eyes tightly. A moment later he passed out.

One Day At A Time

Early the following morning, Sydney awoke to the shining sun casting its warm light through the diamond shaped window of the front door. His eyes slowly opened and the first thing he felt was the throbbing pain within his head. "Ohhh, my head...damn hangover," he said as he slowly sat up straight on the recliner. He stood up and stretched wishing he had a nice cup of black coffee to sip. Unfortunately, coffee was nowhere to be seen. All of this felt a bit familiar to him. *Wait a damn minute...talk about deja vu.* He quickly walked over to the diamond window and peered through it. He expected to see John on the other side, smiling brightly, wearing one of his loud suits. This time, however, nothing greeted him except an empty porch. "I'm not sure whether to be happy...or sad about that. Either way, John ain't coming to fix my hangover this time...Damn, this sucks."

He decided to power through the pain and try to distract himself with unpacking the boxes in the storage room. Picking up each box, he toted them out to the kitchen and placed them on the tiled floor. After all of the boxes were accounted for he embarked on the task of placing everything back where it belonged. As he began to sort everything out, his hangover slowly dissipated and by the time all was put away it was but a slight throb.

Having finally put everything away, Sydney admired his work a moment. Everything was back in it's place. He had even placed some of the refrigerator magnets back up. He stared at the fridge a moment and realized it was missing something special. He reached into his jacket pocket and pulled out the photo of Victoria he had plucked from the old album the day before and hung it upon the fridge with a powerful magnet of a dog bone. He stepped back and admired the photo once again and smiled.

He then walked over to the sink and turned the handle for the cold water. It took a moment for the water to creep back up the long dry pipes. He breathed a sigh of relief when the water went from a brownish color to crystal clear.

As he was watching the water circle the drain in the early morning sun cascading through the window, a knock came upon the front door, startling him. *Oh, lord. Who's out there this time?* He proceeded to the door and peeped out of the window to see his mother standing there, grinning at him. He opened the door and let her inside.

"Good morning, Syd. How are you settling back in over here? Thought I'd come by and check on you."

"I'm alright. I just finished organizing the kitchen."

"That's good. I came by yesterday evening around 6:30 and saw you through the window lying there on the recliner. You looked pretty comfortable so I didn't try to wake you."

Sydney smiled, "Did you now? Well, I appreciate that. I needed the rest. I'll be setting the bed up later on today."

"Good. I hope you'll be alright over here by yourself. I'm going back into work in a little while but I wanted to drop off a little gift for you first."

His mother reached into her pocket and pulled out something thin and black that fit in the palm of her hand. "Here, Syd. This can be an early Christmas present," she said, handing it to him.

He took it and eyeballed it. "OK...what is it?"

His mother's eyes went wide, "It's a cellphone, Syd! Here let me show you how to work it." She took it back and demonstrated how to turn the screen on and how to place a call upon it. "I got it for you yesterday. They had a sale on them at the store and I got one of the people there to show me how to work it. I actually got one too! I got them to add my number to your contacts! See! So, whenever I need to check on you I won't have to come over and bother you. I'd like it if you called me every now and then...just so I know you're alright. I understand you need to sort some things out so I wanted to make things easier for you."

Sydney forced a smile. "Thanks, Mom. I appreciate this. Cellphones sure have changed a lot. I remember my old one…it flipped open. I wonder where that thing is now…I must have lost it along the way somewhere."

"Well, you have this one now and it'll be much better than that old one."

His mother looked at her watch and gasped, "Oh, I gotta go, Syd. I don't wanna be late for work. These phones can do all sorts of stuff. I'll let you play around with it. Have a good day!" She gave him a quick hug and opened the door.

"Hey, hold on a minute. I'll walk you out to your car…" He followed her outside into the cool morning air and saw his neighbor moving some things around his yard. Root Beer raised his hand and called out something Sydney couldn't make out.

"Oh, no. I don't have time to talk to him right now. He'll talk your head off! I gotta go, Syd. Love you." His mother hopped into her purple car and backed up into the street then took off. Sydney watched as she turned the corner and disappeared.

As he stood in the driveway, Root Beer walked over. "She looked like she was in a hurry."

"Yeah, she had to get to work."

"Ah, yeah. She's gotta deal with all those sick people. Hell, I'm one of 'em!" he said laughing.

"Is that right?"

"Yeah, I go down there to Lethe Pharmacy and see her working like crazy while I'm picking up my meds…but anyway, how's the head?"

"When I woke up a few hours ago it was pounding pretty fierce but it's better now."

"You didn't have any coffee over here?"

"Nah, not this time. Too bad I couldn't materialize some…"

Some Things Last...

"Hey, if I could do that I'd probably go for something like a bigger bottle of tequila. Drink myself sober." Sydney laughed and noticed several cats had followed his neighbor and were now poking around in his yard. "You gotta get some coffee over here, man! Next time be prepared. Speaking of which...you free on Monday?"

Sydney looked down as Mr. Green came walking up to him and rubbed against his leg. He reached down and pet him while he softly meowed. "I don't have anything set yet for Monday. Why do you ask?"

"Oh, Mr. Green loves attention. I was gonna get you to come back over. I still feel bad for the other night. I think another good drink will set us straight. After that, it's your turn to supply the tequila. BYOT...Bring your own tequila...and share it with me!"

Sydney continued to pet the cat's shiny black coat as he laughed yet again at the man's foolishness. "Alright, I'll keep that in mind."

"What do you have in your hand there?"

"Oh, this? My mom gave it to me this morning. A cellphone."

"One of those new ones, huh? I still got a flip phone. Works well for me. I don't need to go messing around online too much unless I'm looking for parts for my car," he said pointing across the street. "'75 Oldsmobile Omega! I wanna enter it in the next Lando Fest this coming summer. They have a classic car show downtown each year. I doubt I'd win but I'd still like to do it. I see you don't have a car parked out here. You using Pete and Pat to get around?"

Sydney looked at the empty driveway and for the first time wondered what had happened to his Miata. "Huh, I guess I am. I used to own a Mazda Miata...but we parted ways recently..."

"That's a damn shame. I've seen those cars around. Nice little keychain cars I call 'em. Well, I gotta get back over here and finish what I was doin' but…let me have your number. I'll text ya later on or something."

Sydney forced a laugh, "Um, I don't know my number yet. How do I even check that?"

"Here, I tell ya what…I'll call my phone using yours and then I'll have your number." Sydney handed over his phone and Root Beer entered his number and then handed it back. "My phone's over at the house but I'll have your number now. I'll see ya after while!" Sydney watched as his neighbor returned across the street, the cats in close succession.

Sydney spent the rest of the day setting up the bedroom. During this time, he contemplated just how he was going to see Victoria again and all of the things he wanted so desperately to say. A part of him longed for these things yet another part of him was terrified of what might happen if she rejected him. What would happen then? He wanted to be with her…to be with Vivian…to make up for lost time…but would it be as simple as asking for forgiveness?

Something else he contemplated was reaching out to Victoria's family. They could help him in contacting Victoria…or would they? The longer he thought about it the more he realized they might not want to help him. Why would they want to help him after everything he had done? Could he really blame them if they felt that way? He had broken all of their hearts after all.

They all believed him to be dead…part of him wanted it to stay that way. Until he found out how Victoria felt what exactly was the point of telling anyone that he was alive?

"Was it a mistake for me to come home?" he asked to the empty house as he sat on the edge of his bed later that night. He lied back and stared up at the ceiling fan above him. The bed was comfortable beneath him but he looked to his left to be reminded of the empty spot which Victoria had always filled. There was an emptiness in more ways than one now. Sydney closed his eyes and several tears streamed down his face. He slipped his shoes off and curled up beside the edge of the bed. He was damn tired. After a while, he shut out the noise barking at him from the shadows and eased his way to sleep.

The days passed in a blur and he found himself lost in a fair number of ways. There was no structure to his days. He awoke and kind of floated about the house like a specter from room to room reliving the past and aching for a bygone era.

Sitting to the dining table, he nibbled on a ham sandwich and some potato chips while looking out the window at the vibrant leaves in the tree tops in the distance. As he found himself lost in a bit of a daze his phone let out a loud *ping* that startled him. Not knowing why it had made such a noise, Sydney turned the screen on for the first time since his mother had given him the phone. It appeared that he had received a message. *Wonder if it's mom checking on me*, he thought as he opened the message.

It's Monday. 5:01 pm ok with me. Me you jose &maryjane. Paaartee. - RT

Sydney suspected a wrong number for a moment then remembered his neighbor had invited him over again. He decided to write back.

Is this Root Beer?

A minute later his phone *pinged* once again.

Some people call me the root beer kid. See you at 5. - RT

Sydney let out a small laugh, "So, it *is* him, eh? Well, it'll be nice to get outta here for a bit I suppose…feels like I'm losing it. A little getaway may help me get my shit together…" He looked at the time, '3:35'. He was relieved that he didn't have long to wait.

After finishing up his supper and hopping in the shower, he threw some clothes on and saw that it was nearly time to head next door. He grabbed his jacket and slipped his shoes on then headed outside. Sydney was immediately greeted by cold droplets of rain falling upon his head. *Ah, hell…It started raining. Wonder if the festivities are canceled? Better go find out.*

Sydney walked next door and a faint rumble of thunder could be heard in the distance. He proceeded up the wooden steps into the covered porch and found it illuminated by a string of Christmas lights running along the top corners. Sitting on a shelf in the back was a small radio which was blaring the same classic rock Sydney had come to expect. He knocked on his neighbor's door and waited while an advertisement for an upcoming Thanksgiving weekend music marathon was playing.

The door opened and Root Beer grinned, "Hey, man. You're right on time. Someone must be thirsty. Good, so am I. We ain't sittin' out in the yard tonight. Rain's movin' in and it's gonna get heavier tonight. Oh, did you see the cats sleeping over there beneath the shelf?"

Sydney looked over and saw several cats lying close together passed out. Mr. Green was tucked together in a tight ball against the wall. "Oh, look at 'em all. They look pretty comfy," Sydney said laughing.

"Yep, I got a little heater I turn on sometimes for 'em to get by. They'll be warm and dry at least. Alright, come on in." Sydney obliged and stepped inside.

"Have a seat on the couch. I've got everything laid out…"

He followed him into the living room and saw a small circular coffee table stacked with all sorts of goodies on top. A tall bottle of tequila sat prominently in the middle, the golden elixir within beckoned to him. Next to the bottle sat two cans of beer, two shot glasses and a corncob pipe Sydney recognized using before. "This is quite the spread. Like eating a three course dinner…I see we're going bowling again. Let's shoot for a perfect 300 this time."

The man began to laugh and took a seat on one end of the couch. "Yeah, we're going bowling and going to a Stones concert," he said, with a big laugh. "Oh, I got some lemon slices in the fridge. Go ahead and pour the shots while I get the lemon."

Sydney set the shots up and a minute later the lemon slices followed. "So, I wanted us to look at something while we drink. We're gonna have a little movie night since we can't watch the fire. I got tons of old tapes of movies I recorded off the TV. I got a lot of horror flicks. I know Halloween's over but hell you can watch a horror movie any damn time. I randomly picked a tape and chose Frankenstein."

"You have a VCR?" Sydney said, intrigued. "You don't see those around like you used too. I'm actually in the market for one…"

"You got a tape collection too?"

Sydney's smile faded. "Nah, just some old home movies that I wanna watch."

"Well, I tell ya what…I believe I've got another VCR in my closet on the top shelf packed away. Let me look it over tomorrow and test it out and if it works I'll sell it to ya."

Sydney's eyes lit up as he replied, "Yeah? That'd be cool. Just let me know."

"Sure will. But tonight…we drink!" Root Beer, said as he downed his shot. "Drink…good! That'll make more sense in a little while when we get this movie started…"

The movie wrapped up and Sydney was feelin' fine as expected after the "three course meal" laid out in front of him. "Oh, boy. I need to use your bathroom."

"It's past the kitchen and down the hall to your left. What did you think of the movie, man?"

"I thought it was great," he said, picking up his can of beer and tossing back the rest of it. "Drink…good!" Sydney said, as they both laughed.

Sydney quickly walked through the kitchen and down a darkened hallway. He found the restroom without any

One Day At A Time

issues. His head was a bit swimmy as he finished relieving himself. He opened the door to the bathroom and a photo hanging on the wall across from the door caught his eye. He slowly approached it to get a better look at the person in the dimly lit photograph. Within the aging photo was a pudgy young boy smiling wearing a pair of suspenders that looked very familiar to Sydney. *What the...! Isn't that-* Sydney thought as he stared at the photo.

A moment later the hallway light lit up above him and his neighbor looked at him. "I was just making sure you found the bathroom alright. That photo catch your eye?"

"Yeah, it did. Who's the kid?" Sydney asked, wondering if his assumption was correct.

"That's my son...Junior."

Sydney smiled a knowing smile. "Roland Torfilio...Junior?" Sydney asked.

"Yeah, that's right! ...You know my son?"

"We used to be best friends...way back in the day."

"No shit? Let's have a cup of coffee and you can tell me how you knew Junior."

Root Beer quickly brewed a pot of coffee as Sydney sat to the kitchen table looking out at the rain soaked night outside. The sky briefly flashed and a low rumble of thunder could be heard a moment later. "Miserable night out now..." Sydney said, watching the rain fall upon the window sill. A piping cup of coffee was placed in front of him a moment later as Root Beer took a seat across from him. "Thanks, RB." Sydney, said.

"Ah, call me Roland. I got the nickname "Root Beer" from R&T Root Beer. You can call me Root Beer if you want."

Sydney laughed, "It all makes sense now. I was wondering why you went by Root Beer. That solves that mystery."

"Well, enough about me. How did you know Junior?"

"I met him way back in elementary school. He used to pal around with me and my cousin Al...and my wife Vicky. I knew him for all those years and I never knew he was a junior."

"That's not surprising. We never really saw eye to eye...You say Junior knew your wife?"

Sydney was curious to hear more about why they didn't see eye to eye but didn't want to press the man. "Yeah, it was in seventh grade...1988...I'll never forget that time. We all used to have P.E. and lunch together...good times. On Friday nights he and my cousin Al would come over to my house for our own movie night. Did you remember him mentioning where he would go those nights?"

RB sat a moment thinking back, "Nah, I didn't really keep up with him that well. I was going through some shit back then. His mother and I got into it all the time and I got plastered on Friday nights after my work down at the pier finished up..."

"You worked down at the pier?"

"Miracle Pier, yeah. I helped build the spook house and a few of the other attractions there. Hold on...I got a photo album I can show ya."

RB returned a few minutes later with a thick leather bound photo album and placed it upon the table. He flipped it open and Sydney saw many black and white photographs of people long since passed on. "That's me as a boy. Notice the resemblance between me and Junior," RB said as he handed Sydney the album. Sydney nodded as he could certainly see an uncanny resemblance. He handed the album back over and RB continued to flip through it. "Ah, here we are...summer '88! We started building that spook house for Halloween that summer! Damn, I remember when it was just a shell. Hey, check these out."

Sydney grabbed the album and eyeballed the photos upon the page. "Wow, I remember that place! My wife and I had our first date there…she was so scared she clung to me through the whole thing."

RB laughed, "Sounds like I did a good job setting the place up."

"Indeed you did," Sydney said as he flipped the page.

Within the next set of pages lie several photos that caused Sydney to be taken aback. His old buddy the rude clown from the dunk tank stared back at him. Memories of trying to dunk him came flooding back. "I remember that damn clown…was he a buddy of yours out there on the pier?"

RB leaned over and with a grin on his chin said, "You could say that…HEEEEY YOOO!!! HIGH AND DRY!!"

Sydney nearly spilled his coffee when RB yelled out the old phrase from the past. "Christ alive! *YOU? You* were that clown?!"

RB let out a great laugh, "I did that gig on Halloween a few years in a row back then to make a couple extra bucks and as a bonus I got to say anything I wanted to the people out there. Hope I didn't roast ya in front of your girl that night."

Sydney laughed, "Nah, but you did get dunked by my cousin Al."

"Well, he must have been a good shot. Those dunk tanks weren't easy to trigger."

"This is wild. I can't believe I'm sitting here drunk with the rude clown from Miracle Pier…AND he turned out to be Roland's old man! My mind is reeling right now."

"Don't forget we're neighbor's too…"

"Yes, funny how life works sometimes."

As Sydney continued flipping through the album he came across several photos of Roland taken during their middle school days. He noticed that Roland noticeably appeared to look quite forlorn in them. He turned the page and found that it was the final two pages of the album. They contained a handful of photos of Roland in a cap and gown holding a paper proudly above his head with a large smile across his face. By the look of things these photos must have been some time after Sydney had last saw Roland when they had their escapades downtown. "So, he made it after all, huh?"

"Eh? Oh, yeah. That's when Junior got his law degree. I didn't attend the ceremony. It was up in Michigan. Too far away. He mailed those photos to me afterwards. That was the last time I heard from him. He's a big shot lawyer up north now and doesn't have time to waste with me." RB fell silent and looked out the window while sipping on his coffee.

Sydney sipped on his coffee as well and broke the silence, "...I haven't seen my kid in a long time either. Time's a funny thing...now her and her mom are half the world away."

RB cleared his throat, "I heard a bit about ya from your mom. That she had a son that left a long time ago. I didn't wanna ask ya about it and you don't gotta tell me. Shit happens sometimes...life can lead you to some far off places but no matter how far away you might go, home will always be there waiting for you when you get back."

Sydney forced a smile. "That's true...I just wish my family were still here. I don't know how I'll see them again."

"Where are they now?"

"Paris...France."

"Oh, damn. That's a good piece away. I tell ya what...you ever try lookin' online for her?"

"Online? I don't have a computer..." "You don't need one. You got a phone and from what I saw a new one! You can do all sorts of shit on there. My brother John helped me find some car parts on his phone last year that came from New Hampshire and California! Try looking her up, man.

People can be home as well…maybe she's been waiting for you too?"

RB finished off his coffee and closed the photo album. "Think it's about time we call it a night. I'm feeling pretty tired and by the look in your eye I got you fired up to do some searchin'. Good luck, Sydney."

"Thanks, Roland," Sydney said.

"On second thought…RB will work just fine. I like that. Just don't call me Mr. Torfilio. That was my father's name."

He returned home, shut the door behind him and slipped out of his damp jacket, tossing it upon the recliner. The rain was coming down pretty hard outside now. He could hear the steady rhythm of the drops falling upon the roof. It soothed him as he sat down upon the couch and slid his phone out of his back pocket. *Can I really find Vicky on this thing?* Several icons were upon the home screen. One of them caught his eye.

Internet

He tapped it and a moment later he was taken to a search page. Sydney hadn't messed around online in a long long time. He recalled the last time he had been in front of a computer. He had volunteered to fill in as a receptionist for a week. Waylon's wife, Claire, came down with the flu and they needed someone to man the phones in the office. Sydney thought it would be an easy gig but soon found that Claire didn't mess around quite as much as he'd hoped she did. During that week, Sydney did a fair amount of searches online for particular supplies that needed to be ordered in. He prayed that the process would be a similar one to that.

He touched the search bar and a keypad appeared on the screen. He typed 'Victoria Tesson-Lee' and hit search. A moment later the results showed and many websites lay before him. He scanned through all of the results on the first page but nothing seemed to pertain to *his* Victoria. He decided to hone his search a bit by adding 'Paris' at the end.

Some Things Last...

He hit search and yet again he combed through the results finding nothing connected to what he wanted. He sighed and thought a moment then snapped his fingers. This time he decided to try something a bit different. He typed 'Paris France schools' and saw quite a fair number upon a map of Paris. He was quite amazed at just how many were located there.

He decided to search each schools name accompanied by Victoria's name behind it. It was a a tedious process that kept coming back with no results connected to Victoria...that is until he came upon an bilingual secondary school called Lycee Luitgard. His eyes lit up when he saw Victoria's name listed on the staff page. He eagerly clicked the link and proceeded to the page to see if it really was her. He scrolled down past several of the school administrators and immediately stopped when he laid eyes on a face he'd never forget.

Victoria stood in her staff photo with a look on her face akin to that of Mona Lisa. She looked just as beautiful as she had the last time he saw her. Next to her photo was a list of what Sydney assumed was her educational qualifications. It was all in French and undecipherable to him unfortunately. Despite that, he was very happy to have finally found a clue as to where she was now.

After a few minutes of admiring her photo, he decided to do another search. This time he searched for 'Lycee Luitgard Victoria Tesson-Lee'. What he found within the first search was something a bit unexpected to him. It was a link to a profile with the username of 'VTLee'. This immediately caught Sydney's eye. Beneath the link was the description: "Everyone has a unique story. Write about your life today!" It was an online diary from what he could surmise. Once the page fully loaded he noticed that the diary had been titled, 'Vivre Mon Rêve' and the first entry was dated November 1, 2010. Sydney scrolled down the page and began to read.

"1"

I decided to create this diary today. I doubt many people will care to read it but who knows…This isn't really meant for anyone other than myself anyway. I've been seeing a therapist for a few years now and she said writing my thoughts down would be beneficial to organizing them. Ha, sounds like a cheap way to dole out therapy if you ask me…but maybe Dr. Cook's advice will help?

I'm not sure what I'm going to do. Maybe it would be best if I didn't do anything anymore. Just lie here in this empty room and stare at the walls. I thank God each and every day that I have Vivian to get me up and going. She's been a guiding light in this darkness…but she's just a child and doesn't fully grasp the things that happened back then. She still looks out of her window at night waiting for her daddy to come home. She thinks you're out there having a great adventure just like Uncle Al. It takes everything within me to keep it together long enough to tell her goodnight and run back to the bedroom to cry all over again.

It's been so many years since I saw your face. I still see you in my dreams though. I wish I didn't. No matter how hard I try you still find your way back to me. Mom and dad hate for me to be alone here in this house like this. I'm hanging on though. Maybe you'll be back someday. Was Vivian right? No, that's just ridiculous. I'm tired. Goodnight.

Sydney exhaled as he absorbed everything he had just read. "Christ, this was five years after I'd been gone." Sydney teared up as he imagined Vivian sitting on her bed looking to the sky for some sort of sign he was coming home…but it never came. He tried to compose himself a bit.

There were other entries he needed to read. The next entry was dated December 25, 2010. *Christmas day…oh, boy,* Sydney thought knowing he was in for another punch to the gut.

"2"

Merry Christmas to you. You…you who once meant the world to me. I can remember when it was easy to say I love you. I'd have screamed it for anyone to hear. Then I think about all those years you lied to me and I question just how many of them were real. You finally told me about Sharon…but was she the only one? Were there others? God, I hope not. She was more than enough for what you put her through.

Vivian had a great Christmas. All the family came over here to shower her with gifts. I think on days like this she loves being an only child…As she opened her gifts, I couldn't help but think about you again. How you'd be there watching her grow up with me. She's getting so big. Ten years old. I wonder what you'd think of her. It seems all I'm left with is the wonder.

It wasn't easy for Sydney to finish reading that entry. He had to stop and breath for a minute. He sat upon the couch and realized this was where everyone was gathered that day. He imagined Victoria sitting smiling, watching Vivian happily open all of her gifts. She might have been smiling but on the inside lurked all of these ill feelings.

He had to press onward. There was more to read and he couldn't stop now. The following entry was dated May 31, 2011.

"3"

One Day At A Time

It's summer once again. The trees are green and the flowers are in full bloom. The world is alive with the sounds of new life all around me...yet I feel cold inside. Vivian left this morning for summer camp. She'll be gone a week. It's after one AM now. I'm all alone in this house. I thought I could handle this better but it's not easy. I wanted to go see John and Alexis but they're gone as well. They went to Florida to lay out on the beach for a week. Must be nice. Those two have been together for a LONG time now. I don't want it to sound like I'm jealous or anything...Well, maybe I am. They're down there sleeping in each other's arms while I'm here wrapped around a fucking pillow. A PILLOW! Damn you, Syd. You just HAD to go out for a drink that night. I hope it was worth it.

Today, I spent the day watching our old home movies. At first they made me smile but soon after they made me sick. I watched you say such sweet things to me all the while you were carrying such a huge secret behind that smile. I was unsure what to do with these tapes. I can't destroy them. That would be wrong for Vivian. These are her memories as well as mine. I decided to box them all up and put them away. Maybe one day when she's older I'll give them to her to cherish...but that's not true. I left two tapes out. Those tapes upset me more than all the rest. I can live with the rest but not those two. Not sure what I'll do with them. I've tossed them into a box of your old clothes for now. More shit I can't bring myself to part ways with.

You died that night. I know that. I need to face that. For God's sake...I can't do this anymore. I have to though for Vivian's sake. Maybe I'll go see Dr. Cook tomorrow...

"No, I didn't die, Vicky!" Sydney yelled out. His voice echoed into the empty house. He wasn't sure what he expected. A part of him hoped that maybe somehow a piece of that would echo through the years and find its way to

Victoria's ears that night all those years ago. He realized how foolish that desire was but he thought of everything he'd been through and thought maybe it didn't sound so foolish after all. Either way, he still felt like a piece of trash.

He scrolled down further to the next entry and saw that a while passed between this one. He prayed everything was a bit better. This entry was dated April 2, 2013.

"4"

I got a letter. The letter that I'd been dreading for a long time. I knew that it would one day make it's way here. You truly are gone. Just like Albert. Strange to think he's been gone nearly 15 years. Who'd have thought I'd take your place as the light house keeper. Well, there's not much need for that anymore is there? The both of you are gone...

Vivian still holds onto the idea that you both are on some grand adventure. I can't bring myself to tell her otherwise. At first it was the simple innocence of childhood. She's not a child anymore though. She'll be a teenager later this year! Our little girl is growing up into a beautiful woman. I wish you could see her but I know that'll never be.

The truth is you're dead. Your selfish actions caused three people to die; Albert, Sharon and yourself. Where did it all go wrong for us?

I've made a decision. I'm going to follow my dream. The dream I first told you about the day we met. I'm going to do it! For me and for our daughter! We should have done this together. You couldn't leave this place. Well, I am. I have nothing keeping me here any longer. Au revoir.

Sydney sat for a few minutes listening to the rain pound on the roof. He figured it wasn't going to be easy reading these entries but damn he could feel the anger and resentment emanating from her words. He thought about Vivian and the fact that she was a teenager now. That thought was quite a bitter pill to swallow. He'd missed so much.

After drinking a bit of water and sitting a spell, he decided to continue with Victoria's diary. The fifth entry yet again jumped forward in time a ways. It was dated October 27, 2013.

"5"

It's been over two months now since I left everything behind. All the hurt, all the bad memories. I left it all back there in Lando. It was hard to part ways with some things but I just couldn't take them with me. One thing in particular was that car. The Miata…I was glad to see it go, honestly. After I brought it home from where he left it downtown, it sat in the driveway for years. I had no desire to drive it after I found out that woman sat in there and they did God knows what together. I still feel sick thinking about all the years he looked at me and lied to my face.

When I told Vivian we were moving to Paris she could hardly believe it. She spent the summer learning French and proudly learned a fair bit of the basics. Luckily for her the school she attends is bilingual.

It's been a whirlwind of a time these past six months, (God, has it only been that long)! Getting everything together to come to France was a bit of a nightmare but I DID it! I was quite fortunate to be able to find a job here so quickly and an apartment. I'm loving my new job at Lycee Luitgard. The students have been very well mannered which is a relief. I've felt very welcome here so far and so has Vivvy. We're two girls on an adventure.

Still...I have these dreams of him. They seem to be getting less frequent though.

Sydney had mixed feelings about this entry. Although, he was happy to see that Victoria was doing well as he read the final lines he became upset again. She was no longer writing as if she was addressing him. It seemed he was slipping gradually from her mind. He tried not to dwell on it. Onto the next entry he went. This one was dated January 1, 2015.

"6"

Happy New Year! Looking back at my previous posts I remember how things were. I was in a very bad place back in Lando. Things have changed A LOT over these years.

School has been going super well and I've made some great new friends here in our apartment building. John and Alexis surprised me by coming over to spend the holidays. I haven't seen those two since the day I left and came here. We've had so much fun together but they're going home tomorrow evening.

I was invited to a party to ring in the new year last night by my new friends. John and Alexis decided to dart over for a short while. Vivian stayed upstairs in our apartment. She said she was going to go out for a walk with her friend Elly. She met Elly last year shortly after we moved here. I was worried for her. I know what it's like to move somewhere new and be the new girl. I just wish she'd bring her over for a visit sometime. Every time I ask her about it she says that Elly told her she would come over when the time is right…whatever that means. I'm happy she has a friend. Vivian is no fool so I trust that Elly is a good person.

Back to the party though…it was quite a party. It's been a long time since I tasted alcohol. I rarely drink. I don't like the taste of it but last night I decided when in Rome…or Paris as it were this time! My friend Guy-Manuel played bartender and fixed me up one of his "special sodas". After I'd downed a few he shared with me that they had a splash of vodka in them. I must say they was good.

My friend Edith emailed me a lot of photos from last night. I look a bit out of it in some of them. Here are a few of my favorites…

Sydney's eyes grew wide as he realized this would offer him an amazing look into Victoria's life these days. This party was almost a year ago but still he excitedly hopped up from the couch and decided to take his phone to the bedroom. He wanted to lie back and pour over each of the photos ahead.

Upon getting comfortable, Sydney began to examine each photo with the scrutiny of a seasoned detective. The first few were of a group of people standing around a small makeshift bar. The barman, Guy-Manuel, smiled brightly as he fixed drinks to several people. *Where the hell is she?* Sydney thought, impatiently. He continued onward through the photos and that's when he saw her. She wore a lime green plaid shirt and was holding a pair of teal sunglasses. She was smiling with her eyes closed. Sydney laughed as he looked at her. She certainly looked like she was feelin' fine. As he stared at her a bit longer he noticed that she'd changed. Much like his his own mother had changed, Victoria had indeed aged but she was as beautiful as he remembered. He continued to look through the other photos but gradually drifted off to sleep.

Within the dream, he's transported to that New Years Eve party. Sydney is woken in a comfortable bed by a young woman with short black hair and slowly lead down an impressive velvet lined staircase. Once he reaches the party he turns around to find the woman who lead him there has disappeared. Across the room, he sees Victoria sitting at the bar facing away from him.

He tries to keep a low profile at the party, hiding behind furniture within earshot of Victoria. He hears her voice and her laughter but can't pick out what she's saying. He gets up a bit more courage and watches her in the distance, sneaking glimpses of her from under a white baseball cap he finds on the sofa. He pulls it low to help conceal his face. Taking a seat upon a comfortable antique red leather chair, he sits as Victoria passes close to him. He's petrified that she'll notice him and pulls the hat even further down hoping she won't notice Guy Incognito in the leather chair. She walks on paying no mind to him.

It's at this time, as he breathes a sigh of relief, that Victoria's mother walks by. She on the other hand notices him immediately and says his name quite loud. She removes his hat and outs him as the man who broke her daughter's heart. Sydney sits there feeling as if he were totally naked to everyone.

Guy-Manuel begins talking to Sydney from the chair next to him. He's a friendly man who appears to be in his late thirties. He asks Sydney, smiling, "Why did you hurt Victoria? Did you know she tried to kill herself?" Images of Victoria's wrists bearing grotesque scar marks flash in his mind.   "Why did you do it?" he asks.

"I don't know...I made a really bad decision," Sydney said, struggling to find the words to explain his behavior.

"Do you want her back?"

"Yeah, but I know that will never happen."

He wakes from his dream within the darkness of his bedroom. The queen size bed felt even larger and lonesome. He moved his hand over the big empty space to his right. It was once filled with warmth but now it was empty and cold.

It was the perfect reflection of his life. Sydney felt something underneath his back and raised up and reached for it. It was his cellphone. He turned the screen on and Victoria stared back at him. He tossed the phone away, not being able to look at her any longer. Victoria and Vivian were half the world away and he had no idea when or if he'd ever see them again.

The following day, Sydney awoke around noon to the sound of the wind berating the front of the house. He slipped out of bed and peeped out of the blinds and saw that the rain had finally passed but it was an overcast day. The sun was barely shining through the thick clouds above. By the looks of things more rain was in store later.

He slipped on a t-shirt and pajama pants and decided to make himself a late breakfast. He entered into the laundry nook outside of the bedroom and winced as he stepped onto the cold tile floor. It always was a bit chilly beside the back door. He quickly hopped across the tile into the kitchen and began prepping his meal.

He made himself an egg sandwich and decided to have a bit of potato chips on the side. He took his meal over to the dining room table and took a seat, looking out of the window at the trees blowing in the wind. He watched as a few loose branches came falling down into the backyard. By the looks of things it was in dire need of some grounds keeping. He looked back down at his half eaten sandwich and continued eating becoming lost in thought. *What's on the agenda for today? Well, I need to finish reading Vicky's diary...* KNOCK KNOCK KNOCK Sydney looked over at the front door and saw that someone was out on the porch. He finished up his meal and tossed the plate into the sink and proceeded to answer the door.

He looked through the diamond window and saw it was RB. Sydney smiled and opened the door. "Hey, what's going on?" RB asked.

"Nothing much. I just had an egg sandwich and was enjoying this lovely weather."

RB looked around and smiled, "Yeah, ain't it lovely? We're supposed to be getting some snow come in next week. Blizzard they say. Better get ya more to eat than an egg sandwich over here. I got stocked up on stuff for me and the cats this morning. Hey, how's your head?"

"No hangover today, surprisingly. But...you said a blizzard? In Lando?"

"That's good. Maybe that coffee we had last night helped. It wouldn't be the first time a blizzard rolled through. Remember, we had one back in March of '93?"

Sydney did indeed remember that storm. The power went out for a few days and Albert and his Aunt Milly had come over to stay with them during the storm. He remembered, somewhere buried in a photo album, a photo of the two of them standing beside life sized snowmen they had built. That time felt like the last vestiges of his childhood in many ways.

"Yeah, that was during my senior year of high school."

"Senior year?! Wow, you know you look pretty good to be pushing 40. Good genes I guess," RB said, laughing. "Oh, I was going to say I checked out my VCR in my closet. It works if you want it."

"That's great to hear! Yes, I'll buy it from you!" Sydney replied happily.

"Alright, I'll go get it if you wanna follow me over. I'll bring it out to you."

"Sure, just let me grab that cash for you."

After Sydney grabbed the money he followed RB across the street. He was a bit curious as to why the cats weren't around. When Sydney made it over into the yard he discovered where they were. They were all eating their lunch. Sydney laughed to himself as he stood watching the cats eagerly munch their dry food. He approached Mr.

Green and began petting his soft fur. Greenie mewed at him softly and went back to eating.

"Here ya go, man. I even have a remote for it! Batteries are extra. Nah, just kiddin'. I stuck ya two fresh AA batteries in it. Ten bucks and it's yours." Sydney reached into his pocket and handed off the money. "Nice doing business with ya! Hope you enjoy that thing. It's been sitting in my closet for a good few years. If anything happens to mine inside I might end up buying it back from ya," RB said, laughing.

"Well, I plan on watching some tapes on it here soon. Thanks for digging it out for me."

"No, problem. Think I'll get a bite to eat. Maybe the TV will play some good sports like football or the women's swim team."

Sydney began to laugh. "Hope you find something good to watch. I'm gonna get this back to the house. I'll see ya," Sydney said, returning across the street.

A cold gust of wind jostled Sydney's hair as he closed the door behind him. He could certainly notice the temperature was a bit cooler than the day before but it always got cooler after it rained this time of year. "I haven't got the time to worry about the weather right now. Gotta get this VCR set up."

He connected everything and powered it up. The TVs glass screen slowly lit up a bright blue. Everything was working well so far. He decided to save the mystery tape for last and slid '**Vivian's First Christmas**' into the player. The tape deck groaned to life as it took the tape and began to play it. Sydney fell back onto the couch and watched the screen go black for a moment then the tape began.

"Is this thing on?" Sydney said as he stared into the cameras lens, wiping it with his shirt.

"It looks like it. The red light on the side is on," Victoria said off camera.

"Alright! We're in business. Wave to the camera everybody!" Sydney said as the camera lifted up showing everyone sat around the living room of Victoria's parents house. The camera panned from left to right over everyone as they raised their hands and smiled. The camera then zoomed in and moved to the right and showed Victoria looking down.

"What are you looking at there?" Sydney asked as several people laughed in the background. The camera zoomed out a bit and showed Vivian in Victoria's arms.

She was so tiny! As Sydney watched the tape he couldn't believe how small Vivian really was back then. So fragile and still pink and fresh. She was only a month old at the time.

"This little bundle is Vivian Alexandra Lee and she's very sleepy right now but she has to stay awake because she'll keep Mommy and Daddy awake all night if she sleeps now," Victoria said, laughing.

"You want me to take her for a while, Vicky?" Sydney asked.

"Could you? I'm going to open my gifts now."

"Sure thing. Come to Daddy, Vivvy." Vivian begin to cry as the picture jumped to later that night when the three of them arrived back home.

Sydney remembered he'd decided to film some more after they had gotten back. He wanted to break the camera in and capture more of the day.

"Are you taping again? Come on. I look terrible."

"You look absolutely gorgeous, Vicky."

Victoria smiled, "Look at my eyes, Syd! I'm so tired. I hope Vivian will get to sleep earlier than she did last night."

"I'm sure she will…I'll look after her if she cries out. You can rest."

"That's sweet of you, Syd. You know I'm sure we'll look back on these videos one day and be glad they were filmed. I'm happy that you decided to buy the camera to capture these moments."

As Victoria finished her sentence, Vivian began crying from her bassinet in the middle of the living room. "Uh, oh. Looks like Vivvy needs some attention. I'll take her into our room for the night. Here take the camera, baby," Sydney said.

The camera jumped yet again to the laundry nook outside of their bedroom. The bedroom door was ajar and whoever was filming was quietly inching toward their room. The camera stopped at the crack and a hand gently push the door open.

He immediately recognized the hand as belonging to Victoria. She was wearing the gold ring with the diamond that he'd given to her as her engagement ring. It sparkled in the light as the door was pushed open.

Sydney saw himself on the screen from the back sitting next to Vivian's bassinet. He was looking into the bassinet and reading a book to Vivian. Sydney already knew what book he was reading before Victoria zoomed in on him. He was reading a book called *'The Little Le's in WHO DUNNIT?'*. It was about the only thing that would knock Vivian out for the night and he read it to her almost every night for two years. By the end of it all he could recite the book word for word. Thinking back on it he still could now. The funny thing was it had to be him to read it. Victoria tried reading it but Vivian just didn't enjoy her take on it.

He continued watching as Victoria slowly approached the two of them. Vivian's little arms were flailing and she didn't look very happy. Victoria had come at a good time. He had just started reading the story. Sydney smiled and eagerly sat taking it all in. A wave of nostalgia enveloped him as he saw the front cover of the book.

Cover - Mommy sits to the kitchen table sewing a tiny pair of pants and a -CRASH!- comes from the other room. A surprised look is on her face.

Page 1 - The Little Le's were a funny bunch of kittens. They were always getting into mischief. Hiding Daddy's glasses...

(Daddy looks around for his glasses so he can watch TV and four kittens, The Little Le's, laugh behind his recliner.)

Page 2 - Running up and down the halls...
(All four of them are in a line chasing after Leland, in front who's eyes are huge.)

Page 3 - Jumping onto Mommy's shoulders...
(Mommy is making lunch and Leland and Lela are on her left shoulder. Leroy and Lenny are on her right watching her cook.)

Page 4 - and hiding from Mommy and Daddy.
(Mommy and Daddy are seen in their bedroom looking for The Little Le's. In the shadows of their closet they're all asleep in a ball.)

Page 5 - Mommy sits in the kitchen sewing a hole in little Lenny's pants when she hears a great big crash from the room next door.
(Mommy sits to the kitchen table sewing a tiny pair of pants and a -CRASH!- comes from the other room. A surprised look is on her face.)

Page 6 - Mommy runs into the next room and finds her flower vase in pieces on the floor.
(Mommy looking down from the doorway at the shattered vase and sunflower and water on the floor.)

Page 7 - Daddy comes into the room and looks down at the floor too! "Oh, no! What has happened? Not your new vase!"
(Daddy crouching down picking up the pieces of the vase.)

Page 8 - "Children, get in here this instant!!" Mommy yells, her fur all ruffled.
(Mommy yelling out and looking angry.)

Page 9 - *"Yes, Mommy?" Lela says, shying away from the doorway.*
(Lela's big eyes peak out from around the doorway.)

Page 10 - *One by one the four line up. "Who Dunnit?" Mommy asks, her whiskers frazzled.*
(Mommy points down at the shattered pile that was once her vase. The Little Le's all lined up against the wall like a police lineup. From biggest to smallest left to right: Leland, Lela, Leroy and Lenny.)

Page 11 - *"Leland, what do you have to say?" "Lela did it!"*
(Leland points his little beans at Lela next to him.)

Page 12 - *"Lela, what do you have to say?" "Leroy did it!"*
(Much like Leland Lela points her little beans at Leroy.)

Page 13 - *"Leroy, what do you have to say?" "Baby Lenny did it!"*
(Leroy points his beans at Baby Lenny whose little face is concealed by an over sized baseball cap. Baby Lenny is the shy runt of the litter.)

Page 14 - *"Baby Lenny! What do **YOU** have to say?!"*
"...Daddy did it!"
(Baby Lenny raises his little bean and points it right at Daddy. Daddy's eyes are wide and surprised.)

Page 15 - *Daddy? Did you do this? It seems The Little Le's aren't as mischievous after all!*
(Daddy is seen this time running up the hall with his eyes huge. Mommy and The Little Le's in hot pursuit chasing after him.)

The camera panned back to Vivian who was fast asleep. Sydney turned around and smiled into the camera. "She's out like a light," *he whispered.*

"Who would have thought she'd love that book that much? Thank God your mom found it at the pharmacy and picked it up," *Victoria whispered.*

"I know. I'm gonna go out for a quick drink of water. You get into bed and rest. I know you're tired...so am I." *Sydney arose from his chair and Vivian continued breathing deeply. She was indeed fast asleep.*

"Ah, look how cute! Little tikester," *Sydney said, joyously as he watched Vivian sleeping on the screen.*

The camera cut yet again. This time it was pointed down at the floor for a moment. He watched Victoria's feet as she walked through the house. She stopped and moved the camera upward. The picture came into focus and he could see that she was stood in the dining room looking out upon the living room. Looking through the window of the front door, was himself. "Syd?"

He turned around quickly, "I thought you'd be asleep, Vicky. Don't worry. I was just about to come in," *he said smiling. It was a fake smile.*

"Please come to bed, Syd. I thought you'd be out here watching some TV or something since you didn't come back right away. It's been a while since you were there at the window. It's not good for you."

"But...what if he decides to come home tonight? It's Christmas. I know he'd love to meet Vivian."

Victoria set the camera on the dining room table. She tried to turn it off and thought she had but it was still recording. "Syd, I'm sorry. I just want you to hold me. It's a cold night. You have two ladies who need you. If Albert was coming I think he'd have showed up before close to midnight."

He turned towards the window once more and gave another longing gaze through it then turned around. "Yeah, that's true. Thanks for seeing me through each of these nights time and time *again," he said wrapping his arms around her. "I love you, Vicky. The both of you are my life. I don't know what I'd do without you and Vivian."*

"Syd, you're amazing you know that? You're already a great husband and now on top of that a great father."

"No...Vicky, YOU are the amazing one. You brought our daughter into this world and every time I look into those eyes she looks back at me like no one has before. I wonder what she sees through those big blue eyes of hers?"

"I wonder the same thing, Syd. There's a lot going on behind those eyes."

"Let's get to bed, baby. I'm damn tired."

"OK...Syd? Have you had any nightmares lately? I've just been so tired lately I haven't thought to ask how you've been."

Sydney remained quiet for a moment. "I had one last night. They come and go...don't worry about that. My dreams aren't all bad. You're in some of them. Those are my favorite ones."

Victoria smiled and said, "I dream of you too. The other night I dreamed we were living in Paris. Me, you and Vivvy. We were at a café watching the traffic go by. Vivian was older and had long wavy brown hair."

"Like yours?"

"Yes! It was an amazing dream..."

"Vicky, we'll get there one day. I know it."

"Yeah," Victoria said, as they walked towards the dining room. Victoria noticed the camera and picked it up. "Oops," she said, finally noticing it was still recording and turning it off.

Sydney stopped the tape and wiped the tears from the side of his cheek. *I understand. I shouldn't have been there at the window that night. Damn it! I should have just gone to bed yet I just had to go looking for Al again. She was there for me through so many of those restless nights until the day she found out the truth. The true reason why I had those nightmares. Oh, Vicky...you must really hate me.*

There was something though that made him smile, if not for a moment. Victoria made her dream come true. Too bad he couldn't have been a part of it. He sighed and broke the silence of the room, "Time for the mystery tape." He leaned forward and grabbed the tape, examining it. He was anxious to see what lie upon it but also afraid. *Just what the hell is on here? Christ, it could be anything...*

After ejecting '**Vivian's First Christmas**' he inserted the mystery tape into the player and pressed play. The screen went black for a few seconds then the show began. A title was stretched across the screen.

Sydney And Victoria's Wedding October 27, 1999

He recalled his father had rented a camcorder to capture the day with. *Looks like the old man figured out how to work the text labels,* he thought solemnly.

Under the warm light of the church nave, Sydney stood in front of the altar. His best man was Waylon and next to him was John. Opposite the two of them stood Claire and Alexis.

Victoria and Sydney had decided to have a very intimate ceremony and kept the wedding party limited in number. The people who were invited to the wedding were less than 20.

He stood smiling as the music began playing and the camera turned around to show Victoria, wearing a white wedding dress, walking down the aisle next to her father. He had a proud look on his face as she held onto his arm. The song finished as she reached the altar and took her place across from Sydney.

He remembered being in awe of how beautiful she was.

"Welcome, loved ones. We are gathered here today to join, Sydney and Victoria in holy matrimony," the minister read. The two of them looked so happy staring into each other's eyes.

He wondered to himself why Victoria had decided to leave such a precious memory behind. He continued watching trying to understand.

"By the power vested in me by the state of Alabama, I now pronounce you husband and wife. You may now kiss the bride!" the minister happily said, finishing the ceremony. As Sydney leaned forward and kissed Victoria, everyone began to clap and cheer. The camera turned around for a minute and zoomed in on all that were in attendance.

It hurt him to see his Aunt Milly sitting there with that same blank look upon her face she carried throughout all the days since Albert's disappearance. His mother sat next to her, wiping her eyes with a tissue.

The tape jumped to a large dining hall next. They had rented the gathering hall at Stellaris Cookhouse which was the name of the restaurant within the Lando Inn. There were quick cuts of everyone taking their seat and candid shots of people talking. The camera panned over to he and Victoria chatting with Waylon and laughing.

Sydney smiled brightly as he watched everyone having such a good time.

The camera then cut to his mother sitting at her table, "Harry, are you gonna go around all evening with that thing? You need to eat your supper before it gets cold!"

"In a minute, Lo. I've got some great stuff captured."

"Why don't we leave Sydney and Victoria a message?"

"That's a great idea." His father turned the camera around and smiled. "Hey, Syd, you better take care of Victoria. Don't make me give ya another smack," his father said, laughing. "Seriously though, I wish the two of you all the happiness in the world. You made me proud asking Victoria to marry you. I hope you'll give her everything her heart desires. Oh, and one more thing. Me and your mother are ready for some grand kids!"

"Harry! Don't embarrass them. Take your time you two. Enjoy each others company. Don't rush into it. It'll happen soon enough. I love you both very much," his mother said with a bright smile.

The camera cut again to his father standing up from his table. "Time to go around filming again, Lo. My, you look lovely tonight."

"Harry, don't film me. Go film the bride and groom," his mother said, giggling.

"I will...as soon as I find Sydney. Where's he gone off to? I don't see him in here." He took the camera and walked across the room to where he saw Victoria sitting. "Where's your lesser half, Victoria?" his father asked.

"Hey, Harry. I'm not sure...he said he was gonna step out for some air on the balcony about twenty minutes ago. He seemed a little out of it. He was over at the bar having a drink before he went out."

"A drink you say? I'll go sober him up for you..."

His father quickly proceeded to the balcony and found Sydney sitting on a bench overlooking the pool. As he drew closer, Sydney brought a straw up to his lips and sipped a big gulp from a tall skinny glass. A slight breeze blew into the cameras mic.

"Syd, what the hell are you doin' out here? Getting shit faced? Your wife is inside worried about you!" Sydney continued looking forward ignoring him. "Damn it, Syd. Don't treat Victoria like this!"

"I'm sorry. I just need a minute."

"You've had twenty minutes already. What good's another minute gonna do you now?"

"Look. You can see the Ferris wheel from here. God, I wish I could go back. Al...Sh-Sharon."

"For God's sake...I don't know what the hell you're getting on about. Now's not the time to get all misty eyed over your cousin. Pull yourself together, Sydney, for her sake."

Sydney looked over at his father. "Are you taping this?"

"Yeah, so you can look back on this day and see your old man was trying to help."

"Thanks, Dad. You're right. I gotta get back to Vicky. Enough of this…" Sydney tossed his drink over the balcony, glass and all, and stood up from the bench. The tape ended after that.

Sydney sat upon the couch slouched over in silence for a while reeling in his behavior. "Vicky." That's all he could say. It all made perfect sense to him. After she watched these tapes she must have really grown to hate him even more. He didn't blame her. As he sat with his head held low he hated himself as well. "Vicky, I'm sorry."

He sat for a long time with his eyes closed, waves of sadness crashing against him one after another when out of the silence he heard his phone ringing. He stood up and walked into the bedroom and found his cell phone on Victoria's side of the bed. He quickly grabbed it and answered. "Hello?"

"Hey, man. What are you doin'? Did that VCR work out well for you?" RB asked.

"Yeah, I used it earlier."

"That's good. I don't sell faulty stuff. If I ever sell anything it'll have the Root Beer Kid's seal of approval," RB laughed. "I was just about to sit down for some supper. If you're not doing anything and want a shot later come on over," RB said.

"I might. We'll see. I appreciate the offer."

"No problem. Well, I think my supper is just about ready so I'll catch ya later."

"See ya, RB," Sydney said, ending the call.

When the call ended he saw Victoria's diary on the screen again. He had forgotten to close the page the night before. It all came back to him. He had been looking through all the photos she'd posted from her New Years Eve party. He sat on the edge of the bed and continued looking at them.

The first few were underwhelming shots of random people dancing and drinking at the party. He continued to scroll downwards when he saw a photo that immediately perked him up. It was a candid photo of Victoria sat upon a red leather love seat with another man. She was sitting rather close to him, too close for Sydney's liking. The both of them were laughing and had drinks in their hands. "Who's this fuck?" Sydney said, angrily. He could only see the side of the man's face. Sydney scrolled back up and looked through the previous photos to spot the guy in them but he couldn't find him.

He gave up on the search and scrolled past the photo of the two of them upon the couch and discovered that it was the final photo of the lot. Sydney took a breath and dismissed the guy. He was probably some random dude who wanted to chat her up. Honestly, Sydney couldn't blame the guy.

Scrolling onward, Sydney found yet another diary entry. This one was dated August 25, 2015.

"7"

For the first time in a long time I can say that I truly feel happy again. I've made some amazing friends here in Paris and I can't wait for the new school year to start soon. I love my job!

I have something that I've wanted to say for a few months now, but I didn't want to say it until things were on solid ground. I've met someone incredibly special to me. It's been such a long time since I've felt this way about someone. We met on New Years Eve. We connect on so many different levels.

Vivian isn't fussy on him but I expected this. We've drifted apart lately. I tried talking to her about her feelings. She gave me this horrid look and told me she was going out to see Elly. I hate this distance that's formed between us. She's completely changed the way she looks too. She wears dark, baggy clothes and even has begun to wear dark eyeshadow. Lately, she's holed up in her room playing her video games or out with her friend Elly, whom I still haven't met. For someone who spends so much time inside she has quite a tan like she's been down at the beach! I hope all of this will blow over in time...

Sydney scrolled down to read more but discovered that was the final entry. His phone slipped through his fingers and fell onto the carpet below. "No, that can't be true. This isn't happening." He felt a weight upon his chest and he began to cough. He stood up and began pacing around the room. "Vicky's found someone else!?" He thought about the candid photo again and how happy she looked. "What have I done? She's really moved on..." He continued pacing for a while overwhelmed with the truth until he fell onto the bed and passed out.

He awoke to the bedroom cloaked in darkness. He got to his feet and walked out to the living room. As he entered the dining room he saw a bright blue light enveloping the room ahead. He had left the TV on. He approached the TV and shut it off then took a seat upon the old couch. It had seen better days much like himself.

As he sat alone in the darkness he realized how his life was once so full of happiness yet he was too blind to see it. *My God...why didn't I appreciate those days?* He mused to himself. *Vivian grew up without me. What the hell am I doing here? I was such a fool. Everyone has moved on...yet I can't do the same. For fucks sake, I'm still waiting in this house for Al to come back...Al...You're sleeping with the stars now...just like Sharon. Why couldn't I realize that back then.*

He stood up and walked over to the dining room window and peeped out of the blinds. He looked up into the sky and saw a familiar twinkling star and laughed to himself. A tear rolled down his cheek and landed upon the tarnished wood of the dining room table. *This silence and complete solitude is maddening. I've got to get the hell outta here. I can't go on like this...living each day a prisoner of the past...but where do I go from here? There's nothing left for me.*

Sydney grabbed his jacket from the bedroom closet and then his house keys off of the hook in the kitchen and entered into the cool autumn night. He didn't know exactly where he was headed but he had to get away...at least for a while.

CHAPTER 19
Something To Live For

Sydney entered into the cold night air and began walking down the sidewalk. He had no destination in mind, just the desire to empty his mind. He looked above him for a moment, the moon was nowhere to be seen. The only light above that persisted were several bright stars twinkling brilliantly. He sighed and marched on through the night.

Aimlessly following the sidewalk before him lead Sydney to a part of town he'd never visited on foot before. He believed he was somewhere on the edge of uptown Lando. Out of the darkness he saw a store front brightly lit. He slowly approached its warmly lit facade.

Lakefront Liquor

The name of the establishment was emblazoned on the large sign beside the road. Hung in the front of the store were several neon signs, several of which flickered, for different brands of beer. *Booze, eh? Maybe that'll help me get away from the pain.* He approached the door and opened it. As he did he heard a *BING BONG* inside.

The interior of the store was warm and welcoming to Sydney and all of the shelves were neatly stocked. He didn't know where to begin looking. He walked ahead and saw the tequila section. His eyes fell on a bottle identical to the one he and RB had downed earlier that week. He was surprised at how many brands of tequila were for sale. He thought for a moment about grabbing a bottle of Jose but decided against it. As much as he enjoyed the ride from the tequila, he unfortunately didn't know exactly what to mix it with to ease the bite. He wanted something quick and easy...something he could take somewhere to a bench and forget all his worries.

"You're out late, sir." Sydney quickly turned around to find an older man wearing a wool cardigan stood before him. "Didn't mean to startle ya, son. Just wanted to see if ya needed any help."

Sydney forced a smile, "I'm just looking at the moment. Thinking of having something simple..."

"Simple, eh? How about rum and cola? Kahlua and milk is pretty simple too."

When Sydney heard cola mentioned his mind immediately went back to Victoria. He didn't feel sad in this instance just curious. "How about vodka and cola?"

The shop keep raised a finger, "Oh, yeah. That'll work. Our vodka selection is over here and we have several colas in the coolers up front."

Sydney followed the man to the vodka shelves and was amazed. There were even more brands of vodka than there were tequila. He scanned over the bottles and his eyes fell upon one that had the French flag upon it. *Maybe this is the same kind Vicky drank?* He placed the hefty bottle on the counter and grabbed a bottle of chilled cola and paid. "Thanks very much, sir. Stay warm out there. Those lakefront winds can cut through ya like a knife." Sydney nodded and smiled then entered back into the cold night.

He wandered through the darkness looking for a suitable spot to open his bottle of liquid amnesia until he stumbled upon a park beside Lake Lethe. Sydney had never visited this park, it appeared it hadn't been open for very long. Everything seemed to have that sheen of newness still attached to it. He was thankful to find the park gates open and a walking path which was illuminated by tall lights every few feet. The lights provided a warm glow but even so Sydney prayed that no undesirables lurked in the darkness just beyond the path behind the many trees and bushes.

He walked until he reached a portion of the path beside the lake. Directly beneath one of the lights was a bench just begging to be sat upon. He slid onto the bench and looked out upon the still black water of the lake. Staring out for a moment, he saw a beacon of light swoop across the surface of the water from the opposite side of the lake. *The lighthouse...I almost forgot that thing existed. Been a long time since I've been down here by the water.* He stared a moment longer and watched the beam sweep across the lake once again.

He felt the cold surface of the bench beneath him. It chilled him a bit but he felt the chill gradually fading. He closed his eyes and listened to the faint sound of the lake in the distance.

He was reminded of a day where he had taken Victoria and Vivian to a nearby beach one summer ages before. Vivian splashed on the shoreline in her little striped bathing suit and they had built a tiny sand castle together. He recalled Victoria wore a black one piece suit and waded out in the water up to her chest. Sydney smiled at this memory. They had planned to return to that beach one day soon after but they never did. Life always had a bad habit of creeping along too fast and it was always a case of "we'll do that next week". His smile faded into a frown when he realized that "next week" would never come now.

He took a breath of the crisp air and then delved into his brown bag removing the vodka and cola. It took him a moment to figure out how to open the bottle of vodka. He tried to open it the same as he had the bottle of tequila but he discovered the vodka had a cork top to it. He pulled it open and it let out a soft, *POP*. "Ahh, there we go," he happily said. Raising the bottle in the air, he looked at it as the lighthouse beam passed through it for a brief moment. "Here's to you, Vicky. Whatever you're doing right now. I wish you nothing but the very best in all things," he said,

Some Things Last...

taking a sip of cola and a splash of vodka. The mixture combined into a punch to Sydney's head. "Ah, so it begins. But where do I go from here?" He asked to the lonely air around him. The silence was creeping up on him again and he didn't like it. He took another sip and another and soon found himself in a hazy crazy world.

"Are you alright, buddy?" Sydney opened his eyes and saw an old guy standing over him with a gray moustache. He was wearing a red flannel shirt, a gray fedora and a pair of rubber suspenders.

"What are you doin' in my house?" Sydney asked the man.

"Sir, you're on the beach."

"What are you doin' on my beach?" Sydney looked around a moment and realized just where he was. He was lying beside the lake, the water was almost touching his shoes. "Oh, man. What a night…" The sky was cloaked in dark clouds. He could hear some thunder far off in the distance. He turned his head and saw a row of dense trees peeking over a metal barrier.

It was then that he realized he was beside the park. How he got down here by the water was beyond him. "You don't look so good. Here, let me help you up," the man said offering his hand.

"Thanks, mister."

"Nance is the name. Peter Nance."

"I appreciate the hand, Mr. Nance. This is a bit embarrassing."

"It's a good thing I came down here to do some fishin' today or God knows how long you'd have been lying there before ya woke up. There's supposed to be some storms rolling in tonight. Then it's gonna get *cold*. Arctic air dipping down into the state…Say, is everything alright? If you don't mind me asking."

Sydney smiled and replied, "Thanks for waking me. But maybe it'd been better if you hadn't…"

Sydney began to walk away when Peter called out, "I don't know what you're going through but there's always something worth living for. Remember that next time!" Sydney nodded and found some stairs leading back into the park. There was nothing left for him here nor back at home but he had no place left to go.

Marching along through the windswept streets, Sydney's head felt as if it were two sizes two small for his brain. He cursed at the steady pain emanating from his skull. With each step and each beat of his heart the pain grew stronger. He looked up and noticed that he wasn't too far from his home. Then he began to think that wasn't true. *No, that's not my home. It never was. It was always Al's. I was just keeping it warm for him. All those nights watching the shadows in hopes that he'd emerge from one…Al had the right idea. He never came back. I should have followed his lead…maybe it's not too late to disappear again?*

Sydney unlocked the door and immediately fell onto the couch. He lied there a while with his eyes closed as the late afternoon sun, already dim from the dark clouds, crept beneath the horizon and the night arrived again. A far off sound awoke him from his nap and he realized after a few moments that it was his cell phone ringing in the bedroom. He ran to answer it. He grabbed his phone and saw the ID.

MOM

"Hello?" he answered, bringing the phone to his ear.

"Hi, Syd. You sound tired. I didn't wake you up just now? It's only 5:30."

It felt much later to Sydney, but time didn't have much meaning to him anymore. "I was just taking a nap. What's going on?"

"What's going on? Have you not heard about the big storm that's supposed to move in later tonight?"

"I've heard a few things, yes."

"OK, have you heard that we might get a lot of snow? I went out shopping over the weekend and picked up a lot of food and supplies. I want you to come back here...at least until all of this blows over. You don't have enough over there to sustain yourself for a week or more...which is what the news has been saying about how long the effects of the storm could last."

"Really? It's supposed to get *that* bad?"

"Yes, Syd! I'm coming over to pick you up. We can get something to eat before the restaurants close. I called QL's and they said they would be open until 7:00."

"Alright, I feel if I told you no that you'd come anyway. I'll be ready when you get here."

Sydney hung up without saying goodbye and stood in the darkened bedroom a moment before he heard the rumbling of thunder outside the window. He walked into the kitchen and got a drink of water to wet his dry throat. Turning towards the fridge he saw the photo he'd placed there of Victoria. A moment in time captured in a faded photograph. Sydney closed his eyes and held back the tears that he felt were close to coming to him. He slammed his fist down upon the faux wood countertop and turned toward the window. He stared out of it a few minutes until he saw his mother pull into the driveway. His phone began to ring in his pocket but he already knew who was calling him. He quickly exited the house, locking up behind him, and ran for the car.

"And what would you like to order, sir?"

Sydney looked up at the young waitress and replied, "A dinner all legs, please."

She smiled at him and said, "OK, I'll get your order out soon." Sydney didn't feel like returning the smile. He honestly didn't feel like doing much of anything.

One Day At A Time

"I knew you were gonna order your chicken legs. Ever since you were a baby you *loved* chicken legs. I'll never forget the time we went out to eat and you and Albert were sitting next to each other on your booster seats. You both must have been around two at the time. You ate all of your chicken legs and then you traded your bones to Albert and were eating *his* too!" Sydney had heard the old story many times. His mother hadn't told it very many times since Albert disappeared, however. Sydney wished that she wouldn't have brought it up tonight. Albert had been on Sydney's mind more than enough lately. If by lately you mean the past seven years...or rather seventeen now.

"Is everything alright, Syd?"

Sydney could see the concern in his mother's eyes. "Yeah, Mom, I'm fine. I just had a rough night." He held up his hand, "Before you ask...I don't wanna talk about it."

"Sometimes it's better to talk about things, Syd."

Sydney shook his head and stood up, "There's something I want to see in the other room, Mom. I'll be back."

"OK, but don't be long. Your supper will be out and they'll be closing soon."

When they arrived they had been seated in the smaller front dining room in QL's. Sydney didn't quite care for the atmosphere in this part of the building. It was a bit drab and cold. He mostly saw this room in passing when he was either paying his bill or walking to the restroom.

He entered into the darkened main dining room and felt for a light switch. He was relieved to find one directly next to the doorway. The room lit up a second later and Sydney stared out at the empty room before him. All the times he'd visited here throughout the years came to his mind. The place was a ghost town now in more ways than one. He and his mother were the only patrons in QL's tonight. It seemed everyone else was hunkering down for the impending storm.

It was the first time he'd been in this room by himself. A chill raced through his body as more happy memories flashed in his mind. He shut his eyes a moment and took a deep breath.

He walked across the dining room, his footsteps echoing upon the wood flooring, until he stood before a large mural painted upon the back wall. Throughout all the years that had passed one thing remained constant, unchanged. Upon the mural was a cliff overlooking Lando and Lake Lethe. For the longest time Sydney thought the sun was rising in the distance but looking at the mural now he felt as if the sun were setting. As he leaned closer to the mural, he heard footsteps behind him. "I was wondering why these lights were on." Sydney turned to see the young waitress from before, smiling at him. "You like that mural do you?"

Sydney nodded, "Yeah, I've been admiring it for many years."

"Ah, OK. My grandfather, Quincy Lipton, painted that before the grand opening of this place."

"Is that where Q.L.'s gets its name?" Sydney asked.

"Yep, that's right."

"I had a question...I asked this a long time ago but I'll try again...Do you know the place where your grandfather got his inspiration to paint this?" It felt like a long shot for Sydney but he had to ask.

"Um, if I'm not mistaken I believe he painted it after one of the scenic cliffs by our farm. He always loved hiking trails. Hiking and painting were his two big hobbies...this place was for my mom. He helped her open it and she named it after him."

"Your farm?"

"Yeah, we have a farm on the edge of town."

"Does this farm have a bumpy dirt road beside it with horses and sheep?"

One Day At A Time

"Yeah, that's the scenic drive. A lot of tourists go through there to hike the trails and sometimes feed the horses."

Sydney couldn't believe it. After all these years he'd finally found out where the cliff side was. "Thank you so much…"

"Sarah. Sarah Lipton."

"Right, and Sarah…you wouldn't by chance know the area of your farm where that cliff is located?"

Sarah furrowed her brow and replied, "Nah, not off the top of my head. There's a lot of trails through the trees behind where the horses roam though…but it's not really the best season to go pokin' around up there."

"Right, I understand. I'll wrap up in here in a sec. Thanks again."

"No problem. Oh, and your legs should be ready in another few minutes!" Sarah waved and made her exit. Sydney stayed and continued admiring the mural. He'd already had it in his mind what he wanted to do. Now that he knew where to go nothing was going to stop him.

He finished up his supper and wiped his mouth. "You must have been hungry! You even ate all of your fries…" his mother said, smiling.

"Yeah, I love the chicken here. Best I've ever had." Sydney didn't want to mention to his mother that he'd not really eaten in days. He didn't want her to worry about him.

He looked over and saw Sarah walk out of the kitchen with a broom and dust pan. "Looks like they're about ready to start closing up, Mom."

A flash of lightning illuminated the parking lot outside for a split second and a few moments later a growl of thunder followed it. "We need to be getting home. It's moving in fast," his mother said, standing up from their table. "Syd, I'll get the bill. It's my treat. I'm still so happy that you're home again."

Some Things Last...

He forced a smile and replied, "Thanks, Mom. I've gotta go use the restroom real quick."

Pushing the worn wooden door aside, he entered into the small men's room and stood in front of the mirror. He stared at himself for a minute and spoke, "I can't continue down this road. There's nothing here. I can't see either of them ever again...and that's best for them. They all believe I'm dead so why not just embrace it?"

KNOCK KNOCK! "Syd? Are you about finished? They wanna lock up out here."

"Yeah, I'll be out in a sec!" he said, flushing the toilet. He turned back to the mirror and sighed. "I gotta get out of here. I'm glad I could come back here one last time..."

He exited Q.L.'s and ran across the parking lot to his mother's vehicle. The wind was beginning to pick up and he watched a discarded paper bag be blown across the road and taken away in the breeze. It disappeared into the night as Sydney closed his door. "Alright, let's go home, Syd. Maybe we can find a movie or something to watch."

As she turned out onto the road Sydney said, "Mom, I wanted to ask if you'd let me run back over to the house and get a few things I forgot. Since I might be over for a week I wanted to go grab some old photo albums we could flip through and some old home movies I found."

"We can go right now, Syd. I'd love to see those photos and especially the videos! What kind of videos are they?"

Sydney frowned. "Well, the thing is I was hoping to pack some clothes too...I might be a little bit sorting all that out. Why don't you rest at home and find us something nice to watch. Maybe you could even make some pop corn or something sweet?"

"Well, now, that you mention it I am a bit tired. I worked today and I wouldn't mind curling up on the couch a bit out of this damp air. I'll hop out at home and you can run over and sort that out. Just don't take too long. You don't wanna get caught out in the storm."

"Thanks, Mom. I won't be long."

Twenty minutes later, he parked his mother's car in Albert's driveway. He had stopped thinking of it as his own at this point. He stepped out of the car and looked over at the cold, dark house. Once upon a time, it had been full of life and laughter but now it sat like a tomb. In many ways it was now for he himself felt nothing more than a spectre floating into the night.

He ran for the front door as a bolt of lightning forked across the sky. He was reminded of a certain other storm that had befallen Lando. It felt fitting to him that he'd leave this place much the same as Albert had. He unlocked the door and pushed it aside, flipping the light on as he entered.

Sydney had decided to come back here for one thing and that didn't include packing any boxes of old memories or clothes. He entered the kitchen and knelt down to open the bottom drawer. Within the drawer, he found an old notebook full of blank paper along with a ballpoint pen. *Victoria Tesson* was written on the cover. He ran his finger over the letters and smiled but it quickly faded as he opened the notebook and tore out a single lined piece of paper. He then opened the notebook and began to make sure the pen worked. After a few seconds the black ink began flowing smoothly. He pulled out a chair from the dining room table and grabbed the piece of paper and began writing.

Mom,

Thanks for everything you've done for me. I found what I was looking for here. It wasn't what I was expecting to find. Vicky has moved on and Vivian has grown up. I don't deserve to see either of them again. They are better off without me. I should never have come back here. Maybe staying there with Sharon wouldn't have been so wrong? No, that was the easy way out. Leaving my wife and daughter behind...I don't deserve anything but the darkness that's been chasing me for seventeen years. Soon, the darkness can have me.

Please, if you get a chance, put some flowers on Albert's grave for me...

Sydney

He signed his name and stared at the letter for a few moments when a gust of wind blew against the house bringing him back to what he had to do next. He tossed the pen upon the table and shut off all the lights. He stepped back outside into the cold air and slammed the door behind him, locking it tight.

He rushed back to the car and was about to slip into the driver's seat when a voice cut through the air. "Hey, man!" He turned around and saw RB waving across the road. It appeared he wanted him to come over. Sydney obliged and jogged across the street. "You goin' somewhere? I saw you pull up in your mom's car and wondered where she was. You planning on staying over there across the street? I ask because I got a little extra food if you need anything."

"I appreciate that but...I'm going to see some old friends tonight."

"Old friends? Hope they're close by. This storm's supposed to be pretty bad. I'd advise you to get inside and make sure you got some candles and a flashlight. My power's been flickering already."

"I'll keep that in mind. Can you do me a favor?"

"A favor? Depends on what it is."

"It's not much. Just make sure my mom gets this house key. I'm going away for a while." Sydney held out the key in front of him.

RB eyeballed it then grabbed it. "Why can't you give it to her?"

"I'm going in the opposite direction and I haven't got time to go by there tonight."

"Alright, I'll give it to her when she comes by."

"Thanks…I appreciate it. You know life can be pretty interesting sometimes. I'd never thought one day I'd be drinking buddies with Roland's old man…the rude carnival clown."

RB laughed. "You're still young. You never know what life has in store for you."

Sydney forced a smile. "Goodbye, RB. May the wind forever be at your back." RB smiled but looked a bit concerned.

Sydney returned to the car and found he had acquired another shadow along the way. He heard a soft meow and turned around to see Mr. Green. His bright green eyes were wide and watching him. "Hey, Greenie. You need to go home. It's about to get rough real quick out here." Mr Green meowed softly and walked up to him and began rubbing against his leg. Sydney felt about as low as he had in his entire life but somehow Mr. Green made him feel a tiny bit better.

He bent down and picked up the skinny black cat and began to pet him a bit before he heard, "Come on, Green!" The cat looked across the street and Sydney put him down. Before he ran away, he turned and meowed one final time then sprinted across the road into RB's sheltered porch. Sydney was left alone once again as a gust of wind blew through his hair, chilling him. *There's no more time to waste,* he thought as he finally entered the car and sped off toward the edge of Lando.

Sydney drove in silence as the weather worsened. The car was hit with a strong gust of wind that caused Sydney to almost swerve off of the road but he was damn determined to get where he was going. He exited the tunnel on the edge of town and then saw the observation deck. He looked over for a moment but he couldn't see much through the heavy rain falling in the distance. Sydney didn't care, he wasn't out here sightseeing. He was relieved to see the rain was still at least a few minutes away from him. That gave him time to find his turn off.

He turned left onto a familiar bumpy dirt road from the past. As he turned off he found himself in total darkness. He turned the brights on but they did little to help. This reminded him of the previous time he'd been behind the wheel trying to make his way to Sharon.

Who'd have thought I'd be coming back out here again under these circumstances. Perkins won't be running up to greet me tonight. Is Perkins still alive? How long do horses live? These questions floated about in his mind as he drove along the bumpy road. As he slowly drove a bolt of lightning forked across the sky illuminating the area for a moment. It was long enough for Sydney to get his barrings and figure out that where he needed to be was just around the next bend.

He brought the car to a stop and looked out at the expansive field beside him. On the other side were tall pine trees. *Sarah said the trail was among those trees. Time to find it*, he thought, cutting the car off and leaving the keys in the ignition. He figured the vehicle would be safe there. Someone would come along and find it once the storm had passed. He took a deep breath and hopped out, slamming the door behind him.

The frigid rain immediately soaked him to the bone but he bolted across the field as fast as he could. The sky was swirling all about. He paid no heed to his safety. Any moment a bolt of lightning could strike him down and honestly he felt that'd be alright if that's how he went out. He made it to the trees and took a moment to breathe. He'd no idea where the trail was or what direction to go. "Where the hell is it?!" he yelled at the top of his lungs over the raging storm, now fully upon him.

He tried looking for some sort of marker then something caught his eye, not a marker on the trees but one in the sky. The clouds parted in the distance further up the treeline and a bright star shone through. He felt the star was leading him so he followed. The wind began to pelt him with ice as he walked next to the trees looking for any kind of sign he could spot.

As he ran along the forest, a blinding light flashed behind him for a split second followed immediately by a deafening roar. Sydney fell to the ground and covered his head as the icy rain continued falling upon him. He turned around to see a small fire and a tree split clear into. *Holy hell! I was just standing over there*, he thought as he whipped around and ran forward. He didn't want to dwell on that.

He noticed an opening to a trail with a wooden marker hammered deep into the bark of one of the trees.

Q.L.

The two letters were painted bold and Sydney knew he found what he was looking for. He stepped into the trail head and proceeded on the worn path ahead wherever it may lead.

He desperately followed the trail half frozen and shivering now. It was hard to see in the dark. He was mostly navigating by touch but something else was helping him through this. He didn't understand it but he felt like he was being guided. Soon, he could see a far off light peeking through the trees ahead. He soldiered on, fighting the cold that had gripped his entire body. The light grew closer and brighter until he finally stepped out of the darkness.

He stepped forward and looked out at the view before him. Lando lay in the distance. Its warm lights piercing through the darkness. He could see a few flashing lights far below from what he figured might be an ambulance but no siren could be heard over the gales of wind thrashing against the cliff side. Above the city was that bright star. He smiled as he looked at it twinkling. *Sharon...you're always looking out for me.*

Directly in front of Sydney was a tree. It's skinny branches forked above him. On several of the branches were leaves that were hanging on for dear life. As the wind blew harder, Sydney watched as several of the leaves were plucked from their branches and flew away. He stood watching as the final leaf clung resiliently against the winds.

It remained there for what felt like hours to him then the wind began to die down. Everything grew quiet as Sydney stood still watching the leaf. He hadn't realized it but he had stopped shaking. He was amazed to see the leaf had hung on when all the others had been blown away. He leaned against the tree. He felt so tired all of a sudden. He decided he would sit down a minute and put his back against the tree's trunk.

As he sat there, he saw several small snowflakes float down and land at his feet. He looked up into the branches and saw the leaf was still there. He watched as the snowflakes began to grow larger. He gazed out across the city and his eyes grew wide. Millions of snowflakes, illuminated by the far off lights, fell silently. "How beautiful it is..."he said, in awe. The view from this cliff was even more breathtaking than he could have ever hoped. Icy tears fell from his face as he continued to watch the snow fall.

It was then, as Sydney was captivated by the snow, that the leaf floated down onto his lap. He looked down at it. "Is it time to go, Mr. Leaf?" he said. He slowly grabbed the leaf and slipped it into the inner pocket of his jacket. "OK, I think I'll enjoy the view for a little longer..." He continued looking out over Lando; at the buildings, at the waters of Lethe, at the town that owned him. He watched as his eyes grew heavier and heavier.

He felt himself being lifted. Far off sounds of people talking but he couldn't make out what they were saying. Then he heard a rumble, (an engine)? Then it all went black.

Babe?

Is that you, Sharon? So, we meet again.

Sydney, why would you do this? I thought you were going to live a long life! You have people who love you and need you!

Love me? Need me? Who? Everyone went away. Don't you know that?

No, they didn't! How could you come to that conclusion? What about Vivian?

What about her?! She grew up, Sharon! ...I'm sure she hates me. Is ashamed. How could she not be? Just leave me alone. I want to be alone in the darkness. It's what I deserve after the pain I've caused.

Can you hear me? Follow my voice!

Can you hear her, Syd? She's calling for you.

Who's calling my name?

Listen, closely.

Daddy!? Don't go. Come back!

Is that really her? Is she really calling for me? Where are you, Vivian? I'm here!

She can't hear you, Syd. You have to follow her voice.

Sydney stumbled through the darkness, his only compass being the soft words spoken in the distance. He focused all of his energy on amplifying her voice. He pressed through the darkness and her voice grew louder.

Daddy!? I love you. Don't leave me! Please, don't go!!

He continued forward, listening for the voice to call him but it grew silent.

Where did she go? I know she was in this direction!

He pressed onward then out of the darkness he could see a circle of light. He approached it and saw himself lying in a bed with silk sheets. The sheets were pulled over his body and only his head could be seen. Warm light was shining through the window above the bed.

That's me! What am I doing? Am I dying? No, I-I don't want to die! Not anymore! Vivian is waiting for me! Wake up you son of a bitch! We can't keep her waiting any longer!!

He reached into the circle into the warmly lit room and a blinding light overtook him. It felt warm and inviting. He gave himself over to it. As he faded into the light, he heard a voice.

Good job! Well, I guess this is goodbye. Take care, babe. We'll meet again some day.

CHAPTER 20
Wherever You Go

Sydney eyes slowly opened and it took a moment for them to adjust to the light cascading into the room. He looked across from him and saw a glass door open that lead out onto a balcony. A warm breeze was gently blowing the tan curtain which hung over half of the doorway. He could smell wisps of the sea in the air. *Where...am I?* he thought as the door opened on the other side of the room. He quickly looked over at who walked in. It was a woman with fiery red hair. She wore a bright green pantsuit. "So, you've finally come around," she said, with a smile. She spoke with an English accent.

Sydney couldn't help but smile back. "How did I get here? I can't even remember what happened. Last thing I recall was that tree..."

"We found you on the cliff, Sydney, then rushed you back here."

"We? And how do you know my name? Who *are* you?"

"Ah, how rude of me. I've heard so much about you that I feel we've already met. I'm Elly and as for who else found you...well, they're downstairs. I'll go and get them. We've all been waiting for you to wake up for some time now. Please, allow me to go and get them." Elly smiled and took her leave.

He lied back in the bed not knowing what to expect next. He sat listening to what sounded like ocean waves in the distance. He wanted to get out of bed but he decided to wait and see how things panned out. Even though he had no idea where he was, he felt a sense of great tranquility.

Some Things Last...

A minute later he heard footsteps from the hallway outside his room. They reached his door and then stopped. A moment later the door slowly opened and in walked a young teenage girl that made Sydney's heart swell. For a moment he thought Victoria had come to see him. She wore dark eye shadow and looked at Sydney, unblinking. "So, my message made it through," she said.

Sydney smiled, "Your message?"

The girl stood wide eyed, watching him as if she couldn't believe what she were looking at. "Yes, I lead you out of the darkness…"

"The darkness?" Sydney said, questioningly. He then recalled a small voice calling out to him. A voice he knew all too well. "Vivvy? Is that you?"

The girl's eyes welled up and she ran across the room and wrapped her arms around him squeezing him tightly. "Daddy!" she said, crying on his shoulder.

"Vivvy, I can't believe it! I figured you hated me and were ashamed of the things I've done. I thought for sure you'd never want to see me again."

"I never felt that way! I always knew you were out there and that you'd come back." She hugged him even tighter. Her eyeshadow had begun to run and had left black marks upon his shoulder. "Sorry about your shirt."

"Oh, Vivvy, never mind the shirt," he closed his eyes and held her tight.

A knock came upon the door. Sydney looked up and saw Elly in the doorway. She was smiling brightly. "I don't mean to interrupt the reunion but someone else is out here. They're a little nervous but ready to come in."

Vivian released her grip around Sydney and moved over to the luxurious brown chair next to his bed. She looked over and beamed at him. "Daddy, I know you're going to be shocked. Try not to faint."

Sydney laughed. "Who's out there?" he called out.

"Come on, love. It's time," Elly spoke to someone just outside the door.

Sydney could never have expected who he saw next. It was a face he never thought he'd see again that came around the corner and entered the room. "Hello, Syd. It's been a long time," Albert said, raising his hand and waving.

"*AL?* Al?! Is that *really* you?!" Albert shook his head and smiled. "Oh, Al...am I really alive right now? How are you here? You've been gone for *so* long!"

"Indeed, you are alive. If it weren't for Vivian here you wouldn't be. It was with her help that we found you."

"Her help? How do you mean?"

"We'll discuss that a bit later. You still need your rest, Syd. We don't need you getting too excited. You've been through a lot," Albert said.

"I feel fine what are you talking about. I'll get up right now," Sydney said casting his sheets aside and throwing his legs over the side of the bed. He tried to stand then fell forward. Albert and Vivian caught each side of him. "I guess you're right after all, Al..." Albert rolled his eyes and grimaced as he helped return Sydney to his bed. Sydney began to laugh.

"What's so funny?" Albert asked.

"It took me back seeing you roll your eyes at me, bro." Albert's grimace faded as he broke into a hysterical fit of laughter. Pretty soon the entire room erupted into laughter.

After the laughter had faded, he drifted off to sleep and awoke to find the night had come. A crescent moon hung high above in the window above his bed. He decided he'd have another go at walking. He removed the layers of sheets on top of him and gingerly swung his legs over the side of the bed. He slowly put his weight on his feet and thankfully didn't fall this time.

He walked over to the open door and stepped out onto the small balcony. A warm breeze caressed his cheek as he looked out upon a large beach which was illuminated by a row of lights and what appeared to be a road that dead ended halfway up the platinum sands. Further up from the road were three palm trees swaying in the breeze off of the bay. *Just where the hell am I? Is this where Al's been gone to all these years?*

He exited his room into a large hallway. He slowly walked down the hall, and discovered a flight of stairs. Downstairs he could hear the faint sound of talking. He took to the stairs and quietly descended them.

He found himself in the great room room of the house. "House" was a modest term for this place. It felt more like a palace. He walked forward and heard the conversation more clearly.

He proceeded across the ornate wood flooring. His reflection could be seen upon its pristine surface. He found a set of doors ajar and peeped outside to find Albert and Elly sat beside a pool of turquoise water. The two of them appeared to be sipping on some cocktails wearing identical black silk robes adorned with three golden palm trees. As he watched them, Elly leaned over and began kissing Albert.

He knocked on the side of the door and they both turned to look at him. "What's going on out here?" Sydney said, a toothy grin on his mouth.

"Syd?! You should still be in bed," Albert said, blushing, his brow furrowed.

"Oh, love. I believe Sydney is curious about some things. I think it might be time you and him had a talk," Elly said, touching Albert's brow with her index finger.

Albert sighed, "I think you're right."

"You know I am. Try not to be too long. I'll be upstairs in bed…" Elly said with a wink.

Sydney stepped aside and let Elly walk inside. "See you tomorrow," Elly said.

"Goodnight. Great meeting you. It warms my heart to see my Al with a lady finally," Sydney replied.

Elly laughed, "We've known each other for a *long* time. Albert can tell you all about that. Goodnight, Syd," Elly said, walking back towards the staircase.

He stepped outside into the comfortable night air. He noticed this area was like an inner courtyard surrounded by the high walls of the estate. He walked over and took a seat across from Albert. "I almost hated to break up your little meeting out here but Elly certainly was right. I do have some questions for you. We'll come back to her…Somehow I feel that might take a minute. Let's start with this huge mansion. This is some place, Al. Where the hell *are* we?"

"Paradise, Syd." Sydney stared at Albert for a moment then replied, "Paradise, eh? How 'bout ya narrow that down there, bro."

"OK, *my* paradise. This is the Isle of Elly. This is our home…Me and Elly's."

"So, this is where you ran off to, huh? How the hell did you get here? The cops were looking all over for you."

Albert laughed, "Those fools were wasting their time. They were *never* going to find me. …I must apologize for my abrupt disappearance, Syd. I figured you would have worried about me…but I'd never have figured you would have waited around for me to come home. I heard all about that from Vivian."

"How do you know Vivian? She wasn't born until two years after you left!"

"Hmm, that's quite a story of its own…I think I'll let her tell you that herself. I believe she has a fair bit she'd like to talk to you about…I took her home earlier this evening but she'll be back tomorrow."

"Last time I checked, Al, Paris doesn't have any tropical beaches nearby."

"That's true. I have a way of getting around that though."

Sydney sat not knowing what to say next. He had plenty to say but had no idea where to begin.

"How about a drink, Syd? If I remember correctly you enjoyed sake. Here, have a bottle," Albert said, with a smile.

"Alright, let's hit the bar."

"No need to get up. It's already beside you. I hope you like it chilled."

Sydney turned to his right to find a huge bottle of premium sake sat beside him. The color of the bottle matched the pools water. "How did...wait a fucking minute! *You!* This place! It all makes sense now. Is Elly...?!"

Albert sat with a perplexed look on his face. "Is Elly *what*?"

"You're an *Esper*, Al?" Sydney said, absolutely astonished.

Albert furrowed his brow again, "What's an *Esper*?"

He told Albert the epic tale of his odyssey across the universe and what he'd experienced there upon Esperia. Albert sat listening through it all, eyes wide with amazement. During the tale he had to backtrack to the events that transpired shortly after Albert's disappearance. It was difficult for him to recount everything involving Sharon but he managed to catch Albert up on all the sordid details.

Albert sat completely flabbergasted by what had happened with Sharon. "Wow, you've been through quite a lot. I'm sorry about Sharon."

"Yeah, it's been an adventure to say the least. As for Sharon...She watches me. She's not...gone. I know it was her that helped me make it through the woods to that cliff. I think I might have been struck down by lightning if it weren't for her guiding me...and she was there in the darkness with me. She helped me to find my way back. I was able to hear Vivian's voice because of her. I know that she's OK, Al. She's still up there," Sydney said, looking at the explosion of stars above them.

Albert nodded and smiled. "From the sounds of things I certainly believe that. Stranger things have happened…at least you got to see her again and made your peace with everything. It seems like you had a similar experience to mine…with Sharon being reborn in a sense."

"You experienced that too? So…Elly-"

"Yes, she along with this entire place exist within my mind…but everything is as real as you or I…as you know now yourself. Funny, I recall long ago Elly telling me you'd one day understand. There are things even now that I don't fully comprehend about her."

"I suppose it's good to have a little mystery involved in your relationship…keeps things interesting," Sydney said, with a grin.

"I must agree with you," Albert smiled.

"Another mystery is all this Esper business. I'm wondering…does that make me an alien?"

Sydney began to laugh. "I don't think so, Al. You're a weird fella but not *that* weird." The two of them had a nice laugh over this.

"Maybe it's best not to overthink this stuff. That's become a bit of a motto of mine. It's seen me through some tough times," Albert said.

"I agree. Maybe you're the only Esper on Earth."

"Maybe…on that note. How about we head to bed. Elly's waiting for me. I can feel that she's eager for me to head up. We're going to get Vivian tomorrow afternoon so get some rest. I know she's eager to see you again."

"Alright, Al…I'll be taking this to bed with me. A little late night nip for the nerves," Sydney said, grabbing the bottle of sake.

The next morning, Sydney awoke to the sun filling his room. He tossed the sheets aside and lie in the bright rays of sun. After a short while, he rose to his feet, rejuvenated, ready to take on the day ahead. He had a feeling he was going to need all the energy he could gather for later.

Stepping out into the hallway, he heard a jingle close to the stairs. As he grew closer, the jingling stopped. He slowly approached the stairs and a gray shape leapt out in front of him. It was a cat! "Whoa, you frightened me. Where did *you* come from?" Sydney said, leaning down to pet the cat. He pet the cats soft fur and it let out a pleasing purr. He noticed around it's neck was a collar with a silver bell attached along with a name tag.

LELA

"Lela, huh? Aren't you a pretty one." The cat purred even louder with delight at Sydney's compliment. He gave her a few more neck scratches and then headed downstairs with Lela tailing behind him.

There was a delectable scent in the air that he picked up on once he stepped onto the first floor. He followed his nose through the great room and found it lead him to a dining room. He stopped in his tracks when he rounded the corner and noticed sitting at the table was a young blonde girl. "And who might you be?" Sydney asked.

"Good morning! I could say the same to you but I've heard all about you from Albert and Viv. You're Mr. Lee...Viv's father and Albert's cousin," she said, smiling wide at him.

"Well, you might know *me* but who are *you*, young lady?"

"I'm Clara...and behind you is my body guard, Ducky." Sydney turned around to see a white duck standing directly behind him, eyeballing him, closely. It's little black eyes bore into him. Sydney felt that he was being given an ocular pat down. A moment later Ducky let out a soft quack and waddled over to Clara. "Impressive, eh? Nobody messes with me while Ducky's around! Nothing gets past him. Isn't that right?" she said, kissing Ducky on the top of his head. Ducky closed his eyes and quacked again, happily. Sydney had no idea what was going on.

"Alright, Clara, breakfast is served. Oh, good morning, Syd! Sleep well?" Albert said, entering the room holding a plate of sausages and eggs and diced hash browns. "I see you've met Clara and Ducky…and by the looks of it Lela too. Lovely!"

Sydney looked down and saw Lela rubbing against his right leg. A loud purr coming out of her. "Yeah…about that…" Sydney said as Albert slid the breakfast plate in front of Clara who proceeded to dig in.

Albert left the room and Sydney followed him. "Hey, Al, wait a minute. You can't just gloss over all that."

Albert stopped and turned around. "Yeah, you're right. I'm just in a bit of a hurry to finish breakfast. Elly's in there and we're making it together."

"I'm sure she can manage. Just who is this Clara girl and what's up with that duck of her's?"

"Oh, Ducky's harmless…unless Clara's in danger…then look out. You don't have to worry about that though. Ducky is a good judge of character."

"Alright, what about Clara? Is she…you and Elly's?"

"No, she's not our daughter. We found her on the streets of a small town in Holland some time ago."

"Holland?!"

"You're not the only one who's had adventures, Syd," Albert said with a smile. "We're helping her try to find her sister. She went missing…the two of them were orphaned at a young age. In the meantime we've taken her in here. As you've surely noticed there's more than enough room."

"I see. That makes sense. At least she's in good spirits. She mentioned that she knows Vivian too."

Some Things Last...

"Indeed. They're good friends. Clara usually accompanies us on our trips. I assume you'll be joining us too?"

"Yeah, I wouldn't miss it, Al."

"Good, we'll be leaving after breakfast. There's a bit of a time difference between here and Paris. It's a little later there..."

After Sydney was surprised with a full English breakfast, he needed to go for a little walk. He exited the main entrance into the warm sea air that permeated outside. He walked down to the road that he'd seen from his bedroom window. As he grew closer he noticed the road was enclosed on both sides by marble pillars that matched the architecture of the estate. Every few feet, slightly larger pillars were present and on top of them were the lights Sydney had seen illuminating the beach. They were two glass domes perched upon tall metal frames. He continued down the road and saw a set of stairs which lead down to the beach. He stepped onto the platinum sand and set his eyes upon the bay. *Wow, Al wasn't joking about this being paradise. No wonder the guy never came back*, he thought, smiling, as he walked towards the water.

He approached the shoreline and took a seat, slipping his shoes off and dipping his toes into the cool water which was crashing against the beach. It was the perfect temperature. No surprise there. Staring out upon the bay, he saw a few dolphins jump out of the water a few feet out. Their bodies sparkled in the sun. What surprised Sydney the most was the fact that they were all pink!

BEEP BEEP Sydney was shocked to hear a car horn and jerked his head around to see a vehicle upon the road. In the driver's seat sat Albert, wearing a pair of circular sunglasses. "Oi, Syd, I was wondering where you'd wandered off to! Come on! It's time to go!" Sydney grabbed his shoes and jogged back to the road to see everyone in the car. Elly sat in the passenger seat, Lela was curled up on Albert's lap, Clara and Ducky were in the back.

"Yo, Al, what kind of car is this? I've never seen one like it," Sydney said, admiring the vehicle. It had a two tone paint job. Its hood was painted rouge along with most of the doors. The rest of the body was black. It gleamed in the noon day sun overhead.

"She's a Citroën 2CV Charleston, Syd. I always loved the look of them. Hop in."

After brushing the sand from his feat he slipped his socks and shoes back on and slid onto the white quilted back seat beside Clara. The scent of cherries hung in the air. Sydney noticed an air freshener dangling from the rear view mirror in the shape of three palm trees. He looked up and noticed the vehicle had a black soft top which was pulled back. "Wow, this is nice...reminds me of my Miata, Al."

"What's a Miata?"

Sydney looked around, he didn't recognize the voice. "Is there someone else in here?" Sydney asked.

Albert laughed and Elly playfully pushed him. "Tell him, love."

"Yes, tell him." the voice spoke again.

"Syd, allow me to properly introduce you to Elise. You might recall some of the talking cars from the 80s when we were kids...well she's leaps and bounds ahead of those."

Sydney sat upon the quilted seat and said, "Hello?"

"Hello, nice to meet you, Syd! We met before but you weren't awake. Glad to see you're doing much better!"

"Um, thanks. Nice to meet you too. After all the strange stuff I've experienced lately...a talking car isn't *that* shocking I guess!"

"Alright, now that that's out of the way...let's hit the road," Albert said, turning Elise around.

Some Things Last…

"Don't forget your seat belts!" Elise, cheerily chimed in. Sydney snapped his belt and wondered what was going to happen next.

"This might be a bit much for you, Syd. Hang on. We'll be there before you know it…" He indeed hung on to the seat, tightly.

"Don't be scared, Syd. Ducky will watch over you too," Clara said as Ducky moved next to him on the seat. He let out a deep quack and Sydney actually felt a bit more at ease.

Albert began picking up speed and the palatial estate was quickly approaching. "Al…we're running out of road, buddy."

"Don't worry, Syd," Albert said as he continued gaining speed. The house continued growing closer as Sydney watched. A moment before he thought they were going to collide with the side of the house a bright flash of light came before the car and they entered into a brightly lit space full of swirling colors all around them as they continued forward. Sydney looked out of his window and then up into the "sky" above them.

"Pretty cool, huh?" Clara said. He looked down and nodded at her and saw the colors reflected in Ducky's eyes.

As quickly as they had entered into this space another flash of light signaled its end as they slowly came to a halt in front of a park gate. "We've arrived. That wasn't too bad was it, Syd?" Albert said, turning around. "Would you mind grabbing the top for me. It looks a little rainy here in Paris this afternoon." Both Sydney and Clara helped to return the top to the front of the car.

After securing the top, Elly said, "Right, who wants to go for a swing?"

"We do!" Clara yelled out and quickly exited the car, running for the park gate. Lela jumped up from Albert's lap and hopped on Elly's shoulders as she followed behind Clara, Ducky in her arms.

"What are we doing here, Al?"

"We're meeting Vivian. We're close by her school. She'll be here soon. Care to go for a walk? I can regale you with some of me and Elly's adventures. I'll tell you about the time we visited an arcade in Shinjuku and I beat the high score on one of the machines there that belonged to the local Yakuza boss. Then we found ourselves surrounded by guys in red suits and the boss sauntered in demanding who beat his score...or how about the time I was in San Francisco and met The Duchess. She was a very domineering woman into S&M...but also a nightclub singer who was on the cusp of giving up on her dream of making it big..."

Sydney sat silent for a moment. "What kind of adventures *are* these?!"

"Big ones, Syd. Big ones..."

The two of them found a bench next to a pond and Sydney listened to some of Albert's travels while waiting for Vivian. "Al, I can't believe that Yakuza and you became friends in the end!"

"Goro-san is...an interesting fellow to say the least," Albert said, laughing. "Oh, look, Vivian just arrived," Albert said, standing up waving.

Sydney turned to look at her and saw she was wearing a black school uniform. She quickly ran over to the two of them and hugged Sydney tightly. "Daddy! You're on your feet again!"

"I wasn't gonna stay in that bed, Vivvy. I wanted to come see you."

"I'm so happy you did! Now, you can see Mom again!" Sydney remained quiet. Vivian looked up at him. "What's wrong?"

"I don't know about seeing your mom. It might only bring her pain to see me." Albert excused himself and headed over to see Elly and Clara at the swings.

Some Things Last...

Vivian took a seat next to Sydney on the bench. "We haven't talked about you in a long time...not since right after we moved here. She pissed me off...telling me to stop being a child and accept what had happened. I tried to convince her...I *saw you* that night. I remember it clearly even now. I tucked you in on the couch and kissed your head. I knew something had happened because you were gone all day. I was so happy that you were back home...then I went back to bed and was woken up by this bright light from outside. I ran down the hall to find the front door open and you were out in the yard. I called to you as you floated into the sky but you disappeared into the night. No one ever believed me! I spent years telling everyone my dad was an intergalactic adventurer. At first the kids at school were amazed then when I kept telling them the same story they began to make fun of me. After a while I stopped telling people about you...I stopped talking about you altogether..."

Sydney continued to listen to Vivian's story. "I remember the day we left Lando. It was such a sad day. I didn't let on that I was as sad as I was. It was foggy and gray outside as we drove away from the house. We left early in the morning after daybreak. I fell asleep in the back seat of mom's yellow car."

"Alex..." Sydney said, softly.

"Oh, yeah...she named it Alex. I forgot about that...Anyway, we stopped at the observation deck on the edge of town. I woke up and saw Mom stood beside the concrete wall. Her long hair was blowing behind her in the wind. I quietly stepped out of the car and watched as she took something out of her jacket pocket. It looked like an envelope and she began to rip it up. She held her hands out and a gust of wind took the pieces high into the air. I watched them disappear into the cloudy sky as a bird circled round and round high above. She then turned around and saw me. Tears were streaming down her face. 'Vivian, I thought you were asleep,' she said to me. 'What did you rip up, Mom?' I asked her. She never did tell me but I felt it had something to do with you."

"After we moved to Paris I gradually began to put you away into a little box…I began to wonder if I had simply dreamed that night you'd left…that is until one day I was visiting a playhouse with my class on a field trip…We took a field trip to watch 'The Nutcracker Suite'…after the show I saw a man I immediately recognized with a woman who had fiery red hair. I followed them out to their car but before they left they visited a cafe across the street. I snuck into the car and fell asleep in the back seat waiting for them to return…when I awoke I found myself in the garage of their home…what a surprise I was to them! I told them who I was and Uncle Al was pretty shocked to find out…he was even more shocked to hear you had gone."

"None of that matters now though! When I met Uncle Al that day I knew you would come back eventually…I'm so glad I didn't lose you! If it weren't for that dream…I feel you wouldn't be here now."

"Dream? What do you mean?" Sydney asked.

"In the dream I saw you. You were driving down a dirt road then you stopped and got out and ran through a field as thunder and lightning crashed around you. You made your way to a cliff…and sat down against a tree and fell asleep…The next thing I saw was a policeman finding you. You were frozen stiff and almost covered in snow."

"Were my eyes rolled back into my head?"

"No, they weren't. I'm being serious here. It was the most terrible dream I ever had. The worst part was I couldn't tell Mom about it. I had to wait and tell Uncle Al and Aunt Elly. I know it rarely snows in Lando so out of curiosity I checked the forecast online and saw a winter storm was coming…All I could think of was going back to Lando and finding you.

"After I told them about my dream they agreed to take me to Lando. I had an awful feeling. I wanted to get there as quickly as possible because the storm was already supposed to be there by the time we were going to leave. For the first time Uncle Al let me sit behind the wheel of the car because I had such a precise image in my mind of where you were supposed to be. My dream felt *so* real. It was more of a *vision* than a dream. As clear as a mountain spring. With that image in my mind of the cliff overlooking Lando we loaded up in the car and shortly found ourselves upon that cliff…and you were right where I dreamed you would be except this time you were still alive! I don't know what I'd have done if you hadn't made it. Now, we can be a family again! Just like it was before!"

Sydney put his arm around Vivian. "Oh, Vivvy. I'd love that…but I don't know how your mother would feel about it."

"Let's go find out, Daddy! We all can convince her! Me, you, Uncle Al, Aunt Elly and Clara! Ducky and Lela can help too!"

Sydney forced a smile. "If I see her…It has to be between me and your mother, OK? No one can talk to her about this but me."

"Alright, Daddy. I understand."

He sat there for a while holding Vivian close to him turning her story over in his mind. *How could she have had such a dream about me? …Is she an Esper too?*

Everyone piled into the 2CV and headed for Victoria and Vivian's apartment. Sydney sat in silence as Vivian and Clara chatted next to him. He looked down into the floor trying to come up with what he needed to say. He had no interest in the scenery that passed by.

The vehicle came to a halt once more and Albert parked it. The trip had passed much quicker than Sydney might have wanted but he was actually thankful for that. If the trip

One Day At A Time

had taken a while he might have lost his nerve to traverse the building that loomed in front of him.

He was the last one to exit the car and Albert could see the unease upon his face. "Syd, whatever happens in there, I'm here for you," Albert said extending his hand.

"Thanks, Al. That makes me feel a bit better...still, I'm scared shitless." Albert nodded and pat Sydney's shoulder. "Let's do this thing," Sydney said, softly.

They entered into the buildings warm lobby and Vivian lead them to the elevator. They all piled on and Vivian pressed the '5' button. The elevator ascended the floors and Sydney could feel his heart beating in his ear like a drum.

The elevator arrived at the fifth floor and they all followed closely behind Vivian who lead them around the corner to apartment 502. "I'm going to go in first, Daddy. After a few minutes I'm going to invite Aunt Elly inside then Uncle Al...followed by you. I spoke with Aunt Elly about it last night when I was dropped off. She told me it was finally time to meet Mom." Sydney looked over at Elly who had a knowing smile.

The tension was building as Sydney waited in the hall. Vivian came to the door a few minutes later and motioned for Elly to come over. Sydney tried to listen to the conversation within the apartment but he couldn't hear a word. "Al, my heart is racing. This is like torture."

"Would you like to pet Lela? Her purr is very therapeutic," Clara said as Lela rubbed against his leg. "Yes, I do, actually," Sydney said, picking Lela up and running his hand over her soft gray fur.

The door to the apartment then opened and Vivian stuck her head out. "Come on. It's time," she softly said. Sydney put Lela down and took a deep breath and approached the door behind Albert.

Some Things Last...

The door was ajar as he heard Vivian talking inside. "OK, Mom. Elly's boyfriend is out in the hall...and some friends of theirs. I want you to meet them all. Don't get up."

"Um, alright, Vivvy. It's great to finally meet you, Elly. You're a little older than I expected but that's alright. Let's meet your boyfriend." Sydney heard Victoria say. Hearing her voice made his heart race even faster. Albert pushed the door aside and entered the apartment. A second later Sydney heard, "Wait a second...ALBERT?! Is that you?!"

Sydney thought to himself, *Now or never.* He entered behind Albert and his heart fluttered as it had done the first time he'd laid his eyes upon her. "Hi, Vicky," he said, softly. Victoria's eyes widened and she slumped forward on the couch she was sitting upon.

"Mom?!"

Elly ran over and checked on her. "She's fainted. Understandable reaction."

A little while later Victoria came out of it to see everyone sitting around the living room. "What-what is this?"

"It's a reunion, Mom! Daddy's back and Uncle Al is here too!" Victoria looked over at Sydney then Albert.

"I apologize for the deception, Victoria. Elly and I met Vivian a few years ago but we wanted to keep that between us until the right time came...Today was that time."

Sydney remained quiet in the corner as Albert caught Victoria up on everything. Victoria remained speechless. "It's been wonderful meeting you Victoria but if you don't mind we need to step out for a bit while someone else has a much overdo word with you," Elly said motioning everyone to the door.

"Good luck, Daddy," Vivian whispered and hugged Sydney tightly before she closed the door behind her.

"Sydney? Are you really here? Am I dreaming?"

He took a seat upon the couch a seat over from her and spoke, "I've asked myself the same question a lot lately. Vicky, I'm here. It's great to see you again."

"Syd, I thought you were dead. It's been so long...I waited for you."

"I know. I...read your diary online. Every...heartbreaking word of it."

"How did you find that?! Those were some very personal entries. I mostly wrote them to get shit out of my head. After you...went away...I was left to raise Vivian alone. Do you have any idea what that was like? The questions she asked and how she believed you'd floated into the sky!? Well, are you saying that's what *really* happened!?"

"Vicky...yes, that's what happened. Vivian played it smart by having Elly then Albert come in. I thank them all for helping with that. I believe you seeing Al might give my story more validity. I left that night...but *I* made the decision to leave. I thought it would have been too difficult to stay. No one would have looked at me the same way. Your family...my family...everyone knew what I'd done so I ran. I chose the easier path. All those years we spent together and I tossed them aside. I kept everything from you for so long. You wouldn't have found out about any of it if everything hadn't caught up with me. I was never going to tell you. I've hurt you more than I'll ever know by my selfishness."

Victoria sighed and sat a minute, her eyes closed and her brow furrowed. "Syd, you deserved to feel ashamed for what you did. You were a coward. You didn't just hurt me. You hurt everyone. I can't begin to tell you how my dad felt about everything. He loved you like you were one of his own. The day after I found out about what you did felt like a nightmare. I prayed that I'd wake up to find everything was alright. That didn't happen and things went from bad to worse when you up and left. You might realize what you've done now but what good is that, really? Why did you have to go? Damn you, Sydney!"

Victoria began to weep. Sydney watched helplessly, not knowing what to say. He had flashbacks to other times where he felt just as useless. Her crying began to subside and she began talking. "I spent night after night with you. *Coddling* you after your nightmares all to find out you weren't dreaming of Albert but dreaming about *Sharon* and who knows what else. You put me through hell. Both before and after you left. ...You mentioned you read my diary? I assume you read the entry about my new boyfriend. I'm happier now than I've been in a *very* long time. How did that make you feel?"

"Yes, I read that. It felt like someone punched me in the stomach. It...*really* upset me." Sydney didn't want to tell her just how much it had upset him. She didn't need to know about him trying to kill himself. Truthfully, that was the first moment since everything happened that he had even thought of how close he had come to ending it all. Now wasn't the time to reflect on more of his selfishness.

He pushed his time upon that lonely cliff out of his mind for the moment and asked, "Does he make you feel the way I did?"

"No, he doesn't...but that's OK. He makes me feel happy in *his* own way and he loves Vivian. Despite her feelings against him." Sydney grew quiet again as tears began to well up in the corners of his eyes. He felt like he was on the verge of weeping but he didn't want to put Victoria through that.

"I received your letter in the mail shortly after you'd been missing for a few days."

"My letter?"

"Yes, it was written on stationary from the Lando Inn. You talked about our wedding day and how me and Vivian were your universe...and that you were going to own up to the terrible things you'd done. You said we'd discuss everything later...if only I knew 'later' would mean ten years...I held onto that letter until the day I left Lando."

"Then you ripped it up at the observation deck?"

"...Yes, how do you *know* about that?" she asked, her eyes wide.

"Vivian told me. She saw you ripping a letter up that morning."

"Oh, I never intended for her to see that. I thought she was asleep. When I ripped that letter up it was my way of parting ways with you. I didn't want to carry any of the bad feelings with me to France. Pretty stupid thought I suppose. I ended up thinking about you for some time after we got here. Not much...but every now and then something would make me think of you," Victoria said.

A part of him desperately wanted to grab her and hold her tightly, kiss her and have things be *just like it was before*. Vivian's words echoed in his mind. He knew that wasn't going to happen though. "Where do we go from here, Vicky?"

"I don't know. So many years have passed...It's almost Thanksgiving once again back there. I used to love this time of year but now I hate it. It reminds me of some of the worst days in my life. That being said...to see you again today...it makes me feel better to finally know you're alright. You'll always have a place in my heart, Syd...but I can't be with you again. I gave up on you a *long* time ago. I hope we can be friends...for Vivian's sake. I hope you can find happiness again someday. Meet someone new...make them as happy as you did me once upon a time."

With tears in his eyes he replied, "I understand, Vicky. I hope one day you can look up at the bright leaves and smile again." The two of them stood up and embraced one another tightly in the golden afternoon sunlight that was cascading through the open window across from them. As he held her close, he could hear sounds of the city floating into the room. Sydney felt the distance between them shift. He knew she'd never be there like she was before but he accepted that.

A light breeze rustled the thin curtain that hung beside the window and something curious caught his eye. He slowly approached the curtain and moved it aside.

"What is it, Syd?" Victoria asked.

He set his eyes upon a familiar drawing contained within a black frame. The cliff overlooking Lando stared back at him. In the bottom right corner was a name and year written into the cliff.

JIM '05

"Where did you get this?" Sydney asked astonished to see it again.

"I found it in your Miata on the passenger seat. I thought it was a lovely drawing. I always wondered where you picked it up. I got a frame for it and hung it outside the kitchen a few weeks after you'd been gone. It's the mural in Q.L.'s right?"

Sydney turned around and nodded, "Yeah, it is. I met a guy downtown the night before I left and he drew that for me...I wonder where he is now?"

"Who knows? Maybe he's wondered the same about you? I tell you what..." Victoria said, approaching the drawing then gently removing it from the wall. A shiny nail protruding from the wall glistened in the light reflected from the glass of the frame. "I want you to have this. You always loved that mural. You looked at it every time we went down there for supper," she said handing him the frame.

He took it into his arms and smiled, "Really? Well, thanks for this, Vicky. I'll cherish it. It'll remind me of some things I never want to forget...Good and bad..."

He bid Victoria farewell and left the apartment clutching the frame tightly against his chest. Everyone was standing close to the door, especially Vivian. "Well, Daddy? How did it go?"

"Go on inside, Vivvy. Your mother needs you right now. I'll see you soon…I promise." Vivian reluctantly agreed and hugged Sydney tight before returning inside. "Al?"

"Yeah, Syd?"

"Let's roll."

The group returned to the 2CV in silence. Not asking what had occurred in the apartment. He felt they all had an idea. They stepped out onto the street below and the city lights began to slowly spring to life. When they entered the vehicle, Sydney took his seat behind Albert. Clara and Ducky looked out the window at the passing scenery. He felt they wanted to give him some space which he was thankful for. He honestly wanted to sit in silence reflecting on everything that had occurred recently.

The drawing sat in his lap and he gazed at it once more. He noticed a smudge on the glass and reached into his jacket pockets in hopes of finding something to wipe it off. When he reached into his inner pocket he felt something smooth and cool. He pulled out the object and was amazed to see a leaf. *Mr. Leaf! I forgot I had you in there…I've got an idea. It'll be a good place for you*, he thought as he opened the frame and placed the leaf in the bottom left corner. He then closed the frame and looked at the leaf pressed against the glass. A small grin came upon his face as they cruised along through the city streets of Paris.

They turned down a quiet road then Paris faded away as the brilliant lights enveloped the 2CV once again. Sydney felt he'd never get used to this transition. They reappeared upon the long road on the beach and Albert cruised back to the estate and pulled into the garage. "Goodnight, everyone," Elise spoke as everyone piled out.

Albert laid his hand upon it's hood and said, "Goodnight," as he turned the light off and entered into the mansion.

Sydney took a quick trip upstairs and placed his drawing upon his bedside table. He wasn't very tired so he decided to sit beside the pool gazing up at the stars for a while. He soon found Albert and Elly joining him. "Quite a day, huh, guys?" They both nodded. "Where's Clara gone off to?"

"To bed. She was pretty tired. We tucked her in along with Ducky and Lela."

"I remember those days..." Sydney said. "Hey, what's the date today?"

"Um, November 25th I believe. Why do you ask?"

"I realized something, Al. Tomorrow's Thanksgiving! You know what I wanna do? I want to invite all you guys over to my place and have a nice family dinner. It'll be like old times. How does that sound?"

"Your place? *My old place?* Lord, I haven't been there since...Why can't we have it here instead?"

"Love, that wouldn't be like old times would it? We'd love to come, Syd!" Elly said, frowning at Albert.

"Right...Of course we'll be there! In fact I can help with the food. I'll get the turkey ready tonight...and the fix-ens," Albert said.

Sydney smiled, "Thanks for the encouragement, Elly."

Elly grinned and said, "No problem, Syd. I've never actually been to Albert's old place. It'll be interesting to visit."

The following day Sydney awoke early and met Albert downstairs. True to his word he prepared a huge turkey and everything you could want with it. Everyone chipped in carrying it all out to the car and loaded up the trunk with everything. Once the feast was all loaded up, everyone took their seat except for Albert. "Oh, I forgot one last thing in the kitchen. Give me a minute." A minute passed...then five minutes. Elly went to check on Albert inside. When she didn't come back Sydney had to check on things too.

He quietly entered the house and heard voices coming from the kitchen. "I'm sorry, Elly. It's just...I haven't been back there since that terrible night. I still remember Ma's face!"

"Love, this means the world to Syd. You can't let him down. He's already been through so much..."

Sydney stepped into the kitchen, "Sorry for eavesdropping. I understand how you're hesitant to go back...I know that place wasn't the happiest at all for you. You're aware of what happened to your mom, right?"

"Vivian told me, yes."

"She's at Duke's End now. I haven't seen her...I couldn't. I feel so guilty over what happened to her."

"*Duke's End!?* I see...Syd, why would *you* feel guilty? You only found her like that. I'm the one to blame...and I've spent years trying to put it out of my head. You've helped convince me that I can't run from things."

"What do you mean?"

"I mean I'm going to make things right...soon enough. For now, Thanksgiving dinner awaits us."

The three of them returned to Elise and Albert finally took off towards the dead end road. As they approached the three palms in the distance the island faded away in a burst of color. Albert slowed down and the old neighborhood faded into view. He pulled the car into the driveway and parked it. "Home again, home again, jiggety-jig," Albert said.

Sydney lead the way for everyone to the front door then realized it was locked. "Ah, that's right. I forgot...I need to run next door. I've got to talk with my neighbor a minute. I gave him the key before I left...Why don't you guys run and pick up Vivian while I sort this out."

Some Things Last...

"Alright, Syd. We'll be back soon." A minute later Sydney watched as the 2CV faded away. It was really something to behold.

He proceeded next door and knocked on RB's door. A few seconds later he heard him approaching. "Holy shit. I didn't think I'd see *you* again! Your mother called around looking for you and I told her about what you said. She came and got the key and hauled ass out of there. I'm not sure what happened but...you might wanna give her a call if you haven't already."

"I can't...I lost my cell phone somewhere along the way. Could I borrow your phone to call her. I won't be long."

"Sure, but don't make a habit of it. You gotta be more careful with those things."

He dialed his mother and placed the phone to his ear. She answered after a few rings. "Hello?"

"Mom, it's me..."

"SYD!? Where have you been!!?? I got the police out looking for you. They found my car on the edge of town! Where did you go?! Thank you God! I thought you really gone this time!"

"I'm next door at Mr. Torfilio's place. I lost my phone somewhere."

"It was in the car, Syd! It must have fallen out of your pocket."

"OK, good. I want you to come over...I'll have some people here you wanna see."

"People? What's going on?"

"Just come over, Mom. Bring the front door key. I love you. See you soon." He hung up and went back to the kitchen where RB was sitting to the table. "Thanks, RB...sorry for the trouble." He looked around the kitchen and saw no food nor did he smell anything in the oven. "Hey, what are you doing today?"

One Day At A Time

"Sitting around the house mostly. I might see if there's a football game on."

"Would you be interested in coming next door for Thanksgiving supper?"

RB laughed, "Well, my brother's out of town so I had no where to go this year...sure, man. If you don't mind."

"I don't mind at all. There's enough for everyone and it's all ready to eat."

RB agreed to come over in an hour. He wanted to give Sydney time enough to lay everything out. In the meantime his mother showed up right before Albert faded back onto the street. When she saw him step out of the 2CV with Vivian, she had a similar reaction to Victoria's. Sydney opened the front door and he and Albert carried her inside and laid her upon the couch. She awoke to everyone finishing setting up the meal. "Sydney, what happened? Wait...is that...?" she said pointing at Albert.

"Yes, Mom." A knock came upon the door. Sydney opened it to find, RB standing at the door holding a bottle of tequila. "I didn't wanna come empty handed," he said, laughing. "Alright, let the games begin," Sydney replied, laughing.

That evening, everyone was sat around the dining room and into the living room. Sydney couldn't recall the last time he'd loved Thanksgiving so much. Vivian had invited her mother to join her but she politely declined... but that was OK. Even though she wasn't there he was still happy. He knew that he'd made his peace with her.

"How long have you two been dating?" RB asked Albert and Elly.

"Since we were kids," Albert replied.

"Hey, listen, this might surprise ya but I did more than moonlight as a rude clown down at the pier. I'm also ordained! Maybe I can marry you two someday!" Elly

Some Things Last...

looked at Albert and blushed. Truthfully, Sydney was a bit surprised they weren't married already.

"I'll keep you in mind," Albert said, with a smile. He watched his mother across the room laughing with both Vivian and Clara.

As he finished up the last drumstick he remembered something that he thought everyone would enjoy. "Hey, Vivvy, you remember dressing up as a bumblebee for Halloween? You came running down the hall in your costume and put your arms around my knees. Do you know what you said to me?" Vivian rolled her eyes. "I was your knees! Get it? The bees knees!" Everyone began to laugh.

Vivian spoke up, "God, I was a such a dork." They all looked so happy. It was amazing having the house full of laughter again.

"So, Syd, what will you do now?" asked his mother. "Well, I think I'll go back into carpentry. Maybe I'll get my masters?"

"You're a carpenter? I know a guy who needs some work done...My brother John. I'll give him a ring on Monday."

"Yeah? I'd appreciate that!"

"I'll even waive the finders fee...All I ask is when you get your first check...buy us another bottle of tequila!"

Sydney began to laugh, "You got a deal."

Later that night, RB said his goodbyes to everyone. Sydney saw him to the door. "That was a damn good meal, man. Thanks for inviting me."

"The food was all thanks to Albert."

"Well, my compliments to the chef. I'll see ya after while."

"Yeah, see you later, RB." Sydney watched as RB was met halfway by his cats. Mr. Green turned and looked at Sydney on the porch before running after RB. He smiled and entered the house.

"I wish I could have all of you guys stay the night but I've only the one bed."

"I don't mind sleeping on the couch, Daddy," Vivian said.

"OK, sweetheart but only if it doesn't affect your schoolwork."

"Don't worry about that. I'm all caught up on my work."

Sydney said his goodbyes to everyone as they walked outside. "We'll have to do this again next year," his mother said.

"Definitely. It was lovely meeting you, Lolita," Elly said, hugging her.

"You too, Elly. Where are you guys going now?"

"We've got an errand to run then we're going back home," Albert said.

"OK, be careful. I do so hope you'll visit your mother soon. I know she'd love that."

"Yeah…I'll be seeing her really soon, Aunt Lo. Goodbye for now, Syd. We'll be back for Vivian tomorrow."

"Sounds good, Al," Sydney said, giving him a big hug. "Take care…"

After hugging both Elly and his mother he returned inside to find Vivian already lying upon the couch. She was fast asleep. He found her a blanket and tucked her in then kissed her forehead. She really had grown up into a beautiful young lady much like her mother. He sat watching her for a few minutes then decided to head to bed himself. He was damn tired.

Before he headed for bed there was one thing he wanted to sort out first. He entered his bedroom and grabbed the drawing of the cliff. He'd placed it there earlier that evening after everyone had brought the food in for supper. He recalled Victoria had said she hung it outside of the kitchen. Sure enough, he found a tiny hole in the wall outside the kitchen. He dug out a hammer and a nail from the bottom drawer in the kitchen and as quietly as he could hammered the nail into the same hole and then placed the drawing upon the wall. He admired it for a minute then headed for bed.

He slipped under the cool sheets and lie there for a few minutes. *Today was a good day*, he thought as a smile spread across his face and he fell asleep.

He had a beautiful dream of his father. The two of them embraced tightly. Sydney felt himself crying. They were tears of happiness. He was filled with a great sense of joy. No words were spoken between the two but he felt a great pride emanate from his father. He turned to find Sharon watching him, smiling. He knew they were dead. But it was all right.

He awoke the following morning full of extreme optimism. The room was warm and full of light cascading through the windows. He slipped out of bed and quietly walked to the kitchen for a drink of water. Vivian was still blissfully asleep on the couch and he didn't want to wake her.

He took his glass of water out onto the back deck and sat down looking up into the cloudless sky above. The morning air was still until a few robins flew by and let out some cheerful chirps overhead. *It's a beautiful day...*he thought as he remembered long ago looking up into the sky and watching the birds fly by. *So much has happened since that day. Sharon...Vicky...you'll both be with me forever.*

He knew the days ahead of him weren't going to be the easiest but he also knew that he'd have a little help from his family and friends along the way. He'd made peace with everything and had a renewed purpose...a reason to go on living. It was something he never thought he'd feel again. He smiled as he took a sip of water and decided to wake Vivian from her slumber.

About Dino Jones

Within, his second novel, 'Some Things Last...', Mr. Jones delves into themes of regret, grief, and carrying on in spite of it all.

Dino Jones was born and raised in Sylacauga, Alabama. He's lived in Alabama for most of his life but also lived in Newfoundland, Canada, and Laredo, Texas.

When not reading or writing, he enjoys watching films, playing video games and listening to music. His favorite films include: Blue Velvet and Mallrats. His favorite games include: Silent Hill 2 and Deadly Premonition. His favorite groups include: Genesis and Beach House.

Mr. Jones still has a lot of stories kicking around in his mind and is quite eager to share them. "The gears are always turning up there. I sometimes wish they would stop. New ideas for stories are always around."

The story of Albert will continue…

Quick Thanks

Many thanks for purchasing 'Some Things Last...'!! If you enjoyed the novel and want to share your thoughts please leave me a review on Amazon and Goodreads. All reviews are much appreciated.

amazon.com/Dino-Jones/e/B08J3MNMZR
goodreads.com/author/show/20981755.Dino_Jones

To hear the latest news on my future work follow me on Instagram and Facebook!!

Instagram: dinojones1988
Facebook: DinoJones88

Printed in Great Britain
by Amazon